blood of the FAITHFUL

ALSO BY MICHAEL WALLACE

Other titles in the Righteous Series

The Righteous

Mighty and Strong

The Wicked

The Blessed and the Damned

Destroying Angel

The Gates of Babylon

Hell's Fortress

— blood of the —
FAITHFUL

MICHAEL WALLACE

THOMAS & MERCER

Published by Thomas & Mercer, Seattle

www.apub.com

Amazon, the Amazon logo, and Thomas & Mercer are trademarks of Amazon.com, Inc., or its affiliates.

ISBN-13: 9781477821145
ISBN-10: 1477821147

Cover design by Cyanotype Book Architects

Library of Congress Control Number: 2014913872

Printed in the United States of America

CHAPTER ONE

The sun had dropped into a pool of red and purple flames in the western desert before Ezekiel Smoot emerged from the sandstone maze and approached the back of the temple. His younger brother Grover had received his endowments earlier in the day, and Ezekiel had unlocked the back door of the temple before departing with his wives and the rest of his extended family. It had already been late afternoon, and he guessed nobody would come around and check the lock. When the handle turned in his hand, he knew he was right.

Ezekiel slipped into the cool, dark hallway. His heart was pounding, and he worried that his unauthorized entrance into this holy spot was sacrilege. Five years had passed since he'd first entered the temple at the age of twenty-two to receive his own endowments, and the space still felt mystical, forbidden. But he'd been commanded to enter by a dream. He didn't dare defy it.

The darkness enveloped him, so thick that it felt like hands squeezing the life from his bones. Chances were, his father had flipped the breaker off on his way out, but Ezekiel didn't dare try the light switch and find out.

It was April of the third year of the collapse, and the spring rains were light. To conserve the reservoir ahead of an uncertain summer, the Christiansons cut electricity to the valley at sundown for all but essential uses. And since the only thing that seemed to count as essential was Jacob Christianson's clinic and surgery, a light flickering through the temple windows would arouse suspicion.

So Ezekiel groped his way down the hallway by touch. He had carefully studied the temple corridors that afternoon at Grover's endowment and made a mental map in his head so he wouldn't get turned around and confused. He made his way past the endowment room, the baptistery, the offices, and the hallway that led to the sealing rooms. He found the hall that led to the Holy of Holies, the sacred room beneath the spire of the temple.

A warning voice sounded as he hesitated at the head of the hallway. At first it seemed like his own worries, his own doubts. But the longer he stood rooted in place, the more the warning became an actual voice whispering into his ear.

Turn back. Death awaits those who defy the will of the Lord.

He had to fight it off. Even here, in this holy place, the devil was not without power over the weak-willed and unfaithful. Years ago, Jacob Christianson's brother Enoch had been murdered in these very halls when the Kimball clan made a violent play for control of the church. No doubt the Kimballs had heard Satan's voice then too.

I am not Satan, I am the Destroying Angel of the Lord. Woe be unto those who defy me, for they shall be thrust unto hell.

"Get thee behind me, Satan," he whispered.

The voice faded, but not the sinking feeling of dread. He almost turned around.

Ezekiel's wives would be arriving at the home of his father, Elder Smoot, carrying cornbread, mashed potatoes, and apple pies. The extended family was gathering to commemorate the death of Ezekiel's older brother, Bill, killed last year by a missile strike from a drone aircraft. With so many wives and children filling the Smoot compound to bursting, they wouldn't immediately notice Ezekiel's absence.

His hand went to his jacket pocket, where he had a small flashlight. The few remaining batteries in Blister Creek were reserved for two-way radios and other emergency use, but he'd found a camping flashlight that could be recharged by shaking it up and down for a minute or so.

He resisted the urge to use it. Still too dangerous. The hall had windows.

At last his hands found the carved oak door that opened into the Holy of Holies. He traced the carved sunstone on its surface until he located the cool iron handle.

For a long moment he was unable to move, afraid.

Only the prophet and members of the Quorum of the Twelve could enter the room. Here they met, here they communed with angels. Rumor had it that the Lord himself would hold counsel with the prophet.

"Come on, move."

The sound of his own voice slapped Ezekiel from his paralysis. He took out his flashlight, shook it, then pushed open the door with one hand and turned on the light with the other. The LED bulb cast a thin blue beam across the Holy of Holies. He stepped in and let the door close behind him.

Wooden benches ringed the room. Varnished wainscoting rose above the benches to the height of a man, after which the ceiling disappeared into the darkness, rising into the spire that topped the temple. His light swung to the center of the room.

An aged cedar chest sat in the middle. Various symbols had been carved in its side: a moon with a face, another sunstone, all-seeing eyes, a compass and square. Cherubim, their wooden wings overlaid with gold leaf, perched on either end of the chest like sacred guardians.

The chest had no lock. It needed none. If a man violated the sanctity of that chest, it was said, the cherubim would come to life and rip him apart. Inside lay the sword and breastplate of Laban. Only the One Mighty and Strong could put on the breastplate. Only he could heft the sword in his hand.

Was that man Jacob Christianson? Was he the One Mighty and Strong foretold by prophesy?

Jacob's father, Abraham, the old prophet and patriarch, had died in a violent struggle with the Kimball clan five years earlier, when Ezekiel was not yet married. Any doubts people had about Abraham's son Jacob taking over seemed to have vanished at the funeral, when the young man spoke with power and authority. People were openly weeping, claiming they could hear Brother Abraham's voice emerging from his son's mouth.

But that night Ezekiel had found his own father creaking in his rocking chair on the porch, anxiously tapping a boot. A cloud of frantic moths and other flying bugs assaulted the porch light over his head, but he paid them no mind.

Father looked up and blinked when he saw Ezekiel. "I don't know. I just don't know," he said. "Is he ready? Is he strong enough?"

"Jacob?" Ezekiel asked. He hadn't given it much thought, but his father had long expressed reservations about the younger Christianson.

Father nodded.

"What is your worry?" Ezekiel asked. "That he only has one wife?"

"Yes, that. For a start."

"Can't imagine that will last long. Now that he's prophet, everyone will be happy to offer their daughters."

"They've already offered daughters. Jacob declined to enter plural marriage, says he's happy with Fernie."

Ezekiel stared. "Happy with one wife? That's crazy."

At that time, Ezekiel was still in that anxious point of life when he didn't yet have permission to marry his first woman. Jacob would later eliminate the practice of casting out the excess young men, but back then, until you were given your first wife, there was always the chance you would find yourself among the Lost Boys.

It was natural to be envious of Jacob, with so many beautiful young sisters and half sisters. Men would gladly trade their daughters and sisters for someone like Eliza Christianson. Ezekiel had a dozen sisters too, and plenty of men had wanted to marry Lillian and Lisbeth, but his father and his older brother, Bill, had been the beneficiaries of those trades, not Ezekiel.

It staggered his imagination that a man would be offered wives and not take them. How else would you grow in stature in the sight of the Lord? How else would you fulfill the promise of Abraham, to see your posterity as numerous as the sand on the seashore? Become a king and priest in the world to come? Even a god?

"What are you saying?" Ezekiel asked. "You don't think he's the prophet?"

"Jacob is clever enough, and that fools people into thinking he's wise. And they respect him because he is a doctor. He's a gifted speaker and commands loyalty from his family. And women trust him too."

"None of those are bad things, Father."

Ezekiel was struggling to explain the thoughts churning through his mind. His faith was so absolute that he couldn't understand how Jacob could be left at the head of the church if he had not been called by God. He pulled up a chair and waited for his father to explain himself.

For a long time Elder Smoot did nothing but rock and scowl, his mouth thinned behind his bushy whiskers.

At last he cleared his throat. "Do you know what Brother Jacob said when I asked him if he'd received a heavenly confirmation of his new calling?"

"Did he say no?"

Father grunted and shook his head. "He said to never trust a man who claimed he'd seen an angel. Most likely he was either lying or insane."

A deep worry settled into Ezekiel's gut. "That doesn't sound like a prophet."

"No, it doesn't. Look, I might be wrong. Maybe it's self-doubt. That's no sin."

"For a prophet?" Ezekiel asked. Now his own doubts—not in the church, but in Jacob—were spreading cancerous tendrils through his testimony.

"Even for a prophet. Moses doubted when the Lord called him. And Jonah, before he was swallowed by a whale. Peter denied Christ three times before the cock crowed. And in the Book of Mormon, Alma the Younger was struck down by the Lord before he repented."

Ezekiel felt a little better. "That's true."

The porch door swung open. Ezekiel's mother stood there and both men started.

His mother was a Kimball, but her loyalties now lay entirely with the Smoots, and her husband had been one of the dead prophet's closest allies and confidants. That made her an ally of the Christiansons as well. At dinner, she'd prayed long and hard expressing her gratitude that Abraham had left the church in the capable hands of his eldest son.

From the look on her face it was clear she'd been listening. "Trust in the Lord," she said. "That is all you need to do. Everything else will take care of itself."

Elder Smoot could be a hard man when it came to questioning from his wives and daughters. He had plenty of respect for women's work: cooking, cleaning, child care, managing the domestic economy. And a woman was just as spiritual as a man, Father had said many times. Perhaps more so. But only a fool would trust a woman's advice about the weightier matters of the church or community. That was for men to discuss, men to decide. A woman's job was to follow and obey.

But if he was irritated that one of his wives had interjected herself into the discussion, he didn't let on. Instead he said, "Are the women united? Do they agree that Brother Jacob is the answer to our salvation?"

Mother smiled. "I don't speak for all women. But most are excited to have a young man with energy. We need a strong leader now more than ever."

"No doubt the womenfolk think him handsome," Father grumbled. "And they all want him for a son-in-law, if not a husband."

He rose to his feet with his knees popping. Ezekiel followed his lead.

Mother put her hand on Elder Smoot's arm, and looked back and forth between father and son. "The lights are on at the temple," she said, "and Jacob's car is parked out front. I think he's in the Holy of Holies, wrestling with his testimony. Give him a chance."

Smoot let out a deep sigh. "Very well. He deserves that much."

For a time after the final defeat of the Kimballs, it had seemed that the Smoots would fill the role of rivals to the Christiansons within Blister Creek. Elder Smoot sparred with Brother Jacob and his allies on the Quorum, and resisted every attempt to give women more power in the community and church. But then, at the moment when Ezekiel's father should have hardened his opposition—after the violent death of his oldest son, Bill, on the highway south of Blister Creek—Father seemed to make his choice.

Never mind his dead son. He'd cast his lot with Jacob Christianson. Father had become convinced that Jacob was the One Mighty and Strong, prophesied by Joseph Smith to lead the saints at the End of Days.

And now, in the Holy of Holies, with the light already fading on Ezekiel's flashlight, the time had come to put Father's faith to the test.

Ezekiel reached for the chest. In his dream, the wood had turned hot under his touch until it burned like a piece of metal left baking in the desert sun. But now it was cool, the wood old and rough. He lifted the lid and peered inside. The smell of cedar and old newspaper came out. But he could see nothing; the light was too weak, almost dead now. He held the lid open with one hand and shook the flashlight with the other to recharge it.

In the dream, he had opened the cedar chest to see the sword glowing red and the breastplate white, like the sun. When he lifted the sword, blood had dripped off it. Whose blood, he couldn't say, but he knew, in the way one does in dreams, that he had been the one to do the killing. And he knew that there was more killing yet to do.

It was a terrible risk to open the chest. More terrible still to touch the sword and the breastplate. Only the prophet could touch them.

The cherubim would strike down any other man who dared. And even the prophet was forbidden from wielding them until the Great and Dreadful Day.

If you raise the sword, you are the new prophet. If you are wrong, you will surely die.

Soon there was no more excuse, and he stopped shaking the light and turned it back on. Then he aimed the light and peered inside the chest. His pulse throbbed in his ears, and his breath came fast and nervous.

There was no breastplate. There was no sword. In fact, there was nothing in the chest but a yellowed newspaper.

A nervous, honking laugh burst from Ezekiel's mouth. The dream had commanded him to come here and take up the sword and breastplate. And unlike most dreams, it had not faded over the subsequent days. Instead, he could not stop thinking about it, about what it meant.

"But it was nothing." His voice echoed hollowly in the tall, empty room. "A dream. You are not the pharaoh, and you are not Joseph with the Coat of Many Colors. You are a fool, a dreamer."

He picked up the newspaper. It was the *Deseret Evening News*, with the date of January 4, 1896.

UTAH A STATE
THE PROCLAMATION ISSUED BY PRESIDENT CLEVELAND
ONE OF THE AMERICAN UNION
OFFICIAL MESSAGE THAT AROUSES JOYOUS ENTHUSIASM
IN THE HEARTS OF THE PEOPLE

He tossed it back in and shut the lid of the chest. Then he sat quietly on one of the benches ringing the room as the light slowly faded again. What about the sword and breastplate? Where had they gone?

Brother Jacob must have taken them. Any other man would have died the instant he touched them.

But Jacob had never wielded them. Not when the Kimballs launched a cruel attack to take over the church. Not when the government defiled the temple with armed troops. Not when the time came to drive the starving refugees from the reservoir. Not once had he called down the power of the Lord to help the church. Instead, he always relied on the arm of flesh: modern weapons, allies from the FBI, his own cunning.

Jacob must have taken away the sword and breastplate precisely so they *wouldn't* be used. So that another, more righteous man wouldn't wield them for the purpose for which they'd been created.

Yet Jacob hadn't died upon touching them, either. How was that possible?

Ezekiel had backed his way out of the room and was picking his way down the hallway when the answer came to him. Jacob had touched the breastplate and sword without dying because the Lord had called him as prophet. He hadn't wielded them righteously because he was a *fallen* prophet.

The words from Ezekiel's patriarchal blessing came to his mind. Elder Smoot had laid his hands upon his son's head when the boy was only fifteen. It was a ritual in the church that would give young men and women their lineage through the Twelve Tribes of Israel, as well as pronounce certain blessings and prophesies upon their heads.

"Thy name is Ezekiel," Father had said, "and thou hast been chosen since the foundations of the world for a great and glorious task. For this reason thy mother chose thy name from the Hebrew, the tongue of the prophets. Ezekiel. It means 'may God strengthen.'"

Ezekiel opened the back door of the temple and stepped into the cool night air. It smelled of sagebrush and sand dunes. Somewhere in the sandstone maze of Witch's Warts a coyote yipped.

"May God strengthen," he whispered. "Because I shall be the new prophet."

CHAPTER TWO

Jacob Christianson entered the bedroom carrying his boots, careful to avoid the worst offenders of his loose floorboards. The house was quiet, the children asleep. Fernie had gone to bed an hour ago and was a still shape beneath the covers, her breathing heavy. He eased her wheelchair out of the way where it blocked his path.

He made his way around to his side of the bed and set down the boots with extra care. Then he unbuttoned his shirt and draped it over the chair next to the window. No pajamas tonight. If he made too much noise, he'd wake his wife, and he didn't want her awake until he was in bed with his arm around her. Then, he was sure she wouldn't push him away.

But she stirred when he pulled back the covers. He froze.

"Jacob," Fernie said in a low, wary voice.

"Shh, go back to sleep."

The bed creaked as she lifted herself into a sitting position. Since the accident, Fernie's legs were partially paralyzed, just shy of useless, but she'd become adept at maneuvering herself around without assistance.

"It's Saturday," she said. "You shouldn't be here."

"Jessie Lyn has been in bed for hours, and you know how hard it is to get comfortable when you're pregnant. I don't want to wake her."

"Don't be ridiculous," Fernie said. "She's only five months along. She's barely even showing."

"I'm sure she can wait." Jacob sat down next to Fernie and felt in the darkness until he found her face. He ran his fingers up her cheek and plunged them into her soft, curly hair. "'Be a polygamist,' they said. 'You'll have sex whenever you want.' They promised!"

Fernie laughed. "Quit complaining, mister," she said in that charmingly scolding voice she used. "You know it won't do any good."

"I'm not complaining. I'm maneuvering."

Fernie laughed again, though it sounded more reluctant this time. She was a rule follower, and she had no use for either deception or complaint.

Jacob had little use for either, himself. Once he'd been pushed into a second marriage, caught in a trap at least partly of his own making, there had been no sense fighting. Nobody liked a whiner, least of all himself. And he knew both Fernie and Jessie Lyn were still struggling to adapt. One clumsy move on his part could cut them deeply.

But inside his own head he still railed at the injustice of it. He never wanted this. He'd been fighting a protracted campaign to eliminate new plural marriages for years, and now he found himself the victim of the very thing he'd tried to prevent.

Fernie reached over and touched Jacob's hand. "You know I'd like to. But it isn't my turn. What happens when you finally show up and Jessie Lyn is lying there awake and waiting for you?"

"I'm sure she's asleep."

"No, you're not. Women have urges too. They get lonely."

"Fine, if she's awake, then I'll do my duty."

"A second time? Could you really?"

Could he? Probably not, actually. A decade ago, sure, but he was facing the downslope of his late thirties now, chronically sleep-deprived from his duties and with so many worries on his shoulders. Millions around the world were suffering and dying, and he felt the continual stress of assuring Blister Creek's own survival. He was still a man, he still responded to a woman's touch, but if he went into Jessie Lyn's room after having made love to Fernie, he'd roll over and fall asleep at once. If Jessie Lyn decided to press him—unlikely though that may be—he might be unable to answer the call.

He sighed.

"Go on," Fernie said. "Tomorrow is our night. I promise I'll make the wait worthwhile."

Reluctantly, Jacob headed for the door. There was a certain shame in being turned down by your wife and slinking out of the room with boots and shirt in hand. Knowing she wanted him too didn't help matters.

He was equally quiet when he slipped into his second bedroom. It was a smaller room in the east wing, past the bedrooms where Jacob's teenage sisters and his father's widows slept. The four-poster bed inside had once belonged to his great-great-grandmother Cowley and managed to seem sturdy and timeless as the Ghost Cliffs, yet rickety at the same time.

As much as he tried to prevent it, Jessie Lyn woke up.

"Are you okay?" she asked.

"Sure," he said. "Sorry for waking you."

It sounded stiff and fake as it came out. He leaned over and kissed her cheek.

She rolled toward him. "It's so late. I expected you up a long time ago. There's nothing wrong, is there?"

"You know, the usual worries."

He'd have answered more truthfully had it been Fernie asking.

Jessie Lyn snuggled closer to him. She was still young, her body curvy but firm, even though she'd already given birth once by her first husband. A slight bulge of her stomach hinted at her pregnancy. New life grew inside her in defiance of the collapse of civilization and the death of millions.

He'd hooked her up to the ultrasound last week. She was carrying a daughter. *His* daughter.

Jessie Lyn wasn't beautiful in a classical sense, but had a cute dimple in her left cheek and a shy, endearing smile. She worked hard and without complaint. That was a valuable trait these days, when the community's survival rested on a knife's edge and there could be no shirkers.

According to his sister-in-law Lillian, Jessie Lyn had been Bill Smoot's favorite wife. But widow with a child or no, any of the old patriarchs of Blister Creek would have been delighted to add such a good, fertile woman to their family either for themselves or for one of their sons. He should be grateful.

"Jacob, I can tell from your voice that something is wrong. You can talk to me."

As she spoke, she slipped her hand beneath his undershirt and trailed her fingers along his chest. She eased one leg between his.

Damn, she *was* in the mood. And his body was betraying him, stiffening as her thigh nestled between his legs.

Before marrying her last year, Jacob had slept with only one woman in his life: Fernie. But a decade of marriage and a medical degree hadn't been enough of an education in sexual matters, apparently. He'd been surprised to discover that Jessie Lyn had her own desires, her own, different ways she liked to be touched. She was more enthusiastic during lovemaking than Fernie, but turned shy and embarrassed the moment it was over. It had taken awhile to tell the difference between when she was feeling cuddly and when she wanted something more. He still wasn't sure in this case.

He pulled back slightly. He couldn't sleep with her, not tonight. Not knowing that Fernie was probably still awake in her room, wondering. He'd distract himself.

"I'm going up to the reservoir tomorrow."

"Oh?" She sounded concerned. "To see if the squatters are still there?"

"We know they're still there. I need to know their intentions."

"That's no secret," Jessie Lyn said. "They're waiting for their chance, that's all."

Her voice was tight. She'd lost her first husband during last summer's turmoil and like most of Blister Creek worried constantly about the gentiles who were still lurking above the valley.

"We don't know that," Jacob said. "Anyway, I'll be careful. We're taking the Humvee and a .50-caliber machine gun. But waving a white flag so they know we're not there to attack their camp."

"I don't like it, Jacob. Please, think it over. It's too dangerous."

"We'll be okay. They haven't bothered us and we haven't bothered them for six months. Not since that last skirmish in the fall when they tried to steal those sheep."

And a full year had passed since the major battle, his attempt to clear them from the reservoir altogether. They'd been poisoning the water to catch fish, polluting it with their overflowing latrines. That water flowed into the valley, which risked transmitting to Blister

Creek cholera and other water-borne illnesses of the kind endemic in the world.

But after the battle, the situation had stabilized. The squatters stopped threatening to overwhelm the valley like a plague of devouring locusts. Jacob had expected them to melt away. Once they'd fished out the reservoir and cleared the hills of game, there'd be no other reason to remain in the cliffs. Yet here they were, a year later, somehow still hanging on with no obvious means of doing so.

"But why?" Jessie Lyn pressed. "What possible good could that do?"

"They might have news about the civil war, about the famine. Maybe even about the volcano, if it has stopped or is erupting again. That will give us an idea how long this will last."

"It's going to last until the Second Coming. We all know that."

Do we? Do we know anything at all?

"We do," she insisted, as if reading his thoughts. "We know it."

Jacob didn't know anything of the sort. The supervolcano in Indonesia was a natural disaster that had chilled the climate, leaving famine and war in its wake. All this talk about Armageddon and the Last Days was the fantasy of an obscure desert cult. No doubt there were other religious sects out there that also thought the global crisis could be attributed to their own peculiar theology. Jacob blamed science and human nature.

But sometimes he felt like the only skeptic left in Blister Creek. His brother David was a believer now, almost as devout as his wife Miriam. Jacob's sister Eliza had spoken in church two weeks ago and, while she wasn't exactly breathing fire about the end of the world, she'd made a few comments about faith and God that made Jacob stiffen. Had she found her testimony? Could he stand it if she had?

Which is it? Am I right and everyone else is wrong? Or am I wrong and everyone else is right?

"Jacob?" Jessie Lyn said.

"Hmm? Just thinking." Again, he concealed his doubts. With Fernie he would have been open. "It may be the end, but you know what the scriptures say. No one knows the day or hour of the Lord's coming."

"We know it's close."

"What does that mean, close? Could be ten years. A hundred."

"That's why we stored food and prepared for the worst," she said, her tone soothing. "Why we always tried to be self-sufficient."

"We're not self-sufficient in medicine. I'm out of morphine, have virtually nothing to treat heart disease. No statins, no antihypertensives. I have to use homemade ether for surgery, and I prescribed my last dose of tetracycline the day before yesterday."

"I know." She probably didn't know the heroic efforts he'd gone through to keep their antibiotics flowing. Recycling unmetabolized antibiotics from the urine of people taking them. Now he was trying to raise cultures of penicillin in a mixture of corn mash and rotting melon, with some promise. Still some details to work out.

"And what about vaccines?" he added. "None of the kids are getting their shots. If you want to see what comes next, take a walk through the cemetery. Look at the gravestones from the 1916 polio epidemic, mostly children. We no longer have a vaccine for that, you know."

Jessie Lyn shifted her hand to her belly and the gentle swelling pressing against him there. "That worries me, you know it does. But our ancestors survived it. We can too. And it's a small danger compared to what's happening in the wider world."

"Maybe," he conceded. "But I'm a doctor. I see fifty kids in this valley who haven't had a single vaccination. I've got to do something about it."

"So you'll leave the valley to get medical supplies?"

"In part, yes."

"And the other part?"

He tried to frame it in a way she would understand. "What if there are other saints out there? Salt Lake Mormons who have repented and left their apostate church now that they see what the world is coming to. Maybe God called them to gather to the valley, but they have no way to get here."

That was more than a little disingenuous. Fernie would have seen through it at once. Jessie Lyn seemed moved.

"Oh, I didn't think of that. And you think some of them might be in the squatter camp? They say it's a den of iniquity."

"I don't know. Maybe, maybe not. But I'll find out."

"Well, if you think it's right." Jessie Lyn hesitated. "You'll be careful, won't you?"

"Of course."

"Hold me, please."

He hadn't given it conscious thought, but he'd been drawing away from her throughout the conversation. She still had her arms around him, albeit at a distance now, and pulled herself up to him. He embraced her.

She felt for his face in the dark, and kissed him on the mouth. He thought she would press him for more, but then she rested her head against his chest. Jacob held her and stroked her hair. He was relieved when her body relaxed and her breathing turned deep and regular.

He thought about Fernie, sleeping alone on the other side of the house, and wished he was in her bed and not this one.

CHAPTER THREE

In the morning, when the roosters were still shouting their morning reveille and the air was cool and smelling of ripening cornfields mingled with sagebrush blowing in off the desert, Jacob roused his son Daniel to help him load the truck.

Daniel was thirteen and growing, his body turning long and lean. His voice had started to change. Once the boy had blinked away the sleep and fought off a bout of yawns, he eagerly helped. Using wheelbarrows, father and son hauled out two barrels of flour, several sacks of dried peas, and three buckets of powdered milk. Once they'd lifted them into the back, Jacob covered them with sheets and shut the doors. He sent Daniel in to help with breakfast.

Before going inside himself, Jacob turned toward the Ghost Cliffs, which lay a few miles to the north. The rising sun turned the sandstone orange and gold. With the wet weather of the past few years, the overhangs and fissures had turned green, and a profusion of rabbit grass and other vegetation joined the juniper and bristlecone pine that had grown there since Jacob's childhood.

While he and Daniel had been loading the supplies, the dogs had trotted hopefully around from the back of the house, as if expecting to jump into the truck and go for a ride. Two of them now retreated to the porch, disappointed, but one still stood there wagging his tail.

"Sorry, boy," Jacob said, reaching down to scratch the old dog behind his ears. "No more joyrides for dogs. Those days are past."

All his dogs were either former strays or animals he'd rescued or healed of some ailment or another. This one had been a poor, starved thing belonging to a man Father had driven out of Blister Creek. Abusing his animals, abusing his family. Not unexpectedly, the dog had turned into one of the most grateful, loyal animals Jacob had ever owned. His only flaw was a propensity to tangle with the skunks that wandered in off the desert.

Jacob spotted his brother David on the porch of the house next door, watching. David came down when he saw Jacob looking. The dog trotted over to greet him, then followed him back, still wagging his tail.

"What are you hiding in there?" David asked with a gesture at the truck. He pushed aside the dog, who was helpfully shoving a nose into his crotch.

"I'm having second thoughts about Miriam," Jacob said. "I don't want her picking a fight. Do you think we should bring Lillian instead?"

"Nice deflection." David glanced at the back of the truck. "Well?"

"I'm not hiding anything."

"Of course. And that's why you got up early to haul all that stuff out. You were going to wait until we get on the road before saying anything."

"Am I that transparent?"

"I'm your brother. Of course you are. So what is it?"

"I miss the days when you remembered you were my *younger* brother," Jacob said with a smile. "And you didn't question me all the time."

David raised an eyebrow. "What brother are you talking about? That was never me. So? What's in there?"

"Flour, peas, powdered milk. Not a lot. Enough to show peaceful intentions."

"And spread the word that we're giving away free food. I'm sure that will help."

"I suppose you'd rather charge in, guns blazing."

"I've had enough killing. But why go up at all? What we're doing is working."

"It's working to keep us bottled up. East is an endless wilderness. Go south and west and we run into bandits. That leaves north, past the squatters."

"There's nothing north either."

"There's no way to know from here, that's for sure. But if we get past the reservoir, we're only an hour drive from Panguitch. Don't you want to know what's up there? If there's still a state government or any towns that aren't completely abandoned?"

"Not really. My curiosity these days is mostly about whether or not we can stay alive for another season." David shrugged. "Anyway, there's no rush. We're safe here. We fought our enemies and won. Let the squatters wither and die. Whatever they're living on, it can't last forever. We stay here, the Lord will protect us. We leave, we face the destruction of the world."

"You sound like a fundamentalist," Jacob accused.

"I have a family to protect now. The world has destroyed itself. Then I look around and see this safe place, filled with my people, my tribe. People who fight and die to keep me safe. Of course I'm a conservative in these circumstances. And yeah, suspicious about out-siders. The only question I have is why you aren't."

Jacob drummed his fingers against the side of the Humvee.

"Jacob?"

"What if it's over and we're staying here for no reason?"

"How do you mean?" David asked.

"Say the war has ended. The famine too. The survivors are pull-ing together. We'll go to Panguitch, Richfield, Cedar City. Find the survivors, pull them together. Trade, exchange information. Fight the bandits together. Keep pushing outward until we form a new govern-ment. Maybe just a few towns to start, then the whole state. After that, who knows?"

"Get real, Jacob. Nothing like that will happen. The only thing that will bring peace is the Second Coming. You need to stand up straight and start acting like our prophet. If you don't, the Lord will choose someone who will."

Jacob stared, dumbfounded. With that comment, he knew for certain. He'd lost David.

His gaze fell on the faithful old dog. Still standing there, still wagging his tail. Still hoping to go for a ride. Not that Jacob expected people to be dogs, but couldn't his closest brother, at least, be more trusting? He determined to keep his doubts to himself, at least so far as David was concerned.

"I'm sorry," David said after a moment, his voice softer. "I didn't mean that. I'm worried about this scheme is all. You won't win friends in the squatter camp. They've killed our people, we've killed theirs. No amount of gift giving will ever change that hatred."

"Maybe you're right, but I've got to try."

"You're dead set on this?"

"I am."

David chewed on his lip and glanced back and forth between his brother and the truck. Finally, he sighed. "Okay, then. I'm not convinced, but fine. I'll support you. But don't talk about the food until we're under way. Then you can argue it all you want."

"That was my plan all along. About Miriam—what if we took Lillian instead?"

"There's nothing wrong with Lillian, I trust her. But we need Miriam. If things turn ugly, nobody else gives us a better chance."

"Then talk to her first," Jacob said.

"About what?"

"Make sure she's on a short leash. I'm happy to have Miriam finish a fight, but I can't have her starting one."

★★★

Jacob went inside for breakfast. When he came back out, David and Miriam had already come from next door and were standing by the front bumper of the Humvee, chatting. Miriam had changed out of her prairie dress for the occasion, and wore jeans and a long-sleeve shirt, with a tan utility vest, full of pockets. Her hair had grown out since she'd cut it trying to sneak into Las Vegas, and she wore it in a simple ponytail.

While David and Miriam spoke, she was laying out an array of weapons across the hood: an AR-15 assault rifle, two pistols, a pair of shotguns, plus a zipper case carrying a second rifle, this one fixed with a scope and tripod. Also, various ammo cans and boxes of shells, plus a pile of Kevlar vests. Seeing Miriam's smooth, businesslike movements filled Jacob with confidence. When she wanted to be, Miriam was calm and efficient.

She glanced up as Jacob arrived. "Why'd you lock the truck? I couldn't get this stuff in."

"Habit, I guess."

"What habit? You usually leave the doors unlocked and the keys in the ignition."

"Do I?" Jacob avoided David's gaze and handed Miriam a pair of handheld radios. "I'll load it up. You two test these radios, and make sure the batteries are good. I had to change out one of them the other day—it wouldn't hold a charge anymore."

He opened the back and tossed the vests on top of the blanket concealing the foodstuffs, then loaded the ammo and guns. When he came back around, his sister Eliza was riding up on a chestnut mare.

She wore jeans and a long-sleeve denim shirt, with boots and a baseball cap. Apart from the hat, she was looking suspiciously like a polygamist wife. Even though many other women had begun to wear their hair in shorter, more practical styles, Eliza had been growing her own hair out again. It was now in two long, blond braids that trailed halfway down her back. How long until she came to Jacob asking for a second wife for her husband?

Don't be paranoid, he thought. *You're worked up because of David. Eliza would never do that. And Steve wouldn't go for a second wife either.*

Two of Jacob's younger brothers came out for Eliza's horse, which they led around the house toward the stables.

Jacob and David loaded the rest of the gear in the back of the Humvee while Eliza and Miriam exchanged pleasantries. By the time it was in there, the food under the blanket didn't stand out so much. When Jacob came back, David suggested they pray before setting out. That was a good idea, Jacob said. How about David do the praying?

Jacob opened his eyes midway through the prayer. The others—even Eliza—stood with their hands together in front of them, their heads bowed solemnly. The faith seemed to radiate off them like the heat shimmering from the hood of the Humvee. Each of these people had saved his life before. Yet he felt more distant from them now, more lonely than he could ever remember.

The four of them climbed into the Humvee, Eliza up front with Jacob. Fuel was so precious, the sound of a vehicle so rare, that people hurried out to their porches to watch as they drove through town. Jacob cruised at a slow speed, waving through the open windows to let them know there was no emergency.

"Glad we're not driving past the Smoot house," Eliza said. "Soon as he spotted us he'd raise an army and march it into the cliffs. Just in case."

"I warned Elder Smoot we were going," Jacob said, "and for exactly that reason. I told Sister Rebecca and the Griggs family too. Don't need the alarmists riled up."

They pulled past the temple, gleaming in the morning sun, then drove up the highway along the edge of Witch's Warts. It stretched toward the cliffs in a vast maze of red fins and knobby hoodoos that stood like rows of silent sentinels off the shoulder of the road. Soon they were in the open land with the cliffs looming ahead of them. The highway cut straight to their base, then became a twisting snake as it climbed a series of switchbacks to the top.

Grover and Ezekiel Smoot were guarding the guns at the main bunker halfway up, and Jacob slowed as they approached. A pair of horses loafed in the shade of a lean-to shed on one side of the bunker.

Ezekiel came out to Jacob's rolled-down window, a rifle slung over his shoulder. The young man was in his midtwenties, with the same dark hair and intense gaze as his father. He had a short-cropped beard and thin lips. He wasn't the most handsome man in town, but he carried himself with a confidence that Jacob respected.

"Trouble?" Ezekiel asked.

"Nothing to worry about. A little reconnaissance. Been a long time since I've been to the reservoir, and I want to make sure the squatters aren't up to anything. Has it been quiet here?"

"Dead," Ezekiel said with a shrug. "Need me to come along? Grover can handle the .50-cal while I'm gone."

"Nah, we're good. I'm not expecting trouble."

Ezekiel nodded. "We'll listen for gunfire, just in case."

"Sure, if you hear anything send Grover to Yellow Flats and warn Sister Rebecca. But you stay at the machine gun."

"Got it," Ezekiel said with a curt nod. "God be with you."

After they'd pulled away, Miriam spoke up from the back of the vehicle. "Hey, Jacob. Want to explain all this food?"

"Nothing much to explain. It's exactly what it looks like."

"Looks to me like a gift. Or a bribe. So I guess I have no idea, because it couldn't be either of those things."

"It's a gift," he admitted. "We barely dipped into the food stores last year, and this year we've got a good crop planted and no late frosts."

"No late frosts *yet*," David said.

"Yet," Jacob conceded. "But you'll have to admit the weather seems less . . . *weird*. I think we'll get a solid harvest. We can spare some food."

"It's not a question of whether or not we can spare it," Eliza said. She sounded equally concerned. "You know that. We're trying to shrink the squatter camp, not grow it. How many millions of hungry people are there in the world at this moment, ready to come running the instant they hear we've gone soft?"

"That's the whole point," Jacob said. "We don't have any idea. For all we know, the government has sorted out the food situation."

Some scoffing came from the others at this.

"Anyway," Jacob continued when they quieted down, "people can hardly come running across two hundred miles of desert. And they're not going to do it for two barrels of flour, three buckets of powdered milk, and a few sacks of dried peas."

"I'd rather not find out for sure," David said.

Jacob didn't say anything more, and it seemed that all the objections had been voiced.

They reached the cliffs and the reservoir. It was quiet up here, the water lapping against the shore to their right. The floods had receded from the old picnic grounds, leaving behind a thick layer of mud and sticks. Scraps of clothing lay half-buried in the mud, and a single tent pole stood upright with a plastic garbage bag flapping against the side.

A single cut tree blocked the highway, but there was no sign of gunmen hiding in the boulders that had rolled down from the hills to abut the road. They quickly winched the tree out of the way. David went up top to man the .50-cal behind the gun shield, but Jacob told him to keep the gun pointed away from the camp and into the hillside as they approached, so as not to look threatening.

"Pass up that white sheet," Jacob told Miriam. Then, when Eliza had it, he told his sister to hang it out the window.

Moments later Jacob slowed as they reached the outskirts of the camp. The squatters had dragged more logs across the road and down the shoulder toward the reservoir, with two battered cars without tires pushed up behind to reinforce them. It wasn't a serious barrier—the Humvee could winch it all out of the way—but it might stop them for thirty minutes or more, plus force them to leave the protection of the vehicle and expose themselves to gunfire while hooking up the winch.

The refugees in the camp must have heard the engine, because several hundred came up to line the road behind the barrier, staring toward the approaching vehicle. Plenty of rifles and shotguns in evidence, but no hostile moves. Not yet, anyway.

A year had passed since the battle up here, and little had changed with the camp's outward appearance. There were tents and camper trailers and wagons overturned and converted into dugouts. Nobody had bothered to build anything so substantial as a log cabin or a shack with a corrugated metal roof.

But as Jacob stopped the Humvee in front of the barrier and studied the camp more closely, he noticed a few important differences. First, no latrines near the reservoir. After last fall's bloody battle, precipitated in part because the refugees were polluting Blister Creek's water supply, Jacob had broken the subsequent standoff a few months later to send in another armed excursion. Not to attack, but to deliver demands. Stop fishing with poison. Shift the camp two hundred yards from the water's edge. And move the latrines to the other side of the highway.

The moment someone in Blister Creek sickened from cholera, Jacob warned, he would send his forces into the hills and wipe the camp off the face of the earth. But if the squatters respected the town's water supply, he would leave them be.

The other obvious thing that had changed was the surrounding landscape. Pine and aspen forests had once covered the hillsides above the reservoir. Before the collapse, when the summer sun blasted the valley floor, half of Blister Creek would decamp for the reservoir. They boated and fished and swam, while the cool mountain breeze washed down through the trees, shaking the leaves of the aspens and making the pines sway. They picnicked in the cool shade of the cottonwood trees that grew up to the water's edge.

But the downside of the extra elevation was the bitter cold and snow that pounded the mountains during the winter. It wasn't easy to stay warm up here. By last spring, the refugees had already burned up the picnic tables and cottonwood trees from the park, then moved across the road to attack the woods that grew up the mountainside. Now it looked as though some brutal logging operation had attacked the surrounding hills, leaving thousands of naked stumps. There wasn't so much as a sapling left standing.

"Like goats in a pea patch," Eliza said, taking it in beside him. "It'll be fifty years before this grows back."

Jacob was so shocked by the destruction of their beautiful mountain sanctuary that he was out of the truck before he noticed the other surprising change to the refugee camp.

He was a doctor. His eye naturally went to the children wearing dirty rags for bandages, the old woman bent nearly double by scoliosis, using a ski pole as a cane. A man had a forearm poorly splinted between two flimsy pieces of particleboard. A couple of people were missing limbs. Probably had them sawed off nineteenth-century-style after last year's firefight. But what Jacob didn't see was obvious malnutrition.

These people should be starving. They *had* been starving. He'd seen them last spring, hungry and lean and bony. And when Joe Kemp's band of refugees had come limping into the valley from the south, they'd had that same starved look. Even Steve, when Eliza brought him back from Vegas, hadn't lost his hollow, hungry look for weeks.

These refugees were not fat by any means. Not even well fed. But they weren't starving either. And there were several young children and old adults. Not the sort of people to survive a famine.

Something or someone was feeding these people.

He was about to whisper his observation to Eliza, who had come up next to him as Miriam also stepped out of the Humvee. Only David stayed with the vehicle, up top with the machine gun. But then a man stepped over the logs and approached them.

His filthy, layered clothing, unkempt beard, and matted, dirty hair made him look like the homeless men Jacob had seen in Salt Lake when he was a medical resident. The homeless had slept on cardboard mats beneath the freeway overpasses or had come shuffling out of the Salt Lake Rescue Mission. Most were mentally ill or suffering from a substance abuse problem.

But this man carried himself with a confidence that belied his appearance. He wore a pistol in a nylon shoulder holster, like an FBI agent or police detective. The sight of it made Jacob and his companions stiffen.

"Stay calm, all of you," Jacob said, although the comment was mostly directed at Miriam.

Her typical behavior was to shoot first and then ask questions, except never mind the questions. Who needed to question a dead body? And the dead guy was probably a servant of the devil, anyway.

Thankfully, she remained still, her gun in its own holster. Instead, she met the man's gaze, her mouth drawn tight, then cast a significant glance up to David at the machine gun. A message and a warning to the approaching man. Jacob could live with that.

The man approached warily until he stood about fifteen feet off. "What do you want?"

"I'm Jacob Christianson. I'm from Blister Creek, and I—"

"Yeah, I know who you are. We all know. Now get the hell out of here before you start another war."

CHAPTER FOUR

Jacob stared back at the man, unwilling to simply turn around and go home. The man stared back. His expression darkened further.

"I don't want trouble," Jacob said. "Keep your people back. We'll talk. There's no harm in that."

For a moment he thought the man would resist, and then there *would* be trouble, but then the man turned to the approaching squatters, some of whom were preparing to come over the barrier.

"Stay calm, all of you. I've got this."

"Send them to the camp," Jacob said.

The man glared at him for a long moment, then ordered his people back.

Again, they obeyed, retreating into the camp, some seventy or eighty yards distant. There they massed, watching, whispering amongst themselves. They were still too close. A couple of snipers hidden down there could kill Jacob and his companions before they could reach the safety of the vehicle. But that would be the death of the snipers. First, David would light into them from behind the safety of his gun shield. Then the machine gun would chew through the camp, killing hundreds. And then, when Blister Creek heard about the treachery at the reservoir, they'd mount a full campaign.

"So what do you want?" the man said.

"All I want is to talk. But first I brought you something. Can I give it to you?"

"Yeah?" His eyes narrowed suspiciously. "What kind of something?"

"What is your name?"

"Go to hell."

"It's a name, that's all." Jacob was growing impatient. "Do you want to be enemies?"

"Too late for that, asshole. We tried, you came in shooting."

"You didn't 'try' anything. This is our land, we own it. You invaded, destroying everything and making demands." As soon as the words came out, Jacob regretted them.

Miriam tapped Jacob's shoulder. She leaned in and whispered. "Let me talk to him."

Jacob frowned and gave a slight shake of the head. The last thing he needed was Miriam striking a match to things.

"Trust me."

He glanced at Eliza, who shrugged. Jacob stepped back and let Miriam take the forefront.

"You're former law enforcement," she said.

"What makes you say that?" the man said.

As soon as she said it, Jacob saw what she meant. There was something about the way he carried himself. Confident, poised for action. Jacob hadn't noticed at first, but supposed that Miriam had, and for the same reason that Jacob had been scanning the refugees for medical conditions.

Miriam tapped her chest. "I was FBI."

"Hah, right."

"Special Agent Haley Kite," she said. Her old name. "Salt Lake City Field Office. They sent me to investigate this crazy cult."

"And now you're one of them? How did that happen?"

"Long story."

For what became for Jacob an uncomfortably long time, the two of them flatly regarded each other in silence.

"You know my name," Miriam said at last, without taking her eyes from his.

"Mine's McQueen," he said.

"Steve, I'm hoping."

A slight roll of the eyes. Not the first time he'd heard that. "Whit."

"What?"

"No, Whit," he said, with what might've been the beginning of a smile. "Whit McQueen."

"Almost as good. That's right out of central casting."

"Huh?"

"Whit McQueen. It sounds like Sylvester Stallone's buddy in a crappy old action movie. Is that your real name?"

"Whitney until kindergarten. Fewer fights with Whit."

She nodded. "So I'm thinking cop. Am I right?"

"Army. Military police, so yeah, you're pretty much right. I was at Green River for a while until the army shut down the camp. Caught some bug there. By the time I got out of the hospital, the nearest base was in Denver, and I had no way to get there." He shrugged. "Guess that makes me a deserter."

"Sounds like the army deserted *you*," Miriam said.

"Yeah, more or less."

"Bastards."

McQueen returned a wry smile.

Jacob glanced at her, impressed. She could be such a hard case that he'd almost forgotten that Miriam had gained her reputation in the FBI by infiltrating criminal organizations. It's what had brought her to the saints in the first place, only she'd infiltrated so deeply that she'd never got herself back out again. Here, she'd used that same skill to soften up McQueen.

"Look," she said. "Both sides screwed up last time. You guys were hungry, and we were scared. Some crap started and then got out of hand."

That was disingenuous, considering that Miriam had been among those most strongly advocating the move to destroy and scatter the squatter camp. Her explanation was of the "mistakes were made" variety. Surely, McQueen would see through it.

But no. "I wasn't here yet," McQueen said, "but I heard. Ugly stuff. But I see why you're jumpy. My dad joined the brush war in Kansas, fighting to keep the government from taking his corn. So I understand trying to protect what's yours. I get it."

"That's pretty much it right there."

"You still didn't need to come in here shooting."

"Like I said, we screwed up."

The conversation faltered. McQueen stared at them, seemingly undecided. He glanced up at David at the .50-caliber machine gun, and the scowl refreshed itself.

Jacob whispered to Eliza to bring out the food. Turning back to McQueen, he said, "We brought you something. No obligation. And it's not a lot, but we can't spare much. Not at the moment. It's just to show our intentions are peaceful."

McQueen watched as the three of them hauled out the food and set it in the road. "What is it, wheat?"

"Dried peas. Flour. Oh, and powdered milk."

McQueen's eyes flickered at this last bit. So he had food—that part hadn't impressed him. But powdered milk was something more valuable. Interesting.

"And you don't want anything at all in return?"

"Peace. A chance to go back to before things screwed up."

"Too late for that. But I can tell you that if you stay out of our way, we'll stay out of yours."

"Fair enough," Jacob said. "How are things out there, anyway? Heard anything from the government lately?"

"Government? There's no government."

"What about the army?" Miriam asked. "We know there were irregular troops out there. I'm sure some of those guys are still lurking around."

McQueen shook his head. "Haven't seen anything like that. A few bandits on horse up north of Panguitch, that's about it."

"Panguitch still abandoned?" Jacob asked.

The last time he'd been there was around the time the squatter camp formed at the reservoir. He and David had scavenged the abandoned hospital for supplies. There had been a few ranchers and such still hanging on, but otherwise the town had been taken over by starving dogs and tumbleweed.

"Not a soul in sight," McQueen said. "Other places are the same. Parowan burned to the ground. Tropic is covered with drifting sand. There's no town or settlement of any kind within fifty miles."

Really? Then who is feeding you?

Curiosity was gnawing at him, but he didn't want to put the man on his guard.

"I'd like to drive on through to check things out," Jacob said. "But we'll have to come back this way to get home. So I want to make sure we have an understanding."

"What kind of understanding?"

"That we'll have free passage. That you'll open the highway and won't block it again before we get back."

"Do that," Miriam added, "and we'll have trouble."

"I'm sure he wouldn't do that," Jacob said quickly. "But I want to be clear up front."

"See, I can't allow you through," McQueen said. "Not yet. You want something from us, you've got to give us something in return."

"We gave you food," Miriam grumbled. "And you have no right to block our highway, anyway."

"It's a *state* highway," McQueen said with a smile.

"Which you have already pointed out no longer exists," Miriam said.

"Exactly."

The atmosphere was growing antagonistic again, so Jacob moved to defuse it. "Looks like your boots are worn through. And I'll bet you could use a few wool blankets. I could give you ten. Also, I could probably spare another hundred pounds of powdered milk."

"When?"

"How about Monday?"

McQueen scoffed. "You think I know what day it is?"

"Today is Saturday," Jacob said. "Tomorrow is Sunday, and I can't do it on the Sabbath. So, two days from now. Do we have a deal?"

"Got any meat?"

"Not a lot. But I could bring up maybe twenty pounds of jerky."

"Jacob," David called down from the Humvee. "Are you sure about this?"

"Make it fifty pounds of jerky," McQueen said. "And ten pairs of boots. Twenty blankets. Do that and we've got a deal."

Jacob shook his head. "Not for the right to drive past your camp."

"Then forget it."

"We're going through here." Jacob felt his temper rising. "You can make it difficult. But you can't stop us."

"Yeah? You might be surprised."

"Is that a game you want to play?" Jacob asked. "Fine."

He turned to go. It was only half bluff.

"Come back on Monday," McQueen said when Jacob was half-way to the truck. "Bring that stuff you said. We'll let you up and back one time. After that, we'll see."

Jacob turned back. He met the man's gaze, then slowly nodded. "It's a deal."

★★★

"What a crock," Miriam said from the backseat when they were in the truck and driving down toward Blister Creek. David remained up top at the machine gun.

"What's that?" Jacob asked.

"He was bluffing," Miriam said. "You didn't have to give them a thing. We could have forced them to open the gate for nothing."

"I'm not so sure," Jacob said. He glanced at Eliza, sitting in the seat next to him. "What do you think?"

His sister chewed on her lower lip. "Something was off. I can't place it."

"You know what we do?" Miriam said. "We go home, we gas up Steve's armored car. Grab Lillian, Stephen Paul, and Sister Rebecca. On our way we pick up the Smoot brothers. We can be back here in an hour."

"Then what?" Jacob asked. "Blast our way through?"

"No need," she said. "They'll back down when they see we mean business. If they don't, if they play games when we get back from Panguitch—or wherever you want to go—then we make them pay."

"Oh, I get it," Jacob said. "Tear up their camp again. Mow down a bunch of hungry refugees. Is that about right?"

Miriam didn't answer.

"Is it just me, or did that McQueen guy seem well fed?" Eliza asked.

She'd seen it too, Jacob thought.

"Sure," Miriam said. "He's the head of the camp. If he doesn't eat, nobody does."

"Except there were a bunch of kids and old people too," Eliza said. "We didn't see many people like that in Las Vegas. None of them made it."

"Which means the whole camp is getting fed," Jacob said.

"Hmm," Miriam said. "You're sure?"

"McQueen was nonchalant when we unloaded the food," Jacob said. "The only thing that got him excited was the powdered milk. Then he asked for meat, not more grain. They're not starving."

"I don't see how he could be getting food shipments," Eliza said. "They shut down the camp at Green River because they couldn't feed refugees anymore. So it's hard to imagine shipping it another two hundred and fifty miles."

"The only thing I can think is Alacrán and his irregulars again," Jacob said. "Feeding the camp to be a thorn in our side."

"Yeah, that doesn't make sense either," Miriam said. She'd turned around and was messing with the guns, a sure sign that she was still nervous. "We bloodied Alacrán's nose last time around. We haven't heard a peep from them since last year."

"Are you really going to give them more of our food?" Eliza asked.

"And blankets and boots too? Just so we can use the highway without coming under attack?"

"An attack we could brush off like a mosquito bite," Miriam added.

"The weather is straightening out," Jacob said. "That means there's nothing stopping us from rebuilding, from going out, finding others, and starting it all over again."

"There's nobody out there," Miriam said. "And nothing left to rebuild."

"I've got to agree with Miriam," Eliza said. "It feels like we've fallen into a deep well and can't get out."

"A well is a good place to be when there are bombs going off overhead," Miriam said.

Both women had a point, Jacob thought. Blister Creek had fought through another winter. Most of the modern comforts were gone: flushing toilets, hot showers, cheap electricity for washing and cooking. Clothes that wore out and could be replaced for a few bucks. Internet, telephone service. Even the radio was dead; there was nothing but crackling and the occasional static-filled voice from hundreds of miles away that would appear and vanish like a ghost. Maybe if they had a more powerful transmitter they could reach someone, but so far, nothing. It appeared that the world no longer existed beyond the valley and its reservoir.

Yet Blister Creek itself had adapted. For now.

He was not as confident in their long-term chances. Medicine was a problem. Tools could not be replaced. Even their once vast stores of diesel fuel needed rationing. Some day the hydro turbines would break and the solar panels would stop working.

If civilization as a whole didn't rebuild, the survivors would sink further and further into anarchy and chaos until they faced another

Dark age. It might last for generations. 600 AD all over again, except with millions of guns and endless stores of ammunition.

"Someone has to take the first step," he said. "Why can't it be us?"

"The only rebuilding will come in the Millennium," Miriam said. "But first the world must be cleansed with fire."

"We don't know that."

"Yes, we do," Miriam said.

There was no use arguing with a fanatic, and when Eliza said nothing, but simply stared glumly out the window, he didn't want to engage her either. Frankly, he didn't want to know. If she'd gone down the same path as David and Miriam, then what?

Then he'd be alone.

CHAPTER FIVE

Miriam was in sacrament meeting when the note fell into her lap. Elder Smoot stood at the pulpit, delivering a passionate talk that compared the burning of the wicked in the Last Days to the need to cleanse one's own heart of evil desires. He called on the congregation to open to 2 Peter 3:10. When Miriam opened her scriptures, the note dropped out of that exact spot.

She palmed it and shot a quick glance at David and Lillian. Her husband was reading the scripture himself, while her sister wife was helping Miriam's son Diego search through his own Bible. David's third wife, Clarissa, was nursing her baby, half-dozing in the way of exhausted new mothers.

Miriam shifted her daughter Abigail to her other knee and used the toddler to block the note from the view of David and Lillian. She gave it a quick glance, felt her pulse quicken, then tucked the note into the back of her scriptures.

Smoot's voice turned into a drone as Miriam's thoughts circled the note's contents. When the meeting ended, she handed Abigail to Lillian. "Could you bring her home and get her down for her nap? I'm going to take a quick walk through town."

"Are you okay?"

"Trying to clear my head. Thinking about this thing at the reservoir tomorrow."

Miriam lingered outside the chapel while the congregation dispersed. Women in long dresses and braided hair pushed strollers, while men with beards spoke in earnest tones, discussing crops, speculating on the wars and rumors of wars and other, more trivial issues. Elder Smoot strolled past, his cane tucked under one arm, two of his wives following him down the sidewalk, themselves trailed by a dozen children.

Smoot gave Miriam a curt nod, which she returned. He no longer seemed to believe that she meant to overthrow priesthood authority in Blister Creek, yet neither had he warmed to her as an equal in the community.

Was it you? she wondered. *Did you put the note there on the scripture you intended to read from the pulpit?*

What a strange thing that would be. Elder Smoot, one of the senior members of the Quorum of the Twelve, and full of patriarchal vigor. A staunch opponent of the Women's Council and a man who still offered to trade his daughters to other men in marriage, who told his sons when they could or could not take a wife. Not openly defiant of Jacob, per se, but certainly violating the prophet's intentions.

Miriam waited until the last children had been shooed along by their mothers, the last old woman had hobbled away. When they were gone, she crossed the empty parking lot toward the temple, her scriptures in hand. After making sure nobody was watching, she slipped into the sandstone fins behind the building. Soon, she was out of view, in the deep shadows cast by the looming stones.

Unlike most of the church members, Miriam had not grown up in Blister Creek, and the labyrinth filled her with unease. People could and did get lost among the strange, twisting formations. People had seen dark angels. Conspirators had met beneath the frowning overhangs. The Kimball cult had used Witch's Warts to infiltrate Blister Creek, emerging near the temple to work their evil. Witch's Warts was a strange and savage place, but the only spot where she could be assured of solitude.

So she picked her way a hundred yards or so in, careful to study landmarks, before stopping in a clearing. A giant knee of sandstone rose to her left, while to her right sat a wide, overturned bowl of red stone the size of a house and the shape of a turtle shell breaking the surface of the sand. Behind her, two narrow fins closed in so tightly they were nearly kissing.

A whiptail lizard came strutting and bobbing through the sunny patch in the middle of the clearing. When Miriam moved, it broke into a sprint, flew across a dune, and disappeared down the other side. A crow cawed from deeper into the maze.

Miriam opened her scriptures and removed the note. She read it again.

The Hour of Destruction is nigh. There shall be no rebuilding, no truce, no accommodation with evil. This wicked world shall not know peace until the return of our Redeemer. Then shall the earth be cleansed.

These things thou knowest in thy heart. Error has entered this holy valley, and only the blood of the faithful shall resist the machinations of the Enemy. Yea, even the Father of Lies.

Sundown, Yellow Flats.

Miriam turned the paper over. There was nothing on the other side.

The note wasn't explicitly addressed to her. Maybe it had fallen into her hands by accident. Yet it had been in her scriptures. Her name was written on the title page inside the black leather cover.

Then perhaps it had come to her late. Who was to say that today was the meeting at Yellow Flats? Maybe the note was weeks or months old and she'd missed it earlier.

Except the note had fallen directly from 2 Peter, the exact chapter chosen by Elder Smoot for his reading. That explained Smoot's significant look after church. He must have called the meeting at Yellow Flats, had known Miriam would open her Bible to that spot because it was his sermon and he knew she always followed along in her scriptures.

A year ago she would have crumpled the note and thrown it away. No, she would have shown it to David, and if her husband dismissed it, she would have taken it to Jacob. And if Jacob dismissed it, she would have investigated personally.

The danger of such a thing was obvious. The Zarahemla Compound—her first religious community, and where she had cast aside the errors of her old way of life—had been torn apart by an inner circle of conspirators who thought they knew better than the prophet. Here in Blister Creek, the Church of the Anointing had suffered repeated attack from the Kimballs acting out a similar conspiracy.

This note, Miriam would have known a year ago, threatened more of the same. At best, questioning the prophet was steadying the Ark, as the scriptures put it. At worst, it was a plan concocted, whispered by Satan himself, designed to send doubt and evil into the hearts of men.

A year ago, she was proud to have married the prophet's brother, to have taken the Christianson name. Jacob had repeatedly saved them from destruction, and was evidently the One Mighty and Strong, who would lead the saints into the Millennium.

Then Jacob seemed to lose his nerve. He'd flinched at the violence of the reservoir battle and the subsequent fight to drive off bandits and army irregulars south of town. Maybe all the death led him to think he could compromise with evil. Or maybe he'd proven unable to handle the rigors of plural marriage—heaven knew it wasn't easy—when Jessie Lyn had requested and received Jacob in marriage after Jessie Lyn's first husband died under Jacob's command.

Either way, this mission to Panguitch tomorrow was pure folly. And giving supplies to the refugees was *worse* than folly. You couldn't buy off a plague of locusts. They'd keep eating until nothing remained.

Miriam reread the note. The wind picked up and rustled the pages of her scriptures. She shut the book and set it on a rock, then laid another piece of sandstone on top to pin it down and keep the pages from flapping. Then she dropped to her knees, clenching the piece of paper.

She poured out her heart to the Lord. Should she ride to Yellow Flats? Should she speak with the conspirators? What if they advocated open rebellion against the Lord's anointed?

"If the prophet commands, I'll kill on his behalf," Miriam continued. "I will die in defense of my people." She paused, licked her lips. "But what if he is no longer the prophet? How would I know?"

A simple impression came into her mind. Not a voice, exactly, but strong enough to squeeze the shifting sands of her own thoughts and compress them into stone.

Go to Yellow Flats. Listen. Share your testimony and your knowledge. Then decide.

Miriam rose slowly to her feet. She brushed the sand from her dress. Now that she'd decided, a warm feeling of peace filled her bosom, and this told her she was obeying the will of the Lord.

Her thoughts turned to speculation about the meeting as she picked her way out of Witch's Warts. Sister Rebecca would be there—it was her home. The woman thought of herself as something of a prophetess, and had proclaimed herself the spiritual reincarnation of Henrietta Rebecca Cowley, founder of Blister Creek. And Elder Smoot would be there, she presumed. Who else? What others worried about the spiritual lethargy weakening their leader? Plenty. Maybe every member of the Women's Council and man in the Quorum of the Twelve would be on hand. Every important person but Jacob himself.

Miriam was relieved when she emerged behind the temple to find both the temple grounds and the chapel parking lot next door deserted. There was nobody on the sidewalk, no riders in the street, no people standing on porches on the opposite side of the street to observe her coming out of the labyrinth. She hurried to the sidewalk and then walked casually toward home.

It was only an hour later, sitting at the table as David blessed the food, that she realized she'd forgotten her scriptures in Witch's Warts. The book was still sitting there, weighed down by a broken chunk of sandstone. How had she forgotten to pick it up on her way out?

It seemed like a bad omen.

CHAPTER SIX

After lunch, Jacob rode out to meet Stephen Paul on the highway north of town. He'd have rather been meeting Eliza. Not only for her sharp mind, but so he could test her, see if she was racing down the same pathway of fundamentalism as David. But his sister now lived on the far east side of the valley with her husband, and he hadn't managed to speak with her at church before she'd set off for home.

Although if he was honest with himself, he hadn't tried very hard to track her down. He was afraid of what he'd discover when he questioned her.

Jacob felt more confident when he saw his counselor astride a mare on the north end of the grid of streets that marked the center of Blister Creek. Stephen Paul stood tall and confident in the saddle. He had always been faithful, first to Abraham Christianson, then to his son.

The man was waiting outside the boarded-over windows of a brick building. Over the years, the building had taken turns as town department store, a diner, and a five and dime, but commerce was a relic of the time before the collapse. Now it was town storage. Inside lay old-fashioned plows, crank threshers, grain augers, and other farm tools rescued from barns where they'd been abandoned decades ago and brought here to be refurbished for reuse.

"What order do we take it?" Stephen Paul asked as Jacob trotted up on his own horse.

"Let's start up at the Poulsen place, then the Smoot's. After that, we can hook around the valley clockwise until we finish out by Yellow Flats."

"That'll be what—about five hours to make the circuit?" Stephen Paul said. "That has us finishing around sundown. Sound right to you?"

"It does," Jacob said, reconsidering. "Come to think of it, we're better off hitting the Smoots last, when everyone will be inside getting ready for supper. I'd rather not be riding suspiciously across his land."

"I wouldn't worry about that. It's Sunday, and he's unlikely to be outside working." Stephen Paul adjusted his wide-brimmed hat. "But I suppose it wouldn't hurt. Let's go."

They trotted north in silence for a few minutes. It was not unusually warm for this time of year, but still in the low eighties, by the feel of it. Seasonal for late May. This time the past two years they'd still been facing late frosts, cold rain, and sleet. The heat and dry weather were encouraging. The volcano had done its worst, and now the earth was recovering. Too bad Jacob couldn't say the same for human civilization.

That would happen eventually. It had to.

"Thanks for coming along," Jacob said.

"Of course."

"I can tell you think it's a waste of time. But you didn't argue." Jacob smiled. "You're about the only one these days who doesn't. Even my wives were full of questions as I headed out the door."

"That's what wives do. It's in the job description."

Jacob chuckled.

"Anyway, it's a nice day for a ride," Stephen Paul said, "and I enjoy your company. You make me think. I don't get enough of that these days."

"It's hard to be philosophical when you have to chop fifteen cords of wood to survive the winter."

"Not to mention plowing fourteen hours in back of a mule team. You know, I used to wish I lived back in the nineteenth century," Stephen Paul added. "Forge trails, cut a homestead out of the wilderness. Didn't seem there was much for a man to do these days. That was my biggest gripe when you set up the Women's Council. You know my wife Carol—nobody would say she wasn't as tough and smart as a man. A woman like that *should* be making decisions for the community.

"But you take a man and you drag him into the modern world," he continued, "put him on a tractor, give him a gas-powered log splitter. A snowblower, a chainsaw. Anyone can do that kind of labor. A kid, a woman, my father—he's eighty years old. Then you give women an equal say in running things. Not saying they shouldn't, just that it's a change. What's left for a man? He's not a woman, he can't do the things a woman can do. But he can't do male things anymore either. Not better than anyone else can. See what I'm saying?"

"A little bit, yeah." Jacob wasn't sure he agreed, but he couldn't dismiss the question out of hand either.

"Anyway, no worries now. We all work like draft animals these days, and with tractors gathering dust in barns, a man's muscles are suddenly a valuable commodity." Stephen Paul glanced over with a smile. "Turns out, I don't like that much either. It's exhausting work, wrings the sweat out your body. At the end of the day you want to collapse. Not much energy left for thinking."

"You're making me think right now," Jacob said.

"Good. That's a change, me making *you* think."

They rode the horses down the center of the abandoned strip of blacktop. A distance they'd covered in ten minutes yesterday in the Humvee now took an hour. To the right lay Witch's Warts; to the left, fields of wheat sprouting with tiny shoots of green, laid out in neat rows, laced with empty irrigation ditches, their sluices closed. Shortly, a shimmering steel grain silo squatted near a pair of red-painted barns set a quarter mile off from a white farmhouse with two wide wings. It was the Poulsen compound.

"What do you think, should we tell Brother Poulsen we're on his land?" Stephen Paul asked. "Wouldn't want him spotting a couple of unannounced riders and grabbing his gun."

"Poulsen's not the type to come out shooting. And if he asks, we'll tell him. Besides," Jacob added, "it's not his grain in the silo. It belongs to the church."

A concrete bunker topped with sandbags sat twenty feet off from the silo. During the Federal occupation of the valley at the start of the crisis, the government had stationed gunmen there at all times. After the military pulled out, Jacob had posted his own guards for a time, before withdrawing them for more clearly useful purposes.

To one of the starving war refugees in California or Las Vegas, this silo sitting in the open would have looked almost stupidly unguarded—twelve hundred tons of wheat waiting to be plundered, a couple of chains to cut, easily done with a pair of bolt cutters like the one in Jacob's saddlebags. There were enough calories in that single silo to feed a small town for a year.

But how would you get it out? You'd need a grain truck to move any significant quantity. That required fuel, which didn't seem to exist outside Blister Creek. And you'd need to get past the bunkers that guarded the valley entrances. Say you somehow fought your way past, pulled up in a grain truck, cut the locks, positioned the grain hopper, powered up the grain augers, and filled the truck while the valley swarmed you, then managed to fight your way back out. Anyone who could do that would dispense with a couple of silo guards without much difficulty. So Jacob had figured there was no sense guarding it. He now hoped that hadn't been a mistake.

Jacob dismounted and climbed the feed bin ladder on the side of the silo. He eyed the ports in the grain access doors. "It says 975," he called down.

Stephen Paul had pulled out a notebook and glanced at the figures. He lifted a gloved hand and gave Jacob the thumbs up.

When Jacob was back down, his counselor looked at the notebook. "We were at 1,165 after the harvest, then drew down twice in December, then distributed another fifty tons on March tenth. That should put us at 983, which is close enough."

"Right. A little settling." Jacob nodded to the northeast. "Let's hit the corn silos at your brother's place."

They continued north to the base of the cliffs, then followed the dirt road that cut east where the cliffs met Witch's Warts. It had proved difficult to maintain the rarely used road at the base of the cliffs, and it would have been impassable to a vehicle. Sand had swept across in great drifts, some of the dunes permanent enough that clumps of long, slender rabbit grass had taken root. Later, two huge boulders had sheared from the cliffs and lay like giant toppled dominoes across the roadbed.

They came out in the hills on the east side of the valley. Sand and rock gave way to juniper trees and then flat fields laid across the tan, brown soil on this side of the valley. The corn silos on the edge of Richard Young's property sat behind a chain-link fence, but Stephen Paul produced the keys, and they repeated the survey. Even in the dry climate, corn didn't keep as well as wheat, so Jacob had made a greater effort to rotate this corn through. The levels were lower, but just what the book said they should be, plus or minus two or three percent.

The work was hardly difficult, and Jacob enjoyed the next few hours as they made a circuit through the valley on horseback. They met a few curious saints who wondered what they were doing on a Sunday afternoon, and then ran into Steve Krantz, Eliza's husband, patrolling on horseback near the double set of bunkers that protected their southern flank.

Eliza wasn't with him. Instead, his companion was Larry Chambers, the stray FBI agent Eliza's expedition to Las Vegas had returned. After escaping Vegas, they'd come rolling up the highway in an armored car they called the Methuselah tank after the old prepper who'd modified it into a rolling fortress. Miriam and Steve hadn't cared much for their former partner in the FBI, but hadn't wanted to abandon him either.

Jacob was glad to see Chambers out and doing something. Presumably, he'd be as useful as Miriam or Steve if Blister Creek fell under attack, but otherwise seemed to have few useful skills, and no interest in developing any. And the saints were reluctant to work with him, anyway, being paranoid about outsiders.

The four men met on the highway, the horses stomping and blowing. Steve looked worried to see them here, while Chambers wore a sour expression, like he'd eaten something that didn't agree with him.

Chambers wasn't as strong and powerfully built as Steve, but he was solid enough. He was a former military guy like Steve, a veteran of the Iraq War from before the collapse. Each man had a shotgun in one holster and an assault rifle in the other. With their weapons, their wide-brimmed hats, and the dusters they wore as jackets, the two would present an intimidating sight to anyone coming into the valley.

"Were you looking for us?" Steve asked, brow furrowed.

"No problems, nothing to worry about," Jacob assured him. "We're taking a ride through the valley. I haven't visited most of it since last fall."

That's how he'd left it with the others who'd asked. He was reluctant to explain further. They'd already checked two-thirds of the food stores, and he was growing certain there was nothing missing. Not that it had been the most likely explanation in the first place, but *someone* was feeding McQueen and his squatters. And until Jacob knew who, he wanted to keep his investigation quiet, especially in front of a gentile like Agent Chambers.

"Who's manning the south bunker?" Stephen Paul asked.

"Rebecca Cowley and Lillian Christianson," Steve said, "but it's almost time for a shift change. The Anderson boys are up next."

Steve glanced at the sun as he said this, as if gauging the time of day. Jacob guessed it was almost three. Jacob and Stephen Paul had better hurry if they were going to finish their rounds by sundown.

When they'd put some distance between the two groups, Stephen Paul spoke up. "What do you think about the gentile?"

"Chambers doesn't want to be here, that's for sure. Can't say I blame him. We're a suspicious lot these days. Blister Creek is hardly a welcoming place for an outsider."

"We've got reasons for being suspicious."

"Doesn't mean it's easy for him," Jacob said. "I expect Chambers to take off the first moment it looks safe, but for now I'm glad Steve is giving him something to do. Mostly I've seen Chambers moping around his cabin."

"Way I see it, the sooner Agent Chambers leaves, the better."

"All the more reason to drive up to Panguitch tomorrow and see if anyone else is out there. Maybe he can find somewhere to go."

Stephen Paul grunted. "Can't say I agree with your plan, but it's your choice."

"With what part? Bribing McQueen to let us past or the idea of going to Panguitch in the first place?"

"Either."

They rode a few minutes in silence, before Jacob spoke up again. "How is your father doing?"

"Poorly. Too weak to get out of bed except to go to the bathroom, and sometimes not even then. It's almost his time."

"It wouldn't be his time if I could get my hands on some ACE inhibitors to arrest his congestive heart failure."

"If it's the will of the Lord, he'll die, anyway."

Jacob stared hard at Stephen Paul, who continued to look forward, back up the highway toward the center of town, about a mile north of them now.

As if reading his thoughts, Stephen Paul turned toward him. "These are hard times, Brother Jacob, and there's no denying it. But at the end of the world, which would you rather have on your side—medical science or the power of the priesthood?"

"Why not both?"

"Trust in the Lord, Brother Jacob. Not the arm of flesh."

★★★

Jacob found what he was looking for at the final set of silos. If he'd simply taken the opposite circuit around the valley, he'd have spotted it earlier in the day.

It was almost dusk when he and Stephen Paul came sneaking around the back way onto Elder Smoot's ranch and farm. They dismounted in a dry wash, its sandy bottom glittering with quartz, and tied their horses to a jutting thumb of rock that hung over the wash. Then they proceeded on foot at the bottom of the wash until they were safely past the Smoot compound.

Smoot owned six silos of varying sizes. One double silo held barley on one side and wheat on the other. A third, smaller silo held feed corn. These he used for his own family and livestock, but he was required to report their levels to the church. These checked out, and while Jacob supposed that Elder Smoot or his sons might have been falsely underreporting their harvest, he didn't think so. The yield per acre had been typical, given the climate issues.

Smoot's final three silos lay down a dirt road another quarter mile. These stored communal supplies: wheat, milled flour, and dried beans.

Elder Smoot often relied on his own counsel, and Jacob didn't entirely trust him. Early in the crisis, he'd even suspected that Smoot was preparing to sell a large quantity of the valley's hoarded grain to keep it out of the government's hands. After that incident, Jacob had erected a ten-foot chain-link fence around Smoot's silos and topped it with razor wire. All deposits and withdrawals happened under the watchful eye of the bishop's storehouse.

The padlocks on the gate were closed, the chains intact. And the fence and razor wire looked undisturbed. After a long, tiring afternoon of taking survey, Jacob was only half paying attention when he put the key into the padlock. It didn't fit.

He glanced at the key fob, frowning. "What number key did you say again?"

Stephen Paul flipped open the notebook. "Fifteen."

"This is fifteen." Jacob tried again. "I must have written it down wrong. Let me see that."

The notebook looked correct, and the fob definitely said fifteen on it. Had the fob been changed out? He tried again, thinking maybe that in his exhaustion he'd inserted the key upside down or something. No, that wasn't it. One by one, he went through the other keys. None of them worked.

"I don't get it," Stephen Paul said. "Did we change out the lock and forget about it? When was the last time we checked these silos?"

Jacob looked at the notebook. "Not since last July, when Smoot rotated the flour. It was all good, then, assuming he reported correctly."

"Could be Smoot accidentally broke the key and swapped in a different padlock."

Jacob and Stephen Paul circled the perimeter. Everything looked good from the exterior. No cuts in the fence, no evidence someone had been messing around getting over the razor wire. The three silos sat silently, nothing seeming to be amiss.

But Jacob's suspicions were growing. He went back to the horse and removed the bolt cutters from his saddlebags. When he returned, he cut the chain. It clanked as he dragged it out of the gate.

He climbed the feed bin ladder up the wheat silo, and Stephen Paul climbed the one containing beans. By now it was almost too dark to get a good reading, and when Jacob cupped his hand over the glass port to shield it against the setting sun, he doubted at first what he was seeing.

"One ninety-two," he called over. "The notebook said four hundred something, right?"

Stephen Paul had reached the top gauge of his own silo, and now climbed back down the ladder. He stopped at the lowest checkpoint. "This one's worse. Whatever the beans are at, it's below the lowest gauge."

He tapped the side of the steel silo, which gave off a hollow boom, then descended the ladder, testing the level until he found it. Almost to the bottom.

The third silo—the flour—was more full, but still contained only half what the notebook claimed it should. Jacob turned to catch the dying sun against his notebook and scratched a few numbers. He let out a low whistle.

"How bad?" Stephen Paul asked.

"Roughly, I figure there's enough missing to feed two thousand people for six months. Or nine months on short rations." Jacob flipped the notebook closed. "This is it. This is how the refugees are staying fed up there."

"Why would Smoot do that? He has no love for those people. He wanted to finish the job. He *still* wants us to drive them out or kill them."

"Don't assume it was Elder Smoot," Jacob said. "It might be a coincidence that this is on his land."

Stephen Paul had been looking back in the direction of the Smoot home, even though the compound lay on the other side of a dusty hillock and out of view. When he turned back, his expression was hard.

"Whoever did this must be destroyed."

CHAPTER SEVEN

Miriam had turned from the highway and was halfway to Sister Rebecca's cottage at Yellow Flats when she had second thoughts. She'd prayed in Witch's Warts, she'd received confirmation. Yet the dark feeling settling over her contradicted her earlier impression.

She was about to ride home when the sound of another horse's hooves reached her ears. She turned to see a man coming down the dirt road behind her, tall in the saddle. It was too dark to see his face, but she could see the long shape of a rifle and scabbard tied to his saddle. Miriam unsnapped the holster of her Beretta, but didn't draw it. Then she waited.

The man rode his horse around a cattle guard, and slowed as he approached. "Who is that?" The voice belonged to Stephen Paul Young.

"Sister Miriam," she said. "What are you doing here?"

"I was surveying the valley with Brother Jacob. We finished a few minutes ago."

"Yes, but your home is that way," she said, pointing east.

"And yours is that way." He gestured toward the center of town. "So I could ask the same question."

"I'm here for a meeting of the Women's Council. Nothing unusual in that."

"Is that so? Wonder why the Women's Council would summon me, then."

Miriam eyed him for a long moment. "Come on. Let's see what this is about."

She gave him furtive glances as they rode together toward Sister Rebecca's cabin. If anything, Stephen Paul was less likely to be working against Jacob than she was. The only people more loyal to Jacob were his own family: his wives, his favorite brother and sister, his mother.

I'm loyal too, she thought. *That's why I decided to come.*

Sister Rebecca was rocking on her front porch when they arrived. The woman was in her early forties and never married, so far as Miriam knew, although it seemed that there had been some sort of relationship between her and Abraham Christianson that had nearly led to marriage. She was an attractive woman, independent, and skilled with firearms and fixing old equipment. Miriam had always treated the woman with cautious friendliness.

Rebecca had taken the old, abandoned Cowley cabin on Yellow Flats, and cleared and manured the alkaline soil. She'd pruned the wild apple orchard into shape and now raised pigs, chickens, and cattle. Sister Charity, the elderly mother of the dead Kimball conspirators, lived quietly on the property as well, but the older woman was nowhere to be seen at the moment.

Stephen Paul climbed down and tied his horse to the hitching post in front of the porch. But Miriam didn't dismount.

"Is this it?" she asked. "Just the three of us?"

"No," a deep voice said from the other side of the porch. "There are five. So far."

Elder Smoot and another man stepped from the far side of the porch, where they'd been waiting in the shadows, as far from Sister Rebecca as one could manage and still be on the porch. Rebecca lit a kerosene lantern, and Miriam saw that the second man was one of Smoot's sons, Ezekiel.

Miriam twisted the reins in her hands, prepared to turn the horse around and get out of there. "I might have known you'd be mixed up in any conspiracy."

"There's no conspiracy," Smoot said. "I came to listen, that's all. Anyway, I didn't call this meeting, I was invited. My son too."

"So *you* called it," Miriam said to Rebecca.

"Not me." Rebecca held up a note. "I was warned that visitors would be coming. Figured it didn't hurt to listen. There are some things that have been bugging me for a while."

"They've been bugging all of us, I'd guess," Stephen Paul said. "That doesn't mean this meeting is a good idea." Nevertheless, he trudged up to the stairs, grabbed an empty rocking chair, and sat down next to Rebecca.

"So nobody is in charge?" Ezekiel asked. He turned to his father. "You're the priesthood elder. You can lead until someone else steps forward."

"This isn't a priesthood meeting," Rebecca said.

"What does that mean?" the younger Smoot pressed. "Of course it is."

"Easy, son," his father said.

More hoof clomps, and then another woman rode out of the shadows. Carol Young, Stephen Paul's oldest wife. She gaped at her husband.

"You?" he said, seeming to be equally surprised. "Did you send the note?"

"Not me," Carol said. "Was it yours? Didn't look like it."

"It wasn't me either."

"So *nobody* called the meeting," Miriam said. "Right."

Still, she was intrigued enough that she dismounted and tied off her horse next to Stephen Paul's. She heard the nicker and snort of the Smoot horses around the other side. Carol hesitated, then slid out of the saddle to join her husband.

One more rider arrived. This was Peter Potts, the oldest son of Elder Potts of the Quorum. He was about thirty years old, with two wives and several kids. Before the crisis, the man had been thickening about the waist and thinning up top, sinking into the prosperous lethargy of middle age. But since the collapse he'd thinned down, and the muscles stood out on his shoulders and forearms. He looked ten or fifteen years younger. The same thing had happened to them all, to some extent or other. It was the manual labor, plus the elimination of refined sugars and other processed foods from the diet. Peter had also cut his hair to the scalp and grown a wiry beard, and looked much more formidable.

But Peter also claimed to know nothing about the meeting. And since nobody else seemed to be coming, it was obvious that someone here was lying. Elder Smoot had locked horns with Jacob in the past; he was the obvious choice. But Sister Rebecca kept her own counsel, and Miriam couldn't rule her out either.

Rebecca retrieved another chair from inside the house, and shortly the four men and three women were sitting in uncomfortable silence as the crickets started up around the cabin. The cliffs loomed to their rear, a black gash with a swath of stars overhead that spread like a bowl over the valley.

"This is pointless," Elder Smoot said after about ten minutes. "Go get our horses," he told his son. "We're going home."

"Hold on, Father. Someone must have something useful to say."

"When I saw the Smoots," Rebecca said, "I assumed this would be a gathering of disaffected believers."

"I support the prophet," Smoot grumbled. "Don't anyone claim otherwise."

"We all support him," Rebecca said. A significant pause. "So far as he obeys the will of the Lord."

"And I suppose you think an unmarried woman knows that better than the prophet."

"Don't presume to know what I'm thinking," she snapped.

"Why did you come?" Stephen Paul asked his wife in a quiet tone.

"Because of things you've said," Carol replied. "You've been unhappy. Every time you talk about Brother Jacob, it's to say he's holding back, or he's being soft. That he needs to make hard decisions."

"I always thought a man could share worries with his wife," Stephen Paul said.

"Of course you can. And I've listened. So much that I started to think that Jacob was making mistakes. I thought I'd come hear what Rebecca had to say. I had no idea you'd be here. Really."

"Brother Stephen Paul, do you think Jacob is making mistakes?" Rebecca asked. "You spend more time with him than any of us."

"Maybe, maybe not. He's a smart man, hardworking. He keeps the community running smoothly. But this business at the reservoir—I don't know what to make of it. And I don't see why he needs to get to Panguitch—it seems dumb to hand over food and supplies so we can check out a ghost town."

"So you *do* think he's making mistakes," Rebecca pressed.

Stephen Paul looked uncomfortable at this. "I hate to question the man. Maybe the food thing is a mistake, but I don't know for sure."

"Of course it's a mistake," Ezekiel said. "And why are we surprised? Jacob is only human, he's not divine."

"He's the prophet," Miriam said, unable to keep silent any longer. "The Lord won't let him lead us astray."

"What makes you say that?" Ezekiel asked.

"It's in the scriptures. The prophet may not lead the church astray. Tell him, Elder Smoot," she urged. "Your son seems to need a basic education in gospel doctrine."

Smoot cleared his throat. When he spoke, he sounded hesitant. "The prophet won't lead the church astray—we're promised that. But that doesn't mean he won't try. If the prophet *tries* to lead the church astray, the Lord will strike him down, and a new man will be put in his place."

"Is that what you're advocating?" Miriam was growing angry. This was verging on apostasy. "Jacob has saved us. He defeated the Kimballs, he threw the army out of the valley. He saved my life personally. I took a bullet in the lungs, and he brought me back from death. He's my husband's brother. Who invited me here? What idiot thought I would turn on him now?"

"But Jacob isn't perfect," Sister Rebecca said. "He can't know everything. When he ordered the attack at the reservoir, we almost got wiped out by army irregulars coming up from the south. He didn't see that coming."

"What's more, we never finished the job," Ezekiel said. "It only left the problem for later."

"That's right," Smoot agreed. "We could have cleared out the squatters once and for all. They were bloodied, we could have put them on the run. Now they're dug in, armed, and ready to fight back."

"I've heard enough," Carol said. The shadows hid her face, but her voice was distraught. "This entire discussion is giving me a dark impression. And I don't want to see where it's going."

She rose to her feet and tromped down the stairs from the porch. She untied her horse. "Honey, are you coming or staying?"

"I, um, I think I'll stay a bit longer." Stephen Paul sounded uncertain, worried.

"Follow the spirit," Carol said. "It will speak the truth to your heart." She climbed into the saddle.

As she did, Peter Potts followed suit. "I've heard enough too," he said as he climbed onto his horse. "I won't speak against you, but I won't be a party to it either."

Moments later, he was trotting down the road after Carol Young.

Peter hadn't spoken up until that point, and his sudden departure was surprising. Next to the Smoots, the Potts family had the deepest history of rivalry with the Christiansons. Miriam had assumed that Peter was here because he was already known to have doubts about Jacob. Maybe he'd even called this meeting. He seemed as likely a candidate as any of them.

"How about you?" Ezekiel asked Miriam as the sound of their horses' hooves faded away in the darkness. "Aren't you going to run off too?"

"Not at all. I want to hear your treachery with my own ears. That way I can testify at your excommunication trials."

"Let's all settle down," Rebecca said. "There's no treachery here. We're trying to decide if we need to do anything, that's all. That might mean nothing more than sitting down with Brother Jacob and explaining our fears."

"Jacob would be hurt if he could hear us talking," Stephen Paul said. "He might even offer to step down. But he wouldn't call a church court either. He'd say we had a right to free discussion."

Miriam grunted. That much was probably true.

"What do you think about the reservoir scheme?" Elder Smoot asked Miriam.

"I don't like it at all. Feeding the squatters is the dumbest thing we could do. I don't think we should attack them, necessarily, but for now I say ignore them, keep them from the valley."

"What about getting to Panguitch?" Smoot asked.

"That makes more sense to me. Jacob is hoping he can get medicine, but even more, that he can find some sort of community on the outside. A partner to start rebuilding. I understand why. I happen to think it's a fool's errand is all."

"We're all agreed on that," Rebecca said. "The Second Coming is nigh. There will be no rebuilding. Jacob can try, but it's a waste of energy better spent preparing Blister Creek."

"True enough," Stephen Paul said.

"Same opinion here," Ezekiel said. "But the other thing that sticks in my craw is this business with the gentiles. The ones in the valley, I mean."

"Steve Krantz is one of us now," Miriam said.

Ezekiel shrugged. "So you say."

"He was baptized, he married Eliza in the temple."

"He's still an outsider."

"I was an outsider once too. And Rebecca lived for years outside of the church before she came back."

"It's not about you, or Steve, or Rebecca," Elder Smoot said. "There's

Officer Trost's daughter. She doesn't belong here. She doesn't even pretend to believe."

"She keeps to herself, grows ninety percent of her own food. She's harmless."

"Unless the question is purity of the community," Smoot said. "Then she is not harmless at all."

"And then there's Larry Chambers," Ezekiel said. "As if we need yet another former FBI agent in our midst. Those guys were our enemies for a long time."

Miriam wasn't going to argue that point. It was too tricky to answer. And she wasn't too keen on having Chambers around, to be honest. They should have left him in Las Vegas and let him take his chances there. The way Chambers acted, it was clear he didn't want to be here either. But she didn't think the man was dangerous.

"Now that the gentiles are here, we can hardly kick them out again," Miriam said. "That's a death sentence."

Stephen Paul rose to his feet and tramped down from the porch. The others fell silent. Miriam thought for a moment that he'd grown disgusted and was going to ride off and catch up with his wife. But a moment later he came back up. He was holding a small notebook.

"Jacob and I rode around the valley this afternoon to survey the silos and check the grain levels."

"I was wondering what you meant by surveying," Miriam said.

"I would have told you if you'd asked. I needed to tell *someone*."

"I had other worries on my mind." She nodded at the notebook. "I take it you found something."

"It's what we didn't find." He flipped it open. "We're missing several hundred tons of beans, wheat, and milled flour from communal food stores. Jacob thinks someone has been stealing it and giving it to the squatters."

"What?" Smoot said. "Who?"

"The missing food came from your silos, Elder Smoot. The ones at the back of your ranch."

"Are you kidding?" Elder Smoot exploded, springing from his chair. "Let's go. Get your guns, we'll put an end to it."

Ezekiel grabbed his father's sleeve. "Sit down, we're not going to ride out right now. We don't even know who."

"I don't care. I'll put an end to it, whoever it is."

"Let Brother Stephen Paul explain, Father." Ezekiel pulled on the older man's arm until Smoot finally sat down again, grumbling.

"Why didn't you say so right away?" Smoot asked Stephen Paul. "Instead, you let us go around with all this chitchat."

"Because it was on your land," Stephen Paul said, "and I needed to think it over. Make sure you weren't stealing it to undermine Jacob."

"Of course not! I'd never do that. Anyway, the fence was intact last time I was out there, and the chain and padlock in place. I don't even have a key."

"Neither did we, because someone had replaced the lock. We had to cut the chain to get in."

"Did you see any tracks?" Miriam asked.

"Like a truck, you mean?" Stephen Paul asked. "No, nothing. The road would take you right past the Smoot house, though. So someone in the house would see if a grain truck pulled up."

"There haven't been any trucks," Smoot said. "Or any wagons, for that matter. We've got thirty people living in the house. One of us would have heard something."

"Seems like we'd be the most likely suspects, Father," Ezekiel said. "Someone in the Smoot house, I mean."

"That's stupid," Smoot said. "We'd never do anything like that, and these people know it."

"Someone stole that food," Miriam said. "It would either take a couple of big, noisy trucks to move the supplies, or a whole bunch of people coming and going. Either one of those things make the Smoots look suspicious."

"I refuse to defend myself," Smoot said. "It's ridiculous on the surface."

"What I want to know," Rebecca said, speaking up for the first time in several minutes, "is what Jacob intends to do about it."

"He's going to put Steve and Eliza to investigating," Stephen Paul said. "We talked about Miriam, but . . ." He shrugged. "That seemed to concern him too."

"What does that mean?" she demanded.

"That if you found a suspect, you'd administer frontier justice."

Miriam let out a bitter laugh. "And he wouldn't? He'd shake his finger and scold?"

"He doesn't know what he'd do," Stephen Paul said. "Jacob is deliberate. He doesn't lash out based on emotion."

"So he'll do nothing, really," Rebecca said. "Unless he can catch them in the act."

"Don't underestimate him," Stephen Paul said. "He gets things done in the end."

"The problem with Brother Jacob," Ezekiel said, and his voice was heavy, as if this pained him to say it, "is that we need him to act like a prophet, and he won't do it."

"And I suppose you think you could do a better job," Miriam said.

"Of course not." Ezekiel sounded shocked. "What I want is for Jacob to go into the Holy of Holies and recover the breastplate and sword of Laban."

"Don't speak of that!" Smoot said.

"Why? It's no secret. We all know he must put on the breastplate and wield the sword. This is the perfect time."

Smoot stood up again and paced to the end of the porch. "Yes, but we don't talk about it."

Maybe Smoot didn't, but Miriam had heard it whispered or hinted at by others several times in the past two months alone. This sword and breastplate business was meant to guard against some looming, unstated threat. Miriam didn't know what to make of it, if the objects even existed.

"For all we know, Jacob has taken them out already and is ready to use them as soon as the Lord tells him to," Rebecca said. "That would mean the Second Coming is at hand."

"What, so he can save ten minutes by grabbing them from under his bed?" Miriam scoffed. "Or maybe he wears the breastplate under his shirt and leaves the sword hanging on a hook in the coat closet."

Nobody said anything for several seconds. The bugs were swarming so badly around the kerosene lantern that Rebecca moved it away from her.

Smoot returned from the far end of the porch and fixed Stephen Paul with a significant look. "Maybe you know about it."

"About the sword and breastplate?" Stephen Paul said. "If he's taken them out of the box, he's never told me."

"How about your husband?" Smoot asked Miriam. "Did David say anything?"

"Not to me, no. I doubt he knows. Anyway, I thought we weren't supposed to talk about it. Isn't that what you were just telling us?"

"We're not supposed to *touch* them," Ezekiel said. "But it's not like our tongues will fall out if we talk about them. And if we looked at them, our eyes wouldn't burn."

"What are you saying?" Smoot said.

"I'm saying we should find out if they're in the temple. If our greatest weapons are at hand to face the enemy. Would it hurt us to open the box and have a look?"

There was a moment of dumbfounded silence at this.

"You're not even on the Quorum," his father said at last. "You shouldn't be anywhere near the Holy of Holies."

"But you and Elder Young here could do it. Then tell us what you see."

"I don't know," Smoot said. He turned to Stephen Paul. "Well?"

"I'd only consider it if everyone else agrees," Stephen Paul said. "Even then, I'd need to pray about it. But . . . maybe."

"Let's be clear," Rebecca said. "You want the elders to look, only? Not touch?"

"That's right," Ezekiel said.

"I guess it wouldn't hurt to find out," Rebecca said. "What do you think, Miriam?"

What she thought was that it was beginning to seem like a conspiracy. Maybe a well-meaning conspiracy, with people who thought they were acting in the best interests of the community. They were people who loved their prophet, but thought he needed to be harder, to make difficult decisions. But it was still a conspiracy.

And already she could see errors in judgment. Stephen Paul should have ridden off with his wife and Peter Potts. Instead, he'd told Elder Smoot and his son about the missing food from their silos. If Jacob had wanted them to know, he wouldn't have gone sneaking onto Smoot's property in the first place. So that was a betrayal of trust. Miriam was disappointed in Stephen Paul.

You came too. You prayed about it and decided to obey the summons.

Maybe so, but not so she could betray Jacob. She would never do that. A misguided conspiracy had destroyed the Zarahemla church that had first drawn her to the saints. Why would she tread that same wicked path?

Unless you can do more good on the inside than the outside.

Yes, that was it. If she'd stomped out with Carol Young and Peter Potts, she'd be blissfully riding down the highway with no knowledge of the stolen food, no idea that these others meant to sneak into the Holy of Holies to see if the sword and breastplate were still there.

"I think," Miriam began slowly, "that the two elders should enter the Holy of Holies together. Open the chest and see what they find."

"Then it's settled," Ezekiel said.

"Not yet," Rebecca said.

Everyone looked to Elder Smoot. He was wavering. Miriam could almost read his thoughts. Surely it wouldn't hurt to look, he was thinking. Not to touch, no. But only to look.

"It . . . worries me," Smoot said at last. "I've never touched that chest, never been tempted to sneak a peek. It's like looking into the face of the Lord. If you are not prepared, you will be destroyed."

"You're only destroyed if you touch the contents," Ezekiel said. "Not if you look inside."

"Will you stop talking like you know something?" his father said. "You don't."

"But, Father—"

Smoot's face hardened. "No, I won't be a party to it."

"Wait, are you saying no?" Stephen Paul asked.

"That's right. I won't open the chest, and I won't agree to any plan that has someone else doing it either."

And that proved the end of it. Ezekiel tried a few more times to change his father's mind, but Stephen Paul's interest seemed to fade once his companion on the Quorum had decided. Then Rebecca said she'd go along with Stephen Paul. As for Miriam, she was curious, and since she'd never heard explicitly that opening the chest in the Holy of Holies would lead to certain death, she dismissed this as superstition.

But to her mind this business with the breastplate and the sword was tangential to the real discovery of the night: someone was stealing their food. While Ezekiel fought a losing battle to convince his father that something was wrong at the top of the church hierarchy, she turned her thoughts to tracking down the thief. It shouldn't be too difficult. She was a former FBI agent, after all.

And when she found the thief, she vowed, she would see him brought to a swift and brutal justice.

CHAPTER EIGHT

Despite his understanding with Whit McQueen, Jacob approached the reservoir Monday morning prepared for trouble. He was relieved to discover that the squatters were still willing to cooperate. They'd pulled aside the log gate, dragged away the dead cars, and hauled off the rocks. Nothing but open pavement stretched north from the camp.

Two armed men stood on either side of McQueen in the middle of the highway, but it turned out they were only there waiting to be paid.

Jacob and his brother unloaded the supplies: twenty pounds of jerky, a hundred pounds of powdered milk, ten wool blankets, and a pair of boots. McQueen inspected them, grunted his approval, and waved them on. Soon, they were rumbling north on Highway 89.

"Once you pay the Danegeld," Miriam said when the reservoir had disappeared behind them, "you never get rid of the Dane."

Jacob didn't want to get in another argument about the same thing, so he let it slide. And he refused to let it spoil his good mood, which rose with every mile north along the abandoned highway.

The sky was blue, the sun overhead. Spring flowers bloomed across the desert, and the high country meadows were thick with green grass. Grazing conditions were better than he could ever remember. But there were no herds to graze them. Not a deer or elk to be seen either; the squatters must have eaten or frightened them all away.

Jacob, Eliza, and David were joined by the three former FBI agents in their midst. Eliza's husband, Steve, and Agent Chambers were ex-military as well as ex-FBI. And Miriam could handle a weapon as well as either of them. At the moment, Chambers and Steve were up at the .50-cal, one to shoot, the other to load. Jacob hoped it wouldn't be necessary.

An hour later the Humvee eased into the outskirts of Panguitch and Jacob's hopes collapsed. Even before he saw the abandoned houses, some burned, some with roofs caved in by heavy winter snows, the huge drifts of tumbleweeds disabused him of any hopes. They filled driveways and piled against houses. An elementary school lay almost buried in the spiny bundles.

"If it gets dry this summer," Eliza said, "those tumbleweeds will burn down what's left."

She sat up front with Jacob and had been looking intently out the window during their drive. Like the rest of them, Jacob's sister hadn't left Blister Creek in the past year, and her last experience outside the valley had been an ugly one. No doubt the horrors she'd seen in Las Vegas accounted for her pinched, worried look.

Jacob drove down Main Street. The windows had been broken out of the nineteenth-century brick buildings. Several abandoned trucks sat in parking stalls, their tires removed. No sign of humans or other life. Not even a stray dog wandering the sidewalks.

He pulled to a stop, and everyone got out and stood in front of the Humvee to discuss. Miriam held an assault rifle and studied their surroundings, but nobody else seemed concerned. It was hard to imagine snipers waiting for them up here.

Chambers yawned. He'd been dozing in the back of the Humvee and looked reluctant to have been dragged out. "Well, this sucks," he said, looking around. "I was hoping for something better than this. It's like Nevada all over."

"What were you expecting?" Steve asked.

"I don't know. Fayer was always going on about Mormons and food storage and all that shit. I expected Utah to get its act together."

"So what now?" David asked. "Swing by the hospital and see if there's anything before we head home?"

"We scavenged it pretty hard a couple of years ago," Jacob said. "You really think new stuff has materialized?"

"This sucks," Chambers said again.

"Let's keep going," Jacob said.

"Was that your plan all along?" David asked.

"Richfield is another hour, more or less. It's more of a farming community. Big enough, surrounded by ranches and farms, that they might still be hanging on. If not, we've got enough gas to make it all the way to Salt Lake and back."

"Salt Lake!" Eliza said.

"Sure, why not make a go of it?" Jacob said. "If there's any Utah government left at all, it has to be up there or nowhere."

"But if there is, they'll take our truck," Steve said. "How will we get home again?"

Jacob kept pushing. "We don't have to go all the way. We'll keep going until things look dicey, then turn around. How would they stop us? Whoever we meet won't have enough gas to give chase."

"I don't know," Eliza said, dubiously.

"Let's take a vote," Jacob said. "Miriam?"

Miriam had wandered several yards away and was still scanning the buildings, her gun at the ready. Now she turned with a disgusted expression.

"This isn't a democracy. You're the prophet, you make the call."

"You don't want a say?"

"No, I want you to decide. That's what being prophet means."

"Miriam," David said, with a frown.

"Well, doesn't it? We're on a mission that Jacob chose. Either he's following the spirit, or he's not. If he's following the spirit, then he already knows the answer. If he's not, then we never should have left Blister Creek in the first place."

"One vote for home," Jacob said.

"That's not what I said."

"Close enough." He was irritated with her attitude. "I say we keep going. That makes it one vote for Richfield, one for home. Who else has an opinion?"

"Keep going," Chambers said. "Anyone tries to stop us, we kick their ass."

"One for home, two to keep going," Jacob said. "Steve?"

"Keep going."

"That leaves you guys," Jacob said to his brother and sister.

David looked at his wife, then at his hands when Miriam returned a stern look. "Keep going. This is our best chance."

That made four votes for going and one against, but Jacob wanted to hear what Eliza had to say. She had kept quiet earlier, but now she didn't hesitate.

"I trust you, Jacob. Let's go."

Eliza asked if she could take a turn up top with Steve at the machine gun in place of Chambers. Jacob said that was fine, so the FBI agent took Eliza's place up front next to Jacob when everyone returned to the vehicle.

"It's not a question of trust," Miriam said, climbing in the back-seat next to her husband. "I trust Jacob too. So long as he's speaking as a prophet."

"A prophet is still a man," David said. "He uses the tools he's got."

"You do realize I can hear you, don't you?" Jacob asked.

"That's some kind of blunt tool," Miriam said, ignoring him. "Come on, Jacob can muster a more forceful opinion than that. I've heard him do it before. This wasn't the time for a vote. We're out in the Lone and Dreary World. Satan is abroad in the land."

Chambers made a scoffing sound.

But Miriam continued as if she hadn't heard. "The devil will destroy us in a second if we're not careful. What we need is some real leadership, and Jacob isn't giving it."

Again Jacob considered asking if they'd forgotten he was there, or had just stopped caring, but he didn't want to hear the answer.

"We're going north, aren't we?" David asked. "Isn't that what Jacob wanted? So why was it necessary to lift his hand and say, 'Thus sayeth the Lord'?"

"He doesn't need to do it all the time. But once in a while would be nice."

Jacob sighed and started the truck. He rolled through the streets until he found Highway 89 again and took it north, out of town. This was high desert plain: grass and sagebrush, with wide, expansive views toward distant, snow-capped mountains.

"There's a simpler explanation," Chambers said with a smirk. He pulled out a deck of cards and shuffled them on his lap. "This guy is no prophet. He's the leader of a crazy desert cult."

"Shut up, Chambers," Miriam said. "If it weren't for this cult, you'd be dead."

Jacob shook his head at the bickering. "Let's give it a rest, okay?"

"I'm grateful for that," Chambers continued. "Doesn't mean I believe any of this bullshit."

"Again, shut up," Miriam said. "This doesn't concern you."

"Damn straight it does."

"Do I have to pull over?" Jacob asked, in his best exasperated-father voice.

David snorted. Chambers let out a loud, braying laugh. When Jacob glanced over his shoulder, Miriam had an amused, slightly embarrassed look on her face, as if even she realized how ridiculous the argument sounded.

In the moment of silence, the voices of Steve and Eliza came through from above. They were talking in loud, animated tones. No doubt having their own version of the same argument.

Chambers turned in his seat. "Hey, how about a game of hearts?"

"We don't play with face cards," Miriam said. "Anyway, where did you get those? You didn't have them when you came to Blister Creek."

"Maybe not everyone in your church is as self-righteous as you," Chambers said. "You ever think of that? Anyway, I've seen you play cards. Before you went all fundie."

"Deal me in," David said. "But you'll have to remind me of the rules. It's been a few years."

"We need three players. So unless Jacob wants to play while he drives . . ."

"Fine," Miriam said. "Deal me in."

Jacob let out his breath as they set about playing. He hadn't actually been joking about pulling over. Ten more seconds of arguing and he'd have made either Chambers or Miriam swap with one of the people at the gun to separate them.

★★★

Jacob's hopes rose as they continued north. The tiny towns of Circleville and Junction were abandoned, but when they entered Sevier County, the landscape changed. Some of the ranch houses looked intact, and they came across plowed fields.

"I don't believe it," Miriam said. "Someone is still alive up here."

A few minutes later, a rider paced them on a dirt road running parallel to the highway, but when Jacob slowed, hoping to speak to the man, the rider turned his horse and rode east toward the mountains. So they continued toward Richfield, a larger town on the southern edge of the Sevier Valley.

They made it two more miles before they came under fire. The gunfire came from a rocky hill to the right of the road. Logs reinforced one of those snow fences that were meant to keep drifts from sweeping off the plains to bury the road, and gunmen had taken refuge behind it. Bullets pinged off the side of the vehicle.

Jacob pushed down on the accelerator and left the hill behind. There had been no answering gunfire from the .50-cal above. He was glad for that. If Miriam had been up top, she would have hit that barrier with a devastating return fire. Kill a few people and they'd only make more enemies.

Then the road ended. A four-foot-wide trench had been gouged across the asphalt surface. As Jacob rolled to a stop in front of it, he saw nail strips on either side. Whoever had done this had extended the trench into the field to keep someone from going off the shoulder and driving around. Beyond that lay two barricades of stacked logs, reinforced with dirt berms. Farther up the highway, two yellow school buses overlapped each other to block the highway a second time. None of it would stop a determined tank, but it stopped them.

Past the buses lay plowed fields and undamaged houses, then more barricades, a wooden watchtower, and other defensive measures. This was a real town, with survivors holding on against the collapse. If only Jacob could somehow get in there and communicate with those people. He saw nobody, but knew they must be watching. Surely, they'd heard the gunfire up the road, if nothing else.

"Keep moving," Miriam said, her tone low and warning. From the backseat came the sound of safeties clicking off.

"Where, through fields?" Jacob asked.

"Or back, or something," Chambers said. "But for God's sake, don't just sit here."

From outside came Steve's warning voice. "Jacob!"

Jacob flipped into reverse. He swung the Humvee around, thinking to drive back a few hundred yards, where he could give it more thought. He wasn't ready to give up yet.

But the moment he turned around, a hailstorm of gunfire opened up on the Humvee. It clattered on the sides, dinged against the windows, almost deafening in its ferocity. Jacob tried to pinpoint the gunfire, but at that moment something flashed from one of the barricades on the side of the road. While he watched in horror, a rocket zipped toward them. It flashed over the hood and slammed into the ground eight or ten yards away. It detonated in a flash and bang that rocked the Humvee.

"Jesus!" Chambers screamed. "That was an RPG. Go! Go!"

Jacob was already mashing down on the accelerator. The heavy truck slowly picked up speed.

Only seconds had passed since the gunfire began, but it seemed much longer before Steve opened up with the machine gun. It returned a low thump-thump-thump-thump sound against the chatter of small-arms fire targeting them. An arc of tracer bullets sliced a half circle to their rear, and at once the gunfire diminished. Nobody could keep their heads up against that fire.

David and Miriam opened up through the gun ports with their assault rifles. No more rocket-propelled grenades chased them down the highway.

They continued south until they were past the snow fence where they'd first come under fire. About five miles south of that, Jacob finally decided it was safe to stop. This time when they got out, all had armed themselves, and they were studying the rocks and dry hills lining the road, wary of another ambush. But this was national forest land, uncultivated, covered with sagebrush and juniper trees.

"What the hell was that about?" Chambers said. "Why would they attack?"

"The same reason we'd attack a Humvee rolling through Blister Creek," Jacob said.

"That's different," David said. "The government tried to steal our food. You'd think the gentiles would see a military truck and hope it was help."

"So the government has tried to steal *everyone's* food," Jacob said.

Eliza grabbed Steve and pulled him a few feet away. They spoke in whispers.

Jacob glanced at them, curious, but Miriam was pacing about, looking agitated, and then she came up to him. "I'll bet the military came through already. Probably those blasted irregulars. You either fight back or they loot and sack your town like they did in Colorado City. Like they tried to do to us. That's why those people saw a military vehicle and freaked out."

"Do we fight our way through or go home?" David asked.

Jacob shook his head. "I don't want to fight."

"Too late for that," his brother said.

"I doubt we killed anyone," Jacob said. "They were hunkered down behind those berms, and we only fired back for a few seconds."

He desperately wanted to make peaceful overtures to the survivors in Richfield. Barring that, to get through and find someone less hostile farther north. On the one hand, he was elated to discover that there was still a town organized enough to defend itself against invaders. On the other hand, he hadn't been invading. He'd been turning around to reassess. Yet they'd still tried to kill him.

Or had they? If that grenade had hit, it would have blown a hole in the side of the Humvee. Chances were they'd be dead. But why had they missed? Poor marksmanship? Or had it been a warning shot?

"So what, we go back home?" David asked.

"I say we drive across those fields and flank their defenses," Miriam said. "They can't stop us. We have a heavy machine gun. They don't."

"You don't know that," David said. "Besides, those RPGs are more than enough."

"Dammit," Chambers said. "Why'd they have to shoot? I was almost out of here."

"I say we try again," Miriam persisted.

"Couple of hours ago you thought this was a waste of time," Jacob said.

"Now we've got a chance to get rid of this jerk," she said, hooking her thumb at Chambers. "Look at him. He doesn't want to spend one more minute with us."

"It's too risky," David said. "Too many of us have families. And the prophet. Plus, he's our doctor. It doesn't do any good to get medical supplies if there's no doctor left to administer it."

"This was never just about medical supplies," Miriam said. "Was it, Jacob?"

Jacob twisted one hand around the barrel of his assault rifle, wanting to groan. So close to making contact. If only they hadn't come under fire.

"We can't risk it," Jacob said. "We'll go home."

Miriam dropped her argument. "That's the leadership I mean. Come on, everyone back in."

Eliza turned from her conversation with Steve. "The Methuselah tank could get through that barrier. Knock it down, then we'd have enough horsepower to push those buses out of the way."

From anyone else, Jacob would have dismissed the suggestion. He'd already decided it wasn't worth a battle, wasn't worth more killing. Maybe in another year Richfield wouldn't be hostile and they could try again.

"You think I should swap vehicles and make another attempt?" he asked.

"I don't think *you* should, no. But Steve and I will go." She glanced at Chambers. "And him. One of us can drive. One can operate the machine gun, and one can feed the ammo. The tank will soak up plenty of abuse. Probably even survive a hit from an RPG."

Eliza wasn't talking about an actual tank, but the converted armored car they'd used to flee Las Vegas. Some crazy old prepper had welded on extra armor and gun ports and crammed it with supplies to ride out the collapse. The vehicle was stronger than the Humvee but guzzled precious fuel, so it was rarely started up. Thanks to the preparations of Jacob's father, the church had begun the crisis with hundreds of thousands of gallons of diesel fuel stored in the valley, but three years later, they had barely half their starting supplies. There was still plenty for an important mission like this, but he'd hate to burn so much unless he was sure.

"Jacob?" she asked.

"I'm thinking about it."

"We don't have any kids yet," she said. "It's just the two of us, plus Chambers. If we get trapped outside the valley for a while, it will be fine."

"It's not the getting trapped part that I worry about."

"Why me?" Chambers asked.

"You don't want to leave?" Jacob asked, surprised.

"Not really."

"But you were just griping about losing the chance to get away from us," Jacob said. "We're a bunch of religious crazies and survivalist fanatics."

"Yeah, well. Don't care much for getting killed either." Chambers shrugged. "I've had a chance to reconsider."

Miriam snorted. "Whatever."

"We won't get killed," Eliza said. "Whatever is up there, it can't be any worse than what we faced last year in Las Vegas."

"It was the will of the Lord that we survived Vegas," Miriam said. "I'm not so sure about this."

"Either way," Chambers said, "I'm not going through another firefight if I can help it. I've seen enough of that to last a lifetime. I'm going back with the rest of you."

"Does that mean you'll stop complaining?" Miriam asked. "How about that? You had your chance, you turned back. So now you can shut up."

"We still want to go," Eliza said. "With or without Chambers."

"I don't know," Jacob said. He turned to Steve. "You're on board with this?"

"It was my idea in the first place," he said. "I don't want to abandon Blister Creek, of course I don't. But I need to know if there's anything out there. I think you understand that, Jacob."

"I do."

"Who knows what we'll find? A government, maybe. I still believe in this country. If people don't stand up and start pulling it together again, it'll die."

It was a little late for that. A year ago brush wars had inflamed half the continent. It wouldn't be any better on the outside now. There sure wouldn't be a Federal government with any sort of authority.

But that didn't mean there was nothing left to rebuild. It might start with something as simple as driving to Provo or Salt Lake and establishing contact. Jacob had already been turning this over in his head for months. He wanted to make that trip himself.

"We've taken chances before," Eliza said. "They always turned out well."

Jacob met her gaze. "Except when they haven't. Then people die."

"Trust me, please. Trust in—"

"In the Lord?" he asked.

"In my *judgment*. I want you to trust in my judgment, Jacob."

★★★

A few hours later, and back in the valley, Eliza gave Jacob a hug before she climbed into the Methuselah tank. "Don't worry, I'll be careful."

Jacob tried to keep the concern from his voice. "I trust you and I trust Steve. It's everything else that worries me."

"This beast got us out of Las Vegas. It will do fine." She patted the side of the armored car, which sat at the curb in front of the Christianson house, fetched from the garage out back. It sat as squat and ugly as a horny toad.

"See if you can find a way around Richfield. They'll be jumpy after exchanging fire with us earlier."

"We'll try. No promises."

Jacob handed her his list of medical supplies. "You know the drill. Don't put yourself in unnecessary danger, but if you can find it, this is stuff I need."

"Got it."

Steve was already behind the wheel after having loaded supplies into the truck: food, water, ammunition, blankets, white sheets to wave when necessary. An hour had passed since their return to the valley and the others from the earlier expedition had only just dispersed toward their respective homes, including Chambers, that coward. It was still only midafternoon. That was the surprising part.

In the short time since morning, they'd traveled almost two hundred miles in the Humvee, a round trip to Richfield and back that would have taken several days on horse. And now Eliza and Steve meant to drive all the way around (or through) Richfield before dark. Possibly all the way to Provo by nightfall, if they could manage it. People used to cross such distances with hardly a thought. Now it felt like sending someone across the ocean in a sailboat; you were never sure you'd see them again.

Steve turned the key in the ignition. The engine rumbled to life. He opened the door rather than peering through the tiny slit of bulletproof glass.

"Ready, Liz?"

"One sec." She turned back to Jacob. "Go to scripture study tomorrow night."

"What, the big one at the chapel?"

"Yes, that one. You've been skipping the Tuesday meetings—you don't know what's going on. I was keeping watch on it, but . . . well, I really think you should go. You *need* to go."

Jacob was still wondering what that was about when she climbed into the truck and they drove off. He stared after the vehicle as it rounded the corner and headed for the cliffs. Gradually, the rumbling engine faded in the distance.

After that, he strained against the rustling breeze for a long time, wondering if he'd be able to hear gunfire all the way from the cliffs if the wind blew just right. McQueen had better keep that gate open or there would be hell to pay.

Jacob heard nothing. Eventually, he turned back toward the house, ready to make a dent in his endless list of chores and responsibilities.

CHAPTER NINE

Miriam left the house at dusk, when gold and red still burnished the western horizon, and there was still enough light to ride by. But it was no easy task to slip away without being spotted. Their smaller house was next to the main Christianson compound, and the two families shared stables.

So she sent David next door to keep Jacob occupied, while Lillian kept watch along the back of the house, ready to warn her if someone came around from the front. Neither of them questioned Miriam's destination or her motives for keeping her departure a secret. But she could tell they were bursting with curiosity.

As Miriam rode out, heading north through the fields before turning onto the street, she met Lillian still keeping watch. A look flickered across the younger woman's face, an unstated desire to ride with Miriam and share in her secret. Miriam acknowledged it with a nod. Inside, she felt a flood of affection for her sister wife. Lillian was a good woman, intelligent, hardworking, and loyal.

They had a third woman in the family now. Clarissa Smoot's husband had died in the fight at the reservoir last year and had chosen to join herself and her children to the David Christianson family. She was good-hearted, if sometimes moody, but Miriam figured that most of that was mourning for her first husband and her former sister wives, now scattered among several church families.

Maybe Miriam would feel closer to Clarissa in time, but the new sister wife had a different personality, more feminine, more interested in house and kitchen and childrearing than the other two wives. Nothing wrong with that. It took different types to form a healthy family. But Miriam didn't have much patience for all that female homemaking stuff.

Miriam got off the pavement and onto dirt ranch roads as soon as she could. It was trickier riding here, and the horse moved so slowly and cautiously in the gathering gloom that she thought briefly about dismounting and going the rest of the way to the Smoot ranch on foot. She owned a pair of night vision goggles, but hadn't powered them up in several weeks, and when she'd checked at the house, had been alarmed to discover that the batteries would no longer hold a charge. Three years ago she'd have tossed the old batteries without a second thought. Now, she had no way to replace them.

Instead, she carried an LED penlight that could be shaken in her hand to recharge. Thanks to some forward thinking, these were common in Blister Creek. The only problem was the poor quality of light. Upon hand charging, hers would cast a thin, rapidly fading beam. As weak as it was, she didn't dare use the flashlight while she was in the open, out of fear that someone would spot her.

It took a good hour or more to hook around to the Smoot ranch from the northeast. She bypassed the house and barns, then came onto the hundred acres or so of grazing land that abutted Smoot's fields. Here she tied her horse to a rock behind a sagebrush-covered knoll, then checked her pistol in its holster and slung her rifle over her shoulder. She used the moonlight to find her way to the fenced-in silos, turning on the penlight only when clouds swept in front of the moon.

Once she was sure there was nobody about and the silos couldn't be seen from the Smoot house, she shook the penlight until it had a good charge. Then she walked carefully around the fenced enclosure, looking at footprints.

Boot prints came and went from the dry wash. She presumed these belonged to Stephen Paul and Jacob, who had come through yesterday to inspect the silos. These were visible only where the dirt was soft and sandy, not on the slickrock that penetrated the surface here and there. Unfortunately, they'd walked around so much that she was having a hard time picking out individual prints, or spotting any older prints that might have indicated a third party at the scene. She made her way to the gate. It was chained with a padlock.

A sound behind her caught her ear, something like the scrape of a boot on stone. Then a hiss of a man's breath as she started to move, dropping the flashlight and lifting the rifle in one movement. She groped for the bolt.

Even as she did so, she heard a telltale metallic snick. The sound of a hammer being drawn on a revolver. She had no chance. Someone had come up behind her and already had her in his sights. If she turned, he'd kill her. With that realization, she hesitated, and that hesitation was doubly deadly.

"Don't do it!" a man's voice ordered. He sounded about twenty feet away. "Put down the gun and lift your hands."

She almost gasped with relief as she recognized the voice. "Jacob, it's me. Miriam."

Jacob grunted. "Miriam!"

Miriam turned around, but she couldn't see him. She picked up the light, its beam flickering through the dust kicked up by her shoes. He had to be close, but where?

"Come over here," he said. "You're too exposed."

"I can't see you." Her heart was still pounding.

"Down here, in the wash."

Ah, of course. She found a place where livestock had cut a path down so they could drink when the spring runoff filled the wash. There he was, about ten feet farther down the sandy bottom, where he could peer over the edge toward the silo.

"Now turn off the light before someone sees us."

They were out of view of the Smoot house, so she doubted the light was a risk, but she obeyed anyway. Jacob was a few inches taller than her and so she kicked her foot into the embankment until she'd formed a little place to stand on and get up to his height. She looked over the top of the wash back at the silos, but couldn't see much from this distance with the poor light of the sliver moon.

"How did you know I was here?" he asked in a low voice.

"I heard you, your boots scuffing together or hitting a stone."

"You've got good ears."

"Yes, I do."

"Still, I got the drop on you for once," he said, a measure of satisfaction in his voice.

His tone was friendly, and she didn't take it as an insult. Still, she couldn't help defending herself.

"Only because you were watching for me," she said. "Why aren't you back at the house? I thought you were talking to David."

"He came over to the house to chat about solar panels. My son had saddled up my horse and—" Jacob paused, chuckled. "Oh, I see. You sent David over to distract me so you could sneak out without me seeing you. Only I was trying to get rid of *him* so I could come here myself."

"How did you get rid of him?"

"I didn't, not really. David went on for about twenty minutes. But I rode straight here. You must have gone the long way, based on where you came out."

"Weren't you worried Smoot would spot you?" she asked.

"I had an excuse if I ran into anyone. A bit of minor Quorum business to discuss with Elder Smoot. I didn't, so I came straight back here."

"Clever." She wished she'd come up with her own ready pretext so she could have gotten here first.

"So why are you here?" he asked.

"Checking things out," she said vaguely. "Like you."

"That's not what I mean." Jacob's voice hardened into suspicion. "How did you know to come here, specifically? Who told you?"

There was no use pretending she didn't know what he was talking about. The only reason to come to these silos was if she already knew about the missing grain. Still, she couldn't exactly blurt out what had happened at last night's secret meeting at Sister Rebecca's cabin.

"Someone told me," she said. "Steve and Eliza are gone, so that left me to investigate."

"Who told you?"

"You know, the usual gossipers."

"I don't believe you. Was it Stephen Paul?"

"No, someone else," she lied. "I only found out last night."

"I only found out last night too," Jacob said. "And Stephen Paul was the only one with me. I haven't told anyone. So unless you knew already . . . you're not mixed up in this, are you?"

"No!"

"Shh. Keep your voice down."

"I'm not, and I didn't know already."

"Miriam, tell me the truth."

"I'm absolutely not mixed up in this. Stealing our food and giving it to the squatters? How could you even think such a thing?"

"I wouldn't think it, but you claim Stephen Paul didn't tell you. Yet somehow you knew already."

Miriam was struggling to think of a better lie that would appease him without implicating herself further. The problem was, Jacob knew her too well after all these years. The first time she'd met him, way back when she'd infiltrated the Zarahemla sect, she'd tried to deny that she was an FBI agent. He'd seen through that as well.

Miriam dropped her voice to a whisper. "I told you this morning that I trust you. Now I need you to trust me. God chose you to be His prophet. He chose me to be His destroying angel."

"Don't use that phrase. I don't like it."

"Fine, then His enforcer. I protect this church and this valley. I protect you, Jacob."

"So you're here to what?" he pressed. "Enforce? What does that even mean?"

"I was going to use the penlight and walk around, see if I could figure out who is stealing from the silos. I have my suspicions, but I need to be sure. What are you doing?"

"Waiting for the thief to steal food. He should be here soon."

Miriam stiffened. "What makes you think it will happen tonight?"

"There's a lot of missing food. Do you know how hard it is to ship it out of here? Unless you've got trucks, and I don't see how that could happen."

"Or mule-drawn wagons," she said.

"That would be even more difficult. Wagons couldn't cross the desert from here, they'd have to backtrack to the road. We're talking dozens of shipments. Slow and noisy. Someone would have spotted them by now."

"Then how does the thief manage it?"

"It's like eating an elephant," Jacob said. "One bite at time. In this case, one bite each and every night, or near enough. That's what it would take. I was going to wait to see who, if anyone, showed up."

"You must have suspicions."

"Everything points to Elder Smoot. This is his land, and the Smoots usually man the bunkers at the switchbacks up to the cliffs, since they're the biggest family on the north end of town. It's a shorter ride for them. That means they'd have the easiest job smuggling the food out of the valley." Jacob hesitated. "But it seems too simple, too obvious. And too risky for him."

"Someone would check these silos sooner or later," she agreed, "and then he'd have to answer. It would be a terrible chance to take."

"Besides, Smoot is hostile to the squatters," Jacob said. "He'd rather burn the food than see it fall into their hands."

"Got to agree with him there."

"Then who do you think it is?"

"Chambers," Miriam said without hesitation.

"Because he's a gentile?"

"Because he hates us, Jacob. He hates everything we stand for. And he resents that we're still alive and kicking and the rest of the world has gone straight to hell."

"He needs a better motive than that."

"I don't know. Maybe it's his ticket out of the valley."

"He had his chance this afternoon," Jacob said, "and he refused to go north with Steve and Eliza."

"Maybe because he wanted to keep stealing our food."

"Again, for what purpose?"

"Remember how Chambers was yawning this morning? How he drifted off to sleep in the truck? When's the last time you saw him out and about during the middle of the day?"

"Yesterday, patrolling with Steve, in fact." Jacob shrugged. "But no, I don't see him out and about much. That doesn't prove anything, only that he's lazy and disgruntled."

Miriam was growing exasperated with Jacob. Was he blind to the way the world worked? Chambers was stealing from them because he hated the church. And he was jealous.

"Fine, since you're so smart, who is stealing the food?" she asked. "If it's not Smoot and it's not Chambers, then who?"

"I don't know."

They fell silent. It was a clear, still night, growing colder as the thin desert air bled off the daytime heat. But the sand at their feet was still hot from the baking it had taken during the day. A coyote yipped to the east, answered moments later by another yipping, this one more distant. The coyote population had exploded in the surrounding deserts over the past three years, and it was a running battle to keep them from devouring entire flocks of sheep. A few more years and the wolves too, would return, and then things would get interesting.

An hour passed and Miriam was getting tired from standing up. She was about to suggest taking turns watching while the other person sat, when her ears caught the sound of a high-pitched mechanical whine from the desert side. Like a two-stroke motorcycle engine. She hadn't heard that sound in a long time.

The engine was gradually growing closer, but cut out when it was still a half mile distant. Far enough from the Smoot compound, she thought, that the distance and the hillock would keep the sound from the house. Whoever it was must be walking the final distance.

Something occurred to Miriam. She tugged on Jacob's arm so she could whisper in his ear.

"The padlock," she said. "You cut the chain yesterday, so you must have replaced the lock. His key won't work, and he'll know we're on to him."

Jacob whispered back. "I took the padlock to the shop and drilled out the tumblers. Any key will open it. Then I popped it and put it on a new chain. He'll never know."

Good thinking. She settled down to wait.

About fifteen minutes passed before the sound of bouncing tires and a rattling of wood on wood caught her ear. A shadow approached the silos, pulling another shadowy object. There was enough moonlight from the crescent overhead that she was fairly sure it was a man, but not enough light to pick out his features. And what was he pulling?

He rattled the chain link as he felt for the gate. Then came the unmistakable sound of a rechargeable flashlight magnet shaking up and down in its solenoid. He turned on the light so he could fit the key into the lock. It was only on for a second, but that was enough. The light reflected off his face and his immediate surroundings.

And then she knew.

CHAPTER TEN

Miriam watched with righteous fury rising triumphantly in her breast. She was right!

Larry Chambers. The bastard. He was pulling a handcart with an aluminum scoop shovel in it. The handcart had a hitch on the end.

She reached slowly for her rifle, which she'd propped against the bank to her right. Jacob grabbed her wrist and held it. She relented rather than struggle. But not without frustration. She hadn't planned to shoot Chambers. Not if he surrendered.

In a moment, Chambers was inside the chain link and she lost the opportunity for a good shot, anyway. But as he moved to the nearest silo, she saw also that he was trapped. No doubt he was armed, but they could hold him at the gate. He'd be unable to get through the chain link or over the coiled razor wire up top.

Again she tried to pick up her gun. And again Jacob stopped her. What was wrong with him?

She grabbed his head and dragged it down so she could whisper fiercely in his ear. "I won't kill him," she promised, pleading. "I swear."

"No. We're letting him go."

Dammit!

Chambers was messing around with a door or hinge of some sort. Miriam wasn't a farm girl; she didn't know how these silos worked. It seemed there was a way to get out foodstuffs for testing or simply to remove a small portion without using one of those big hoppers to fill a truck or wagon. He scooped a shovelful of what sounded like dried beans into his cart. The first scoop rattled like pebbles in a can, then it was quieter as he worked.

It took three or four minutes to fill the cart. When he was done, he shut the panel on the silo, hauled the cart through the gate, and locked it again. He moved slowly, his breath loud, the cart crunching now over the ground with its heavy load, instead of bouncing.

Miriam waited, teeth clenched, while Jacob held out an arm to keep her from snatching her rifle. She felt coiled like a rattlesnake, ready to strike. It was all she could do to keep from scrambling out of the wash, saying the hell with the rifle, and going after Chambers with her pistol instead. But as the minutes passed, the tension eased from her body, and she trembled when the adrenaline had drained away. The cold air raised goose pimples on her arms.

The engine started up again and disappeared east into the desert.

The instant it was gone, she wheeled on Jacob. "What's wrong with you?"

"Cool down," he said.

"That's what I've been doing, cooling. For the last twenty minutes. Pointlessly. I could have taken him at any point. What are we doing, letting him rob us? Don't you care?"

"Miriam, will you calm down?" He sounded so even and measured, but his tone only made her more irritated. "Chambers isn't going anywhere. He'll come back tomorrow. And the day after that. A few more bushels of wheat and beans isn't going to make a difference."

"Are you crazy? It makes a huge difference. That food is life and death."

"Not for us, it's not. He's been doing it for months and we never noticed. That means we can take our time while we figure out what he's up to."

"We know what he's up to. We saw it with our own eyes. And we know he's trading or giving it to our enemies. What more do we need?"

"We need the big missing piece in the middle between the stealing and the giving," Jacob said.

Miriam turned it over in her mind and shortly saw what he was driving at.

Some of the pieces were easy enough to put together. What Miriam had taken for a motorcycle was undoubtedly one of the ATVs that had been used among the farms and ranches but were now gathering dust in barns and sheds for lack of fuel. That meant Chambers had found a place to steal gas too. Where? It was so precious, every liter was rationed and measured.

More likely grain ethanol, she thought. He probably had a still hidden somewhere on his property, and he had a ready supply of wheat right here.

Chambers would drive onto Smoot's land from the desert, hauling the cart by hand the last half mile so he wouldn't be heard. Once he filled it with stolen grains or beans, he'd hitch it to the ATV and drive it . . . where, exactly? South, west, and east would take him nowhere but mountains or desert, even if he could get past the bunkers guarding the approaches to the valley.

That left only a direct approach to the Ghost Cliffs, but it was well protected and in the open. Even if Chambers wasn't spotted getting to the road, the highway would take his vehicle past Yellow Flats. Sister Rebecca would hear him driving past every night. Twice—coming *and* going. She could practically snipe him from the porch of her cabin. Then he'd still have to get past the bunker guarding the switchbacks up the reservoir.

"Now do you see?" Jacob asked. "We don't know how Chambers is moving the food out of the valley. And we don't know why he's doing it either."

"It doesn't matter how or why. We only need to stop it from happening again. The rest of it is not important."

"It's important to me," Jacob said firmly. "If this goes beyond Chambers, if there's a conspiracy, I need to know. And if there's a secret path in and out of the valley, I want to find it."

"Chambers will tell us. We'll ride out to his cabin tomorrow and take him at gunpoint. Then we take him back to the chapel and interrogate him. If we need to be rough to make him talk, all the better. He deserves what he gets."

"And after that?"

"A short trial. A quick punishment."

"We don't have a court. We don't even have a jail."

"We're not putting Chambers in jail," she scoffed. "This calls for frontier justice. That's the law these days. The law of survival."

"So hang 'em high. Watch him twitch in the wind. Sure, why not?"

"We can't do nothing."

Jacob sighed. "Miriam, please. Eliza and Steve are gone. You're the closest thing to law enforcement I've got. I need your help. But I can't have you waging a holy war every time you see some injustice or other."

She clenched her jaw and glared at him. That it was dark and he wouldn't be able to see made no difference. Her anger and frustration had reached the point of boiling.

"Fine," she said at last, through gritted teeth. "I'll come out tomorrow on horse to look for tracks for the ATV, see where they go."

"I know where they go already."

Miriam blinked. "You do?"

"They go to the base of the cliffs. Here, in the desert. They can't go up the switchbacks for all the obvious reasons, and anything west of the highway is too close to Yellow Flats."

"Yeah, I already figured out that part. So, what, he climbs the cliffs by hand, a couple of hundred pounds of beans strapped to his back?"

"He doesn't have to," Jacob said. "Only the food needs to reach the reservoir."

"Well, sure. But how does that change things? It can't fly up."

"Let's say Chambers shovels the food into sacks. Then he drives his ATV into Witch's Warts where the maze abuts the cliffs. Someone up top throws a rope over the edge and hauls up the sacks of food by hand."

"By hand? That has to be three hundred feet."

"More like four hundred."

"That's a lot of rope," she said. Still, the idea intrigued her. "How would they get the rope up and down without it snagging on something? It's not a straight drop to the bottom in most places. There are crevices, overhangs, trees clinging to the side. And then they'd have to haul it up four hundred feet. Multiple times."

"They've got plenty of manpower for hauling—that's not a problem. As for keeping the rope from snagging, I don't know. I figure we'll go out tomorrow night and wait for him to show up."

"Where? There's a good three miles of cliff front we'd have to watch. And it's not much of a moon. It will be dark."

"Yes, but we can hear the ATV for a good mile. We each take a spot and wait."

"If we get there early," Miriam said, warming to the idea, "we might even be able to find tracks in the sand. Most likely he's going back to the same place every night."

"Good, now you're thinking. To deal with the darkness, we'll bring along night vision goggles."

"My batteries won't hold a charge anymore," she pointed out. "I'd swipe the radio batteries, but they use double A, and the night vision takes triple A."

"I've got batteries."

"They still hold a good charge?"

"Non-rechargeable, unopened. Eliza and Steve brought them from Las Vegas. They were in the prepper supplies left with the Methuselah tank. I've been saving them for an emergency."

"Great, that will make a big difference. I'd better come by tomorrow afternoon and get them. I'll want to test out the goggles in the basement, make sure they're still good and the batteries have a charge. After that, when do you want to leave? Right after dinner?"

"Tomorrow is Tuesday. Scripture study at the chapel."

"I can skip the meeting," she said. "It's not mandatory."

"Actually, I wanted to go myself."

That surprised her. "Really, you want to go to scripture study?"

"Am I not allowed?"

"Of course you're allowed, but I haven't seen you there for months. Not really your thing, is it?"

"I should go more often, but I'm busy."

"But why now?"

"I got to thinking," he said. "Seems there's a big crowd hanging around the chapel these days. Like you said, it's not mandatory, so why so many people? I thought I'd see what the fuss was about."

"Okay, sure."

Miriam thought about what she'd seen at meetings lately. Jacob wasn't going to like what he discovered. He must have suspicions or he wouldn't be going tomorrow, of all times. His brother or sister must have said something to him.

"I know you attend with David and your sister wives," Jacob said. "But do you think you could slip out midway through?"

"Of course. They knew I was heading out tonight, but nobody asked for details. They won't tomorrow either."

"Good. It'll be dark around eight thirty, more or less. I'll take the pickup truck so we can go faster. We'll leave about seven, seven fifteen—that will give us time to hide the truck and hike along the base of the cliffs before dark, looking for tracks." He straightened, stretched. "Go get your horse. We'll ride back together."

As soon as Miriam was away from him, climbing up the wash and then picking her way back to where she'd left her mount, she started to reconsider. Jacob's plan was reasonable, the sort of thing she might have proposed herself back in her FBI days. Like going on stakeout. They knew the culprit, they knew he wasn't going to escape. What was the problem?

She untied her horse from the rocks where she'd hidden it. It was fortunate Chambers hadn't discovered the animal. He must have driven his ATV not far from here. If the horse had whinnied or nickered, Chambers would have realized he was being watched. Maybe he *had* realized. Miriam climbed into the saddle and picked her way slowly back the direction she'd come, toward where Jacob was waiting.

The problem is you don't trust Jacob.

She didn't trust Jacob, and he didn't trust her. He wanted to ride home with her to make sure she didn't go after Chambers. Because Jacob knew that she was itching to deal with the man now. And why not? It was the right thing to do.

She remembered what Ezekiel had said at their secret meeting at Sister Rebecca's cabin.

The problem with Brother Jacob is that we need him to act like a prophet, and he won't do it.

Miriam had no intention of joining a conspiracy against Jacob. It would take more than a few misgivings to turn her against her prophet, it would take a divine command by the mouth of the Lord or one of His angels. But that didn't mean she couldn't protect Jacob from his own weakness. His misguided sense of mercy.

This was not the time for mercy. This was the time for justice.

Ahead, Jacob waited for her, horse and rider a dark silhouette against the star-studded sky. And when she saw him, Miriam made a decision.

She'd go with Jacob tomorrow to search the base of the cliffs. But when the time came, she would put a bullet through the head of Larry Chambers.

CHAPTER ELEVEN

As Jacob pushed Fernie's wheelchair to the chapel the following night, he decided he really should attend Tuesday scripture study more often, if for no other reason than it would give him a chance to spend more time with Fernie.

Not that they were remotely alone. Three of Father's widows accompanied them, including Jacob's own mother, together with several of his unmarried half sisters and brothers. David and his wives and children met them out front of the house, and together they formed a large clump walking down the sidewalk. They met other families, and by the time they reached the chapel, Jacob and Fernie were in the middle of a crush of thirty or forty people.

But it felt like cheating (in a good way) to be with Fernie, and not Jessie Lyn, on a night that was technically scheduled for his second wife. Jessie Lyn had stayed home to work in the garden while kids cleaned up after dinner. Jacob had no aversion to Jessie Lyn; he could have helped her tie tomato plants and enjoyed her company. But he ached to spend more time with Fernie.

As he helped her into the pew, he shooed aside one of his sisters so he could sit next to his wife. His mother sat on his other side, and she of course wanted to chat. And Eliza's mother—one of Father's other widows—wanted news about her daughter. Nothing yet, he assured her. She'd been gone only a day, and only the most optimistic scenario would have had her returning right away. And then there were all the people who came to shake his hand and thank him for coming.

At last Elder Smoot arrived. He walked up the aisle, leaning on his cane. Smoot seemed to need it only during meetings, but it was hard to deny that he looked far more the Old Testament prophet than did Jacob. His dark beard and sharp gaze gave him a deep, intense aura, and he was old enough to carry a certain gravitas without being so old as to seem feeble. He seemed much like Jacob's father had been, in fact.

Smoot spotted him. "Brother Jacob. I didn't know you were coming."

"Last-minute decision. I had a free evening for once."

"Come up front, you can preside."

"No, I'm not here for that. You go ahead and lead the meeting."

"I can lead it if you'd like, but you should come up front. I can't have you sitting down here while I'm up there presiding." Smoot gave him a smile. "It looks bad."

Fernie squeezed Jacob's hand and said with her expression that it was okay. And by now half the people in the chapel had broken from their whispered conversations and were looking at him. The others on his aisle stood, and he reluctantly left the Christianson pew and accompanied Smoot to the stand. Other men from the Quorum joined them: David and Stephen Paul, plus Elder Griggs.

Jacob sat next to his brother, facing the audience. Smoot shook hands with the other elders before taking the lectern. The audience hushed. Smoot waited while Elder Potts came up front, leaning on a four-legged aluminum cane that he most certainly *did* need. His son Peter helped the frail old man up the stairs, then took a seat next to him facing the congregation with the rest of the men on the stand. The chapel was full, people standing around the edges where they couldn't find seats.

David whispered in Jacob's ear, "It gets a little weird. Try to have an open mind."

Jacob waited for his brother to explain. But then Smoot opened with prayer. After that, the congregation sang Jacob's least favorite hymn, "We Thank Thee, O God, for a Prophet." It seemed obligatory at any meeting he attended, and only reminded him of how little he felt like a prophet.

After that, the meeting started off normally enough. Jacob hadn't expected anything different in spite of Eliza's warning. In spite of what David had whispered.

Smoot's son Ezekiel came up to the stand to read from the scriptures. It was a chapter from Revelation—end-of-the-world stuff. Nothing unusual about that.

"'And when he had opened the seventh seal, there was silence in heaven about the space of half an hour. And I saw the seven angels which stood before God, and to them were given seven trumpets. And another angel came and stood at the altar, having a golden censer, and there was given him much incense . . .'"

Ezekiel's words turned into a drone. Jacob was watching the congregation. They seemed especially rapt. No young children out there, unlike Sunday's sacrament meeting, but some teenagers sat among the adults. Every face stared, wide-eyed, at the reader. No eyes drifted closed, no women knit, no men fiddled with ties. Nobody followed along in their own scriptures either, which was unusual on the sur-face, but hardly cause for alarm. Strange things at scripture study? Like what? This was more of the same.

Church meetings of any kind were rigid, well-regulated affairs. Whether they involved business or scripture study, they followed a set schedule. Even the temple rituals, with their mystical elements, fol-lowed an identical script each and every time. Only testimony meet-ings could be quirky, with members occasionally bearing testimony not of the gospel or the scriptures, but of the US Constitution or of some strange vision one of his ancestors had seen about the end of the world. Once, before Jacob's father died, an old woman had gone on for about twenty minutes about how the government was putting rat poison in ice cream, until finally Father had tugged her sleeve and suggested she sit down. But that sort of thing was rare, even at testi-mony meeting.

Things had been different in early Mormon history. New doc-trines sprang from Joseph Smith's mouth as the spirit moved him. Angels appeared to church members at the Kirtland temple, and peo-ple spoke in tongues. When Brigham Young was speaking at Joseph Smith's funeral, it was said that he had taken on the appearance of the murdered prophet, had spoken with Brother Joseph's voice.

Jacob wondered how he'd slip out midway through the meeting, as he'd promised Miriam. It wouldn't be so easy from up on the stand. Everyone would take note. He picked out Miriam to discover his sister-in-law staring at Ezekiel with her eyes wide. Her lips were mouthing something. Other people's lips were moving too. That was odd.

Suddenly, from the audience, a woman cried out, "Praise the Lord!"

Jacob flinched, startled. After a lifetime of well-ordered meetings, the unexpected outburst was like a jolt.

Another woman cried out. A man rose to his feet in the front pew. He lifted his hands above his head, but said nothing as tears began to run down his cheeks. He continued staring at Ezekiel. A woman stood and did the same thing. A teenage girl cried out, "Heavenly Father, save us!"

Through this, Ezekiel kept reading. Or so Jacob initially thought. Suddenly, his ears tuned in to the young man's voice. Ezekiel wasn't speaking English, he was babbling. Speaking in tongues. His voice rose in pitch. More people cried out in the audience.

Speaking in tongues was rare these days, but not unheard of. Never in a church meeting, though. Suddenly, half a dozen people in the audience erupted into their own chattering babble. Shouts sounded from every corner of the chapel.

"Save us from the fire!"

"Burn the wicked!"

"We are the faithful, Lord! Do not shed our blood!"

"Jesus Christ! I'm here, Lord!"

"Heavenly Father, save us!"

Men wept. Women threw themselves convulsing to the floor. Other people collapsed, caught by family and neighbors before they brained themselves on the pews in front of them. Half a dozen people broke out in ragged song: "Come, Come, Ye Saints." More people shouted and babbled in tongues. Above them, Ezekiel's voice rose to a high pitch. Behind his son, Elder Smoot was trembling, tears running down his face.

As Jacob watched, stunned, the chapel had changed from a calm Mormon meeting into a wild, charismatic revival. This wasn't scripture study. It was a mass psychotic event. He could almost picture the fMRIs of their brains, the neurons firing like mad in their frontal lobes as they were swept along in the revival, while parietal lobe activity faded away. They were no longer individuals; they were one with the Holy Ghost and their fellow saints.

His own family was as caught up in it as anyone. Fernie lifted her hands above her head and shouted a prayer. One of his teenage sisters whipped her head back and forth, her braids coming undone and thrashing about her face. His mother and Eliza's mother clung to each other, weeping ecstatically. Other family members danced and sang or threw themselves to the floor.

Horrified, Jacob tore his eyes away and turned in alarm to his brother to see what he was making of all of this, only to discover David's eyes rolled back in his head and his mouth hanging slack. He'd fallen into a trance.

Jacob rose, shaken, to his feet. He made his way down from the stand between the rows of pews, pushing through the people clogging the aisles. Hands grabbed for him, people begging him to bless them, crying out in joy that the prophet had come among them. Others shook and spasmed without seeing him, or lay writhing on the carpet as if caught in epileptic seizures. He pushed through the doors and stood in the hallway, breathing heavily. The tumult continued behind him, muffled by the doors. He kept going.

In a moment he was in the open air and striding toward the sidewalk. Outside, everything was so quiet. So normal. A dog barked a few blocks away, and from the south came the whinny of a horse. Somewhere, a man was chopping wood. Elsewhere, a woman called for a child to come indoors. The temple sat quietly to his right, white and clean, the golden angel on top silently blowing his horn. The heat shimmered from the street while the sun dipped low on the horizon, already stained red and orange.

The church door opened behind him and Miriam came out. She was wearing a prairie dress, but as she came down the stairs, he caught a glimpse of jeans beneath it. And she wore sturdy shoes.

Miriam eyed him, not unsympathetically, it seemed. "So, now you know."

"How long?"

"A few months. It started slowly. The last few weeks people have been more worked up."

"Is anyone leading it?" he asked.

"It's spontaneous. People know the end is near. They want to be prepared."

Jacob started walking toward the house. "They're afraid. I understand."

"Of course they're afraid. Aren't you?"

He let out a bitter laugh and picked up his pace. "More than I was an hour ago, yes. Now I'm terrified."

Miriam caught up with him. "Why?"

"Because it's clear now. I'm alone."

"No, you're not! We're all with you. Every single one of us. Everything we do. Everything you see—everything!—even when people argue with you. Those are your followers. We're tools in your hands. All you have to do is wield us."

Jacob shook his head, angry with himself. He shouldn't have let Eliza and Steve leave. They would have listened.

"Jacob, you can do this. Take us in your hands. Shape us, tell us what to do."

"I didn't ask for this. I didn't ask for any of it."

"Of course you didn't ask. The Lord called you."

"My father died, that's what happened. Then I was next. I should have said no."

"You think you had a choice?"

"These are my people. I was their doctor, the one they looked to. And I knew I could change things. Stop them from driving out the boys. Stop trading women like cattle. Stop the crazy—"

"You're not listening to me," she interrupted. "The Lord chose you—you had no say in the matter. The world has changed. The old rules don't apply. The sooner you figure that out, the better."

No, he wasn't listening. He wasn't trying to convince her. Like there was any point in *that*.

Instead, he was arguing with himself, the stupid decisions he'd made. When he agreed to take over after his father's death, it was only so he could lead his people into moderation. Bring them to the real world, into civil society. Into the mainstream. And it had been working too, until the real world refused to cooperate. Until it collapsed. Now that it was gone, his people were clinging to their most fanatical beliefs, swept up in a howling sandstorm of religious hysteria.

Fernie. David. Miriam. Probably even Eliza. All of them gone.

CHAPTER TWELVE

Jacob maintained a glum silence as he and Miriam brought the pickup truck out of the garage and drove through Blister Creek. She tried to encourage him with a few words about their upcoming mission, but he refused to answer.

Miriam had never quite understood her brother-in-law. From the first time she'd met him, back when she was living farther north in central Utah as part of the Zarahemla community, she'd seen his remarkable potential. He was bright, he was educated. He was fair-minded, and could consider other points of view, sometimes to a fault. It led him to pull back when a situation called for ruthlessness.

But so much of what she saw was potential. Leadership potential. Spiritual potential. Always potential, never realized. When the situation needed him to raise his right arm to the square and call down the wrath of the Lord, he demurred.

They swung past the cemetery and came up the east side of Witch's Warts on the ranch road that ran parallel to the rocky formation. Jacob slowed when they were still a mile from the cliffs. Here he pulled off the road where a flat stretch of slickrock rose from the sand and forced the road to bend away from it. He drove across the slickrock for about twenty yards, then came down just before it climbed into a fat, tortoiselike hump. He drove through the packed sand until he had the truck around back of the stone and out of sight.

Once there, Jacob turned off the engine. The trust level in Blister Creek was such that he usually left his keys in the ignition, but Miriam suggested that he pocket them. On the off chance their quarry discovered the truck hidden back here, she didn't want to make it any easier for the man to tamper with their vehicle.

"That's it, then," he said. "There's nothing to be done for it now."

"We're not that far from the cliffs," she said, confused. "We can walk the rest of the way."

"That's not what I mean." He gave her a look, then opened the door and climbed out. As they dropped the gate on the pickup truck, he added, "What am I supposed to do, step down and hand the keys to Elder Smoot?"

"What kind of talk is that?"

"If there's any time the church needs a level head at the steering wheel, it's now."

"Absolutely."

Yet it worried her that he sounded unconvinced. Like he was trying to talk himself out of running from his responsibilities.

They spent a minute changing their clothes from the Sunday

best they'd worn to the chapel. Miriam stripped off her dress. Underneath she wore a sensible denim shirt and jeans, and she'd worn sneakers to the church. Jacob stripped off his tie and white shirt and had grabbed a tan, long-sleeve shirt when he climbed out of the truck. He took off his church shoes and replaced them with boots from the back of the truck. He grabbed two light jackets and handed one to Miriam.

When they were more suitably dressed, Jacob dragged a backpack with an aluminum frame from the back of the truck and handed it to Miriam. She checked it over to make sure he'd packed everything. A canteen hung in a side pocket. Inside was a box of ammunition for her pistol, a folded-up solar blanket, a first aid kid, and some beef jerky in a Ziploc bag. Night vision goggles. A rechargeable LED flashlight. A package of AAA batteries, the blister pack cut open when Jacob had tested them.

"And that's how you see yourself?" she asked. "A level head? Nothing more."

Jacob responded with a grunt. He got out the handheld radios and flipped them on briefly to test them, before turning them off to conserve the power in the rechargeable batteries.

"You didn't answer," Miriam prodded.

"No, I didn't." He put away the radios, one in each pack. "They don't hold a very good charge anymore, so leave yours off unless it's needed. You know, if there's one supply I regret not stocking up on before it was too late, it's more and higher-quality batteries."

"I thought it was medical supplies, antibiotics, and all that stuff."

"That too. But in that case, I saw it coming and grabbed what I could. I blew it with batteries, and that would have been easier to acquire." Jacob shrugged. "Doesn't matter. Between the rocks and the cliff, we're unlikely to get much use out of the radios, anyway."

She checked her pistol in its holster, then grabbed the KA-BAR military knife that she'd tossed in the back and threaded the sheath through her belt.

Jacob had his own pack, plus an AR-15 rifle with a scope. Miriam reached for the rifle, but he shook his head.

"We're not shooting anyone. We're going to watch, that's all. Then, when it's time to move against Chambers, we'll do it in broad daylight."

"That's my call to make."

"No, really, it's not."

Miriam put her hands on her hips and fixed him with a look. "Which one of us is the former FBI agent?"

He smiled. "As you said, the world has changed. The old rules don't apply."

"Hah. All right then, let's go."

They returned to the road instead of trudging through the soft sand. Miriam listened for the sound of a two-stroke engine and kept an eye out for riders or people on foot, but saw nobody. There was still a bit of daylight left. If Chambers followed the same schedule as last night, it would be at least two hours until he stole the food, and then he'd have to drive out here.

A jackrabbit came tentatively onto the road ahead of them. It spotted them, sat staring as if transfixed until they were only a few feet away, then exploded toward the sagebrush on the opposite side. Later, a big spiny lizard with a brilliant turquoise throat studied them from its perch atop a rock. It did a few warning push-ups as they passed before retreating to a crevice. A raven landed atop one of the sandstone fins and croaked insistently until they were out of sight.

"The desert doesn't like people," Miriam observed. "The animals don't, anyway."

"Tell that to the skunks who keep raiding our compost bin and spraying my dogs. They love us."

"Doesn't it ever surprise you we ended up here?" she asked. "Who came into the Blister Creek Valley and thought this was a good place for a settlement?"

"I know exactly who—I've read her diary. It was about hiding from Federal authorities so they wouldn't get arrested on polygamy charges."

"I know all about Grandma Cowley's diary," Miriam said. "But still, of all the places. This isn't the most remote, or the most desolate, but it's some crazy combination of the two. You'd think in the past hundred and twenty years someone would have pulled up stakes and moved somewhere better. Even the old Montana or Alberta communities were green and lush compared to this."

"I happen to like the desert. It's wild and beautiful, and the air is clean. Take a look at the cliffs," he said with a nod toward the sheer sandstone escarpment looming ahead, the late sun casting it in burnt reds and orange, streaked with black desert varnish. "Who could get tired of that view?"

"Sure, they're beautiful, if you like that sort of thing. But that's missing the point."

"Which is?"

"The cliffs are a natural fortress. So are the mountains, the desert. You couldn't build a better citadel than the one God provided in the Blister Creek Valley."

Jacob gave her the side eye. "This again?"

"Admit it. It's no coincidence that we ended up in the safest, best-protected place in the entire country. The Lord led your ancestors here. He knew. He prepared a sanctuary for His people and He kept it hidden from the world."

"You know what would have been easier? If God had simply told the Indonesian volcano not to blow its top. None of this would have been necessary."

"It's in the scriptures, Jacob. The world has to be broken and destroyed for the Lord to return in all His glory."

"It didn't have to happen *now*."

He was still arguing, but at least he was more cheerfully obstinate. More like his old self. He'd seemed shaken when she found him outside the chapel. That had worried her.

"What would it take to convince you?" she asked. "Jesus himself appearing to you telling you it was the end?"

"Maybe. It would certainly help. But that hasn't happened yet."

"Have you asked to see Him? Dropped to your knees and poured out your heart so that the Lord would come to you in person?"

Jacob stopped. "So, former FBI agent. How are your keen observation skills now?" He pointed to the ground. "You were so busy pontificating you almost walked right past it."

At their feet, a set of knobby tire tracks left the road and cut across the sand toward a fissure between two sandstone fins. The tire marks were visible for only a few yards, then the wind had swept the sand into rippling waves, more peppered with the tracks of lizards and stink beetles than evidence of Chambers passing in the night.

She grunted, annoyed that she'd missed it.

"There's a metaphor in there, somewhere," he said.

"Yeah, yeah. I get it."

★★★

Miriam was happy to let Jacob take the lead in entering Witch's Warts. She came after him through a pair of sandstone fins, following the tire tracks, and almost at once found herself surrounded by an intimidating maze of fins and columns, passageways through the stone that opened promisingly, then ended in cul-de-sacs that forced them to retreat.

Here and there they came across more tire tracks, but it was not an easy trail to follow. The tracks would disappear for a stretch where the wind had run its shifting fingers over the sand. Then they'd find a sheltered spot and see it crisscrossed three or four times.

She'd expected to use the nearby cliffs as a guide, but the fins were so close together and so tall that she couldn't see the cliffs at all. Jacob seemed to have a better sense of direction among the rock formations, but he still halted regularly to study their surroundings. Once, he stopped for what seemed like five minutes, staring at a single hump of sandstone the height of a two-story building.

"Are you lost?" she asked nervously.

"Not yet." He pointed at an angled line of light and shadow that slashed across the stone. The darkness crept up almost imperceptibly as the sun fell. "See that angle? Right there is southeast. Back that way is where we left the road."

"Really? I must be turned around."

"It's easy to do in here." He returned to studying the pink sand. "Let's see if we can find those tire tracks. This seems like a good path through to the cliffs."

They still couldn't find a clear set of tracks, but to Miriam's relief, they popped out of the labyrinth a few minutes later. There, looming above them, were the Ghost Cliffs. They cut in a line from west to east along the extreme northern edge of the valley. Boulders lay tumbled around the base, most of them old and weathered, but others jagged, their colors fresh.

The upper reaches of the cliffs were still bathed in light, with the blue sky overhead, but here at the bottom Miriam and Jacob stood in late-afternoon shadow, save for a stray shaft of light that found its way in a straight line through Witch's Warts.

Miriam shifted her backpack to get to her canteen. "We're running out of daylight," she said, after taking a swig. "Do you want to split up? You go west, I'll go east?"

Jacob nodded. "Sounds like a plan. But stick to the cliffs. I don't want you going back into the maze and getting lost."

"Trust me, I won't." She hesitated. "You want to get out the radios?"

"No point to that. Only chance of a signal would be to climb one of the boulders, and even then it would only work if the other person was in the clear as well."

"So how do we communicate? I hate to shout—if someone is out here, he'll hear us too."

"You see anything, you come back to this spot." Jacob slapped his hand on a boulder the size of a school bus. "Otherwise, we'll meet here when it gets dark."

That gave them only fifteen or twenty minutes before they'd have to turn back for the boulder, so they set off without further discussion. Jacob went west, while Miriam cut to the east, studying the ground for tracks as she walked. She saw no evidence of tire tracks in the few places where there was enough space to maneuver a small vehicle. By the time she'd mentally ticked off fifteen minutes, she had no better idea about where Chambers would approach the cliffs than when she'd left.

On the way back to the prearranged rock she studied the cliffs instead of the ground. That was the other limiting factor—finding a place to toss over the rope from above. Maybe she'd spot something up there. Something, or some*one*. But there was no movement; all was still except for a pair of blue scrub jays squabbling in the air overhead.

Vegetation clung to the cliff in spots: shrubs and grasses, with the occasional juniper tree, its roots clinging to the rock, its branches twisted and stunted from the wind. A bristlecone pine stuck out at an angle a few dozen yards above her head. One green branch grew from a mass of bare trunk and branches, the dead part as lifeless as driftwood. A tree of that size might be hundreds or even thousands of years old.

In spite of the vegetation, the overhangs, and the gullies eroded by seasonal runoff, there were more spots than she'd initially guessed where someone might toss over a rope without it getting snagged. She examined them as she approached, but couldn't see any one location that stood out. Chambers could have any one of a dozen places pre-arranged, then wait for the rope to swing down from above. Worse, it was now dark enough that she might have stumbled right past a rope without spotting it.

By the time she returned to the boulder, she was frustrated and irritated.

Jacob was arriving at the same time, his rifle slung over one shoulder, and his backpack hanging from the other. He set them both down when he spotted her. "Anything?"

"Just my own tracks. Hope Chambers isn't looking for them. You?"

He shook his head.

"Let's go back and wait at the silo," she said. "If you're right and he shows up every night it should be easy enough to grab him. Like we should have done last night."

"I want to see what happens here. There's only so much cliff. I figure if we divide up, listen for the ATV, and keep watch with the night vision goggles, we'll be sure to spot him. Then we'll know how it's being done."

"Why do you care?"

"Miriam, someone has found a way to smuggle food out of the valley. Don't you want to know how?"

"Not really. It doesn't matter, so long as we put a stop to him."

"What if it's more than one person?"

"It's not. It's Chambers acting alone in the valley, then that McQueen guy who put him up to it. But it's not like McQueen is going to rappel down the cliffs every night. We stop Chambers, we stop the smuggling."

"Taylor Junior got into the valley by climbing down the cliffs. He found a fissure and worked his way down."

"Taylor Junior grew up in Blister Creek," she pointed out. "And he was insane. You'd have to be to climb down the cliffs in the middle of the night. Chambers is not insane, he's a greedy backstabber. A coward. I say we hoof it back to the silo. It's a sure thing. Unless," she added hopefully, "you're getting a spiritual prompting telling us to stay."

"No spiritual prompting. At least, I don't think so. The only prompting is my own head telling me to find out how Chambers is doing it. Besides, there's no guarantee we'd reach the silos in time, not if we have to sneak up to them again. Anyway, if we can't find him here tonight, nothing is stopping us from trying again tomorrow."

"Those are good points," Miriam conceded. "Okay, then. Let's get out the night vision."

CHAPTER THIRTEEN

"The spirit repelled him," Ezekiel Smoot said. "It literally shoved Jacob out the door."

He studied his father's troubled expression, wondering, worried that he was pushing the older man too hard and too fast. Elder Smoot stroked his beard with one hand and rubbed the brass beehive on the end of his cane with the other. He still sat in a chair directly behind the podium, where he'd been throughout the church meeting.

The chapel had emptied and the lights were flickering. There were strict regulations about electricity use in the valley, but people would be arriving at home, turning on just one light so they could see to light a lamp, or justifying why they needed to run this electric pump or fire up that semi-licit appliance. It was the sort of behavior that led to brownouts. In fact, Ezekiel or his father should have already flipped the breaker on the chapel. With the sun down and the solar arrays off, that left the turbines at the reservoir, but they produced a limited quantity of electricity.

Smoot seemed to notice the flickering lights at the same time. He used his cane to lever himself to a standing position, but carried it under his arm as he made for the switches. Out in the hall, they briefly turned on one more light so they could find the box and flip the breaker, and they left through the front door without locking it. There was no need.

Ezekiel caught his father's arm. "I need to show you something before we go home."

"Brother Jacob was uncomfortable," Smoot said. "He wasn't repelled."

"And what would possibly make him uncomfortable?"

"I was uncomfortable at first too. The Lord's house is a house of order. When the spirit seizes an entire congregation of saints, it looks like chaos, bedlam. I had to surrender to the spirit to understand it. Jacob hasn't done that yet."

"Did you see the look on his face?" Ezekiel asked.

"No, I didn't."

"Disgust and fear."

"That doesn't make sense. Why would the prophet be disgusted and afraid?"

"Exactly."

"I'm getting sick and tired of this," Smoot growled. "Stop hinting around like a gossipy old woman. Say what you mean or shut your mouth and leave off with your apostasy once and for all."

His father's righteous tone was intimidating. As a boy, Ezekiel would have cowered. Only his older brother, Bill, could stand as a man when Father used his patriarchal tone. But doing so had earned Bill respect in Father's eyes. And now that Bill was gone, nobody else in the family could do it. It fell on Ezekiel to seize that for himself.

"Wake up," Ezekiel said. "You know what I mean. You know it in your heart."

"Show respect, boy."

"*You* show respect. I'm the one being led by God. You're the one fighting the obvious. Why, because of some misguided loyalty to Jacob's father? Abraham Christianson is dead. His son is leading the church into the gaping jaws of hell."

If there was ever a time for Smoot's anger to explode, this was it, but instead he fell silent. The two men stood a pace distant, studying each other through the near darkness.

"Good," Ezekiel said. His heart was pounding. He felt like he was staring down a mountain lion. No time to show fear. "Now listen to me. Brother Jacob *was* called by the Lord. We all know that. But it's clear to anyone with ears to hear and eyes to see what has happened since then."

He paused, waited for his father to again demand answers. But the older man didn't speak.

"Jacob is a fallen prophet," Ezekiel said.

Smoot let out his breath in a long, drawn-out sigh. "I don't know. I can't see it. Why would the Lord let that happen?"

"Why would the Lord take away Eliza and her gentile husband at this exact moment, if not to get them out of our way?"

"So, what? So we can remove Brother Jacob from office? What about Brother David?"

"Jacob's brother is one of us."

"He is?" Father sounded surprised. "What about Sister Miriam? Sister Rebecca?"

"They're with us too."

"Jacob's wives?"

"They won't like it, but they have no power in the community."

Ezekiel was anxious to get his father off the sidewalk and around back of the temple, but his father seemed to have regained his confidence.

"But Stephen Paul Young does have power, and he's an ally of Brother Jacob."

"He's with us too," Ezekiel said.

"Ha!" Smoot said. "That's where you're wrong. I spoke to him this afternoon. He said he was sorry he'd ever gone out to Yellow Flats, that it was a sin to speak about Brother Jacob behind his back. He said if there's any fault it's with us, not with Jacob. That we need to stand beside him. So now I know you've been shoveling manure this whole time."

Ezekiel had been bluffing, and now his father had caught him out. Worried that he was about to lose the argument before he even had a chance to show Father what he'd hidden in Witch's Warts, he stumbled into an even bigger blunder before he had a chance to think it through.

"Don't worry about Stephen Paul. I'll take care of him."

"Take care of him?" Smoot roared. "Why, you little—he's a good man. If you lay a hand on him, so help me I'll—"

"Shh, keep your voice down."

"Damn you, I will not. If this were the old days, I'd drive your sorry hide to St. George and dump you in the Walmart parking lot. That would be the end of you. You'd be cast into the Lone and Dreary World. A Lost Boy."

"Father—"

"No, I won't listen. I've got to take shift at the bunker tonight, and a long ride ahead of me to reach the cliffs. I have no more time for this nonsense." Smoot turned toward home. "If I were you, I'd fall on my knees tonight and beg the Lord for forgiveness. And thank Him for Brother Jacob, who is a more merciful leader than you deserve."

Now terrified, Ezekiel backtracked from his earlier boast. "No, Father, no. That's not what I meant. I'm not going to hurt Stephen Paul. I'd never do that. I'm going to *talk* to him. I have information, new information, that will change his mind."

Smoot stopped. "What information could you possibly have?" Skepticism dripped from his voice. "This whole business is of the devil."

"I don't expect you to take my word for it. I'll show you." Ezekiel nodded toward the temple.

"If you think I'm going into the temple with you at this hour . . ."

"Not *in* the temple, behind it. Witch's Warts. I need to show you something."

Smoot wavered. Ezekiel wanted to push, but didn't dare. He'd misread his father more than once already in this conversation and didn't trust himself to get it right this time.

"Okay," Smoot said at last. "But this had better be good."

Ezekiel set off without waiting for his father to have second thoughts. When he reached the back of the temple, he groped in the shadows until he found the shovel he'd left propped against the back wall. The blade scraped against the foundation stones.

"What have you got there?"

"It's a shovel," Ezekiel said. "There's something buried in Witch's Warts."

"I don't have time for this. I told you, I've got to man the north bunker."

"It will only take a minute. Trust me."

"What is it? A body? Some old bones?" His father sounded nervous. "You know I don't like to go in there."

"Shh. Come on."

The stones stood in the darkness like silent sentinels, seeming to frown on the two men as they entered.

The truth was, Ezekiel didn't care much for the sandstone labyrinth either. Like many of the other kids of the valley, he'd played around the outskirts as a boy, using a screwdriver to carve his name into a sandstone hoodoo, or scrambling up a hump of red rock after a lizard. One afternoon in spring when he was about nine, he'd found a huge mass of writhing racer snakes retreating into a fissure ahead of the falling sun. He'd been afraid to reach his hands into all those snakes, but he couldn't let them go either. He ran for his older brother, Bill, who grabbed a bucket, a pair of gloves, and a couple of clothes hangers that they'd bent into hooks as they returned to Witch's Warts. But when they got back, Ezekiel couldn't find the spot even though the brothers searched until darkness. Bill accused him of lying, but the younger brother was adamant. He knew what he'd seen.

Ezekiel hadn't been dumb enough to venture past the first few rows of stones, but he hadn't been afraid of Witch's Warts either. Not like some kids. Then, when he was eleven, there was a terrifying incident with the Kimball boys that put him off the place forever.

A summer cloudburst had overflowed the banks of Blister Creek and filled the sandy wash that flowed out of Witch's Warts on the south end, near the cemetery. The next day, when the temporary stream evaporated, Bill and Ezekiel followed it into the labyrinth to look for quartz crystals and flint arrowheads that sometimes washed out during storms. Once, their cousin had even found a twenty-dollar gold piece from the nineteenth century lying glittering on the surface as if it had fallen from a hole in someone's pocket only moments earlier.

Two hundred yards into Witch's Warts from the south the ground began to rise, and they had to climb a stretch of slickrock to get back to the wash. Eroded potholes in the stone still held several inches of water, and in them they saw hundreds of squirming tadpoles. After a storm, spadefoot toads would drop their eggs in the holes and then the tadpoles would race to turn into toads and bury themselves in the sand before the hot sun evaporated the water and baked them to death. The brothers were squatting over the holes, poking the tadpoles with their fingers, when a shadow fell over them.

Ezekiel turned, his heart suddenly in his throat. Two other boys stood on the rock ledge above them, where the water had cascaded over the edge to flow into the wash below.

He thought at first it was Jacob Christianson and one of his younger brothers—Enoch or David, probably. But when he stood, shielding his eyes, he saw it was Gideon and Taylor Kimball Junior. A knot of worry worked into his gut.

Normally Ezekiel felt safe when hanging around his brother. Bill was thirteen, about the age of Taylor Junior, and bigger, but Gideon was older than both and already long and muscular. More a young man than an older boy. But he didn't act like a man. He was feared as a cruel bully by every kid in the valley except for Jacob Christianson, who was close to the same age and seemed to intimidate Gideon. But Jacob was in Canada that summer, Ezekiel remembered suddenly, working on the Christianson ranch in Alberta.

"What are you pussies doing?" Gideon said with a sneer. "Jerking off down there?"

Bill tugged Ezekiel's elbow. "Come on, let's go."

But before they could get away, the Kimball boys slid down the slickrock to where the Smoot brothers were standing over the potholes.

"Look what we found," Taylor Junior said. He held something round and white in his hand.

It was a human skull.

CHAPTER FOURTEEN

Ezekiel had gaped at the skull in Taylor Junior's hands. Terrified, yet fascinated at the same time.

"Where did you get that?" Bill asked, his eyes bugging.

Gideon grinned. "We found some guy buried in the sand. Rain must've washed him out. Some of the body was eaten by animals a long time ago. The rest is like a mummy. Must have been there forever."

"Was it an Indian?" Ezekiel asked.

"Wouldn't you like to know?" Gideon said. "Should we show 'em, TJ? I don't know if they can take it. They look like they might piss their pants already."

Gideon took the skull from his brother and thrust it at Ezekiel, its eye sockets staring, as if it would frighten the younger boy. But by now, Ezekiel was more intrigued than anything.

"Want to see the body?" Taylor Junior asked. "It's just up there."

The thing about the Kimballs was that they weren't always nasty. Sometimes they did cool stuff too. They built the snow forts in winter, made homemade fireworks, and Gideon had once showed Ezekiel and Bill an abandoned mine in the foothills on the east side of the valley. He claimed it was a diamond mine, and several boys went climbing through the narrow tunnels with flashlights looking for gems. Father later said (after he'd given Ezekiel a belt whipping for going into the dangerous abandoned mine) that it had been a silver mine back in pioneer times, except nobody had found much.

And the skull tempted him. There was nothing cooler than finding stuff from the old days: a wagon wheel or bleached cow skull in the desert, an Indian pot in a crumbling cliff dwelling, an abandoned cabin. Even discovering a rusting, sandblasted hulk of a long-dead Ford truck made him itch with curiosity.

"Come on, Zeke," Bill said. "We gotta get home before supper. It's just a dumb old skull."

"What, are you scared?" Gideon asked with a sneer. "Afraid of ghosts?"

"I'm going home," Bill said. "Come on."

Without waiting to see if Ezekiel would follow, the older Smoot brother made his way back down toward the wash. Ezekiel was torn. But when he looked at the skull with its gaping, hollow expression, he had to see what the Kimballs had found.

So instead of doing the sensible thing and going after his brother, he followed Gideon and Taylor Junior and climbed up the fissure. From there, they continued along the wash. The sand was still damp where the encroaching stone fins forced the wash into a narrower, shaded channel, with stone rising twenty or thirty feet on either side to shade it. It was so narrow that the three boys had to pass single file, with Ezekiel taking the lead. At the end it grew so tight that he had to squeeze sideways to get through. The walls were damp and cool. This seemed to be where the wash had originated that later flowed past the cemetery to join Blister Creek.

When he was able to face forward again, he glanced down to find his footing over a jutting hump of stone and saw, curiously, that there were no other footprints. Nobody had come this way earlier. Where were they taking him?

Ezekiel turned to look over his shoulder and saw that he was alone. When had that happened? Gideon and Taylor Junior had entered the fissure too. He'd heard them behind, scraping over rocks and crunching on the sand. Yet at some point they'd turned around and retreated out of sight.

"Guys?" he called. His voice reverberated hollowly through the narrow stone fissure.

No doubt they meant to spook him. He was more irritated than anything.

"It's not funny. I'll just go back again. I'm not lost or anything. Guys?"

Gideon leaned over from on top of one of the stone fins, thirty or forty feet above him. He smirked down at Ezekiel. Gideon must have backed out again, then climbed up the sloping sandstone fin. No doubt Taylor Junior was up there too.

Ezekiel opened his mouth to say something. But there was something cunning in Gideon's expression, and he suddenly thought better of mouthing off. Let them have their stupid games. Ezekiel turned around to pick his way back through the fissure.

He hadn't gone more than a few feet when he heard the sound of stone scraping stone. He glanced up and what he saw filled him with terror. Gideon and Taylor Junior were heaving their shoulders into a loose piece of sandstone. It was a large hunk about the size of Ezekiel's slender torso. Before the boy at the bottom had a chance to move, it was falling down on him.

Ezekiel had no chance to run as the stone plummeted into the fissure. His arms flew over his head in a futile attempt to protect himself, and he waited to be crushed.

But the rock hadn't been aimed at his head. Instead, it cracked and boomed as it rattled off the stone fins, then came to a rest wedged into the fissure some ten feet away. Gideon and Taylor Junior laughed above, then they disappeared.

At first Ezekiel was merely relieved, and determined to get back to his brother as soon as possible. Until he tried to get back down the fissure, when he realized that the wedged stone had blocked his return. He'd have to go around.

Now furious, biting his lip so he wouldn't mouth off to the Kimball boys and bring them back to torment him again, Ezekiel made his way to the end in the direction he'd originally been traveling. Once out in the open, he stopped. And stared in dismay.

The giant stones rubbed one against the next on either side of the passageway, making it impossible to simply go around and return to his starting point. Due to a further quirk of geography, all the fins dove sharply into the ground on this side. He couldn't climb over the top of them either. Ahead and in front lay a tight, but passable maze of fins, humps, and columns. All of it led deeper into the labyrinth instead of back toward the cemetery.

He studied the position of the sun in the sky, trying to figure out his points on the compass, but that left him more confused than ever. He'd have to cut around and see if he could turn himself back toward the wash and the cemetery. It wouldn't be easy. What if he got lost? He might be out here for hours. No sooner had the thought entered his mind than his mouth felt dry and parched, as if by suggestion.

Ezekiel decided to go left. Behind a series of short fins and knee-like protrusions the height of a man lay a taller rock formation shaped like a horse head on one end and a double camel hump on the other. The terrain seemed more open in that direction, which he hoped would provide opportunities to find a path back toward the cemetery.

But when he got around the fin and stone columns, he discovered that the collapsed part between the fins wasn't a passage, but a fissure about six feet wide and twenty feet deep. The back end of the second camel hump connected with the narrow fins behind it to form a sheer, impassable wall. If he'd had more courage, he'd have taken a running start and leaped the chasm, but the thought of that made his knees shake. Instead, he moved in the shade of the giant horse-head formation, only to come around and find another tight clump of sheer rocks angled in such a way that he'd be funneled farther than ever away from his goal.

He stood staring, heart pounding. Deeper into the labyrinth, or back the way he came? Seemed there was no choice but to continue. But already he was disoriented and frightened.

He thought of the skull in Taylor Junior's hands. Eye sockets gaping, the bone white and bleached by the desert sun, the flesh devoured by wild animals. He pictured himself lying dead on his back, sinking into the sand, eyes staring at the sun while crows landed to tear off his lips and nose with their sharp, gleaming beaks.

A desperate prayer came to his mind.

Heavenly Father, please help me get out of here. Please, please, please.

He hadn't yet said *amen* when a voice called through the thin desert air.

"Ezekiel! Hello?"

It was his brother Bill.

Ezekiel almost wept with relief. When he could find his voice, he screamed back. "Over here! I'm over here! Bill!"

Bill shouted something back and Ezekiel had to scream for him to repeat it.

"I'm not moving!" Bill said. "Don't want . . . lost. Come . . . voice."

"I'm coming!"

Bill kept shouting while Ezekiel picked his way through the angled fins. For a few desperate minutes he thought he'd be forced deeper and deeper until he could no longer hear his brother's voice, but then the labyrinth thinned in what he thought was the west. He was able to climb over the top of an enormous hump of slickrock, jump a narrow fissure—this one no more than two feet wide—and then slide-scramble down a steeper slope of slickrock, grabbing onto sagebrush clumps to keep from tumbling out of control. Moments later, he came around another fin to find Bill there with his hands cupped to his mouth, shouting.

Ezekiel's eyes watered up, and it was all he could do to keep from sobbing. He rushed at his brother to hug him, but Bill pushed him away, laughing.

"Whoa, don't be gay." Nevertheless, he looked relieved. "What happened? Where'd you go?"

Ezekiel told him, then asked where Gideon and Taylor Junior had gone.

"The jerks had bikes in the cemetery. They jumped on and rode off to town. I knew when I didn't see you that they'd done something and I'd better come back and find you or Dad would kill me."

Ezekiel started to shake. It was only the desert. Only rocks. Only a few miles from home. And Bill had known where he was. The town would have organized a massive search. He wouldn't have been lost for more than a few hours. He hadn't been in any real danger.

"I hate them," Ezekiel said. "I hope they die."

"Don't worry about it. They'll get their reward."

What Bill meant, Ezekiel thought all these many years later, as he led his father into Witch's Warts behind the temple, was that everyone expected Gideon and Taylor Junior to end up as Lost Boys, denied wives and driven from the community. Bill surely hadn't known that their "reward" would be a pair of violent deaths.

Ezekiel studied the rock formations behind the temple and tried to pick out landmarks.

Gideon had died a few minutes' hike from here, killed by Eliza Christianson. He'd tried to abduct her as his wife, and she'd split his skull with a hunk of sandstone. And Taylor Junior had died even closer, maybe a hundred yards away. He was killed in a violent struggle with Brother Jacob.

"I'm not going any farther until you tell me what this is about," his father said.

Ezekiel ignored him and used the thin light of the moon to search the clearing between two giant humps of sandstone. He took his shovel and poked tentatively at the sand. After five or six pokes, the tip clanked against metal. He shoveled away sand.

Smoot came over. "What is that? What are you doing?"

Ezekiel had cleared away the upper sand, but didn't want to damage the contents of the hole, so he rammed the shovel into the pile he'd excavated and dropped to his knees. He scooped away handfuls of sand, tugging gently at the burlap sack to get first one side free, then the other. His father squatted next to him.

"Stand back unless you want to die," Ezekiel said in a sharp voice.

"What are you talking about, let me—" Suddenly, Father stopped and scrambled back. "No! You didn't."

Ezekiel rose, heaving out the burlap sack, which clanked, metal on metal. He set it on the pile of sand next to the shovel. Then he opened the mouth of the sack and reached inside. There was no need to wave his father back—the older man was a good dozen feet away now.

Ezekiel's fingers closed on a sword hilt. He eyed his father one last time, then drew the weapon out of the sack. He held it up and turned it so the older man could see the moonlight glint off the metal.

"Father in heaven," Smoot said, his voice pinched and terrified. "Forgive me. Do not smite me. Please, I beg thee for forgiveness."

"Why would He smite you?" Ezekiel asked. His confidence had increased even as his father seemed overcome with terror.

"Because I am a fool. A blind, wicked fool. I told you not to enter the Holy of Holies. But I should have known. I should have guessed you'd do it anyway. As your father, I should have stopped you."

"I received a vision, Father. I was only obeying what I saw."

"I don't believe you."

"And you wouldn't have been able to stop me, because I have been called by the Lord. Not even the hosts of Satan could have stood in my way."

Ezekiel set aside the weapon and pulled out the other object. It was heavy and flat, with cords dangling off the end.

"The breastplate of Laban," his father whispered.

"I woke at night," Ezekiel said, after setting this object down too, "and I found myself barefoot walking up the steps to the temple doors. I passed through the dark halls of the temple without seeing, but led by the spirit every step of the way."

"Sweet heavens."

"Even then, I wasn't sure I was not still dreaming until I stood in the Holy of Holies, my hands resting on the cedar chest. There were no electric lights, no candles. But the carved cherubim were glowing with a white heat, so bright I couldn't stare at them. That's when I came fully awake. I knew I had been led there, but in my fear worried that I'd been tricked by Satan. If I opened the chest, I would be destroyed. But what could I do?"

"I—I don't know."

"I had no choice."

Ezekiel had rehearsed these words in his head again and again. Like most of the men on the Quorum of the Twelve, Elder Smoot was more practical than mystical. But he must have thought about the sword and breastplate a thousand times. He must have wondered why Jacob didn't wield them. Why, if Jacob were the One Mighty and Strong, he seemed so spiritually weak.

"So you . . . took them?" Smoot asked. "And buried them here? Why?"

"I cannot tell you the things I saw, the beings who spoke to me. But know this, the Lord has commanded me to take these things. The final battle is approaching. I will wield the sword and breastplate when the forces of Satan descend upon our valley for the final time. I will cast aside the enemy and the Lord will enter our midst in all His glory. And then I will lead the saints into the Millennium as their prophet."

Smoot drew in his breath. "Brother Jacob is our prophet."

"Jacob *was* our prophet," Ezekiel corrected. He approached his father, who flinched. "Jacob *was* called. Of course he was. But he turned away when given difficult commandments. When ordered to repent, he hardened his heart against the Lord. And so the Lord chose someone more worthy. I'm not perfect—you're my father, you know that. But I will obey the Lord, my God, and that is why He chose me. Because I will obey without question."

"I don't believe it. I *can't* believe it."

"Father, listen to me." Ezekiel took the older man by the shoulders. "The spirit repelled Jacob. It literally pushed him out the doors. It's terrible, it makes me weep, but you can't deny it. Our leader is a fallen prophet. The blessing of the Lord has been taken from him."

"And you . . . ?"

"I have strapped on the breastplate and not died. I have held the Sword of Laban in my hand and not been smitten by an angel. No other man may do this and live. No man but the One Mighty and Strong."

"I don't . . . I can't."

"Touch the sword if you doubt me. Pick up the breastplate. You know what will happen."

His father pulled away with a groan and put his fists to his temples. "I don't understand. Jacob saved us. His people love him. What do we do? Tell him to step down?"

"Father, no," Ezekiel said. His father's anguish touched his heart. "You don't ask a false prophet to step down. What if he refuses?"

"Then what? Drive him from Blister Creek?" Smoot let out a harsh bark. "Send him into the world to take his chances?"

"Our people are too soft-hearted, too loyal. They would never let him go. And his wives would fight for him, Miriam and David. His sister, Eliza, when she returns."

"You said Miriam and David were with us. Are you lying?"

"They're with us," Ezekiel said. "But it's one thing to ask them to stand aside while we force Jacob to stand down. Another thing for them to watch us drive Jacob out of Blister Creek. Their loyalty will blind them to the will of the Lord."

Ezekiel turned away from his father and walked slowly back toward the objects he'd dug out of the ground. He picked up the blade and turned it over in his hands, his heart heavy. He took no pleasure in any of this. He turned around to face his father.

"The Lord told me what to do," Ezekiel said sadly. "The Lord commanded me to find Jacob Christianson and cut off his head."

CHAPTER FIFTEEN

Miriam listened for Jacob as he moved through the darkness west along the base of the Ghost Cliffs. When she could no longer hear him, she picked her way slowly to the east. There was just enough light that her straining eyes could pick out the forms of the larger boulders to her left. To the right lay the inky blackness of Witch's Warts.

Periodically, she put on her night vision goggles and climbed one of the boulders or sandstone fins to see how far her view carried.

The best spot was on a hump of rock shaped like a two-story loaf of bread. It took a few minutes to find a way to climb the thing, but when she got up top, she knew she'd chosen the right place. The rock offered the perfect combination of height and isolation that would allow her an expansive view both east and west. Too bad she didn't have the rifle; she could have propped it right over her backpack and enjoyed a wide range of fire.

But Jacob had insisted on taking the rifle with him. She understood, she got it. He didn't trust her, and probably with good reason. She wasn't here to screw around. She was here to stop Chambers.

The stone was warm, but the breeze picking up from the cliffs already had a bite to it, so she zipped up her jacket and made sure she knew how to get to the solar blanket if it kept growing colder. She checked her pistol ammunition by feel, then ate some beef jerky, even though she wasn't hungry.

Miriam turned on the goggles. The black turned to pale green and cast stones into sharp relief. The eyes of an animal glowed up at her from the sand below. A jackrabbit. She scanned the cliffs, both above and below. Nothing unusual caught her eye, but it was early yet.

There was probably some overlap with Jacob's position to the west, so she mostly looked east. Every twenty or thirty minutes an animal would pass along the desert floor below her. Some she recognized—a coyote, a mule deer—but some of the smaller animals were furtive, creeping shapes that she couldn't identify.

It had been several years since Miriam had sat on an extended stakeout, but she found her emotions following the same pattern as the hours crawled by. At first her attention was sharpened like a knife drawing back and forth across a whetstone, until it was well honed.

But the edge dulled as time crawled by. First, her mind started to wander, thinking about her baby, her husband. Then thinking about her parents and her brother and wondering if they'd survived the war on the West Coast. She hadn't heard from them for years, not since her mother and father tried to stage that ridiculous intervention to get her out of Blister Creek, believing she'd joined a cult. Right, like Miriam was that weak-minded. But surely her parents would think about her on occasion, wonder what had happened to their daughter.

It filled her with an unexpected longing. Not regret for her path in life, exactly, but the sense of something lost.

Miriam yawned and forced her attention back to the business at hand. One difference between tonight and the old FBI stakeouts was that she'd have had a gallon of black coffee on hand. The Word of Wisdom prevented hot drinks, but a little caffeine would surely come in handy about now.

She was growing drowsy again when a high-pitched whine caught her ears. She was instantly alert. A few seconds passed before the whine cut out. She couldn't pick it up again, no matter how she strained. But she was certain of what she'd heard. It was the same ATV as last night.

No, there it was again. Definitely to the southeast this time. Faint, but clear. She looked, but couldn't see anything through the tumble of Witch's Warts.

Could Jacob hear it too? Probably not; he was a mile or so to her west. Her hand went automatically to her backpack, where she found the radio and turned it on. After a moment of hesitation, she turned it off again.

"Can't risk it," she said aloud. Even in a whisper, her voice startled her. Strange thing to voice the words instead of thinking them. "Chambers knows what frequency we use. What if he's listening?"

Don't lie to yourself. You know what you're doing.

Well, yes. She knew. She wasn't worried about Chambers listening in on a radio. The truth was that she didn't want Jacob to know she'd heard the ATV. She wanted to handle Chambers on her own.

A flashlight appeared on the edge of her vision, flaring white in her night vision goggles like a miniature sun. Miriam's heart took a leap like a startled rabbit.

Staying low, leaning against her backpack, she slid the goggles to her forehead to have a look. Her naked eyes took several seconds to adjust to the darkness. The light was nothing but a small penlight, a good two hundred yards away. It disappeared behind rocks, only to appear again.

Miriam put on the goggles and dialed down the intensity so she could see the man behind the light. Only it wasn't one man, it was two. One man had the flashlight; the other was pulling the cart through the soft sand. The cart was heaped with bulging sacks.

Two men? There was a second traitor?

The light kept coming toward her along the cliffs until it was about fifty yards away. Then it blinked out for good.

Miriam turned up the goggles. The two people stood by the cart, discussing something in voices too low to hear. Without taking her eyes from them, Miriam touched a hand to her pistol holster, then to the knife sheathed at her side. She crawled backward in the darkness, looking for the rainwater fissure that had helped her scale the rock.

She climbed down to the sandy valley floor and walked slowly through the darkness, pressed against the stone, the goggles still on. The men weren't looking at her, instead turning their gaze up the cliff, but she still took no chances in her approach. Kick a pebble, stumble into sagebrush, and they'd whirl around and turn on the flashlight.

She moved from boulder to boulder until she was about forty feet away, where she squatted behind a rock not much bigger than an overturned garbage can. Both men wore sidearms, but that only mattered if they could get their guns out and locate her in the darkness. She eased the pistol from its holster. From this distance, with this much time to aim, she could hardly miss. Two shots. They'd go down, one after the other.

But who was that second person? Definitely a man; he had a beard and a masculine posture and height. But through the green glow of night vision, she couldn't tell any more than that.

It could be anyone.

Anyone? Even David? Would she shoot her own husband if she thought he were smuggling food out of the valley? Of course not, most especially because he'd have a damn good reason for doing . . . well, whatever he was doing. Anyway, it wasn't David. She felt ashamed that the thought would even cross her mind.

Beyond that, who? Maybe one of the squatters, who'd infiltrated and was helping Chambers steal their food. Miriam had to find out who and why before she killed the man.

"There it is," one of them said. It sounded like Chambers. "Get the rock."

The two men grabbed one of the large rocks at their feet and wrestled with it until they got it turned on its edge. There was a rope tied around it, which Miriam had missed in her earlier search. One of the men tugged on the rope, which she could now see stretched up the cliff into the darkness. So Jacob had been right about the rope, although she couldn't figure out why the men didn't untie it from the rock. Then suddenly, and to her surprise, the rock heaved off the ground. It soared up into the darkness until she lost sight of it.

A minute later, a wooden barrel came dropping silently from above. When it reached the ground, the two men tossed out skull-sized chunks of rock from the barrel until it was half-empty, then they heaved it on its side to empty out the rest of the rocks. When that was done, the men filled it with sacks of what she presumed were foodstuffs from the cart.

The thing was a primitive elevator. Instead of relying on brute strength to lift the food several hundred feet, there would be a pulley above, working by sending down a counterweight that would provide most of the lifting power for the barrel. Lift the rock to lower the barrel, or lower the rock to lift the barrel. A little extra muscle power would even out any difference in the weight of the two objects.

Miriam was still turning this over in her head when the men stopped loading. They'd tossed in roughly half the sacks of food, and at first she wondered why they didn't top off the barrel. Then, to her surprise, one of the men helped the other climb into the barrel on top of the sacks of grain.

"You good to go?" Chambers asked. No question now it was him.

"Yup," the other man said in a low voice.

Only one word; it wasn't enough to identify the man.

Chambers jerked twice on the rope. A second later, the barrel inched off the ground, before it began to rise at a more rapid pace. Miriam watched, fascinated and alarmed, until the barrel disappeared out of sight. A minute or two passed, and the rock reappeared from above and settled on the ground.

The elevator system was crude, but effective enough to move thousands of pounds of food out of the valley. The limiting factor was the pace of theft from the silos and the transport to this spot.

What was even more worrying was what the elevator might be used for besides transporting food: people. Send twenty men down from the squatter camp, one at a time, and they could do serious damage to the church's food supplies. Maybe they already had. Or worse, send a small army down one night, maybe forty or fifty men, then have them fan out across the valley, murdering people in their sleep.

Miriam clenched her jaw. This would end. Now.

There was no guarantee that the second man would return. But there was no saying he wouldn't either. Quietly take care of Chambers here, then she could wait for the second man to either come back, or not. If he did, she'd kill him too.

She was barely thinking of Jacob as she returned her pistol to its holster and slid her KA-BAR knife from its sheath. No time to argue with him about this. Time to act.

Miriam rose from behind the rock. Chambers was still staring up, almost turned completely away from her, but not quite. He was taller than her and stronger, ex-FBI, around thirty years old. Miriam was confident, but not stupid. There was no guarantee that if she grappled with him she'd come out on top, knife or no. No, it had to be a quick thrust, the knife plunging into his back before he had a chance to respond.

She closed to fifteen feet, then ten, then five. Then he was in reach. She sprang at him.

Chambers must have felt something, heard something, sensed her somehow. He whirled as she came at him.

Miriam was already stabbing down with the heavy military knife as he flinched out of the way with a shout of alarm. The knife hit and hit hard. But not into his back. Instead, it thrust into his upper shoulder, the blade meeting resistance on bone as it slid in. But when he twisted away with a cry of pain, the knife wrenched out of Miriam's hand. Chambers swung blindly with his other arm. His forearm whooshed past, almost catching her on the side of the head with a lucky blow.

By the time Miriam regained her balance, Chambers had the knife out of his shoulder. His left arm hung limp. His right swung and slashed at the darkness with the knife.

She got back until she was well out of his reach, then stopped and watched him without moving. Inside, she was furious with herself for failing at the job. He'd moved too quickly.

Chambers dropped the knife and drew his pistol. "Kite, you bitch. I know that's you."

"My name is Miriam."

He snapped off a shot into the darkness in the direction of her voice. But she'd expected it and had ducked the instant she spoke. The shot would have gone wild anyway, she thought. Her own gun was in hand, and now that he'd fired at her, there was no longer a question of keeping silent. But she wanted to know. She returned to the protection of the rock where she'd crouched watching the two men.

Chambers stood panting, staring hard into the darkness, looking this way and that.

"You must have dropped your flashlight," she said. "Too bad."

He fired again in her direction. It didn't hit the rock, let alone threaten her in any way.

Miriam chuckled. "You're a terrible shot. And I have night vision. I can kill you any time I like."

"So do it, bitch."

"Who is the other man? I'll let you live if you tell me."

"Liar."

"Tell me."

"Go to hell."

Miriam was getting tired of this. And she wanted him down before the people up top decided to send someone back down in the barrel. So she lifted the gun and took careful aim with her pistol. Right at his chest.

"Last chance," she said.

He lifted his gun in her direction. This time he steadied his aim, and it looked more like a plausible shot in the direction of her voice. She didn't wait to test his aim. Her finger squeezed the trigger. The gun barked in her hand. Chambers fell.

The shot was good. She didn't need to go over to know the result. If he was still alive, it was only temporary.

Miriam now had two worries. The first was that the second man would come down in the barrel looking for her. The squatters could probably fit two men in the barrel once the food was unloaded. If they had flashlights, they might even get off a couple of good shots before she brought them down.

The second worry was Jacob. He'd have heard the gunfire too, and would be hurrying in her direction. Whatever she did, she needed to act before he arrived and ordered her to stand down so he could argue about what she'd done.

Still holding the gun and looking through the goggles, Miriam made her way cautiously to Chambers's prone body. His gun lay in the sand a few inches from his outstretched hand. She kicked it away, then picked it up and flipped the safety before tucking it into her pants. After casting a final glance at Chambers, she returned her own pistol to its holster.

She reached the rock that had descended from the cliffs and touched at the rope. It was taut. There was some weight on the other end. But the stone wasn't rising yet either. She made a quick decision and reached for her knife, only to find her sheath empty.

It took a moment to remember that Chambers had torn it out of his shoulder, then dropped it when he drew his gun. She searched the ground around him, finding it only when she rolled him onto his back. It had been beneath him. She picked up the knife.

"What have you done?" a voice asked behind her.

She whirled to see Jacob turning on his flashlight and shoving his night vision goggles to his forehead. He dropped to his knees and fumbled with the buttons on Chambers's shirt.

Miriam turned back to the rope. "He shot first."

"There's a knife wound here!"

Miriam grabbed the rope and sawed. A few quick strokes and she severed it. Something clanked on the rocks above.

She sprang away. "Get back!"

They both retreated as the barrel came tumbling out of the darkness, spitting rocks. It slammed into the sand. There was nobody in it, only rocks. Someone had apparently been filling it to add ballast for a return trip down, but nobody had climbed in yet. Ah, well. She'd wrecked their system all the same.

"Dammit, Miriam. What are you doing? What's going on here?"

"You wanted them coming down on us in the darkness? For that matter, turn off that light. They're only a few hundred feet above us. Now that I cut the rope, they'll know it's not Chambers down here."

Jacob obeyed, then put on his goggles and stared down at the body.

"Aren't you going to try to save him?" she asked. "Pull bullets out of the wicked and all that crap you do?"

"Like the time you got shot through the lungs and I kept you from drowning in your own blood? Is that the kind of crap you're talking about? Anyway, he's dead. You put a 9-millimeter slug right through his heart."

"It was his choice. Like I said, he shot first."

"I saw the knife wound, remember? So I think you came up and tried to kill him first."

She'd already concocted a story about how she'd tried to take Chambers prisoner with the knife, but she didn't have a chance to tell it. A rifle fired from above them. As they scrambled for cover, a handgun snapped more shots. For the next few minutes they crouched behind a rock while gunfire blasted down from the cliffs. At least four different weapons were firing, as far as she could tell. Possibly five.

Miriam and Jacob had only partial cover, but the gunfire wasn't aimed. Only one shot even came close, ricocheting off one of the fins of Witch's Warts at their rear and then whizzing past her ear.

By the time the enemy stopped firing, Miriam had changed her mind and decided to tell Jacob the entire truth. While they remained crouched, she confessed everything she'd done and everything that had gone through her mind as she'd done it.

"There was no rush," he said when she'd finished. "We could have stayed in the shadows tonight, maybe even studied them for two or three more days. Then, when we were ready, waited here and arrested them when they arrived."

"Who was that second guy? Why did he go up top if he was only going to return later tonight?"

"What did he look like?"

"He had a beard." She shrugged. "I didn't see much else."

"Man with a beard. That's really useful." Jacob sounded disgusted.

"Could be Whit McQueen. He's military—maybe he knew Chambers from back when. Or they made some sort of pact. I tried to find out, but Chambers wouldn't tell me. All I know for sure was that he was an enemy. That's why I didn't want him to get away."

"That's exactly what happened, thanks to you. He got away. I'll say it again—there was no rush."

"Don't be blind. The end is here."

"Sure, of course." His voice oozed sarcasm, and this made her angry.

"We need a leader. Word gets out that the prophet has gone soft and what do you think happens?"

"Why don't you tell me?"

Miriam stopped, suddenly made wary by the sharp tone of his voice. He suspected something. Jacob was a smart man, and his mind was working things over.

"Well?" he pressed.

"Never mind, forget it."

"You're holding something back. What?"

"Nothing," she lied. "I'm worried is all. You saw the meeting tonight, you know people are worked up."

They came out from behind the rock. Miriam searched Chambers's body. She found keys to the ATV in his front jeans pocket. The only other interesting thing she found was a nearly empty pack of stale-smelling cigarettes. That was a risk. Nobody in Blister Creek smoked, so the cigarettes must have come from outside the valley. If he'd been caught with them, if he'd even smelled of cigarette smoke, people would have turned suspicious and hostile.

"I don't think it was McQueen," Jacob said when she'd finished searching the body and they'd returned to the safety of the rocks. "I mean, it could have been, but that's not the most likely scenario."

"Do you think we have a traitor?"

"Doesn't have to be a traitor, only someone who thinks he knows better. He comes up with some scheme that seems perfectly logical and then goes about in secret to execute it. Know what I mean?"

Miriam looked away, uncomfortable. She cleared her throat. "Who?"

"I don't know yet. But I'll find out by morning."

CHAPTER SIXTEEN

Elder Smoot stared out from the north bunker, looking down and across the valley toward Blister Creek. He struggled to maintain his focus. His son Grover lay in a sleeping bag, snoring softly, getting some rest before his father woke him for his turn as spotter. That left Smoot alone with his thoughts.

Only a few hours had passed since Ezekiel had dragged him into Witch's Warts, and Smoot's mind had been in turmoil ever since. His son's plans were almost too horrific to contemplate.

The Lord commanded me to find Jacob Christianson and cut off his head.

If Jacob was a fallen prophet, and Ezekiel had been lifted to take his place, then it was the righteous thing to do. After all, the Sword of Laban had been used for such a purpose before. It was an ancient relic from The Book of Mormon, wielded by the hand of Nephi to behead Laban and allow the faithful to recover holy scriptures and then escape Jerusalem for the Promised Land in the Americas.

But if Jacob had *not* fallen into apostasy, if he was still favored by God, what then? Not only would Ezekiel's plan fail—the Lord would never permit it—but Smoot's own complicity would damn his soul to Outer Darkness. One could not turn against the Lord's Anointed and survive.

But Ezekiel had the sword. He had the breastplate. How to explain that?

The alarm sounded and startled Grover from his sleep. Smoot told the boy to settle down, then turned on the spotlights and looked uphill. A mule deer stood frozen in the switchback above them, its huge ears turned toward the bunker. A large doe. After a few seconds it regained its senses and bounded back up the road and out of sight. Smoot turned off the lights.

David Christianson had rigged an ingenious electronic system to assist in guarding the highway. Using a solar panel for recharging, an array of car batteries, and two old home-security systems, he'd crisscrossed the road in several places with invisible infrared beams as motion sensors. When activated, a bell would ring inside the bunker. Smoot could then illuminate the road with two spotlights.

It was a good system, but in the past year it had delivered nothing but false alarms. Mostly larger animals like mule deer or coyote triggered the sensors, but occasionally even a skunk with an upraised tail could do the same. These days, the alarm didn't even raise Smoot's heart rate. Grover didn't seem to wake completely, and was soon snoring again.

Smoot's thoughts had returned to Ezekiel's strange and frightening pronouncement when a light caught his eye from down in the valley. He looked through the slit running along the valley side of the concrete bunker. It was one of several narrow gun ports that enabled

360-degree fire from the .50-caliber machine gun. On this side it presented a wide, sweeping view of the valley from a vantage point roughly halfway up the cliffs, where the bunker snugged into a crook beside the snaking highway.

There was only a sliver of moon, and the valley had been resting in a pool of inky blackness beneath a glittering bowl of stars. The single light stood out.

Some miscreant, he thought at first, disobeying the brownout regulations. Then another porch light turned on, then the lights of a third house. He took out his binoculars. They were full size, 10x50 power, and strong enough to pinpoint the rough location within town if you could hold them steady. The lights were on at or near the Christianson compound. More lights. Entire households, rousing themselves. Then, to his surprise, he spotted lights from a vehicle.

The vehicle cut east through town, moving at a steady clip. Another vehicle started up, this one making for the highway. Soon, it was driving north, toward the bunker.

Smoot nudged Grover with his toe. "Hey, wake up."

"Huh?" Grover climbed groggily out of his sleeping bag. "My turn already?"

"There's something wrong."

Grover sat upright. He sounded instantly alert. "What is it?"

The boy came over to the gun slit. Smoot handed him a second pair of binoculars.

"Well, look at that," Grover said. "That's never a good sign, is it?"

It was a stretch to say that Grover's personality had changed after his adventures in Las Vegas last year. Grover had always been a sensitive, feminine boy, and sadly, Smoot thought he would stay that way. Grover preferred the piano to riding, would rather read a novel than go target shooting. He still liked to read plays aloud with his teenage sisters. Well, at least Smoot didn't think anymore that the boy was a homosexual. That was something. The pathetic way he'd mooned after Eliza Christianson was evidence enough.

Grover's desires had been hopeless from the start. Eliza was in her midtwenties and had been engaged to Steve Krantz, the former gentile. Grover was nineteen and weak and scrawny next to Krantz. Yet that hadn't kept the boy from moping about the house for a week after Eliza got married.

But since then, Grover had at least grown a spine. He asserted himself around his brothers, rode through the valley with David Christianson to learn electrical and mechanical skills. Heck, that was plenty useful. And Smoot was no longer worried that if the squatters attacked, Grover would curl into a ball and whimper until it was over.

More houselights came on throughout the town. A streetlight blinked on.

"They're going to cause a blackout," Grover said. "This time of night, we choke flow through the smaller turbine."

Sure enough, the lights began to flicker. The fools.

But just when Smoot thought Grover would be proven correct, people in town began to respond to the flickering. Soon, more lights were turning off than turning on. Still, a wave of lights was moving through town as one house after another woke. Multiple flashlights and lanterns added to the movement, bobbing along as they traveled through town. And now he counted six different vehicles, all burning precious fuel as they radiated out from downtown.

Smoot turned on the radio, risking some of their own precious electricity, this stored in batteries. He checked to be sure the radio was tuned to the correct frequency. Almost at once, he heard a woman's voice.

"Hello? Blister Creek? Come in, please." The frequency was strangely filled with static, given that town was only a few miles away.

When the woman cut out, Smoot responded. "This is Smoot at the north bunker. What's going on down there?"

"Hello? It's Eliza Christianson."

"Sister Eliza? Are you back already? When did that happen?"

He held the radio receiver in one hand and was still staring through the binoculars, which he held with the other. His first thought was that Eliza's return explained the chaos below, some alarming news she'd brought from the road. But why hadn't she descended from the reservoir and passed his checkpoint?

"I can hear someone, but there's too much static," she said. "Listen, I'm in Salt Lake. We made it safely. I've been trying to reach you."

This got his attention. She'd made it all the way to the state capital. The thought was so surprising—Smoot hadn't even believed Salt Lake was still standing, let alone that Eliza and Steve would reach it safely and then get to a radio—that he momentarily forgot about the turmoil on the valley floor.

She must have a more powerful radio than his. This one was seventy-five watts, enough to transmit across a hundred miles, maybe a little farther. But Salt Lake was a good two hundred and fifty miles away as the crow flies.

Eliza started to say something about a war and fire, but then her voice faded away. He waited impatiently for her to come back.

As if he didn't have enough to worry about, the buzzer sounded. Another damn animal had tripped the motion sensors outside. Grover lowered his binoculars and moved to flip the switch and turn on the spotlights.

Smoot waved his hand at Grover. "Never mind, it's just another coyote. Keep watch on the valley." Then, into the radio. "Hello? Can you hear me?"

"Elder Smoot, is that you? I can hear you now."

"Who is in charge up there? Is it still Governor McKay? If I were you, I'd—"

"Hello?" she said. "Are you still there? I lost you again."

The bunker door swung open and a figure appeared from the darkness. Smoot dropped both the binoculars and the radio receiver. He dove for the firearms in the gun rack on the side wall next to the filing cabinet.

As he did, he recognized his blunder. That last warning had been no animal. It had been an intruder from the reservoir. Even after a hundred false alarms, he should have turned on the lights and checked it out. But with the movement in the valley and Eliza's unexpected presence on the radio, he'd been distracted from his duties. What a foolish, careless mistake.

But even so, the bunker door was locked. Or should have been. He couldn't imagine that he'd left it unlocked. Even as this thought crossed his mind he saw that the man bursting in from the darkness held something in his hand. A key? A gun? It was too dark to see.

Grover reached the weapons first. He snatched a shotgun from the rack, pumped it once, and started to turn.

"Don't shoot! It's me!"

Smoot flipped the switch and turned on a small, twenty-lumen CFL bulb that dangled from a wire overhead. His son Ezekiel stood in the doorway, panting and wheezing for breath. Sweat drenched his shirt and trickled down his forehead to bead in his beard.

"What the devil?" Smoot said, stunned. His mind was reeling. "Ezekiel, what are you doing?"

"I almost shot him," Grover said, his voice shaking. He lowered the shotgun. "I almost killed my own brother."

Smoot took the gun from Grover's hands, disarmed it, and replaced it on the rack. "Grover is right. Why didn't you call out?"

Ezekiel shook his head. He was still gasping, trying to catch his breath. He came over and picked up one of the pairs of dropped binoculars, then turned off the light and plunged them back into darkness.

As the older of his two sons stared down at the valley through the binoculars, Smoot remembered the radio. He picked up the receiver.

"Hello? Sister Eliza?"

There was nothing on the other end. Damn.

Ezekiel turned. "You were talking to Jacob's sister?"

"She called from Salt Lake."

"What is going on?" Grover asked his brother. "Why are you here? And why are you out of breath?"

"Because I was running, obviously."

"All the way from the valley?" Grover scoffed. "Wait, you weren't, were you? Not from the valley. You came down from the cliffs. That's what triggered the alarm, not an animal."

Ezekiel ignored his brother's questions. "How much did she hear? Did you drop the radio before you said my name?"

"I think so," Smoot said. It was all a blur. "Anyway, Grover is right, isn't he? You were up above, weren't you? Please don't tell me you were talking to the squatters."

Ezekiel was at the gun slit, looking through the binoculars again. He let out his breath. "Someone is coming."

Smoot looked out. Two pairs of headlights were racing north from the center of town. In reality, they probably weren't going that fast, but compared with the long, slow ride on horse that Smoot and his son Grover had taken, they seemed to be flying. Another six or seven minutes and they'd be at the bunker.

"Were you?" Smoot asked.

"What?"

"Were you talking to the squatters?"

"We'll argue about that later, not with Grover in the room."

"Anything you can say, you can say in front of me," the younger brother said.

The other two men ignored Grover as the two vehicles below stopped on the road. One swung west, toward Yellow Flats. The other continued north up the highway, toward the bunker.

"They don't know," Ezekiel said, relief in his voice. "They're checking everywhere, not just here."

"That doesn't help when everywhere includes us," Smoot said. "Whatever you were doing earlier, I take it you don't want it known."

"Listen to me," Ezekiel said. "You need to do exactly as I say. Otherwise there will be trouble."

"Father, no," Grover protested. "I don't care what he wants, don't agree to it. He's mixed up in something terrible."

"Stay out of this," Smoot said.

"But Father—"

"Quiet!"

Smoot hesitated. He could turn back now. Refuse to participate in whatever lie or scheme that Ezekiel had concocted. Grab the shotgun and force his son to sit in the corner until the truck arrived, then tell them everything. That Ezekiel had come running down from the reservoir. That Ezekiel was planning to kill Jacob while Eliza and Steve were out of town.

But Smoot had already taken too many steps down this path, starting with the meeting at Yellow Flats, and then going with Ezekiel to Witch's Warts to look at the sword and breastplate.

And Ezekiel was his son. His *oldest* son, now that Bill was dead. Smoot couldn't betray him on mere suspicion.

"Father," Ezekiel said, his voice growing desperate.

Smoot made his decision. He pointed his finger at Grover. "You. Out of the bunker. Go!"

CHAPTER SEVENTEEN

Jacob had stopped the lead pickup truck at the turnoff to Yellow Flats. David had pulled up next to him in the second truck, with the two vehicles idling side by side in the highway, and asked if there was a problem.

"Miriam spotted a man climbing into the barrel," Jacob explained, "but only women live at Yellow Flats."

"I thought you wanted to check everyone."

"I do. We need to know where this stops. I need to verify that everyone is where they are supposed to be, and that nobody sneaks back into the valley while we're not looking."

Jacob didn't need to add that he didn't entirely trust Rebecca. Of all the women in the valley, she was the most like Miriam, a shoot-first sort of person. What's more, Rebecca also believed she had some strange ties to the nineteenth century that made her some kind of prophetess. Or so she claimed in her more manic phases. If Miriam hadn't been so insistent that Chambers's confederate was a man, Rebecca would have been high on the suspect list.

"What do you want to do?" David asked.

"Come with Miriam and me to the bunker. Send Lillian to Yellow Flats alone."

David shrugged and turned to his second wife. Lillian and David had a quick conversation that Jacob couldn't hear, then David climbed out carrying his rifle. Lillian slid across to the driver's seat and turned down the ranch road toward Yellow Flats.

When David had squeezed into the front seat and the three of them were headed north again, Miriam scowled first at Jacob, then at David.

"I don't need a babysitter," Miriam said.

Jacob gave her a sharp look. "After what you pulled at the cliffs? I'm not so sure about that."

"Oh, please."

David broke in. "It won't hurt to have a third person on hand in case anything funny happens."

"I can handle anything the Smoots try to pull," Miriam said.

"What if they 'pull' a .50-caliber machine gun?" Jacob asked. "That's what they've got up there."

"Fine, but if they're going to do that," she said, "a third person won't stop them. They could mow us down in the road and claim they saw a strange truck and panicked."

"For all they know, it's their own family coming to check on them," Jacob said.

"Unless someone has radioed to warn them."

"In which case, there are witnesses. And once we're out of the truck," he added, "it's going to be a lot harder to claim it was an accident."

"So we need three people?" she asked.

"Killing three of us is harder than two, no matter how tough and nasty one of those two thinks she is."

Miriam grunted at this.

"Okay," David said. "We're all on the same side, right?"

The lights of town reflected in Jacob's rearview mirror as the turmoil of his pronouncement continued to roil through Blister Creek. He had left his remaining family members to organize a complete accounting of every person over the age of sixteen in the valley. Jacob's half brothers Joshua and Trevor were speeding toward Stephen Paul Young's house, where Jacob's counselor on the Quorum would organize a sweep of that side of the valley. In the center, he'd already roused the Griggses, the Davidsons, and the Madsens. Their adult members vetted, they'd joined in the census.

After that, he'd joined Miriam, David, and Lillian in driving toward the north bunker and Yellow Flats in a pair of pickup trucks.

"So you think the Smoots are behind this?" David asked.

"I don't know," Jacob admitted. "What do you think?"

"The Smoot house seemed normal when we arrived, nothing weird going on. And when we get to the bunker, I'm not sure how we'd be able to tell."

"It's been, what? Ninety minutes since we left the base of the cliffs?" Miriam added. "Plenty of time for him to run back along the cliffs and get down to the bunker. Then pretend nothing happened."

Jacob had been busy during those ninety minutes, but not so busy that the wheels hadn't been turning in his mind. First, he and Miriam had left Chambers's body at the cliffs, located and disabled the ATV, and then jogged back to the truck so they could organize a rapid search of the town. If someone was missing, he intended to find out before the man had a chance to sneak back into the valley by some alternate means.

During that time, pieces started to come together, beginning with Miriam's knowledge about the missing grain. How had she known about that? Directly from Stephen Paul, or from someone else? And then there was Jacob's alarming experience at the scripture study earlier in the evening. The scripture study had morphed so quickly into an old-time revival meeting that it must have been going on for weeks, or even months. Speaking in tongues, people falling to the ground, overcome by the spirit—that sort of transformation didn't happen overnight.

If not for Eliza's warning, Jacob would still be stumbling blindly as his people turned into fanatics and mystics. Even then, his sister must have known for some time without telling him. The same could be said of David, Fernie, Miriam, and any number of other people who might have warned him. Not one person had.

"Is Elder Smoot in on it?" Jacob asked.

"What do you mean?" David said.

"Your conspiracy. Does he know?"

"Huh?" David sounded legitimately confused.

Jacob glanced at Miriam. She stared straight forward, her brow furrowed, a deep, unreadable expression where her face caught the reflected light of the dashboard controls.

"Miriam, it's time to talk."

She looked at Jacob. "What? Sorry, I was thinking."

"Quit screwing around. What's going on?"

"There's nothing going on," David insisted. "Nothing we know about, anyway. If Smoot is up to something, it's all his doing."

"I don't believe you. I think you know something." He said this not to David, but to Miriam.

They'd reached the cliffs, and Jacob followed the twisting road as it climbed the switchbacks. The headlights reflected off the squat concrete bunker above them before the building fell temporarily out of sight. Then they were rounding the last bend and pulling to a stop next to the bunker.

"Miriam," Jacob said in a sharp voice.

"What?"

"Tell me the truth."

"There's nothing going on. Nothing I know about, anyway. If Smoot was the other man we saw tonight, it's a mystery to me too. And if he was, I intend to stop him."

Jacob was still suspicious, but enough of Miriam's confidence had returned that his certainty wavered. The problem was that he was paranoid, and why not? There was nobody left who would listen to his doubts. Maybe there was no conspiracy.

Spotlights bathed them in cold white light as they exited the truck. They grabbed weapons and strode up to the door without waiting to be challenged. A bulb flickered on inside. They entered to find Smoot at the light switch, his son Ezekiel sitting up in his sleeping bag, yawning. The younger man's hair was mussed, and he wasn't wearing his shirt, only his white church undergarments.

Ezekiel blinked at the light, glanced at the newcomers, then back to his father. "What's wrong? Why are they here?"

"I don't know," Smoot said. "Something is happening down in the valley. Bunch of lights and cars. Brother Jacob?"

"You let me sleep through it?" Ezekiel said.

"Where is your other son?" Jacob asked.

Smoot gave a confused shake of the head. "Which one?"

"Grover. They said he was up here."

"No, it wasn't his night."

"That's what they said at your house."

"You must have heard wrong. It was supposed to be my son *Garrison's* night, but he'll be up here tomorrow instead."

"I'm pretty sure they said Grover," Jacob said. "You, Ezekiel, and Grover. I remember, because I was surprised that it was three of you and not two." Jacob looked to Miriam for confirmation. "Isn't that right? Were you in the room at the time?"

"No, I was downstairs talking to the women," she said. "But that's what you told me back in the truck."

"Whoever told you made a mistake, then," Smoot said. "It was always just the two of us. I'm sure if you go back, you'll find Grover in bed. How long were you at the house?"

"Not long enough, I guess," Jacob said.

Jacob was doubting his earlier assumption that Smoot would be involved. Neither of these two gave any sign of having been anywhere but in the bunker. It even *smelled* like they'd been here, like sweat, from continual occupancy of the bunker through the heat of the day.

In any event, it couldn't have been Grover Miriam had spotted at the cliffs. The young man didn't have facial hair, and she'd clearly spotted a man with a beard.

David poked around at the guns on the rack, inspecting the ammo cans sitting next to the mounted machine gun.

"Are you going to tell me what this is about?" Smoot asked. "Why is everyone in such an uproar down there? Why did you drive up?"

"Someone spotted—or thought they spotted—intruders," Jacob said.

"Really?" Smoot sounded dubious. "They didn't come through here. That's for sure."

"So you haven't heard or seen anything strange?" Miriam asked.

"Nothing unusual. Typical stuff. The motion sensors got tripped a couple of times. Mule deer. Hardly worth mentioning."

"Didn't even bother waking me up, in fact," Ezekiel said. "But what about the radio? That *did* wake me up. You forgot about that, Dad."

"That's right," Smoot said. "After I got the call, I tried to radio town, but nobody was picking up. Then I saw the lights and—"

"Wait, someone radioed from outside the valley?" Jacob interrupted.

"Yeah, your sister."

"Eliza!" David exclaimed.

All thoughts of the intruder vanished from Jacob's mind as Elder Smoot told them about the call. It had been short and frustrating, with Smoot struggling to communicate back, because of insufficient power from Blister Creek's end, but it seemed that Eliza and Steve had arrived safely in Salt Lake City. And they didn't seem to be in any danger. Jacob took a deep, relieved breath.

"And what's it like up there?" he asked. "Is there still a functioning government?"

"We didn't get to that point," Smoot said. "Sorry, I tried to ask, but she was struggling to hear me. She kept fading out."

"My dad was too busy asking about the roads and bandits along the way," Ezekiel said. "I told him to find out."

Smoot blinked. He opened his mouth, closed it again, then finally said, "I was getting to it. I didn't know she'd only be on for a minute. Then we lost her."

"And that's all she said?" David asked. "Did you try to call her back?"

Smoot cast a quick glance at his son, then shook his head. "No. I told you, we didn't have enough power. We only broadcast with seventy-five watts. I didn't think there was much of a point."

Jacob wanted to have a go at the radio anyway, so he spent the next couple of minutes messing around on different frequencies that Eliza and Steve would know Blister Creek used. Nothing came back.

"Come on," Miriam said at last. "We've got other places to check."

"Stay alert," Jacob told the Smoots. "Keep an eye on both directions, down to the valley and up into the cliffs. If something trips the detectors, don't assume it's an animal. Go check it out."

★★★

"Elder Smoot was lying," Miriam said when the Christiansons were back outside and climbing into the truck.

"How do you know?" Jacob asked.

"Trust me, he wasn't very good at it. When his son made that comment about the roads, Smoot was caught flat-footed. He'd already claimed Eliza couldn't hear him, but then his son seemed to contradict him."

Jacob started the truck and drove slowly back down toward the valley. Lights were on at Yellow Flats to the west. That would be Sister Rebecca and the other women roused by Lillian.

"Smoot said Eliza *struggled* to hear him, not that she couldn't hear at all."

"And think about the timeline," Miriam continued. "Eliza calls on the radio, waking Ezekiel up. No way he hears that and goes right back to sleep. Smoot then tries to raise Blister Creek, sees lights in the valley. You're telling me that fifteen minutes later Ezekiel is still in his sleeping bag? He didn't bother getting out to take a look through his binoculars?"

When she put it that way, it did sound suspicious.

"And did you notice that the bunker door was unlocked?" she added.

Another good point.

"So you think they made up that part about Eliza?" David asked. He sounded upset. "She never called in the first place?"

"Who knows?" Miriam said.

Jacob gave it a moment of thought. "Forget the radio, why wasn't Ezekiel out of the sleeping bag in the first place to see what was going on in the valley?"

"He was still in the sleeping bag," Miriam said, "because he's all hot and sweaty from running down from the cliffs. It's got to be five miles from where that elevator came up, around the back of the reservoir, and down to the bunker. He didn't want us to see that he'd been running."

"It smelled strong in there," David said. "I thought it was because men had been sitting in there around the clock. Men who no longer take regular showers."

"It always smells rough," Jacob said. "But a little worse tonight, I think."

"A lot worse," Miriam said. "I noticed right away."

"Then why didn't you say something?"

"Because you keep hammering on me to play it cool. Didn't seem to be any rush, and it would have been hard to prove, anyway."

"Hmm."

Jacob wasn't buying it. So *now* she was turning cautious?

He stopped the truck when they reached the valley floor. "I'm trying to decide. Do I check out Yellow Flats or drive back up to confront the Smoots?"

"What would you do that for?" David asked.

"Yeah, let's go back to town," Miriam said. "Maybe something has turned up."

Jacob shrugged. "Maybe something has turned up at Yellow Flats too."

"There are only women out there," she said.

"I'm not so sure. I haven't been out there for a while. But you're probably right." Jacob shifted out of park and turned the truck around to head north again.

"What are you doing?" Miriam asked.

"I told you, I'm going to confront the Smoots."

"Don't do that. It's dangerous."

Jacob hadn't yet started driving again and now he turned on the cab light so he could study Miriam's face. "And you know this . . . how?"

"I don't know anything more than you do. It's a guess."

"You're lying," Jacob said. "I know you think you're good, but I've learned to catch you out. And I'm sure you're hiding something."

David looked back and forth between his wife and his brother, a confused expression growing on his face. "Will someone please explain?"

"And you," Jacob said to David. "I thought I could trust you."

"You can! I swear before all that is holy. I don't know anything about this. Miriam, what is he talking about?"

"David doesn't know," Miriam said. Her voice was calm, all pretense stripped from her expressions.

"Know what?" David asked.

"Turn the truck around," Miriam told Jacob. "They're probably watching, and I don't want them to think we're going back up."

"You'll tell me?" Jacob asked.

"Not here. At the house."

Jacob turned back toward Blister Creek, and soon they were entering town. People stood on porches and gathered at the chapel and in front of the temple. A man on horseback flagged them down, wanting to give and get information. Jacob kept it short. But others found him, needing instructions.

It took a good fifteen minutes before they were parking in front of the two Christianson houses again—Jacob's larger one, inherited from his father, and David's smaller, newer home next door, part of the roof still covered in tar paper from when they'd lost a source of roof shingles midconstruction. Jacob turned off the truck, but left the keys in the ignition. He climbed slowly out of the vehicle.

Fernie was on the porch in her wheelchair, and when he spotted her, he came up to tell her everything was okay, but to keep people out of the kitchen and dining room. David and Miriam followed him inside. There was plenty of creaking upstairs, voices of women and children from the hallway. He shut the door to the dining room and kitchen and pulled up a chair at the table.

David sat next to him, his movements weary. Miriam paced back and forth from the kitchen to the dining room two times before Jacob told her to knock it off and sit down. She sat next to David and patted his hand. David wouldn't look at her.

"Tell me everything," Jacob said, lighting a candle. "I'll forgive any lies you told me before, but do not lie to me now."

Miriam nodded slowly. "But before I do, there's one thing I want to know."

"Yeah?"

"Have you ever looked into the chest in the Holy of Holies?"

CHAPTER EIGHTEEN

Elder Smoot watched the lights of Jacob Christianson's truck while Ezekiel paced back and forth across the bunker floor behind him. His son was biting at his fingernails and muttering to himself.

"Where are they now?" Ezekiel asked. "What are they doing?"

"They've stopped in the highway. Maybe they're thinking about going to Yellow Flats. No, now they're driving toward town."

"Can you see Grover on the road yet?"

"I can't, but it's dark."

"Dumb kid will be poking along like he's got all the time in the world," Ezekiel said. "I'll probably catch up with him. Maybe I should go around. I'd rather he didn't see where I'm going."

Smoot's mouth felt dry. "Does that mean . . . *tonight*?"

"I don't have a choice. Should have brought the sword with me, then I'd have been able to do it here. I didn't know it would be Jacob."

That raised a good question. Why hadn't Ezekiel had the sword with him when he'd come stumbling into the bunker? Wasn't that the sort of thing that a divinely inspired assassin should have known? If the Lord truly meant for Ezekiel to hack off Jacob's head, that was.

"No, that wouldn't have worked," Ezekiel said, as if to himself. "Too risky. Three of them, all armed. One was Sister Miriam. That lady doesn't mess around."

"And you still think David and Miriam are on our side? That they'll magically come around after you kill Jacob?"

"I don't know, I really don't." Ezekiel looked up. The light was dimming, the batteries already losing juice. It cast Ezekiel's face in an eerie glow. "The Lord hasn't shown me that part yet. One thing I do know. It's too dangerous to wait. I have to move tonight."

A shudder worked through Smoot's body. "We should pray about this again. To be sure."

"Jacob was suspicious about Grover. He knew the kid was supposed to be here. What was I supposed to do? I couldn't risk that idiot blurting out that I'd just come down from the cliffs."

"I still don't see the rush."

"What if Jacob goes to the house and arrives before Grover returns? Imagine Grover showing up to find them standing on the porch. He's too stupid to tell a good story."

Ezekiel was wrong about that. Grover's problem wasn't intelligence. If they could have trusted him to lie to the Christiansons, they wouldn't have hidden him outside in the first place, with instructions to grab his horse from the shed and race for home the instant Jacob left.

Ezekiel pulled on his sweat-stained shirt and buttoned it up. "I'm going." He grabbed a rifle from the rack and slung the strap over his shoulder. "When I get home, I'll gas up the truck in the garage. Then I'll find Jacob and finish the job."

Smoot's heart was hammering in his temple.

"I'll be back in a few hours," Ezekiel added. "I want you ready to go when I arrive."

"Go where?"

"I saw it in a dream, Father. Things will be ugly for a few weeks. We'll wait at the reservoir. That's why I've been helping them. We'll need a refuge."

"This dream, you're sure it comes from the Lord? It wasn't . . . the *other* kind?"

Ezekiel grabbed him by the shoulders. Smoot's son looked more confident now. "You saw the sword and breastplate. You know the truth. Now trust me."

"Wait—" Smoot said, miserably.

But Ezekiel was already turning away. He shoved open the heavy metal door and let it slam behind him. Moments later Smoot heard the whinny of a horse from outside and hooves clomping down the road.

Smoot sank to the cool concrete floor. He thought about Jacob, no doubt settling in at home while people brought him reports from around the valley. Holding court at his dining room table. Jacob's father, Brother Abraham, had met with his elders at that very table.

Smoot remembered something Abraham had said to him back during the Kimball attempts to seize control of the church.

"If anything happens to me, look after my son. Jacob needs a guiding hand."

Smoot imagined his old friend glaring down from the heavens, eyes blazing with righteous fury. He pressed his fingers to his temples.

The door swung open and he looked up with alarm. It was his younger son, Grover, standing beneath the dimming lightbulb.

Smoot sprang to his feet. "What are you doing? You were supposed to ride back to town. What if Jacob shows up at the house?"

"Then Mother will confirm that I'm up here with you."

"Damn you."

"I'm not the one who will be damned, Father."

There was something so grim in Grover's voice, so uncharacteristic, that Smoot stopped the angry retort that was rising to his lips.

"How much did you hear?" Smoot asked.

"All of it. I hid my horse up the hillside and squatted below the gun ports while you and Ezekiel talked. I needed to know what was going on."

"You shouldn't have done that."

"I heard him mention the sword and breastplate. Did Ezekiel go into the Holy of Holies and open the chest?"

"How do you know about the chest?"

"Everyone knows. It's church lore. They talk."

"Well, they shouldn't. It's sacred information, and should stay within the walls of the temple. Anyway, it's more than lore. It's gospel, it's prophesy. When the forces of Satan mount their final assault on the saints, the One Mighty and Strong will strap on the breastplate. It will protect him from blade and bullet. The Sword of Laban will cut through anything. It will cleave the enemy and smite him unto death."

"I know the story," Grover said. "That doesn't mean Ezekiel is the one to use them."

"He already claimed them. If he weren't the One Mighty and Strong, he would have died the instant he stretched out his hand."

"And you saw the sword and breastplate with your own eyes?"

"Yes, I did. Well, mostly. It was dark."

"Where were they, in the temple?"

"No, they—" Smoot stopped, scowled. "It's none of your business. Your business is to stay out of this. When it's over, I'll tell you what to do." He reached over and flicked off the light to conserve the batteries. "Now go home."

"No."

Smoot's face flushed with heat. "What did you say?"

"You won't tell me what to do," Grover said. "You have fallen into sin and error and lost whatever moral authority you might have possessed."

"I would be careful if I were you. You're close, boy. Very, very close."

"Close to what?" Grover laughed, his voice echoing hollowly in the bunker. "Are you going to excommunicate me and drive me from the valley? Listen to yourself. You're colluding to murder the prophet. Then, when the church rises against you in righteous anger, you'll flee town to hide at the squatter camp. Hide there until you have the force to come back and take control. And you have the gall to say that *I* am close? That *I* should be careful?"

Smoot didn't respond. It sounded ugly when put that way.

"So my brother has befriended our enemies," Grover said. "The ones who tried to slaughter our people. Ezekiel has a safe place among them. He has apparently been sneaking in and out of the valley, like a Gadianton Robber from The Book of Mormon, forming secret combinations. Making evil plans to overthrow the servants of God. And you—"

"Enough!" Smoot roared. An ugly feeling was squirming in his belly like a nest of snakes crawling from their burrow.

But Grover continued. "And you are a part of it. Have you seen the sword and breastplate? It was dark. You saw nothing. They do not exist. You have been deceived."

The dark feeling had spread until Smoot's limbs felt like jelly, his knees buckling. He now doubted everything.

Had he been deceived? Or was he being deceived now?

★★★

Smoot and his son rode Grover's mare down from the switchbacks, Grover in front, and the father in back. The horse snorted complaints at having two people up on her saddle. It was a tight fit, but they pushed her to a trot and made decent time. About a mile out of town she began to tire from the pace, and they hopped off and abandoned the horse to continue the rest of the journey on foot. Grover was young, and Smoot had a hard time keeping up with his jog.

They slowed to a walk only when they reached the straight, gridded streets of town. Smoot's breath whistled, his lungs burning. The past few years had hardened his body, and he was in better shape than he'd been since his twenties, but there was no denying that age had dug its bony fingers into his body. In two months he would turn sixty.

He watched Grover striding along, breathing heavily but not gasping. Only nineteen and strong. Smoot had underestimated his son. This one had moral courage to match his youth. When had that happened?

People were coming and going, riding horses, zipping past on bicycles. A car hurried down the street, its beams blinding them as it rounded the corner. A large crowd had gathered in the chapel parking lot that abutted the side of the temple. There were flashlights and lanterns, and if the Smoots approached too closely, he worried someone would recognize them and call them over.

So Smoot nudged Grover's shoulder and led him back up the street to the vacant lot on the north side of the temple. Here they crossed through the sagebrush and broken hunks of sandstone until they were behind the building.

It had been only a few hours since Smoot had been here with his other son, but it still took a few minutes to find Ezekiel's clearing, then another careful search to locate the disturbed ground. Father and son scooped at the sand like a pair of badgers digging for prairie dogs. A minute later, Smoot's hand touched something hard and he fell back as if he'd been stung.

His stomach turned over. He'd half expected to find the hole empty.

"You're still alive," Grover said. He climbed to his feet and brushed sand from his knees. "Pull it out."

"Why don't *you* do it if you're so cocky?"

"You brought this upon yourself."

"I saw something," Smoot insisted. "A sword, a breastplate. If you're wrong, if they're real, I will die."

"And if you're wrong, Jacob will be murdered in cold blood, innocent before man and God. Wouldn't you risk your life to save the prophet?"

"Of course."

"And your soul?"

"Grover, why don't you pick them up? You're sure, I'm not."

His son faltered. "I—I'm not sure. Not completely."

"Then what are we doing here?"

"You're an Elder of Israel. An apostle in Zion. On the way into town you admitted a dark feeling, said you thought it was wrong what Ezekiel was planning."

"That could mean anything. Maybe you're the one leading me astray, not Ezekiel. I haven't seen an angel, haven't had a vision. I don't know what any of this means." Smoot clenched his hands, torn with confusion and fear. "Why don't I know what to do?"

"Trust your conscience, Father. And trust the Lord. Would He smite you for doubting the word of a man who tells you to kill the prophet?"

"That man is my son."

"All the more reason to prove his words for yourself."

Smoot turned back to the hole. The crescent moon was right overhead, and it gave enough light to see the mound of sand they'd excavated and the hole, a darker shade than the surrounding desert.

It felt like weights were dragging on Smoot's feet as he returned to it. He dropped to his knees and thrust his hands into the hole, closing his eyes as he did so. He grabbed the edge of burlap and dragged the bundle, clanking, out of the hole, then left it on top of the mound of sand.

"Now open it," Grover said.

Smoot breathed heavily. His eyes were open now, staring hard at that dark bundle. His heart felt like it would explode from his chest. Trembling fingers found the mouth of the sack and opened it.

Now is the moment of thy destruction, when the destroying angel appears to smite thee for thy wickedness. Thou shalt not tempt the Lord, thy God.

But when his fingers closed around the flat, cold metal of the blade, nothing happened. He drew the weapon out and let it fall. Then he took out the breastplate. It too fell from his grasp.

"Nothing happened," Grover said. "You see. Now what are they?"

Wondering, still lightheaded, Smoot lifted up the breastplate—or what he'd thought was the breastplate. He held it up to the moonlight, then passed it to Grover.

"It's a metal bucket, sawed in two," Grover said. He laughed. "The shape of a breastplate, nothing more, with holes punched in it and leather strips tied off to look like straps. What about the sword? A plow blade?"

"No, not that." Smoot picked it up by the handle and turned it over. It was sharp, but only on one side. "A machete. One of the ones we use for hacking scrub oak around the watering hole."

"So my brother lied," Grover said. "That settles it."

"Now you know my secret," Ezekiel's voice said from the darkness behind them. He stood a few yards distant, one hand resting on the stone fin to his right, where he had apparently been listening to the others scheme.

The man stepped into the moonlight toward his father and brother. He was armed.

CHAPTER NINETEEN

"Yes, I looked into the chest," Jacob told Miriam and David. "About six months ago, I entered the Holy of Holies and opened it."

They leaned toward him, silent, expectant.

Jacob shrugged. "There was nothing."

David frowned. "Nothing at all?"

"Nothing of value. Some old newspaper from the nineteenth century. I took it out to study. In better light I could see discolored marks where objects had sat on the newspaper, presumably for decades. Do you remember the Jupiter Medallion Gideon Kimball wore? There was the outline of that—that's apparently where he got it. He was always sneaking in and out of the temple. The medallion must have been undisturbed in there for decades before he touched it. If there was anything else, then he'd taken that too."

"Or maybe the sword and breastplate *were* there," Miriam said, "but the Lord lifted them away to protect you. If you had touched them before your time—"

"If God worked that way, he'd have killed Gideon before he murdered my brother," Jacob said.

David frowned and picked at the soft wax oozing down the side of the candle. He had a distant look in his eyes, no doubt remembering the horrible way the Kimballs had butchered Enoch in the Celestial Room of the temple. They'd all been close: Eliza, Jacob, David, Enoch. Out of all the many children of Abraham Christianson, those four were the most alike—the questioners, the independent-minded.

"This doesn't make sense," Miriam said. "If the sword and breastplate of Laban were not in the chest, then where were they?"

"It makes perfect sense if you assume there were never any ancient relics to begin with," Jacob said.

The frown deepened on her face. "Of course there were."

"According to what? It's not scripture, it's not written down anywhere. It's never mentioned from the pulpit, except as hints. The rest is rumor and oral histories." Jacob shook his head. "But I'm not going to argue that now. I answered your question. Now it's your turn. Everything you know. Spit it out."

Miriam began slowly, describing how she'd found the note in her Bible. She'd gone out to Yellow Flats reluctantly, she claimed, and only so she could keep an eye on whatever plot others might be hatching. Several other people had arrived, and she named them now.

Jacob had already guessed Stephen Paul—this was how Miriam had discovered the information about the missing food at the Smoot silos—but it was disappointing nonetheless to hear that his closest counselor had been involved. Stephen Paul's wife too. Plus Sister Rebecca and Peter Potts. Add in Miriam and the two Smoots, and you had seven.

"A strange number," Jacob said. "The Kimballs always had a dozen men, trying to form a full quorum. Like a shadow government to take over the church."

"Maybe Elder Smoot asked others and they balked," David said.

"It was his son pushing the rest of us," Miriam said. "I didn't see it at the time. But I'm sure, now. This was Ezekiel's plan, not his father's."

"But the rest of you stayed. You listened, you colluded." Jacob rose to his feet and walked past them to the end of the table. He didn't know what to do. Didn't even know if he could trust these two.

"We didn't collude," Miriam protested. "Carol Young and Peter Potts left almost before the meeting started. They were angry, and fully loyal to you. The rest of us stayed and argued. Even Smoot argued with his son. I was only sticking around so I could get an inside track on any treachery."

"What about Stephen Paul?" Jacob asked.

"He was upset. He ended the meeting, said he'd heard enough."

"So why didn't any of you tell me?"

"The meeting was only Sunday night," she said. "I needed a couple of days to process it all."

"A lot has happened in two days." Jacob thought about what had happened just since sundown. "A lot has happened in a few *hours.*"

"So what do we do?" David asked.

"There's only one thing to do," Jacob began, reluctantly. "We have to confront Elder Smoot and his son."

★★★

Smoot stared at Ezekiel as his son entered the clearing with a pistol in hand. There was something stiff about the way the young man carried himself, but the gun hand wasn't trembling. He didn't look afraid.

"And now that you know my secret, what are you going to do about it?"

Ezekiel didn't say this to Grover, but kept his gaze fixed on his father. He was underestimating the boy, just as Smoot himself had done earlier in the evening.

"Why did you lie to me?" Smoot asked.

"Would you have obeyed if you'd known it was junk? If you'd known the sword was a rusty garden tool, and the breastplate half a bucket?"

"I didn't obey you, anyway. I came to find out for myself, and saw that it was a lie."

Smoot didn't point out that Grover was the one who had convinced him to touch the supposed relics. His younger son stood to one side, still ignored by Ezekiel. The boy was only a few feet from one of the passageways that led deeper into the labyrinth.

Go. Run away. Save yourself and get help.

Instead, Grover stood fixed in place, staring as Ezekiel took another step closer with the gun. Grover needed to wake up and get out of here before his brother did something stupid.

"So you never touched the sword and breastplate, did you?" Smoot asked.

"I went to the temple, to the Holy of Holies. The Lord told me in a dream to take them. That much is true."

"When?"

"A few weeks ago. Late April."

"You never said a word about this dream. You should have told me before you went in alone."

"They weren't in the chest. Jacob had already taken them out, probably hidden them so they wouldn't be used. Satan must have warned him I was coming. That's when I knew he was a fallen prophet."

"You lied to me once. How do I know you're not lying now?"

"We can be in the Holy of Holies in five minutes," Ezekiel said. "Would you like to see?"

"Yes."

The word came too quickly, was too obviously an attempt to buy time. And Ezekiel didn't move.

"No, you don't need to see," Ezekiel said. "You don't need to do anything except go back to the bunker and wait for me."

Smoot let out his breath. So Ezekiel didn't intend to kill him. His son was swimming in deep waters, but he was not a natural killer. There was still a chance to talk him down.

"Come home with me," Smoot urged. "It's late, a lot has happened. We'll sleep it off and discuss it tomorrow when our heads are clear. A good night of rest with your arm around one of your wives will do you wonders."

"We already discussed this. Jacob is suspicious. If we wait until tomorrow, he's likely to show up with an armed posse to carry me off. I have to do it tonight."

"Then why did you come here?" Smoot asked. He caught Grover edging backward, finally moving, and resisted looking at him. "There's no sword to do the job."

"There's a machete."

"You're going to hack off Jacob's head with a rusty garden tool?"

"That's the sanctioned penalty for apostasy. Cutting the apostate's throat from ear to ear. Blood atonement—it's a mercy."

Smoot stared, his mind churning at the horrible thought of his son hacking Jacob to death, trying to sever his throat. Then something occurred to him. "You're lying again. You've got a gun. I'll bet you were halfway to the Christianson house when you started thinking about how many people would hear a gunshot. That's the only reason you want the machete."

Ezekiel took a half step back and Smoot knew that he'd guessed right.

"Miriam and David live next door," Smoot continued. "Jacob's teenage brothers sleep under his roof. Half the town is out and about and would be on you like a pack of dogs. You couldn't fire a gun." He held out his hand. "And you can't fire one now either. Two hundred people are in the chapel parking lot on the other side of those rocks. They'll come looking the moment they hear gunshots."

Ezekiel backed away, the gun still aimed at his father's chest. Smoot stepped toward him.

"Don't do it," Ezekiel said. "I'm warning you, I'll shoot."

"No, you won't. I'm your father." Smoot made a grab for the gun.

But Ezekiel was younger and faster. He ducked out of the way before Smoot could grab his wrist. He brought the gun up and when his father stumbled past, swung it around and pistol-whipped the older man across the temple.

A flash of pain burst inside Smoot's head. He stumbled, tried to keep his balance, but he'd lost control of his limbs. He fell hard.

"Dad!" Grover cried out behind him.

Smoot rolled over, trying to recover from the blackness crowding his vision. He hadn't been knocked unconscious, but his head felt like his brains had been scooped out and replaced with hot sand. He fought his way to his knees.

Ezekiel and Grover were struggling. The younger brother had snatched up the machete, and now the two men were fighting for control of the weapon. Ezekiel lowered his shoulder and shoved his brother backward. Grover dug in his heels and seemed to stop the push and was about to turn the tide.

Then Grover put a foot behind him to try for a better place to brace himself than the soft sand, and he stepped into the hole. His foot twisted, he cried out, and fell. Ezekiel threw himself on his brother.

Smoot reached his feet, then staggered and almost fell again. The world seemed to be swaying, and the figures wrestling in the moonlight too far away.

Ezekiel came up on top. He held the machete in his hands. He lifted the weapon above his head. Grover, lying on his back, lifted his hands to stop the blow.

Horror swept over Smoot. "No," he tried. The word was soft, without force. Then, louder, "No!"

Ezekiel swung the blade. It hit the outstretched hands with a crunch. Grover screamed.

The older brother let out a feral scream and pulled back the machete. He swung again and again. Grover bucked and screamed and writhed. Ezekiel swung again.

At last Smoot reached them. But Ezekiel was on his knees and turned and kicked at his father's legs. Smoot staggered back. His head was clearing now from the pistol-whip, and it only took him a second to recover. By now Ezekiel was regaining his feet. Grover still struggled feebly to crawl away. Ezekiel lifted the machete, this time from behind his shoulder. He swung in a huge, devastating arc. It struck Grover across the back of the neck.

Ezekiel wrenched the blade out as Smoot came staggering in. He fell over his younger son, sobbing, cradling the boy's head. Grover was moaning, still alive, but his head flopped, nearly severed. Blood gushed onto Smoot's hands.

"No!" Smoot wailed. "Please, Lord, no! Help me, please. Father in heaven, please, don't let this happen."

He turned and through tear-filled eyes saw Ezekiel staggering backward. Blood dripped from the end of the machete and down the older brother's arms. He shook his head violently.

"I didn't want to. I never meant to do it."

"Put it down!" Smoot bellowed. He rose to his feet, trembling with rage and grief.

"Grover made me do it. He made me!"

The boy groaned. Unbelievably, he was still alive, his bloody hands trying to push himself up. Maybe there was still time. Brother Jacob was only a few blocks away with his surgery. There was hope. If the blow hadn't severed the artery, if it hadn't cut through the spine, Jacob could—

A long, terrible shudder worked through Grover's body. He fell flat and didn't move.

When Smoot turned around, Ezekiel was fleeing the scene, machete in hand. Smoot's head was still throbbing, and he knew he would never catch his older son. If Ezekiel ran straight to the Christiansons', he'd be there in a few minutes. Smoot had to stop him.

"Heavenly Father," he prayed out loud. "My son is dead. Lift Grover up, bring him forth on the morning of the First Resurrection. I have sinned, but do not allow thy prophet to die because of my error. Give me a—"

He was praying with his eyes open, still staring in the direction that Ezekiel had disappeared. But now his eyes dropped to the ground, as if guided there by divine command. There, glittering on the sand beneath the moonlight, was Ezekiel's pistol.

Smoot snatched it up. He checked the safety and aimed the weapon at the sky. He squeezed the trigger and fired. Then he screamed for help. He kept firing and screaming until the magazine was empty.

Smoot was halfway out of the labyrinth when the first anxious people found him. At their head was Stephen Paul Young, who began demanding answers.

"It's Ezekiel," Smoot gasped. "He's gone to murder the prophet."

CHAPTER TWENTY

"Confront the Smoots?" Miriam asked. "That's weak. What about arrest them, shoot them if they resist?"

Jacob didn't let her bait him. "Tomorrow afternoon there's a Quorum meeting at the temple. David and I can question Elder Smoot after the meeting. Get him away from Ezekiel, see what he says when he's alone. Maybe he'll crack."

Miriam scowled. "We could be at the bunker in twenty minutes. Settle this once and for all."

"In the most bloody way possible, sure." Jacob was still standing, but no longer felt like pacing around the table. He returned to his seat. "And I want to give Smoot a chance."

"Please be clear," David said. "A chance to what?"

"To step back from the edge." Jacob turned from his brother and gave Miriam a hard look. "Smoot is not the only one who stumbled next to a precipice."

"I wasn't stumbling," Miriam scoffed. "And neither were the rest of us. Nobody went along with the Smoots in the end."

"Nobody came to warn me either."

"We were just talking. It didn't amount to anything."

"Jacob is right," David said in a quiet voice. He broke off a piece of wax from the side of the candle and rubbed it between his thumb and index finger with a thoughtful expression. "It was a conspiracy all the same. You didn't act against them, so they assumed they could move without opposition. Then Eliza and Steve left without knowing anything was wrong. They wouldn't have done that if they'd known."

Miriam seemed more troubled by her husband's disapproval than Jacob's. She addressed David's comment with a pleading tone. "You were worried too. Everyone is. Jacob isn't—he wasn't . . ."

"No, he wasn't," David said. "We all need him to do more."

Jacob felt the bite of those quiet words. He was doing all he could. He'd never asked for this, never campaigned to be prophet. It had always been assumed he would take over. And in the past, his successes were accounted to divine guidance, while his failures were discounted as human frailty. Jacob didn't have a big ego about such things; he didn't need, didn't *want*, praise. It seemed in the past they'd respected him for his quiet leadership; now they thought it made him weak.

But he wasn't going to argue that now.

"We'll go in the morning," he said firmly. "We'll give Smoot a chance. Maybe he's no more involved than the rest of you. Maybe he knows nothing about the theft of our food. Maybe it's all his son. If Ezekiel was working alone with Chambers, we'll deal with him separately."

"In what way?" Miriam asked. "Will you give Ezekiel a slap on the wrist? Twenty hours of community service and a stern lecture?"

"Ezekiel is a traitor and a spy. I'll do my duty."

"Finally," she said.

It wasn't the appropriate time to discuss punishment, when Ezekiel Smoot hadn't even been apprehended yet, let alone brought before a church court. But Jacob was thinking exile. They could drive him into the southern desert with a little food and water and a promise to shoot on sight if he returned.

He rose to his feet, ready to go outside and see if he could get an accounting of whether anyone else was missing from their beds tonight, when the front door banged open.

People had been coming and going from the house during the entire conversation, and he'd heard the voices of women and children. At one point he'd heard his mother calling up the stairs, then his brother Joshua arguing with someone. It must be two a.m., but once roused, the town was taking time to settle back down. Only there was something different this time. With the banging of the door, voices raised in the front room. Shouts. Fernie screamed. Something was wrong.

Jacob shoved open the door from the kitchen, his heart rate accelerating. Someone had turned on the lights in the hall toward the front door, and after sitting in the dim candlelight for so long, he had to squint while his eyes adjusted.

A bearded man stood in the hallway. He held a sword in his hand. No, not a sword. A machete. Blood gleamed along the edge of the blade. It soaked his hand and sleeve, and smeared across his denim shirt. More blood and sand plastered his face, as if he'd been rolling in it.

It was Ezekiel Smoot, but he looked transformed. He stood staring down the hallway, eyes blazing with a violent intensity. Jacob had seen that look before. It was the look worn by Gideon Kimball. By the men who'd set off a violent confrontation with the FBI at the Zarahemla Compound. By Taylor Junior. By Jacob's cousin, Alfred Christianson, just before he'd detonated a Winnebago filled with explosives and killed thirteen soldiers in a suicide bombing.

That same look had gripped the church members at Tuesday's prayer meeting. It was religious fervor, capable of turning any sane man or woman into a weapon ready to kill in the name of God. And now Jacob was staring into that abyss yet again.

Will it never end?

Ezekiel had pushed past Fernie and several other women as he'd entered, and violated the Christianson home. No enemy had ever done that before. Ezekiel spotted Jacob, and moved toward him.

The women now came in from behind him, crying for children to run, warning people upstairs, shouting for help. Fernie wore a look of fierce determination as she rolled down the hallway in her chair, head lowered.

Drawn by the tumult, one of Jacob's young sisters came racing down the stairs, but stopped at the bottom when she came face to face with Ezekiel. Annalane was ten, slender with blond braids, looking just like Eliza had as a young girl. She took in the blood and the knife and her eyes widened in terror. She screamed, her high-pitched wail seeming to carry on forever, though some part of Jacob knew that the entire scene from when the man had opened the door to now had lasted no more than a few seconds.

Ezekiel ignored the screaming child and stared at Jacob. Fernie slammed into him from behind. His knees buckled, and he braced himself. Fernie pounded at his back with her fists, but he paid her no attention. He lifted the machete and took another step toward Jacob.

"Move!" Miriam cried behind Jacob's shoulder.

She had her gun out and was aiming past him, but Jacob blocked her. He wouldn't stand aside and let her shoot. His wife was there, his sister, any number of other women and children in the hallway behind. And even if Miriam's shot was true, other feet came pounding down the stairs. If one of them slammed into Annalane, she'd be knocked right into the path of the bullet.

Ezekiel pulled back the machete and made as if to spring. The blade was ugly and caked with blood and sand. It had killed someone tonight already. The next blood spilled would be Jacob's own.

Jacob raised his right arm to the square. "Ezekiel Smoot!"

Ezekiel stopped as if hit by a blow. He blinked, seemingly stunned.

"In the name of Jesus Christ, drop that weapon!"

Jacob's voice didn't sound like his own. It was too strong, too powerful. It sounded like his father's. Righteous fury burned through his veins. For an instant he felt every inch a prophet of God.

Every voice in the house died. People stared, gaping.

Quickly, before the spell could break, Jacob stepped forward to disarm Ezekiel. But the movement seemed to shake the young man from his paralysis. He turned this way and that, looked past Jacob to Miriam, who would surely be standing over Jacob's shoulder with her gun leveled. Then he turned on his heel.

Ezekiel shoved past Fernie's wheelchair as Jacob sprang after him. A crowd blocked the doorway. Ezekiel swung his machete to clear them. He hacked a woman across the arm and swung at a boy who fell back as the blade swished dangerously past his ear. Jacob fought to get through. Behind, Miriam barked orders. People moved out of her way.

Outside, Ezekiel kept slashing and jabbing to open a passage through the gathered people. Another woman fell, an old man too, hit on the side of the head as Ezekiel hacked at them like they were troublesome brush blocking his path. People were racing up the street and sidewalks from the direction of the temple, shouting warnings. There was Stephen Paul. Elder Smoot too, almost as bloody as his son. Was that his blood on the machete? Couldn't be—he was still on his feet.

Many of the newcomers were armed, and they tried to aim rifles and shotguns at Ezekiel as he fought his way through. He had almost reached the street.

"Everyone down!" Miriam shouted.

Some people dropped to their bellies, but there was too much noise and most people hadn't heard. Jacob took up the call. David too.

Ezekiel swung open the door to Jacob's truck. He jumped in and slammed the door shut. And then, to Jacob's horror, the truck started up. He had left his keys in the ignition. Of course he had. Damn it!

The truck peeled down the street, scattering people who had been crossing from the other side. If they hadn't moved, no doubt Ezekiel would have run them down.

Miriam stepped into the street and lowered her pistol at the back of the fleeing truck. She emptied her magazine. The glass exploded at the back of the cab. But the truck didn't stop. Moments later, it disappeared around the corner.

Elder Smoot came up beside Jacob. His face hung slack, his head drooping. "My son. My son."

"Who did Ezekiel attack?"

"His own brother. Hacked Grover to pieces."

The words were like a slap. "Grover is dead?"

Smoot tried to speak, but he couldn't find his voice. He collapsed to his knees, sobbing.

It was ugly news. But hearing it gave Jacob a twinge of hope that was followed by guilt. When he'd spotted the blood dripping off

Ezekiel's machete, his first, horrible fear was that one of his own family members had died. One of his wives or children. A brother or sister.

People were sobbing and traumatized on the Christianson lawn. He scanned the crowd, noting injuries, his subconscious already plotting triage. He spotted David's wife, Lillian, and pointed to the garage door. She nodded and ran toward the side of the house to get the door open and prep the clinic for surgery.

Jacob looked down at Smoot. "Did he kill anyone else?"

"I don't think so."

"Where did he go?"

"I don't know. The reservoir, maybe."

Miriam and David stood a few feet away, having an animated discussion with Stephen Paul, who shortly sprinted back toward the chapel. Miriam was reloading her pistol as she came to Jacob's side.

"Stephen Paul went for his truck. We're going after Ezekiel."

"Don't kill him," Elder Smoot said. "Please."

"Sit down and shut your mouth," Jacob said.

Miriam glared at Smoot as he obeyed. "We'll do what it takes," she said.

A groan at Jacob's back reminded him of his primary duty. Injured people lay across the grass, with family and friends down by them, crying, pressing hands to wounds to stop the bleeding. Ezekiel had cut at least six people as he hacked his way out of the house and through the crowd.

"Is the bunker manned?" he asked Smoot.

Smoot looked at his boots. "No."

"You're in charge," Jacob told Miriam and David. "The first thing is to man the bunker. Second, find Ezekiel and stop him."

"Like I said, we'll do what it takes," she said.

"But don't leave the valley."

"I'll find that bastard wherever he's gone."

"No. That's an order. Do not go into the cliffs."

Miriam stared back, defiant. David reached for her arm, but she shrugged it off.

Jacob hardened his voice. "Miriam Christianson, you will stay in the valley. If you leave, I will excommunicate you, do you understand?"

Men and women had been gathering around him, trying to get his attention so he'd look to their injured family members. It was all he could do to keep from running to help, but he couldn't turn away until he had Miriam's compliance.

"Miriam," he said. "You will *not* leave."

She clenched her teeth together. A vein pulsed at her temple. But at last she opened her mouth and said the words he needed to hear.

"Thou sayest."

CHAPTER TWENTY-ONE

Ezekiel was shaking so violently by the time the truck reached the base of the cliffs that it was all he could do to control the stolen vehicle. His hands were damp with sticky, coagulating blood. The machete sat like a black, malevolent thing on the passenger seat. The interior of the truck had a thick, metallic smell to it. That smell was Grover's blood.

Sweet heavens, I killed my own brother.

In his mind he saw Grover's outstretched hands imploring him not to do it. Heard the boy's scream as the heavy blade hacked into his arm, shoulder, chest, head. Then the final, devastating blow.

He closed his eyes against the horrific images and missed the curve of the switchback as the highway wrapped its way back around in its ascent. His tires went onto the shoulder, kicking up gravel.

Ezekiel's eyes flew open and he slammed on the brakes. He stopped a few feet short of the edge.

The truck headlights thrust into the empty sky over the edge. There was a hundred-foot drop below. A split second longer and he'd have gone over.

For a moment he thought he heard a deep, chuckling voice in his head. The owner of the voice had distracted him and nearly sent him to his death. And then thrust his soul into the depths of hell.

Save me, it's the destroying angel!

But as quickly as the impression came, it faded away. He was no Kimball; he was not insane. Ezekiel backed slowly onto the highway.

He beat the heel of his hand against his forehead. "Get a grip."

Down on the valley floor, he could still see plenty of lights in the center of town, even vehicles moving around, but to his surprise, no vehicles racing up the highway after him. Not yet. When he realized why, he almost laughed.

Jacob, that pathetic weakling. Instead of immediately commandeering another vehicle and sending an armed party after him, he had no doubt been distracted by all the wounds left by Ezekiel's machete-waving flight from the Christianson house. Jacob would be more concerned about stopping bleeding and stitching wounds than stopping his enemy.

Ezekiel hadn't cut down all those people to delay pursuit. He'd done it simply to escape. He'd burst into the Christianson house hoping to find Jacob alone or maybe with one of his wives, but instead, the house had been full of women and children, some of whom tried to stop him. Ezekiel was already shaken from his plan when Jacob came out with Miriam behind him, armed. And all Ezekiel had was a machete. He'd had to flee and then cut his way through a dozen innocents to get to Jacob's truck.

Miriam. That bitch. What a mistake to call her out to Yellow Flats the other day. She was as treacherous as a snake. She'd already killed Chambers and would have more murder in her heart after seeing all those injured people. She'd forced Ezekiel to cut past them—didn't she see that? Of course not; she'd only blame him.

Miriam would come after him, he knew. But as he waited and no pursuit materialized, he guessed that Jacob must have stopped her, at least temporarily.

"There," he said, feeling calmer. "You see, you have time."

But not if he sat here idling in the truck like an idiot. He got back onto the road and continued up the switchbacks. Moments later he came upon the bunker, empty since they'd abandoned it earlier in the night. He was starting to grow worried about the reaction of the gentiles at the reservoir upon his arrival. Earlier in the evening, after riding the supply elevator up, he'd been speaking with McQueen when gunfire sounded at the base of the cliffs.

The gunfire meant Chambers was in trouble down there, and McQueen's men were filling the barrel with ballast to send Ezekiel back down when someone sawed the rope. The counterweight gone, the barrel had plummeted to the bottom. No doubt it was Miriam. She must have killed Chambers.

As soon as the elevator was cut, McQueen and his men went crazy. They fired down at the base of the cliffs until they'd wasted their ammunition on hand. Then they'd turned on Ezekiel and angrily insisted he go down and keep the food coming.

Ezekiel had been only too happy to get the hell out of there. He'd been an uneasy partner in the alliance from the beginning. Giving the squatters Blister Creek's precious food was no different than feeding rats. They were vermin; they would only multiply if fed.

A few weeks ago, after he'd infiltrated the Holy of Holies to search for the sword and breastplate, he'd been troubled by the ramifications. They were missing, and the Lord had ordered Ezekiel to replace Jacob at the head of the church, but He had not provided any way for him to do so.

It must be known to all that Ezekiel had done the killing. If he secretly cut Jacob's throat, the leadership would simply fall to the senior member of the Quorum of the Twelve, Stephen Paul Young. Ezekiel was not even a member of the Quorum, let alone in line to assume the mantle of prophet. But if Ezekiel tried to assemble a collection of allies first, an alternate power structure, he'd be denounced and attacked. The Kimballs had attempted that strategy, and it had led to their death and disgrace.

A few nights after his entry into the temple, he'd gone outside at night, confused and unable to sleep. There had been a full moon, and it cast the ranch in a pale, ghostly light. He walked past the barn, listening to the lowing cows before continuing down the trail toward the tool shed, several hundred yards from the house, and midway to the grain silos. There, he came across a wheelbarrow filled with tools that someone had carelessly left outside. Probably one of Ezekiel's lazy brothers.

One of the tools was a machete that made him think of the sword he'd been searching for in the temple. He picked it up and felt the heft of it in his hand. For a long moment he stood there with the weapon and imagined what it would be like to kill Jacob. It wasn't the Sword of Laban, but it would serve the same purpose.

He was returning the machete to the wheelbarrow when the sound of a distant engine caught his ear. He stopped, frowning. The engine was somewhere to the east on their own grazing lands. Who the devil would be out at this hour? He started walking toward the sound when it quit.

But by now his curiosity was raging. And his suspicion. There was nothing in that direction but the silos and open desert beyond. He followed the ranch road to the silos, where he crouched in an old, weed-infested irrigation ditch to wait. Soon enough, Larry Chambers appeared, the former FBI agent quite visible in the full light of the moon. He'd come to steal grain.

Ezekiel simply watched and waited instead of confronting the man. It couldn't be an accident that Ezekiel had been outside, unable to sleep, turning over the problem of Jacob, when Chambers appeared with his cart and shovel. There had to be meaning to it.

And then it hit him. This was the solution to his problem.

The next day Ezekiel rode out to Chambers's cabin. He carried several quarts of near-pure grain liquor in his saddlebags. Normally it was distilled for fuel, but he figured it would be a valuable trade good for the vermin at the reservoir. Like most gentiles, they'd be drunks and alcoholics, no doubt.

Once at the cabin, Ezekiel made his proposal to the suspicious FBI agent: He'd help Chambers and the squatters get everything from the valley they needed to survive. In return, Ezekiel needed to make contact with the camp. He needed to arrange for sanctuary for when he'd killed Jacob Christianson. Chambers agreed. Rather quickly, in fact.

Ezekiel wasn't stupid; Chambers was playing his own game. The man was currying favor with the squatters—he was a gentile, like them, and a natural enemy of the church. Maybe he meant to weaken Blister Creek from within. Maybe the ultimate plan was to let the squatters flood into the valley and overwhelm the saints. Drive them off, enslave them, kill them. Murder the men and take their women as sexual slaves. Some evil or other. The exact manner of that evil wasn't important.

Once Ezekiel was prophet, he would do what Jacob had been too soft to do: kill every last man, woman, and child in the squatter camp. Only then would the threat be eliminated. Meanwhile, he would use Chambers as their motives overlapped.

Ezekiel was still convinced that the plan would have worked if Miriam hadn't shot Chambers at the base of the cliffs. A few more weeks to gather the faithful, convince important people that Jacob was a fallen prophet. All that had been thrown in chaos the moment the gunshots sounded and Miriam cut the rope to the makeshift elevator.

But even after Ezekiel descended from the reservoir to the bunker where his father and brother waited, he'd believed there was still time. He could come into the valley before Jacob had organized, finish the ugly business, then flee with enough weapons and food supplies to buy off McQueen's camp. Later, when Miriam and the rest quieted down, he'd return to Blister Creek and take over. They'd be desperate for a leader. Only now he was doing the fleeing, Jacob was still alive, and he had nothing to trade. He needed something or McQueen would turn him away in rage.

So when Ezekiel reached the abandoned bunker, he stopped the truck and ran inside. He hauled out the spare guns and ammo cans first, then returned from the truck with a toolbox he'd found in the back. He unbolted the .50-caliber machine gun that was mounted at the gun slits, slung it over his shoulder, and hauled it back to the truck, where he put it in the back with the other weapons.

Now he was set. He had a machine gun, several other weapons, and hundreds of rounds of ammunition. That should satisfy McQueen.

When he climbed into the truck, he eyed the dark, bloodstained machete on the seat next to him. It had an ugly, malevolent air to it. When swinging it earlier, it had been easy to pretend that it really was the Sword of Laban and not a sharpened ranch tool. Now it looked like neither, but some horrible weapon wielded by a murderer. He couldn't stand to look at it anymore, so he shoved it under the seat. As soon as it was out of sight he felt better.

Ezekiel slowed the truck when he reached the top of the cliffs. He flashed the truck lights and inched up the highway. He honked his horn. Gunmen would be watching; if they thought he was a threat, they might open fire.

A few minutes later, when the headlights illuminated the gate across the highway, he slowed even further, until he was traveling at a creep. He honked and flashed, and rolled down his window to wave. Figures came out of the darkness armed with rifles and shotguns. They surrounded the truck, some twenty or thirty men and women in all.

A figure stepped forward from the pack. He was filthy and bedraggled, but with a straight back and strong arms. It was McQueen.

"It's only me," Ezekiel said, relieved. Of any of the squatters, McQueen seemed the most practical. Some of these people were survivalist fanatics, and they scared him.

McQueen looked past him into the empty passenger seat. "Where's Chambers?"

"Dead. Sister Miriam shot him."

The man's face hardened. Chambers and McQueen had enjoyed a good rapport. Had almost been friends. They were both gentiles and former military men, and would think of nothing holy or sacred, only how to survive, how to take.

That hard look made Ezekiel anxious. He wasn't sorry about Chambers's death. The man had disgusted him, was nothing but a tool to get what he wanted. But he'd been useful for protecting Ezekiel from these savages.

"I brought you some stuff," Ezekiel said nervously. "Look in the back."

McQueen glanced in the back, then ripped open the door, seized Ezekiel's shirt, and dragged him out of the truck. He threw him to the ground, where Ezekiel lay, terrified of all the people now surrounding him, their sneers showing how badly they wanted to smash in his face with their rifle butts.

"Don't kill me! I brought you guns."

"Screw guns," McQueen said. "Where the hell is our food?"

★★★

Sister Lillian served as nurse and Jacob's two wives managed the patient flow, with Jessie Lyn triaging the patients according to their severity of their injuries. Fernie calmed family members, found beds for postoperative patients, and did everything else to keep the external environment orderly.

Nellie Haws was Jacob's most serious patient, suffering a savage abdominal wound that cut all the way through the transverse abdominis. Doubling the risk, Nellie was thirty-five weeks pregnant. There were a few anxious minutes trying to stanch the blood flow when he thought he should perform an emergency C-section, but he got her stabilized.

After that, he gave morphine to two children screaming in pain from deep gashes across their arms, then helped an older man, one of Jacob's neighbors from down the street, who'd suffered an ugly slash that had taken off his left ear and broken his jaw. An inch lower and the blow would have severed the artery in his neck. Jacob reattached the ear, then reduced the fracture by realigning the shattered bone into its original anatomical position, before fixing it in place with surgical pins. This was more like carpentry than the delicate work he'd performed reattaching the ear. After that, he returned to the children to whom he'd given morphine. They were now quiet and whimpering. He sutured their wounds and sent them home with their mothers.

It was morning before he'd finished his work. He was less than satisfied with the results. He was saving his remaining 4-0 sutures for facial injuries, and so had stitched a woman's palm with larger 3-0s, which would leave a noticeable scar. He'd set a fractured ulna in homemade plaster, judging the severity and manner of the break not by X-ray, but after painfully kneading at the poor kid's arm. His X-ray machine had broken, and its repair had proven beyond his brother's mechanical skills.

A bucket held the bloody tools of his trade, and he sent these off with Jessie Lyn to be washed and sterilized. Everything must be reused, even the blood-soaked gauze. He took off his mask, removed and folded up his gown to be washed, and scrubbed his hands in the sink with soap to get rid of the smell of latex that would otherwise cling to them for hours.

The clinic was mostly empty, but one of the children was still there, lying on the hospital bed next to the garage door, moaning while her mother dabbed at her forehead with a wet cloth. She was the kid with the broken arm.

Jacob turned away, frustrated he couldn't give her more morphine. But he was running low on analgesics, and even when he'd seen the collapse coming, hadn't thought to acquire seeds to cultivate his own poppies. One of several mistakes that were obvious in retrospect. What he wouldn't give to send a message back in time a couple of years. He looked around the room, noting each and every deficit of his clinic.

Fernie wheeled into the room. Her eyes were bloodshot, and wisps of hair had come loose from her thick braid. But from her sympathetic look, he knew he must appear even more haggard. She glanced around his operating room and sighed.

"How many times will we suffer this?" she asked. "Will the Lord show us no mercy?"

It was an unusual statement of doubt from Fernie, who was usually the one comforting him, urging him to faith and patience, and not the other way around.

"Hundreds of millions are dead around the world. Maybe billions. We're the lucky ones."

"I don't feel lucky," she said. "I feel miserable."

He gave her a hug. She leaned her head against his arm.

"Don't give up faith," he said.

"You're one to talk. What faith do *you* have?"

"I have faith in our people. Our preparation, our community. The love we have for each other."

"Jacob, that's what I don't understand. This attack came from our own people. Not gentiles, not outsiders. Our own people. Again. Why?"

"The scriptures say even the elect will be deceived."

She looked up at him with a hopeful expression. "Do you believe that?"

"I do. I don't know why or what it means, but people do terrible evil and claim they're obeying the will of the Lord."

Fernie kissed his hand. "Go up to bed. You look exhausted. I'll handle things here."

"The children are okay? The rest of the family?"

"Yes. Everyone else is accounted for. Nobody is missing across the entire valley."

"I didn't think they would be. It was clear we'd found our enemy. How about Ezekiel? Has he turned up?"

Fernie shook her head. "David and Miriam radioed from the bunker while you were in surgery. Ezekiel got away. And he apparently stopped at the bunker to steal the .50-caliber machine gun and the ammunition on his way out."

Jacob rubbed his temples to relieve his throbbing headache. Of course the gun would be missing. By the time Ezekiel reached the cliffs, he'd have been able to look back and see that pursuit was lagging. That had given him time to loot the bunker. The .50-cal would end up guarding the squatter camp. Imagine trying to assault it now.

"I've got to go to the bunker," he said.

"No, you don't. Stephen Paul already drove up with the Humvee to replace the gun. He swung by the house about fifteen minutes ago, told me you didn't need to worry."

"It's not just arming the bunker that has me worried. Miriam will be on the warpath."

"You told her not to leave the valley. Everyone heard you say it."

"All that was before we knew Ezekiel had stolen the machine gun. She'll be itching to snatch it back or destroy it before the enemy has a chance to dig it into some fortified spot. Then Stephen Paul will show up with the Humvee. Gassed up and ready to go. Miriam, David, Stephen Paul—a full crew. She might see that as divine sanction."

"Call her on the radio. Tell her."

"You call her. Tell her I'm on my way and not to move a muscle until I arrive."

Fernie started to protest, but he put a hand on her shoulder and cut her off. "I can't risk that she'll start more bloodshed. This clinic can't handle it. This *doctor* can't."

Jacob was outside, blinking against the sharp morning light, before he remembered that Ezekiel had stolen his truck. Fortunately, several other vehicles were parked in the street in front of the house. Men stood around, discussing the evening's events in animated terms. They were the ones who had driven around the valley looking for anyone who might be missing. Now they wanted information from him. He didn't have anything to give them.

Instead, he commandeered a truck, resisted offers to ride with him, and drove off through the streets of Blister Creek. Soon, he was passing the chapel and temple on his way north toward the bunker.

Most of the Smoot family was gathered out front of the temple. People were crying, hugging. Few of them bothered to look up as Jacob drove past.

A figure lay on the grass in front of the temple. A bloody sheet covered it. Grover Smoot.

★★★

Jacob's worries were assuaged when he arrived to find the Humvee parked in the road outside the bunker, while David and Stephen Paul were up top of the vehicle, unscrewing the machine gun from where it was fixed behind the gun shield.

It was a gorgeous morning across the valley. A brilliant sun rose in a blue sky unmarred by cloud or contrail. The mountain ranges rimming the valley to the east and west still had snow on their highest peaks, but in the valley itself, the fields had taken on a patchwork of various shades of green. The fields contrasted with the red sands of the desert and the vast swath of bare sandstone formations of Witch's Warts that ran from the Ghost Cliffs down the center of the valley.

While the men worked, Miriam was scanning the cliffs above them with a pair of binoculars. A sniper rifle with scope jutted out of the bunker, but there didn't appear to be anyone inside manning it. It looked like just these three plus Jacob.

Miriam lowered the binoculars as Jacob shut the truck door. "Fernie called. She seems to think you should be in bed."

"We all should be. I'm inclined to radio and have different people sent up. Someone who actually got some sleep last night."

"Can't guess who that would be. Nobody slept much last night, I'll bet." She returned to studying the cliffs.

"Did surgery go okay?" David asked as he and Stephen Paul walked past carrying the machine gun and toolbox toward the bunker.

"I don't know about okay, but everyone survived." Jacob thought about the figure beneath the bloody sheet. "Except Grover Smoot."

"Well," Miriam said, when the other two men were inside the bunker with the gun and tools. "Grover served his purpose."

"What's that supposed to mean?" Jacob demanded.

Miriam's expression softened. "Sorry, that came out wrong."

"Grover did nothing to deserve this."

"I'm sorry," she said again. "I didn't mean it that way. Grover almost died on the road to Las Vegas last year. He was supposed to be manning that rifle to keep that sniper off our butt. Then Officer Trost took the gun out of his hands. And was killed. I was angry about that—Trost was more useful to our needs. It should have been Grover who died."

Again, so little compassion in his sister-in-law. Was everyone a tool to Miriam?

"But later I started thinking," she continued. "The Lord must have saved Grover for some purpose. Now he has served that purpose."

"Please tell me you're not claiming that Grover died so we'd know Ezekiel was a killer."

"Of course not." She gave Jacob a look. "I collared Elder Smoot after you went in to surgery. I thought he might have an idea of what Ezekiel was thinking. Smoot told me it was Grover who stood up to Ezekiel. That's why he was killed."

Miriam explained how Ezekiel had convinced his father that he'd retrieved the sword and breastplate from the Holy of Holies, that he'd been called as the new prophet. Only when Grover convinced his father to dig up the supposed relics had Smoot realized he'd been duped. The two brothers had struggled, and in killing Grover, Ezekiel seemed to lose his mind. He set off on a mad charge to the Christianson compound. Grover's death had shocked Elder Smoot out of his stupor, and he raised the alarm.

"So you see," she added, "Grover saved your life. That was why the Lord preserved him outside Las Vegas last year."

"Grover had more purpose in life than to save me from an assassin."

"Of course he did. That wasn't his *only* purpose—I never claimed it was. And he'll receive his reward in the world to come."

"I sincerely hope so." Jacob's anger deflated. "But his death is still a tragedy in the here and now."

"Eliza will be devastated. She liked that kid." Miriam looked sorrowful. "Come on, let's get inside and out of the open."

Jacob followed her toward the bunker. "Thanks for obeying. I was worried I'd get up here to discover you'd gone tearing off in the Humvee."

"You gave me a direct order," she said. "I'd never go against that. Besides, I've got a better idea now."

CHAPTER TWENTY-TWO

The interior of the bunker still smelled vaguely of body odor. Jacob's eye fell on Ezekiel's sleeping bag where it lay partially unzipped in the middle of the floor. Boots had left their dusty prints on the glossy nylon surface.

Jacob knew he was lucky. If he'd come to the bunker alone, Ezekiel might have murdered him then and there. Maybe even with David at his side. But Miriam's ruthless reputation was well known. He glanced at her as she opened the filing cabinet and realized he was lucky to have her on his side, and not as an enemy. His own destroying angel.

Stephen Paul and David had finished mounting the machine gun from the Humvee and were testing its range of motion. When they finished, David went out to retrieve cans of .50-caliber ammunition from the vehicle.

Miriam seemed to have found what she was looking for in the filing cabinet. She retrieved an unopened blister pack of batteries and set them onto the desk next to her night vision goggles.

"I thought you didn't have batteries," Jacob said.

"Not for personal use. We kept these up here as emergency backup for the flashlight. Don't want to go stumbling around in the dark with one of those crappy LED flashlights you have to shake. They'll work for the night vision."

"Dammit, I left mine in the truck," Jacob said. "Now Ezekiel has them."

"Yeah, that's a problem," she said. "With any luck your batteries are almost dead. How long were they on?"

"Hard to say. I lost track of time out there." He stopped. "What do you mean, stumbling in the dark?"

She shrugged. "It can't be helped if he has them. I'll have to take my chances."

David came in carrying two of the heavy cans by their handles. "Take your chances? I don't like the sound of that. Jacob, what is she talking about?"

"I have no idea," Jacob said. Then, to Miriam, "Well?"

"We're lucky Ezekiel didn't get the batteries," she said, which didn't answer the question. "He must have come through here so fast he didn't have time to grab everything. Or he forgot. That Son of Perdition had a lot on his mind." Miriam reached into the cabinet and fished out some flares. "He could have used these too." She pulled open a lower drawer. "And the grenades are still here too. That's lucky."

"What about these plans?" Jacob said. "What are you proposing we do?"

"You won't do anything. The three of you will stay here and man the bunker. I'm going to infiltrate and reconnoiter. Alone."

David straightened from feeding a belt of ammunition into the gun. He didn't look happy. "I see no point in that."

"You can bet things are exciting up there," she said. "A polygamist shows up covered with blood, carrying a machine gun. That will get them riled up."

"They already know him," Stephen Paul pointed out. "He and Chambers have been handing over our food for who knows how long."

Rather than argue with Miriam, Jacob pulled up a chair to listen.

She glanced at him, as if waiting to see if he'd contradict her, then turned back to the other two men. "They'll be scared of us, for one. Are we angry? Are we going to attack them again? And what will they do if we don't? Sit up there and starve now that we've cut them off?"

"Maybe they'll pull out," Stephen Paul said. "Give up."

"Be about time," David said.

"And go where?" she asked. "It was our stolen food that kept them alive. That's all. They have no other options."

That was true, and yet that same food had kept the peace for almost a year. What now that the supply was cut off?

"So they might come down demanding more food," Miriam said. "Or try to take it by force."

"I have to ask," Jacob said, "if it took us so long to miss the stolen food, how critical was it, anyway?"

"Pretty damn critical," David said. "Maybe not now, but soon."

"You don't know that," Jacob said. "Last year we nearly fed ourselves with what we grew. Barely dipped into our stores at all. I'll bet this year we pull it off. The weather seems almost normal again."

"It's the End of Days," Stephen Paul said. "This is a lull."

"We're all agreed on that," David said.

"No man knows the day nor hour," Jacob reminded them. "That's what the scriptures say."

"You're not going to convince us," Miriam said. "We all know this is the end."

She was right insofar as he wasn't going to get anywhere arguing about the end of the world.

"So what then, you'll sneak into camp, have a look around?" Jacob asked. "Or are you going after Ezekiel specifically?"

"Why not both? I can get into that camp easily enough, play my role. If I go at night, when it's dark, I can pose as just another refugee. I'll look around and see if they're sheltering Ezekiel. Maybe they want nothing to do with him. Maybe he fled into the desert with whatever he could grab. But maybe he's there. If he is, I'll either drag him back if I can, or kill him if I can't."

"I don't like it," Jacob said.

He looked to David, sure that his brother wouldn't let his wife do this crazy thing. But David was scratching at the stubble on his chin, the look in his eyes saying he was considering it.

"Are you serious?" Jacob asked him. "You want to leave your children without their mother?"

"That's not going to happen," Miriam said, confidently. "The Lord has a purpose for me."

"Yeah, and He did for Grover too. Isn't that what you were saying? His purpose was to die?"

"The Lord has protected her before," David said. "He'll protect her again, assuming she is following His will."

"Ezekiel knows everything about Blister Creek," Stephen Paul said. "We can't leave him up there scheming with our enemies."

Jacob cast around for some other possibility. "How about we offer to trade? They give us Ezekiel, and we give them food."

"Haven't they stolen enough?" Miriam said. "And you want to give them more?"

"It would be worth it."

"Besides," Stephen Paul said, "what if they don't agree to the trade? What if they keep Ezekiel and demand food, anyway?"

"Then we put the gun back on the Humvee," Jacob said, "wait for Eliza and Steve to return in the Methuselah tank, and mount another attack on the camp. We'll take Ezekiel by force."

"Only now they're armed with the stolen machine gun," David said. "And who knows what else. For all we know Ezekiel and Chambers had been sharing out our weapons for a long time. Instead of a few hunting rifles like last year, we might be facing fully automatic assault rifles, improvised explosives, and whatever else they've stolen from us."

That was a good point.

"How about a compromise plan?" Miriam said.

"What kind of compromise?" Jacob said.

"I'll infiltrate the camp tonight." She held up a hand as he started to object that this wasn't a compromise, it was the same plan. "Just to look, not to attack. If Ezekiel is gone, then no worries. We forget it. We assume he's fled into the desert and there's nothing we can do. In that case, I'll reconnoiter, get a better idea of whether they have, in fact, stolen weapons from the valley. That information would be valuable in and of itself."

"And if Ezekiel *is* there?" Jacob asked, warily. "What will you do?"

"Nothing. I'll come back and tell you." She shrugged. "That's it. We'll have another argument, but with better info."

It was hard to argue with that. Her proposal was reasonable, in fact. Still dangerous, but at a level of danger that he could accept. And it didn't involve more violence.

"What do you guys think?" he asked the men.

"Got to be fifteen hundred people up there," Stephen Paul said. "How will you even find Ezekiel?"

"Easy," she said. "I'll look for Jacob's truck. No way Ezekiel takes his eyes off it. It's got three-quarters tank of gas, could get someone two hundred miles. Until he knows what's what, he won't leave it and risk someone stealing it. And if the truck is not there, it will be obvious he took off."

"Unless they took it from Ezekiel by force," Jacob said.

"In which case they'll probably have him tied up somewhere. That should be easy enough to find out too."

"That makes sense," Stephen Paul said. "Sure, I think you should go."

"David?" Jacob asked.

His brother hesitated a moment longer, gave a worried glance at his wife, then nodded. "I say we go for it. I trust the Lord will protect her."

"Good," Miriam said quickly, "then it's settled."

"Hold on," Jacob said. "When will you go, tonight?"

"Sure, tonight. I'll stay right here until then. We won't want to leave the bunker short-handed, anyway. Why don't you go home, look in on your patients, and get some rest. We'll come find you when I've returned."

He tried to decide if she was attempting to deceive him. He'd have a hard time telling if she were. What if he drove down to the valley only to learn later that she'd waited until he was gone, remounted the machine gun, and talked Stephen Paul and David into rushing the squatter camp? He couldn't risk it.

"I think I'll stay here. None of my patients have life-threatening injuries. Lillian is there to render post-op care. I'll radio town later to make sure everything is okay."

"What about sleep?" she said. "Don't tell me you're not exhausted."

"No more exhausted than the rest of you."

"Sure you are," she insisted. "None of us spent half the night in surgery."

"You seem to be trying awfully hard to get rid of me."

"Fine, then. Do what you want," Miriam said. "I figured you had more important things to do than guard duty. But stay or go, it doesn't matter to me."

Jacob held her gaze. "Thanks, I will."

★★★

They decided to alternate keeping watch and resting. Nobody wanted to touch Ezekiel's sleeping bag, but fortunately David had thought to grab a couple of bags from the house before he'd left. He hauled Ezekiel's out to the truck and unrolled the other two on the floor, unzipping them to open flat, since it would shortly be too warm to climb inside.

In truth, Jacob was exhausted, and happily accepted the first sleep shift. David flopped onto the second bag and yanked off his boots. Miriam and Stephen Paul handled gun and watch duty while the brothers napped.

It was still cool lying on top of the sleeping bag where it touched the cold concrete, and Jacob pulled the edge of the unzipped bag over his legs. His mind was racing. If only he could get an hour or two of sleep, he'd have a much better time of it tonight. Gradually, his mind calmed.

Some time had passed when he woke up, and the light cut a different angle across the floor. He was sweating from the heat that had invaded the tight quarters as the sun pounded down on the bunker roof overhead. Outside, insects buzzed from the dry brush that grew on the hillside around them. David and Stephen Paul sat near the gun slits, speaking in low voices about the amount of grain and beans needed to sustain all those squatters. Miriam was gone, but he was so fuzzy-headed that this didn't register fully at first.

Jacob climbed to his feet. His mouth felt like cotton. Stephen Paul handed him a sweating canteen, which he gratefully accepted. David acknowledged him with a nod, then picked up his binoculars and looked through the bunker slit up at the cliffs.

"How long was I out?"

"Four, five hours," Stephen Paul said. "It's still early afternoon."

Jacob looked around. "Where's Miriam?"

"Don't worry," David said. "She went back to town is all."

Jacob was suspicious about this, but David showed him that the Humvee was still parked outside, though the pickup truck was missing. She wouldn't have taken the lighter pickup to the reservoir.

"They radioed from home," David explained. "I guess the kids are upset, so Miriam went back to check in with the family. Then I figured she may as well sleep in her own bed for a few hours while she was down there. Better there than the hard floor."

Jacob yawned and rubbed at his neck. "Floor's not so hard if you're tired enough."

"You were out of it," David said. "Snoring like a pig."

Stephen Paul had picked up on the yawn and made it his own, and Jacob remembered that his counselor hadn't slept yet. He told the man to take his turn getting some rest, then got on the radio to check in with Blister Creek.

Ostensibly, it was to tell Lillian—the one who picked up on the other end—to send up food to the bunker with Miriam, but really to verify that Miriam was where David claimed she was. Lillian said she was asleep in her own bed.

David watched him with raised eyebrows when he got off the radio. "Did you think I was lying?"

"She's a free spirit, David. She follows her own counsel."

"Don't I know it. But she's also a mother and a wife. She was worried about her family."

"You've got to have misgivings about this scheme of hers."

"A little," David admitted. "But she seems to live a charmed life. Or a protected one."

"Everyone alive could say the same thing." Jacob glanced at Stephen Paul. The man was already asleep. "It takes a lot of luck to survive war and famine. Every survivor everywhere has a charmed life, right up until they're killed like everyone else."

"Does that mean you're having second thoughts?"

"I don't know. Maybe. Still seems risky."

"You sent Eliza to Salt Lake. What about that?"

"She's a free spirit too," Jacob pointed out. "Anyway, Eliza didn't go alone. Steve went with her. I'd send someone else with Miriam—you, maybe, or Lillian—but I think she'll be safer infiltrating on her own." He hesitated. "So you *don't* have misgivings? None at all?"

David shrugged.

"You're not worried she's going to get killed?" Jacob pressed.

"Look, can we talk about something else besides whether or not my wife is going to die?"

"Yeah, of course."

"It's like you're *trying* to wind me up or something. Get me freaked out."

"I didn't mean to. I'm sorry."

David grunted.

After that awkward exchange, the brothers spent the next hour in silence, studying the cliffs or simmering in their own thoughts. After a while, David radioed Blister Creek again.

Miriam came on the line, and Jacob finally received his confirmation that she hadn't, in fact, slipped up to the reservoir to have a go at the squatters.

When David was done with the call, he set down the receiver and cleared his throat. "I shouldn't have snapped at you. I'm sorry."

"No problem. I know how I must have sounded."

Another uncomfortable pause, then David said, "Hey, do you remember that time we were camping in the desert and fed those foxes?"

"The time you screamed your head off?"

"It was your fault with all that ghost stuff."

They'd been out with Grandpa Griggs in Goblin Valley. Three brothers: Jacob, Enoch, and David. Jacob was the oldest, David the youngest. Grandpa was asleep. Jacob had been telling ghost stories to the younger boys, getting them worked up with a tale of a grizzled prospector whose body was found in the desert, dried to a mummy, his eyeballs and nose eaten by vultures. They said his ghost still wandered these parts.

Suddenly, David squealed in terror. Jacob looked up to see glowing eyes at the edge of the firelight. Enoch saw it too, gasped, and scrambled back toward the tent.

Jacob smiled at the memory. "Poor guy was just hungry. He and his dozen brothers and sisters."

"Whose brilliant idea was it to feed them hot dog buns, anyway? Was that Enoch's?"

"No, it was mine," Jacob admitted.

"That's right. And when we ran out of buns, you made me sneak into Grandpa's camper to get a bag of potato chips. We had six or seven foxes by then, all wanting to be fed."

"Then Enoch started putting potato chips on Grandpa's chest," Jacob said.

David laughed. "Remember Grandpa's expression when he sat up to find a fox staring him in the face?"

After running through the fox story, Jacob and David talked about other camping trips, the adventures and misadventures of life in the valley. Lizards caught, arrowheads discovered. The time David almost drowned in the reservoir, or when they went sneaking out the back door with an entire box of ice cream sandwiches, only by the time they found a safe place to eat them, the ice cream was already melting into a sticky goo. Kids weren't very supervised back then, and they'd had their run of the entire valley. Of course, that meant mishaps. Broken bones two miles from home, or stupid stuff they did, like climbing crumbling rock at the cliffs or wandering deep into Witch's Warts.

"Yeah, I'm worried about Miriam," David said at last. "I'm worried as hell. I'm worried every time she puts herself in danger. I know she seems hard and determined, but she's the one who has kept me sane in all of this. Every time I get depressed or lose faith, she lifts me up."

"She's a good woman."

"I love her so much. I don't know what I'd do if I lost her."

"You won't lose her."

"I hope you're right."

Stephen Paul stirred, cleared his throat, and the brothers fell silent. He got up, stretched and yawned, and came over to take the final chair next to the gun slits.

"All clear?" he asked.

"All clear," Jacob confirmed. He glanced at the angle of the sun in the sky. "Looks like it's about six, six thirty."

About half an hour later, the rumble of a truck caught their ears from the direction of the valley. A few minutes later, Miriam pulled up.

She'd grubbed up her appearance. Her hair was greasy, her face covered in grime that seemed to rub right into her pores. She wore a filthy, oversized denim jacket torn at the elbows, and men's jeans with frayed cuffs rolled up above her scuffed boots. A man's belt had been cinched to hold up the jeans, but it only made her look thin and starved. Which was exactly the look she was going for, Jacob realized.

Miriam carried in a cooler from the back of the truck. "Fernie packed us a nice picnic dinner. Ham sandwiches, potato salad." She raised her eyebrow. "No ice cream sandwiches, though, melting or otherwise."

David started. "How did you know about that?"

Miriam set the cooler on the floor and walked over to the radio and picked up the receiver, then thumbed the switch twice to get it to pop up. "The switch sticks on this thing."

"So you heard our entire conversation?" David asked.

She nodded, then bent and kissed him. "I love you too. And you can stop worrying. You're not getting rid of me that easily."

CHAPTER TWENTY-THREE

Miriam had one final argument with Jacob before they left the bunker. He wanted her to go up unarmed, which she thought was ridiculous. Jacob's thinking was that if she were caught, the squatters would be less likely to harm her if she weren't carrying a weapon.

In the first place, she had no intention of getting caught. In the second, she might need to use the weapons preemptively. That was something he would not understand, and she had no intention of explaining.

Miriam opened her denim jacket to show him the pistol. "You'd have to look right up under my arm to see it. Nobody is going to get that close."

"What about your knife?" Jacob asked.

"What about it?"

"We can see it bulging under your jacket," David pointed out. "Every time you move, there's a hard object visible on your back."

"That's only because it's not dark yet. Once it's dark, it will be as good as invisible. Anyway, I don't hear either of you complaining about the night vision goggles. That looks just as bad if I'm caught." She had them tucked under her arm.

"But you need those," Jacob said. "You don't need the weapons."

The three of them stood in the road while Stephen Paul remained in the bunker manning the machine gun. The dying light of the sun had cast pale yellow beams across the valley floor and streaks across the face of the Ghost Cliffs. The sun was now descending in a ball of fire behind the western mountains. Ten more minutes and it would be dark enough to move without worrying about watchers in the cliffs.

Miriam would just as soon have set off alone from the bunkers, but Jacob and David insisted on accompanying her up to the reservoir and waiting for her there. The two brothers unloaded rifles with scopes from the Humvee.

She joined them around the back of the vehicle and grabbed two more magazines for her Beretta. She put one in each front pocket of her jeans. Then, to be sure, grabbed another and stuffed it into the left pocket of her denim jacket.

"Guys, stop worrying," she said when she saw Jacob and David watching anxiously. "I've done this sort of thing before. I'm confident."

"Confident?" David said. "Or overconfident?"

"Don't try to psyche me out, it won't work."

"We're not doing that," Jacob said. "We just need to be sure."

Miriam glanced up at the sky. Still too much light. Five minutes, maybe, then they could go. "There is one thing you could do for me," she admitted. "I could use a priesthood blessing before we set out."

"Good idea," David said, nodding.

"Jacob, could you?" Miriam asked.

"Of course."

She had expected an argument. But maybe Jacob saw the psychological benefit of sending her in with a blessing, or maybe cracks were forming in his armor of doubt. She could only hope.

They did it right there, with Miriam standing in her filthy clothes in the middle of the road. Jacob and David put their hands on her hair, which she'd rubbed with dirt and bacon grease to simulate a woman who hadn't bathed in weeks, like the filthy squatters from the reservoir.

After opening the blessing, Jacob got right to the meat of the matter. It wasn't exactly what she'd been hoping. She'd wished in her heart that he would call on divine strength to flow through her veins, that she would have the power to lift her hand and smite their enemies. What Jacob gave her was something different.

"Sister Miriam, thy life has value beyond measure. The wisdom of thy counsel to thy brothers and sisters in the gospel, the love thou hast for thy husband and children. Their love for you in return. And to all of the community, thou art a shield and a protector."

She didn't miss the implication. A shield. Not a sword. Defensive, only.

Except Jacob spoke with such power and confidence that she was reminded of his prophetic calling. If she disobeyed him, would she be going against Jacob? Or against the Lord?

"Insofar as thou art faithful and true, thou shalt be protected from harm. No bullet shall pierce thy breast, no hand touch thee in wrath. Being faithful in all things, thou shalt return to thy people without a hair harmed on thy head. These blessings and exhortations I close in the name of the Holy Redeemer of Israel, even Jesus Christ, amen."

"Amen."

"Amen," David added in a husky voice. His eyes were damp. "You heard him. Not a hair harmed on your head. I'm holding you to it."

She hugged him, then eyed the sky again. "It's time."

★★★

The crowd surrounded Ezekiel, jeering, spitting, and cursing him. He lurched in terror from one brutal shove to the next. The mood was tense, coiled. They wanted blood, and they wanted his. Their anger was bewildering, though he'd heard it building for hours.

All day McQueen had kept him with his hands and feet bound, sitting with his back against the tires of the pickup truck. The camp itself was in an uproar. As the day passed and his tongue thickened with thirst, the sun beat relentlessly on his face, and the mood grew more and more ugly. People would come to stand behind the single guard, pointing and shouting at him.

They seemed to be blaming him for Chambers's death. That was ridiculous. Ezekiel had been up top when it happened. Chambers wasn't one of the squatters anyway, just a rogue FBI agent who'd struck up a friendship of convenience with their leader. Ezekiel knew their food supply was cut off, and these people were already thin and hungry, but surely they weren't living so hand-to-mouth that a single missed meal or two would send them into a rage.

What kind of crazy fanatics were they?

When late afternoon had arrived, McQueen and three armed companions came up to where Ezekiel sat at the tire of Jacob's truck, eyed him with a look of disgust, and ordered him to his feet. He struggled to stand after so many hours in a cramped position, his hands and feet still bound. One of the armed men grabbed the rope around his wrists and dragged him up. A young woman with short, hacked-off hair slapped Ezekiel across the face when he voiced a protest.

McQueen ordered the rope untied from his ankles, but left his hands bound behind his back. Then they'd driven him to the center of camp, where the crowd had gathered. McQueen pushed him into the center, and the crowd had begun to shove at him. He stumbled back and forth, exhausted and frightened, even as the fury of the mob grew.

"Please," he begged. "What did I do?"

A teenage boy slugged him in the stomach and he doubled over, gasping. An old woman jerked his head by the hair while another woman spit in his face. More blows rained down on his head and shoulders. A well-placed kick to the thigh knocked his feet out from under him and he collapsed. They yanked him back to his feet. More blows followed.

This was how they meant him to die, he realized with terror. Each and every one of them taking revenge for all the indignities suffered over the past few years: the war, the famine, the wretched treatment at the military-run refugee camp, the evacuation of the camp, and the desperate struggle across the desert. More had died in the crossing. More still from starvation and disease at the reservoir. Exposure in winter, violence as the desperate turned on the desperate. They must have thought that if they could only reach Blister Creek, with its food and safety, they would survive.

Except Blister Creek had turned them away, even tried to wipe out their camp instead of sharing food like good neighbors. Then, when Chambers offered a lifeline, the polygamists of the valley had cut that off too. There was no way to get at the valley, but here was Ezekiel, bound and helpless. He knew all of this instinctively, yet it felt so unfair.

A blow smashed into his temple and he fell facedown in the dirt. This time they left him down. He was helpless to protect himself as the mob closed in to finish him off. Kick him to death.

McQueen barked an order for silence. The shouting and cursing from the crowd diminished, then died altogether as he roared his orders again. McQueen and several others pushed back the mob.

"Don't kill me," Ezekiel begged as they hauled him to his feet. "Please, I'll do whatever you want."

McQueen slapped him across the face. "Shut up."

Ezekiel hung his head. He was shaking and wouldn't be able to stand if they weren't holding him up.

"The rest of you, go," McQueen told the mob. "We'll deal with this one later. For now, you know what to do."

Just as McQueen and his armed companions had marched Ezekiel into the camp, now they marched him back to the truck again. He regained some of his strength as he walked.

"They'd have killed you," McQueen said. "Don't forget that."

He pushed Ezekiel into a sitting position with his back against the rear driver's side tire. McQueen stood above him, his hands on his hips, looking down with a scowl.

"Do you have water?" Ezekiel asked.

McQueen nodded at the short-haired woman who had slapped Ezekiel earlier. She trotted back to camp and came up with a faded green soda bottle half filled with cloudy water. Ezekiel glugged it down.

"Any food? I'm so hungry I can barely stand. Even a bite or two, anything."

McQueen let out a barking laugh. "If you'd said that in the camp, they'd have killed you. Look at you, so fat and lazy. It makes me sick."

Ezekiel didn't have an ounce of fat on him—too much physical labor these days for that. But compared with the hungry, lean figures he'd seen in the camp, he must look that way to them.

"That's why you're angry, isn't it?" he asked. "Because there's no supper tonight."

"There's never enough to go around. Someone always goes hungry. We don't have a single meal saved up—how could we? But tonight there will be nothing."

"Give me time," Ezekiel said. "I'll find a way back into the valley. And when I do—"

"Don't insult me, you polygamist freak. I know what you want. Chambers told me everything."

Ezekiel blinked. "What?"

"It's a power struggle, that's it. You think I don't know? You killed the head of the cult, didn't you? That's what all the blood on your hands is. Now you want to hide until it's safe to go back and take over."

Ezekiel started to protest. But that would be stupid. He was in enough danger as it was. They despised him already. What if they knew the blood was from his own brother? That his allies had turned against him? That Jacob Christianson was still alive and vigilant down below?

"And when you claim your place as head of the cult, what then?" McQueen asked.

"It's not a cult. It is the church of God."

"I know what you'll do," McQueen said, as if he hadn't been listening. "You think I don't? I'm a survivor—I'm nobody's fool. Chambers would have kept feeding us, but you? You'd cut us off in a heartbeat. That's right, as soon as you're head of the cult, you'll let us starve."

It was hard to argue with his logic. Certainly, Ezekiel had no intention of keeping these locusts feasting on their grain. It was only Jacob's weakness that had allowed it in the first place.

"I brought you a machine gun," Ezekiel said. "And ammunition."

McQueen smiled. "Yes, you did. And I'll put it to good use, don't you worry."

"Doesn't that count for something?"

"Yeah, it will keep you alive. That, and your knowledge of the valley. You can show us around when we get there."

Ezekiel licked his lips. "You're going down?"

"You cut off our food. You've left us no choice."

"Why are you here?" Ezekiel said. "We never said we'd help you. We can barely take care of ourselves. Why didn't you go somewhere else?"

"There is no somewhere else, you idiot. Now sit there and be good. We'll have work for you later." He nodded at one of the men, who was armed with a shotgun. "Keep an eye on the polygamist."

The short-haired woman looked up at the sky. "It's almost dark. What if he makes a run for it?"

"Tie up his feet again," McQueen said. When that was done, he nodded. "Now stick him in the truck. If he opens the door, blow his brains out."

A few minutes later Ezekiel found himself bound and shoved into the truck cabin. The sun was vanishing behind the western mountains. Another twenty minutes and it would be dark. He was thirsty again and his stomach growled uncomfortably. Outside, the guard with the shotgun leaned against the side of the truck and looked down at the commotion still roiling through the camp.

Ezekiel took advantage of the man's distraction to inspect the truck cab. They'd taken Jacob's night vision goggles from the passenger seat, but a glance revealed a glint of blood-stained metal below the seat. They'd neglected to search the truck. The machete was still down there, the cursed blade that had killed his brother.

So McQueen meant to attack Blister Creek tonight. By then Jacob would have the bunker manned again. And he'd replace the gun with either the one from the Humvee if he was still in a defensive posture, or a gun taken from one of the other bunkers, if he meant to use the vehicle for his own assault. There would be a battle.

Several people came trudging up from the camp a few minutes later carrying a variety of plastic jugs and containers. Someone had a hose and a funnel. While the man with the shotgun watched, they siphoned the gas out of the truck. As each container was filled, its owner trudged off, but not back to camp. Rather, up to the highway, then south in the direction of Blister Creek, following the road as it stretched along the reservoir.

That was interesting. And alarming, at the same time. Where were they carrying all that fuel?

When the fuel scavengers were gone, the man with the shotgun returned to watching the camp, his back to the truck. Someone in camp lit a fire.

Keeping an eye on his guard, Ezekiel used his toe to ease the machete out from beneath the seat. He tried to get it turned onto its side so the sharp edge would be facing up, but this proved impossible with his hands bound behind his back and his feet tied together.

With a final glance at his guard, now in shadow as it grew dark outside, Ezekiel lay down across the seat bench. He twisted his shoulders until he got his hands on the floor. He groped blindly along the carpet until his fingers found the blade. It took more struggling to lift the knife up to the seat. When he had done so, he waited with the machete hidden beneath his body in case the guard opened the door and demanded to know why the truck was rocking from all of Ezekiel's movement.

After several seconds of silence Ezekiel breathed a sigh of relief and began again. He twisted the machete until the blade was against the cord binding his wrists. Then he went to work sawing through.

CHAPTER TWENTY-FOUR

Miriam, Jacob, and David hiked up the switchbacks in silence. It grew darker and darker as they snaked higher. By the time they reached the heights it was night. The moon, now waxing from the crescent of the past couple of nights, would be brighter in the sky than it had been, but it wouldn't come up for at least an hour or two.

The three of them stood in the cool breeze that washed down from the higher mountains above. Miriam shivered, glad to have the denim jacket. The night was quiet. No insects or birds up here. The trees were all gone, and only tumbled boulders marred the landscape, spilling right up to the edge of the road. To the right of the highway lay the wide, inky pool of the reservoir. It would take twenty or thirty minutes to round the reservoir on foot and reach the squatter camp from the opposite side. She figured that was a safer bet than approaching directly from the highway.

Miriam turned on the night vision goggles just long enough to verify that no figures were lurking in the darkness. "All clear."

Jacob pointed to the left of the highway. "We'll take position behind those rocks and wait."

"I'll be awhile."

"Don't linger. Just go through the camp, look for Ezekiel, anything else you see that might be out of the ordinary, then come back. No heroics, no side adventures."

"I know what to do."

"Give me a minute with Miriam," David said to his brother. "I'll meet you at the rocks."

As Jacob left for the boulders, Miriam and David picked their way along the dirt road on the south shore of the reservoir.

"Are you planning to follow me all the way around?" she asked.

"I've half a mind to, yes."

"You've got nothing to worry about. I've done this sort of thing before, and against worse odds."

"I wish you'd give this up. It's not worth it. Not to me, it isn't. Not to your kids."

"It's just reconnaissance."

"You keep insisting. It's less convincing every time you say it."

"Oh, come on, what are you talking about?"

"You may have fooled Jacob. Barely—he seems suspicious. But I'm your husband, and I know you. I know what you're thinking."

"I'm not going in with any preconceived ideas," she said, truthfully. "But if I see that traitor, if I have the chance, I'll do what must be done."

"Insofar as thou art faithful and true, thou shalt be protected from harm. That's what the blessing said."

"And I will be."

"You told Jacob you were going to reconnoiter. He's trusting you to keep your word. If you go against that, how will you claim you were faithful and true?"

"I'll be faithful and true. But maybe not to what Jacob is expecting."

"So you're trusting your own wisdom, and not the prophet?"

"I'm trusting my own *inspiration*," she corrected. "What the spirit tells me directly."

"Jacob gave you a blessing. That *was* the spirit speaking."

"There are two ways to interpret that blessing. One is Jacob's way. Caution, compromise. Hold out and things will blow over."

"And your way?"

"Not my way, the Lord's way. The world is ending. You know it, I know it. Everyone in Blister Creek knows it, even Ezekiel Smoot. Everyone except Jacob. Either everyone else is right and Jacob is wrong, or Jacob is right and we're all wrong. Every single one of us, wrong."

"I believe this is the end," David said, "but I don't know it."

"I do." She put her hands on his shoulder. "And I know that the Lord has chosen me to protect this valley. A shield, yes, but sometimes a sword too. And even as I protect our people, so will the Lord protect me in turn. I know this."

"But I *don't*," he insisted, as stubborn as ever. He took her hands from his shoulders and held them. "Miriam, I really don't."

"There's one way for you to know for sure," she said, as something occurred to her.

Even as the thought came to her mind, a shiver worked itself down her spine at the implications. Was that a whisper of doubt in her mind? She pushed it aside.

"If I'm right, if this is the End of Days, I'll destroy our enemy and return unharmed this very night. If I'm wrong and Jacob is right—"

David stiffened. "Thou shalt not tempt the Lord thy God."

"I'm not tempting Him. I'm trusting Him. My life is in His hands." Miriam took a deep breath and began again. "If I'm wrong and Jacob is right, if this is nothing more than a natural disaster, then the Lord shall remove me for my folly."

"Please, don't say that."

She nodded. "Then this very night shall mine enemy smite me unto death."

★★★

Miriam continued alone. Last year they'd used this road to circle the reservoir in the Humvee and attack the camp from the back side and she wasn't surprised to see that the squatters had taken steps to render it impassable to vehicles and horses.

Every few hundred feet a trench had been cut across the road. In other places, logs blocked the road. Once, she almost stepped on a nail strip thrown across the road, but was traveling with the night vision goggles and spotted the dark stripe against the dirt. She stepped gingerly over it, watching for other traps or snares. It occurred to her that with McQueen in charge, a former military man, they might have improvised mines to catch the unwary. Was she heavy enough to trigger them?

Heavenly Father, guide my steps.

The light of a small fire flickered on the far side of the reservoir, but otherwise the camp was dark. The arrival of spring must have come as a welcome relief for the refugees. With the hillsides denuded and firewood farther and farther away, it must have been a frigid, miserable winter up here. The lucky lived in dugouts or campers, while others would have suffered through the cold in tents or beneath propped-up tarps. Some must have died. Many of the survivors no doubt wished they had.

Why didn't they go away? Blister Creek couldn't help them; the church members had enough worries caring for themselves. It wasn't fair for them to stay up here starving and freezing, their presence making the saints of the valley struggle with fear and guilt.

Listen to yourself. Have you no compassion? These people are suffering.

Miriam shook her head. Compassion was a trap. It would have been kinder for Jacob to drive the refugees away the moment they'd arrived rather than to leave them up here, filled with hope. And then Jacob's compassion had made the treachery of Chambers and Ezekiel possible.

She slowed when she came within a few hundred yards of the camp. She could see the sentries through her goggles. Two people sat behind a barricade of logs, their heads and rifle butts poking up. A third person lurked to one side, this one wrapped in a blanket, his back against a tree stump. He was either asleep or sitting so still she might have missed him with a more casual examination.

Miriam took out her pistol. She swung to the right of the road, then crept up to the sentry at the tree stump. The camp had chosen their guard positions well; it was the narrowest point between the reservoir and the hillside.

But she was quiet and careful, and he didn't turn toward her. She passed behind the man at the stump, no more than a dozen feet away at the closest, moving step by step, placing her feet with extra caution so she wouldn't kick a stone or crunch gravel. The man cleared his throat and she froze. But he didn't move or look in her direction.

It took several minutes before she was past the sentries and approaching the outer tents of the camp. One final survey showed numerous people milling around the camp or gathering at the fire, but no more sentries. She turned off the goggles and shoved them into an inner pocket of her jacket.

That had been surprisingly easy. She'd learned how difficult it was to maintain an endless vigil, but she'd expect to find the camp still in turmoil from the loss of their food source last night, plus Ezekiel's no-doubt unexpected arrival.

A panel truck sat directly ahead of her, its tires missing, a tarp stretching from the side to form a crude canopy over the ground. Someone's home, but it was dark and quiet, and she thought it would be a good place to hide and study the camp from closer range. She stepped up to the back bumper.

"Hold it, there," a woman's voice said. A figure stepped from behind the truck, a rifle or shotgun in hand.

Miriam's stomach flipped over, and she had a hard time not grabbing for her pistol. She forced herself to remain calm. "Holy shit, you scared me."

"What are you doing, where did you come from?" The woman sounded nervous. And young.

"Chill out, it's just me."

"Who?"

"Someone thought they saw something, so McQueen sent me around the reservoir to check things out. Of course it was nothing. Look, I already checked in back at the checkpoint. Are you going to give me crap too?"

Without waiting to see if the woman would challenge her further, Miriam resumed walking toward camp. She didn't know if the young woman was watching her or if she'd already turned back to study the road emerging from behind the reservoir, convinced by Miriam's casual behavior that she wasn't a real intruder.

Again, the long months since the last attack on the reservoir worked to Miriam's advantage. They must have had a million false alarms. And it was still a camp of strangers—no way to know all fifteen hundred people, or however many they were now.

Miriam walked between rows of tents. A harmonica wailed somewhere to her right, accompanied by the strum of a guitar that seemed to be missing a string. The wind picked up, flapping tents and snapping the edges of poorly secured tarps.

Someone, presumably McQueen, had drawn out the campers and tents from the water's edge and arranged them in rows, with footpaths between. It looked more like an actual, organized refugee camp than the chaotic jumble of the previous year. To keep the Humvee from simply driving through and mowing people down again, they'd buried tree stumps in strategic places. Those would trip up any vehicles, but posed no obstacle to an intruder on foot.

The moon rose behind the mountains to the northeast, and she could suddenly pick out figures. Two people sat on lawn chairs in front of a tent, smoking. She saw the harmonica player and his guitar-playing friend. A woman sat next to the guitar player. Maybe she was his wife. Maybe she'd come to listen to the music.

A man stood down by the shore, fishing. Miriam couldn't imagine there were any fish left after all this time. Even if they were no longer poisoning the lake to send fish floating to the surface, surely they'd used every other tactic to catch and eat the last few fish. She couldn't see any trout leaping for flies in the moonlight, or the little pools of water that showed them stirring below the surface. No doubt any other animal that could be eaten had been, from deer and rabbits down to crickets and meadow voles.

Fifteen or twenty people stood around the fire in the center of camp. She expected to see some of them cooking, but there were no pots and nothing going in and out of what she now recognized as a crudely built bread oven sitting to one side. All the bread in that oven, she realized, had been made from grain and flour pilfered from Blister Creek.

But why weren't they cooking anything now? Could they already be out of food? They must have truly been living day to day if less than twenty-four hours after Chambers's last delivery they had nothing whatsoever to eat.

Well, sure. A thousand, fifteen hundred people. What did a person need to survive, maybe a pound of grain per day? Even adding what they could hunt and fish from their surroundings, that stolen food had been barely enough to keep them alive.

The discussion at the campfire rose in volume. It was animated—almost, but not quite an argument. She was suddenly sure they were discussing Ezekiel and Blister Creek. Food supply gone, now what do we do? And will those polygamist whackos attack us again?

Miriam was itching to get closer and eavesdrop on their conversation, so she wandered back and forth through camp, coming at the clearing from several directions. But she couldn't find any way to approach without stepping into the firelight. She didn't see Ezekiel, so she didn't worry about getting recognized. But with so many men and women, it wouldn't take long to figure out that *nobody* knew her. Two seconds after that there'd be trouble.

Instead, she gave up and went looking for Jacob's truck. She picked her way through the tents until she found a fifth-wheel trailer up by the road, two of its windows broken out and taped with old newspapers instead. There was nobody lurking around it, and so she pressed herself against the side and put on the night vision goggles, dialing them down to compensate for the moonlight. She looked up toward the highway.

Jacob's stolen truck sat off the shoulder of the road, several yards down the muddy slope, roughly a hundred yards distant from the edge of camp. A man with a long-barreled gun stood guard. He wore a long, scraggly beard, but he was too skinny and short to be Ezekiel. She was wondering where to look next when she spotted movement inside the truck cabin. There was someone in there. And that could only be one person.

There was her quarry. She'd found him, a prisoner inside the pickup truck. And the truck sat isolated from the camp, with only one guard standing watch. Miriam allowed herself a smile.

The Lord had delivered Ezekiel Smoot into her hands.

CHAPTER TWENTY-FIVE

Miriam put the goggles away as she looped back into camp. She needed to think about what to do and couldn't stand here gawking while she did. She kept her head down as she walked back through. After a few minutes she cut back around to get another look at the truck.

If there had been any doubt before, it evaporated when she saw the posture of the armed guard relative to the pickup truck. The man wasn't guarding it from outsiders, he was there to keep the man in the truck cabin from getting out.

And look at how they'd placed the truck. Off the road, but set apart from the camp. They didn't want Ezekiel in their midst, not while they argued about what to do with him. Ezekiel had probably driven up covered in blood and making demands. They'd taken his keys, told him to stay in the truck, then put someone to guard it.

But yes, they'd have taken the keys. That burst her fantasy of simply jumping inside, holding Ezekiel at gunpoint, and forcing him to drive back to Jacob and David. They could hold a church court instead of Miriam executing him on the spot; Jacob would like that. The guard would be collateral damage, but that couldn't be helped. But no, not if Ezekiel didn't have the keys. Probably McQueen had them. And who knew where he was or if she could even get to him.

By the third time she circled through the camp, she was sure the guard was alone. She'd inspected the truck from several angles and had a chance to look along the edge of the camp to make sure nobody else was keeping watch.

Go back. Tell Jacob what you've seen. Let him decide.

It was a strong impression, seemingly coming from nowhere. She froze, uncertain if she were hearing her own doubts or the warning of the spirit.

Insofar as thou art faithful and true, thou shalt be protected from harm.

"I *am* faithful and true," she whispered. "Always."

It was too good an opportunity to pass up. If she went back, Ezekiel would escape. McQueen and his fellow squatters would find a way to put him to use after they'd gained the valley floor. Maybe they'd mount the .50-cal on the truck, or maybe they'd aim it down from the cliffs while others assaulted the bunker from the road. Maybe they'd even try the rope trick on the cliffs again. Either way, once they reached Blister Creek, Ezekiel could show them every weakness, every vulnerability.

And here she was. One guard plus the traitor. Easy.

But she couldn't use her gun. She was too close to camp and too far from where Jacob and David could help her escape. There would be other guards south on the road, and she'd have to run that gauntlet with an uproar caused by her gunfire.

Two women walked past carrying firewood toward the fire ring at the center of camp. When they were gone, Miriam reached under her denim jacket and eased her KA-BAR knife from its sheath, then walked with it tucked and hidden along the inside of her forearm.

She strolled out of the camp toward the pickup truck sitting quietly by the highway. Forcing herself to walk at a normal pace, which felt almost melodramatically slow, she approached the truck with no attempt at stealth. The guard spotted her and watched as she approached.

"Hey," she called. "I have something for you. Are you hungry?"

The guy snorted, as if the question were not worth answering. But he sounded eager when he spoke. "What have you got?"

"Some guy came in from the mountains from cutting wood and turns out they'd trapped a couple of squirrels. Gamey, but it's fresh."

"In other words, the same old slop," he said with a chuckle. "But I'll take it."

He propped his gun against the back of the truck as she approached with her left hand outstretched as if it held something. The man's weapon was a double-barreled shotgun. Definitely for keeping the truck occupant under control, not protecting the vehicle itself from outside attack. But at short range it could turn her to hamburger. Only now his gun was out of reach as she let him step the last few feet toward her. Deluded by his hunger, that mistake would prove to be his death.

Miriam waited until the man reached out his hand, then grabbed his wrist and yanked him forward. He staggered, off balance. She swung the knife around with the other hand and thrust up and in.

He gave a surprised yelp as he came up against her. She shoved the knife into his belly as hard as she could. The force of his movement and her thrust got the first two inches in. Then she pushed off with her feet while hooking him around the neck with her left hand and dragging him down. A groan came out of his mouth and the knife slid up to the haft, all seven inches of blade now under his rib cage. She jerked it viciously back and forth as his legs went out from under him. When she pulled the blade out, he was dead at her feet and her hand was slick with blood.

Miriam shuddered and allowed a moment to recover as she looked down at him. The poor fool had been doing his job; he wasn't to blame. If she could have spared him, she would have. But it was life and death, the people of God arrayed against the forces of Satan. Circumstances had forced her hand.

A quick glance at the camp showed nothing amiss. Figures moved about in the darkness, but nobody cried out or ran toward her. The guard was dead on the ground. Out of sight. If they looked toward her, they would see only a solitary figure moving in the moonlight outside the truck, exactly as expected.

What now? Sneaking up and gutting a guard was one thing. Trying to knife Ezekiel in the confines of the truck cab another. Miriam was strong for a woman, but Ezekiel was a man and a rancher, six feet tall with broad shoulders and arms. In the open, she had no doubt she could take him, but the cramped space would negate her advantages in training and maneuverability.

And she couldn't shoot him here. Not so close to the squatters. She had to get him away from camp first.

Miriam sheathed the bloody knife and walked slowly around to the opposite side of the truck so she could come in from the driver-side door out of view of the camp. She couldn't risk someone catching a glint of moonlight off the door window as she opened the truck. When she passed the back bumper, she grabbed the shotgun propped where the guard had left it. She confirmed that both barrels were loaded.

There was one final concern as she reached for the door handle. Had Jacob set the cab lights to turn on automatically when the door opened? She guessed not—that would be a risk to the battery at a time when it would be hard to recharge—but she wasn't sure. If so, the cab light would attract interest from the camp, and she'd have no choice but to shoot and run.

Miriam took a deep breath and swung open the door. No lights came on. She aimed the shotgun into the darkened interior, her knee holding the door open. The moonlight caught movement in the interior. A person had been lying down on the bench seat and now raised himself to a sitting position.

"Don't move," she said.

The man inside made a small, frightened noise in the back of his throat. "Don't shoot me."

Miriam's heart leaped in triumph. Yes. It was the apostate and traitor.

"Ezekiel Smoot. You will come with me."

"If I do, will you kill me?"

"No," she lied. "We'll go back to Blister Creek."

"And they'll kill me there."

"Brother Jacob will make that decision, not me. He is a merciful man."

She meant to give him hope. He must know that the others in the Quorum of the Twelve and the Women's Council would be calling for his death. Slit the throat of the murderer so that his blood would atone for his crimes. But Jacob would argue for compassion. If Ezekiel came peacefully, he had a chance. Or so he would imagine.

"You can't shoot me," he said after a few seconds. "It will make too much noise."

Miriam hardened her voice. "I can and I will. The prophet sent me to bring you back. If I must die to obey him, so be it. The Lord will welcome me on the other side of the veil with open arms."

"You're a woman! You've got a husband and children. You can't throw your life away."

"And I will see them again someday. Try me, Ezekiel. I already killed your guard. I will kill you too."

None of this was a bluff. She lifted the gun to shoot.

"No! I'm coming, I'm coming."

Miriam stepped back two paces while he came out. Her movement was automatic, muscle memory from years of FBI training, from all those drug raids. Give sufficient space so that if the enemy did something stupid, he'd have no time to close before she could fire.

That training saved her life.

Ezekiel came out attacking. Shockingly, he still had his machete, and it was this that he swung in a wide arc toward Miriam's head. It hadn't occurred to her that McQueen would leave Ezekiel armed. But she wasn't so shocked she was left without time to pull the trigger. Indeed, her finger was tightening automatically before she remembered not to shoot. At this range, the shotgun would blow a hole right through him. But then the entire camp would come running.

Miriam ducked to one side as the blade whooshed past her head. Ezekiel was off balance, his charge hasty and without skill. She sidestepped him and smashed him in the ribs with the gun butt as he stumbled past.

He came back around, flailing madly. His technique—or lack of it—may have served him well hacking through an unarmed crowd of children and their mothers, but it was helpless against Miriam's training. She again ducked aside and this time bashed him on the kneecap. He stumbled and fell with a cry, and she hit him between the shoulder blades. He fell flat on his face.

Miriam dropped the shotgun, reached behind her back, and whipped out the KA-BAR knife from its sheath. She drove her knee against the small of Ezekiel's back as she fell on him. Then she grabbed his hair with her left hand and yanked back his head. At the same time she reached around with the knife and jerked it across his throat.

The blade bit deeply, and Ezekiel's gathering scream turned into a gurgle and a spasm that nearly pitched her off. Blood gushed onto her hand. He flopped violently. She got the knife free and dragged it across his throat one more time to be sure.

Miriam threw herself backward, gasping and panting from the exertion. Ezekiel struggled on, but within mere seconds he was stilling. His hand twitched, still holding the machete. Then he lay motionless, his throat cut, his blood spilled onto the ground through a severed artery in his neck. The manner of his death hit her.

Without meaning to do so, Miriam had rendered the blood atonement on Ezekiel Smoot. His crime of apostasy was so great that only the spilling of his own blood would allow him some measure of mercy in the world to come. Otherwise, his soul would be cast into Outer Darkness for all eternity.

"You're welcome," she whispered. She wiped the knife clean on Ezekiel's pant leg, then sheathed it as she rose to her feet.

In spite of her hard words, she felt shaky and sick. It was one thing to kill a gentile, another to cut the throat of a man she'd known for years. A saint. Fallen, yes. Apostate, certainly. But still a member of her own community. It took effort to fight down the churning sensation in her gut.

Her left leg hurt, and when she felt at it with her hand was surprised to discover a ragged hole in her jeans, and a superficial, but painful, cut along her thigh. She had no memory of being struck, but he'd apparently grazed her with the machete on one of his lunges. But it was nothing, wouldn't even require stitches.

Miriam put on the goggles and turned them on. She looked down at the camp. All quiet. Nobody had seen or heard a thing. That was a small miracle in and of itself.

She mouthed a silent prayer as she picked up the shotgun and checked to verify that her pistol hadn't come dislodged from its holster in the struggle.

Miriam felt better as she reached the road and slipped south along the highway, her goggles still on and nobody appearing between her position and where David and Jacob waited. A surge of triumph rose in her breast, and she remembered her earlier prophesy.

If I'm right, if this is the End of Days, I'll destroy our enemy and return unharmed this very night.

A smile touched her lips. David had taken it as a boast. Maybe it had been, a little, but going into camp to kill her enemy hadn't been the time for false modesty. It had been the time to shore up her courage.

"I knew it," she whispered. "It truly is the End of Days."

She was so caught up in these thoughts that she almost didn't notice the movement on the opposite side of the highway. When she saw it, she froze.

That side of the road had once been a park and picnic area. A grassy slope had stretched from the highway down to the reservoir. On hot days, people would flee the oppressive heat of the valley and enjoy the shade of the hundred-year-old cottonwood trees in the park. They would picnic at tables while their children played on the grass or dove from the docks to swim in the reservoir. People would launch fishing boats, and a couple of families even had motorboats for waterskiing.

Those days were long gone. The cottonwood trees had fallen when the squatters arrived. The grass had first grown wild and weedy in the unusually damp weather, then died, unwatered, when the climate turned dry again.

There were a dozen people milling down the slope from the highway, standing around something the rough shape and size of a camper van, only it had strange things sticking out from it at angles. People were circling the vehicle, checking these items. Someone else lay on his belly up top, screwing something down.

Miriam approached cautiously, still looking through her goggles. She had no cover, and there was a small risk that someone would spot her against the moonlight. But it was still plenty dark, and their attention seemed focused on their labors. When she'd crossed the highway, she dropped to her belly and crawled down the dirty, weed-covered slope like an infantry soldier inching beneath barbed wire.

The vehicle was indeed a van, or had been. The objects fastened around the side were bits of metal and boards, together with sandbags and tires—anything that could be attached to give the vehicle protection from gunfire and explosives. The man up top was fastening down the stolen .50-caliber machine gun. McQueen had put together a crude version of the Methuselah tank that had carried Miriam and her companions safely out of Las Vegas last year. And as soon as she recognized what it was, she also knew what they intended to do with it.

They meant to assault Blister Creek that very night. Cram the van full of gunmen and run the gauntlet past the bunker and thunder down the highway into town. Or seize the bunker and let the rest of the squatters pour into the valley under cover. Take Ezekiel with them, no doubt; the traitor could show them whom to take as hostages, how to get to the food.

Maybe McQueen had been working on his plan for months, or maybe he'd just slapped it together only today after Ezekiel delivered the gun and fuel into his hands. Either way, this was a disaster. At the moment, only Stephen Paul was at the bunker, with Jacob and David hiding behind the boulders with their rifles. The two brothers wouldn't be able to stop it, and Stephen Paul would be hard-pressed to hold them off alone until he could summon help.

She was torn in two different directions. On the one hand, she could run down the highway, find her husband and brother-in-law, and they could make for the bunker to see if they could hold the highway while they called in reinforcements.

But a better plan would be to attack the van herself. If she'd had Jacob's .308 sniper rifle with its night vision scope, she could do it from here. She didn't, but she did have a shotgun with two shells and her Beretta with spare magazines. Her night vision and the element of surprise would give her the upper hand. She could circle them, killing, until the squatters brought reinforcements up from the camp. By then, she'd be on top of the van with the machine gun and pouring fire into their midst. After she was done, there would be no more threat from the squatters. Now, or ever.

Take out the man on top first. That was the key. Get him before he could bring the machine gun to bear and sweep it across the slope on full automatic. The man was on his stomach, so she didn't have much of a shot from this angle. She needed to get closer. Then she'd need to spring to her feet at the last moment and charge.

And so it was that Miriam found herself squirming forward on her belly, ready to assault a dozen armed men and women. She couldn't remember ever making a conscious choice to press the attack.

CHAPTER TWENTY-SIX

As Miriam crawled through the darkness, ready to leap to her feet to make a charge at the gunner atop the van, she saw that reaching the machine gun would be harder than she'd imagined. What she'd taken at a distance for the bubble top of a camper van was a row of sandbags. The vehicle was a standard van, flat-topped, but they'd built a protected machine gun nest up top. The man wasn't on his belly, as she'd assumed, but sitting behind the sandbags. She needed to get even closer to pull off a good shot.

Voices reached her ear. A man called for another man to pass up one of the ammunition cans Ezekiel had stolen from the bunker. The second man opened the double doors at the rear of the van. The interior had all its seats pulled out, and on closer inspection seemed more like a panel truck than a passenger van.

There were two people inside, one of whom pushed out the ammunition can toward the man calling for it. Suddenly, she saw her opening. From the inside, only a thin metal shell protected the machine gunner from below.

Miriam jumped to her feet and broke into a sprint. She was sixty feet away, then forty. Still, they were too concentrated on their efforts to notice her. Only when she was twenty feet away, eating up the last few strides, did the man turn from lifting the heavy ammo can to the man up top. He looked at her, and his eyes widened as he seemed to take in the sprinting figure, the gun, maybe even the night vision goggles. He shouted and grabbed for something. A gun, perhaps. He never reached it.

She was only five feet away, with the doors open in front of her. There was the man reaching for his weapon, plus two more inside. All within range of the shotgun. She fired into their midst. The first man fell without a sound. Two others screamed in pain from inside.

Without waiting to see if her shot had delivered a lethal blow, she leaped into their midst and into the back of the open van. She collided with bodies. She rolled onto her back, steadied herself long enough to aim straight up through the roof, and pulled the trigger. The roar was deafening in the enclosed space.

The shot was straight and at close range. She knew at once that it had blasted straight through the flimsy roof and into the body of the machine gunner. He would be dead or dying. All she had to do was get up top and take control of his weapon.

Miriam tossed aside the empty shotgun and grabbed her pistol as she fought through the writhing, injured bodies she'd blasted on her initial approach. There were weapons lying around, but she didn't know if they were loaded, and didn't have time to find out. She had to get out of the enclosed space inside the van.

She came out firing her Beretta. Her first bullet hit a woman with short hair. The woman's rifle went off as she fell. The shot missed, but the flash of light and angle of the gun was enough to stop Miriam's heart. The bullet must have zipped past her head. She turned, firing twice more at a man who threw himself to the ground a few feet away. This missed, and he rolled over, lifting his own weapon. Miriam ducked around the back side of the van as he fired. Glass shattered on the windows of the open door.

There were two more people on the side of the van next to the reservoir. She shot one of them point blank in the chest, and the other in the back as he turned to run. Neither was armed, and she ran around the front, stumbling over yet another man, this one dropping to one knee with an assault rifle. But his back was turned to her, as if he'd spotted the fighting on the opposite side, ducked to ready himself, and been caught unaware from behind.

Miriam did a little dance to disengage her legs from him. He swung out, grabbing for her ankle. She threw herself backward. As she fell, she shot him in the head. After that, he presented no more trouble.

She had regained her knees when the enemy finally recovered and began to return fire. Bullets pinged against the van: handguns and semiautomatic rifles. She flattened, afraid she was about to be killed, but it was clear the firing was blind. They couldn't see what she'd done, and it was doubtful they'd even figured out there was only one gunner. Instead, they seemed to have retreated up the hillside and were blasting away at her position. Which was a grim enough situation to find herself in, but hardly fatal.

Miriam reached down to grab the assault rifle from the man she'd shot in the head. When she looked at his face, she stopped. He had a drawn look, with deep-set eyes, now holding the glassy stare of the dead. A scraggly beard. It was Whit McQueen. She'd killed their leader.

His weapon was an AR-15, converted to full auto, with an extended magazine. One of Blister Creek's own, no doubt given to them by Ezekiel, that bastard. She checked the ammo. One magazine: sixty bullets. Satisfied it would serve her purposes, she put away her Beretta and took stock of her situation.

One dead outside the van, two more inside the van, wounded and perhaps dead. Another dead person at the machine gun. Then there was the woman she'd killed with the Beretta as she exited the van. Two more men killed as she came around the side of the van. Plus Whit McQueen, with a bullet through the forehead.

Miriam had already hacked down half of their assault team, and one of them was the camp leader, the man who had no doubt hatched this vile plan. Maybe they could recover and would mount another attack, but it wouldn't be tonight.

Meanwhile, the gunfire had died down, but she had no illusions. The survivors had regrouped and would be waiting for more people to join them from camp. The entire reservoir would have heard the gunfire and would be running toward the battle, laden with more weapons. She had to get out of here or she would die. That meant abandoning the plan of reaching the machine gun, but so be it. She'd done plenty of damage already.

Miriam came around the front of the van to find two men creeping in the other direction to get to her. But they were groping blind, their free hands feeling the van, their eyes open and staring into the darkness. Miriam wore night vision goggles and could see them clearly. She squeezed the trigger on the assault rifle. Gunfire snarled out the end on full auto, catching her by surprise.

Damn!

The two men fell, but she'd wasted several bullets and nearly lost control of the weapon in a haphazard spray of gunfire. She switched to semiauto and began stalking toward the road, keeping an eye on the knot of people to the northwest, who had their guns trained in her direction but didn't seem able to see her.

Then her eyes turned south and caught a glint. Someone was trotting up the highway from the direction of the cliffs, a rifle in hand. It was not David or Jacob. A woman, she thought.

The glinting object had come from the woman's eyes. Miriam had caught a reflection off a pair of night vision goggles. They must be the pair that Jacob had left in the truck, and Ezekiel had stolen. And now this woman had them, and she was looking right at Miriam, able to see her as easily as Miriam could see the woman.

All these thoughts went through Miriam's head as the woman dropped to one knee and lifted her rifle in Miriam's direction. Miriam drew down in response. But she knew at once that she would not get off a shot in time.

★★★

It had been at least an hour since Miriam had vanished into the darkness. Jacob and David were taking turns staring down the night vision scope attached to the .308 sniper rifle.

The brothers had taken refuge behind one of the boulders that lay like giant marbles alongside the road, spending a few minutes to build a little bunker of small rocks next to it. The makeshift bunker sheltered the man at the rifle, while the other brother sat next to him with his back at the boulder. Whenever Jacob was at the scope, David wrung his hands and asked anxiously if he could see anything. It was driving Jacob crazy.

Finally, he moved away from the gun and said, "Maybe you'd be happier if you just stayed at the gun instead of taking turns."

"Can I? Great."

David lay down at the gun and mumbled a prayer, something about the Lord guiding his aim so that he would strike down his enemies.

Why not pray that the scope was properly calibrated while he was at it? That the Lord retroactively align the factory machinery that had manufactured the ammunition, so the bullets would have precise tooling and the exact correct amount of powder in each casing? Hate to misfire under such critical conditions, after all. Heck, why not pray that their enemies each suffer an acute myocardial infarction? Kill them by good old-fashioned heart attack. That would be even more useful.

But Jacob kept the scoffing to himself. He waited until his brother had finished praying. "Since when have you become so devout? Seems only yesterday you were living in Las Vegas, wanting nothing to do with Blister Creek."

"You lured me back. I'd have never come home if it meant living under Father's thumb."

"And here I thought you'd stuck around so you could get inside Miriam's pants."

"Hah. Well, that too."

"When did it happen, all at once?" Jacob asked.

"My testimony? Little by little. First, I only wanted to ease my doubts. It sucks living in the middle of religious people when you don't believe any of it."

Tell me about it, Jacob thought.

"Then I started *wanting* to believe. That's the first step, you know. Everything else comes in a hurry." David glanced up from the scope. "You should try it sometime."

"What makes you think I haven't?"

"You know what it was? I was spiritually blind when I was in Vegas. It was all that stupid stuff I was doing—gambling, strippers, drugs. Especially the drugs. I needed to get free of that crap first."

"Meth is an elegant-looking drug," David continued. "Little crystals, sophisticated-looking product and delivery system. A man smoking a pipe. Not like a heroin junkie shooting poison into his veins."

"At least at first," Jacob said. "I've seen a few heavy users. Not pretty."

"Exactly. And I was on the fast track. Another year and I'd have been dead."

"I'm glad you're not."

"I'll always be grateful to you and Eliza for tracking me down. And to Miriam for giving me some tough love, a good slap in the face."

"But have you ever thought that maybe you're trading one kind of drug for another?"

David's voice turned wary. "How do you mean?"

Jacob ran his hand along the boulder. The surface was pockmarked with bullet holes, and he realized this must have been the same spot where his people had taken refuge when the Kimball cult made their final attack on Blister Creek, using the same Humvee now parked at the bunker with Stephen Paul.

"The meeting last night," Jacob said, more carefully this time. Had it only been last night? So much had happened since then. "People were throwing themselves on the floor, frothing at the mouth, their eyes rolled back, screaming gibberish."

"Surely you felt the spirit."

"Hmm."

"Nothing at all?"

"Not really. A shared hallucination—that's what it felt like. And I was the only one awake. I used to think you were awake with me. Guess not. I'm not even sure about Eliza anymore."

David was quiet for a long moment as he scanned the road ahead. "What are you waiting for, Jacob?"

"Peace and quiet. A return to normal."

"That's all behind us now. There is only staying faithful until the Lord arrives in all His glory."

"Great, wonderful."

"You don't *want* the Lord to return?"

"No, I don't."

"But why? The Millennium will be a wonderful time. No death, bounty for all. Peace across the land. The lion and the lamb shall lie down together. Who wouldn't want that?"

"It's the pain and suffering that precede it. The death of billions."

"Most of the hard stuff is behind us now."

"Behind us? What the hell do you think we're doing up here? Grover Smoot was murdered by his own brother not twenty-four hours ago. And a dozen others hacked up with a machete. Your wife is out there right now. They'll kill her if they catch her sneaking into their camp with a gun."

"Not a hair harmed on her head," David said, firmly. "That's what your blessing promised. And I for one believe it."

Jacob wanted to scream. David had taken a beat-up hydro turbine and used it to rig together an electrical grid for the valley. He'd mathematically calculated how much manure and biochar they needed to generate annually in order to maintain soil fertility in perpetuity with zero input from rock fertilizer. How could David be so smart and yet flip a switch and turn off his brain when it came to matters of faith and religion?

Those words from the blessing had come out of Jacob's mouth. He'd made them up!

Insofar as thou art faithful and true.

That was meant to remind Miriam that she was not supposed to mix it up with Ezekiel and McQueen, but to reconnoiter and come back. But of course she and David had both seized on the part of the blessing they liked, then molded the rest of it to suit their pre-conceptions. Why was that a surprise? Jacob should have known better.

It was time to step down. Jacob's hopes of turning the church away from polygamy, or at least softening its edges, had proven illusory. Hell, he'd been trapped into a second marriage himself. And what good was empowering women within the community if most of them decided they wanted to conform to the same patriarchal hierarchy that had plagued Blister Creek since its founding? Even the men and women he'd surrounded himself with had all taken hard turns toward fundamentalism.

Not that he could get away. There was no escaping Blister Creek, unless it was alone, and he'd never leave his family or force them to abandon their homes, their brothers and sisters in the church.

But that didn't mean Jacob had to pretend to lead while they lurched ever further down a path he could not follow. When Eliza returned, he decided, he would tell the church that they'd have to find another to lead them. From now on, he would be Blister Creek's doctor, not its prophet. It was a calling he'd never asked for, deserved, or fulfilled.

He was imagining how this would happen, thinking of the relief he would feel when the weight of responsibility lifted from his shoulders, when a gunshot boomed from up the road. It sounded like a shotgun. A split second later, another shotgun blast, followed by a pistol barking off shots.

And then almost immediately after, several different weapons, all going off at the same time.

"Miriam!" David said.

And before Jacob could stop him, his brother had leaped to his feet and snatched up the sniper rifle on its tripod and was running up the road toward the squatter camp. Jacob grabbed the second rifle and ran after him.

CHAPTER TWENTY-SEVEN

As soon as Miriam realized the other shooter would get the first shot, she dropped and rolled, even as she lifted her weapon. With no time to aim properly, she flipped to full auto and let off a spray of gunfire in the general direction of the shooter.

The other weapon fired. Something punched into her shoulder. Miriam was on her knees, firing again on semiauto before she realized she'd been hit and her left arm and shoulder no longer seemed to be working. There was no pain.

The other shooter scrambled back from the road and dropped to her belly. Miriam held the gun up with one arm while her other hung limp. It still didn't hurt, but a strange numbness was spreading out from the wound. Some deeper, more analytic part of her brain said she was in that brief window, like when you smash your thumb with a hammer, when everything is numb. In another instant there would be raging pain.

The distance between the two shooters wasn't great, perhaps a hundred yards to where the other shooter was down and trying to bring her gun to bear. It would have been an easy kill had Miriam been able to steady the weapon with her injured arm, even with the target presenting such a low profile. But holding the weapon with one arm, knowing she had only one chance, Miriam needed either luck or a divine hand.

Father in heaven, guide my shot.

She fixed the other woman in the scope. The enemy was trying to get a bead on her in the opposite direction. Miriam's finger squeezed. The gun kicked against her shoulder and she lost her aim. She had no visual confirmation that she'd killed her enemy.

The pain from the gunshot finally hit. It was like a clawed hand reaching into her shoulder, shredding muscle and tendon, crunching bones in its fist. She gasped and stifled a scream.

Only pure adrenaline got her to her feet with the rifle in hand. She turned and ran back toward the van, forced to trust that her shot had done its work. If she'd missed, a second gunshot would slam into her from behind and she would go down, dead. She reached the van safely.

When Miriam came around the vehicle, she found two more armed men, their eyes darting this way and that at the bodies on the ground, searching in the blackness for the one lurking there to kill them. Miriam still held the assault rifle in her good hand, and shot them both from point-blank range. Then she dropped the heavier, more unwieldy assault rifle and drew her Beretta, which she could more effectively wield with one hand. She sank to the ground with her back against the front tire and popped out the magazine. Gripping the pistol between her knees, she reloaded it with one hand and put away the partially used magazine.

Every movement made her wince. She felt lightheaded. A quick and excruciating probe at the wound showed that it had gone straight through. High velocity, apparently; different ammo would have torn her up worse. But that didn't mean she wasn't in trouble. In the short term she was bleeding fairly heavily, and together with the pain she'd have a hard time fighting off her enemies. In the long term there was a hell of a lot of damage in there. Jacob could save her life if she could get to him in time, but he didn't have the tools in his clinic to do a modern job of fixing her up properly after such a serious wound to bone, muscle, and tendon. She might permanently lose function in that arm and shoulder. That was an awful thought. But first, she had to extract herself from the dire situation at hand.

Gunfire started up again from the south. It blew out windows and tires on the van, and bullets struck the ground all around her. She struggled to a squatting position, and came around the back side of the van where she had more shelter. To her relief, she spotted the woman with the night vision lying motionless in the road where Miriam had dropped her. But that was only a reprieve; several figures were hurrying south along the road toward the body. She had to stop them before they recovered the goggles.

It was too far for a good shot with the pistol, and when she fired a few shots, she only managed to drive them off the road without hitting any of them. Several of the shooters kept blasting away at the van while half a dozen others continued north toward the downed shooter. More people came running from the direction of the camp.

Miriam fell back behind the van. Once they got those goggles, she'd be in trouble. Either a new sniper would wait for Miriam to present herself while the others provided cover, or the goggles would enable them to pinpoint her location and encircle her. They'd figure out first thing that she was alone and injured.

She cast her glance upward, where the .50-caliber machine gun waited, protected behind the sandbags. If they weren't fools and had loaded the correct belt of ammo into the gun—and McQueen was former military, so she guessed he'd done it properly—the belt would contain tracer bullets to guide the fire. Get up there and she could sweep across the road, mowing them down where they stood.

But when she struggled to a standing position, she found she couldn't lift her left arm above her waist. There was no way it would support any weight. And she simply wasn't strong enough to climb to the roof without the full strength of that shoulder.

Miriam waited until a lull in the firing, then edged around the van. Her only hope now was to make a run for it, cradling her injured arm, snatch the goggles from the dead sniper before anyone else reached them, then flee down the road toward the safety of David and Jacob. But as soon as she poked her head around the vehicle, a fresh hail of bullets rattled against the van. She ducked back to safety.

A frustrated groan escaped her mouth. This was grim. Very grim.

Then, from the south, came more gunfire, blasting north along the road. It wasn't aiming at her.

★★★

Jacob raced to keep up with his brother, who flew down the road with little apparent concern for gravel or potholes that might trip him up and break his ankle. Gunfire flashed from the north and northwest, all targeting a dark shape off the shoulder of the road. From this distance, it was impossible to see if it was a rock or an overturned cart, but it must be serving as shelter for Miriam.

David pulled up short. "Change weapons!" He grabbed for Jacob's semiautomatic rifle and handed back the .308 with the night vision scope. "Take them out."

"What are you doing?" Jacob asked.

"I'm going after her."

That would be a terrible risk, with David running right into the teeth of that gunfire, while Jacob sniped from a distance. David might be caught in the crossfire. But Jacob couldn't protest. If it had been Fernie out there, nothing would have stopped him from going after her.

Jacob flattened himself on the ground and set the gun on its tripod. The pavement was still warm from the stored heat of the sun, and as it seeped into him he felt his pulse slowing, his emotions easing. It was the same steady, clear headed calmness that swept over him when he gloved up for surgery, looked down at a gaping wound, his mind picking out a severed vein or cataloging internal organs: liver, kidney, gallbladder, pancreas.

Only this time he was picking out figures on the highway, armed with rifles and handguns, some shooting toward the object to his right, which turned out to be a van. There was a chance that the scope had been hit or jostled during David's run, so Jacob took aim first at the chest of the nearest figure, which presented the largest possible target.

Jacob fired. The gun thumped. The figure fell.

Slowly, keeping calm, he unlocked the bolt to open the breech and eject the spent cartridge as he chambered another round. He picked out another figure, this one a woman standing in the middle of the road, emptying her pistol at the van. He dropped her too. The rest of the people on the road scrambled for cover.

He turned his scope toward the van. There he spotted Miriam, crouched behind the front tire of the van, a pistol in one hand, her goggles on. She glanced toward him, no doubt wondering if he were friend or foe, then turned and fired back toward camp.

She didn't steady her pistol with both hands, firing instead with only her right. Her left arm hung limp and wounded. A gunshot to either the upper arm or shoulder. For a moment Jacob's thoughts turned to the difficulty they'd have getting her down to the bunker and the Humvee, and from there to the clinic. There Jacob faced another surgery without the benefit of X-rays, only a primitive groping at the wound to see what injuries he could diagnose by eye. But first he had to get her out of there.

The fiercest gunfire was now coming from closer to the camp. These attackers also had a better angle at the back of the van. This was the biggest threat to take out Miriam, but he'd have to fire over and through both Miriam and David. As Jacob was trying to pick out one of the distant figures, his brother passed as a blurry figure across his scope.

"Dammit, get out of there."

Frustrated, unable to take the risk, he aimed the gun back to the highway. The men and women on the road were moving again. He hit two more, but one of them seemed to be only clipped. The man dropped to the ground with the others and continued on his belly. The scope must be out of alignment, a flaw that manifested itself only now that he was shooting at more distant targets. If he could figure exactly *how* it was out of alignment, he could adjust his shots accordingly.

He paused to load more rounds into the weapon. Then he picked out the lead, crawling figure and aimed first high, then low. Both shots missed, but he saw where the low shot had hit the pavement, which was an important clue. The next time he aimed high and slightly to the left. Bull's-eye.

Still, the figures kept moving north, not toward the van, but up the road. Why? What were they so desperate to reach in that direction? There was no cover. They were only keeping themselves in reach of his sniper rifle, a danger they wouldn't be able to see by the thin light of the moon.

Five of the survivors turned their guns in his direction and started shooting wildly. A bullet smacked the pavement nearby. He shot one of them, then hazarded a look at two of the squatters now bent over a body on the ground.

The dead person wasn't somebody Jacob had shot. Miriam must have taken the shooter down. Perhaps the person was only wounded and crying for help. Like David, the enemy was desperate to rescue one of their own.

That was the sort of storytelling that crippled his will and made it hard to finish the ugly business he'd started. So Jacob hesitated. Then, as they flipped over what looked to be a dead woman, he saw that he'd been wrong. One of them pulled off a pair of goggles from her head and put them on. That's what it was.

They had his night vision, which he'd foolishly left on the seat of his truck before Ezekiel stole it. There was no sign of his truck, but here were the goggles, ready to peer through the darkness and get a clear shot at the shooter tormenting them from the road.

He took aim and fired.

But the man was moving, others crossing in front of him. The shot either missed or hit someone else. The man grabbed a gun with a scope and took aim from one knee. But Jacob now had more time to aim. Bullets still blasted wildly in his general direction, but he ignored them, concentrating only on the man with the goggles. The man was still moving his weapon, trying to find the enemy. Jacob would get the first shot.

Then two big, blurry figures staggered in front of his scope, one supporting the other. They were David and Miriam, stumbling down the highway toward him. Jacob no longer had a clear angle.

CHAPTER TWENTY-EIGHT

Miriam's hopes leaped when she realized that the shooter south on the highway was not targeting her, but her enemies.

They'd come for her. David and Jacob, hearing the shooting, had come running from their hiding place. Twenty minutes ago, after taking care of the apostate, she would have scoffed at the thought that she'd need any sort of help. Now, crouching frightened and helpless behind the van, with a throbbing, crippling wound in her left shoulder, she almost wept with relief to know they'd come.

The rifle snapped regularly, but with little urgency. Perfect. Steady shots, carefully taken. Given a few minutes, the rifle with its night vision scope would devastate the forces arrayed against her.

The main threat was the increasing gunfire from the direction of the camp, which came at her from the rear and behind the van where she hid. The shooters wouldn't be able to see her as long as she kept still, and they weren't particularly close, but there was enough gunfire roughly aimed in her direction that it was only a matter of time before someone caught her with a lucky shot.

Miriam glanced back down the road, silently willing her rescuer to target the camp so she could get clear. A man staggered off the highway, a few hundred yards distant and running toward her. He carried a rifle. She recognized him by his gait.

"David," she whispered, both relieved and yet terrified for him at the same time.

She came around the front of the van with the Beretta held in her outstretched right hand. Most of the gunfire from the opposite side of the road was directed at the shooter—Jacob, she now understood—but at least one person seemed to have spotted the figure running in the darkness. He aimed a pistol at David.

Before he could fire, Miriam took aim and fired. It was a long shot for a pistol held in one hand—a good seventy-five yards—but her bullet found its mark. The enemy fell.

David stumbled out of the darkness calling her name.

"Over here!"

He found her and grabbed her in a fierce embrace that made her cry out in pain.

"You're hurt," he said.

"Not as bad as the other guy, believe me." She gritted her teeth at a fresh wave of pain. "I got Ezekiel too."

"I don't care about that. Let's get out of here."

"Sounds good to me."

"Hands and knees," he said. "We'll crawl along the shore while Jacob holds them down with the rifle."

"No hands and knees. I can't do it. In fact," she said, though it grated her to admit it, "I'm fading fast. I can't go running either, not for long. We'll have to get up to the highway where it's flat."

"There are shooters up there."

"God will protect us. And Jacob will too."

"Give me the goggles."

He put them on and cursed as he took stock of the forces arrayed against them. For Miriam, the darkness was almost a relief.

"We're okay," David said, though he didn't sound like he believed it. "Everything will be fine. I'll swing around the front, take out as many as I can, and hope Jacob does the rest. You get up to the highway and move as fast as you can. We'll protect you."

"Sounds like a plan."

Not a very good plan, but she couldn't see any better option. And every second they waited only increased the number and organization of the forces arrayed against them. Time to place their trust in the hands of the Lord.

He kissed her forehead. "I love you, Miriam."

"I love you too. Now go!"

David sprang to his feet and ran around the front of the van at a crouch, the goggles on his head and the rifle in hand. Then he disappeared into shadows, nothing but a moving black shape ahead of her. She stumbled after him, blind and helpless. This is what the enemy felt. It was terrifying.

Flashes lit up the road, the camp, the shoulders of the highway. No way to tell friend from foe or even do more than pick out the general direction of any one party. The blindness grew more debilitating with every step. Her hearing struggled to fill the void. Bullets pinged against the van behind her like ball-peen hammers against a sheet of metal. Shouts came from the direction of camp, but the enemy on the highway was eerily quiet.

Miriam was almost to the road when gunfire sounded from a shooter a few yards ahead of her. She stifled a flinch, knowing it was only David, picking out the biggest threats, one by one.

"Miriam," he said. "Go!"

But she was still struggling to find her footing on the slope up to the shoulder of the road. The pavement must be close, she knew, but she hadn't reached it. And her head was swimming, the wound in her shoulder aching with a pain that felt like icy cold and the stab of a red-hot poker in turns. She reached the highway and stumbled. Regained her feet.

The gunfire sounded hollow now, like she was at the bottom of a well. She staggered forward. David took hold of her good arm and hauled her along.

"No," she tried to say. "Keep firing."

But the words came out in a slur.

"Faster," he urged. "You can do it."

He was carrying most of her weight now, having draped her good arm over his shoulder. She'd dropped her pistol at some point, but didn't remember it falling from her fingers.

Hold on, she told herself. *Keep moving. You can't stop now.*

Miriam's worries dropped away: her role as protector of the valley, her love for David and his love for her. At that moment, she could think only of her children. They needed their mother. Diego, Abigail. One adopted, one the child of her own womb. She loved them both fiercely, equally. They needed her in different ways, but they both needed her. And she needed them.

That consuming need propelled her, forced her legs to keep churning. Gunfire sounded all around, but no bullet hit them. They were protected from above. Ahead, she could see a figure lying flat on the pavement. He was shouting at them. Something about moving off the highway so he could get a shot. Who was that? David? No, her husband was holding her up and dragging her along. It must be Jacob. They were drawing closer. Another few steps and they'd reach Jacob and safety.

I'm going to make it. I'm going to live.

Then a tremendous blow slammed into her back and she fell.

★★★

When Miriam and David blocked his view, Jacob scrambled to move himself and the gun so he'd have a different line of sight through the scope. He shifted several feet to the left, and flattened on the pavement to take fresh aim.

He dropped three enemies in quick succession, but none of them was the person with the goggles. Where was he?

Jacob glanced away from the scope to check on the progress of David and Miriam. His brother had Miriam's arm draped over his shoulder. Her other arm hung limp and her head drooped. Her feet staggered along. The two of them weaved across the road like a pair of drunks, no more than fifty yards away.

"David, move!" he shouted. "I need a clear shot."

He looked in the scope again. Two men stood firing assault rifles haphazardly down the highway. Another had dropped to one knee and took more careful aim. A glint of reflected light from this one. The goggles.

Jacob squeezed the trigger. At that exact moment, a flare of light came from the muzzle of the other man's gun. David and Miriam fell in a jumble on the pavement.

From his rear came the growl of a diesel engine, the crunch of tires. It was a vehicle closing rapidly from the direction of the cliffs. No lights. Ahead, David shouted in fear or pain. More people closed in on the road ahead of Jacob. He didn't dare let up, not even to look back at the vehicle that rolled to a stop behind him.

He fired three more times. Then, to his relief, the door slammed shut behind him and a gun fired on full auto, shooting over Jacob and down the highway. It was Stephen Paul. The gunfire was as random as the enemy's, but it scattered the squatters from the highway in a way that the sniping had not. Jacob dropped two more people, including one who tried to recover the night vision goggles. By now he must have killed seven or eight people, but still they were boiling out of the camp by the dozen.

"Give me the rifle," Stephen Paul said. "Go get them."

Jacob left the other man with the sniper rifle and ran forward at a crouch to get to David and Miriam. His brother had extricated himself and was on his feet trying to lift Miriam, who lay sprawled in the road. Jacob grabbed her legs and the two brothers hauled her back. Stephen Paul continued to fire the .308.

"Get her into the truck," Jacob said to David when they were behind the rifle.

While Stephen Paul sniped, they got Miriam into the back of the Humvee. A bullet pinged off the metal near Jacob's head. He barely heard it; his mind was churning as his fingers probed the wounds in the darkness.

"We got her in!" David shouted at Stephen Paul, his voice tight and frightened. "Let's go!"

Stephen Paul grabbed the weapon and jumped to his feet as David climbed in with Jacob and Miriam and pulled the door shut. The Humvee swung around the highway, backed up to make the turn, then raced down the highway. Bullets dinged off the vehicle.

"Give me light," Jacob said.

The light came on, and he blinked, blinded after so long in the darkness. While he waited for his eyes to adjust, his fingers worked to unbutton Miriam's shirt. His eyes finally adjusted at the same moment he got the shirt peeled back from her torso. Beside him, David gasped.

There were two wounds. The first had struck her from the front, and made a mess of her left shoulder—damage to the scapula near the glenohumeral joint. The second had entered from behind, passed all the way through, and left a gaping exit wound that had torn through her right breast. As the bullet passed through her chest cavity, it had dissipated energy along the wound track, sending a shock wave through her body. Already, her blood covered Jacob's hands and pooled onto the carpeted truck bed.

Miriam's eyes were open, flickering. Bloody spume bubbled through her lips.

A sob escaped from David's mouth. He reached for her.

"Stay back," Jacob snapped.

He rolled Miriam onto her side to look at the entry wound. He followed its trajectory from the small hole through the serratus posterior muscle left of the scapula, to where it emerged from her breast. He pictured the lungs, drowning in blood. His heart sank.

And she'd already lost blood from that first hit. They were twenty minutes from his clinic, so poorly outfitted these days that he doubted he'd be able to stabilize a wound like this if it had happened in his front yard.

"Do something!" David pleaded.

Jacob chewed his lip. He took a deep breath, getting ready to tell David the awful news. Then Stephen Paul pulled to a stop. He jumped out of the truck. They must be at the bunker, and he had run in to man the machine gun in case the enemy came for an attack.

"Go," Jacob told his brother. "Drive the truck. Get me to the clinic."

David jumped from the back. An instant later, they were careening down the switchbacks to the valley floor.

"How is she?" David cried.

"Shut up and drive."

Jacob pressed against the larger exit wound with the heel of his right hand. With his other hand, he felt for her pulse. Already, he couldn't detect a radial pulse, but putting his fingers to her throat detected a feeble carotid pulse. That meant her blood pressure was already below sixty and falling.

There was nothing he could do but stare at Miriam as the moments of her death approached minute by minute. Even though they were flying down the highway at top speed, it seemed to take forever before David screeched around a corner and Jacob knew they'd reached the center of town. Moments later, the vehicle jerked to a stop. David raced around and threw open the doors.

Jacob stared at Miriam. Her eyes were glassy and the blood bubbles had stopped moving at her lips.

"Let's go," David said. "Get her inside. For God's sake, don't just sit there."

Miriam was limp. No further pulse could be detected. Jacob released the pressure on her chest. Blood oozed slowly from the exit wound, but there wasn't enough pressure left to force it out.

"What are you doing?" David cried.

Jacob looked up at his brother, throat tight. "David."

"Please, you saved her before." His voice was pleading, sobbing. "Remember? She was shot through the lung. And you pulled her out of it. You saved her!"

"It wasn't like this."

"You have to try!"

"I'm sorry. She's already gone."

"She can't be. She didn't even—" He swallowed hard. "—didn't even say goodbye. I can't—no."

David was shaking. Outside, a dog was barking, and doors opened and closed. Voices.

"Use the priesthood," David urged. "You're the prophet. You can close her wounds, bring her back. Have faith!" He'd taken Miriam's hand and squeezed it while staring at her with bugging eyes. "Jacob!"

"I'm so sorry." Jacob felt numb, like he was dreaming. This couldn't be happening.

"Give her a blessing," David begged. "Please."

"Yes, okay. Help me get her onto the lawn."

They carried her out of the back of the Humvee. Women came from the Christianson houses. One was Lillian, who let out a cry when she saw Miriam and came running. Lillian's sister-in-law, Jessie Lyn, grabbed the young woman and held her tight. David stumbled at the curb and fell, but two women grabbed his arm and held him up, while another caught Miriam before she hit the ground. Together, the men and women eased Miriam onto the grass. David threw himself on top of her, weeping, kissing her forehead and mouth, his tears dripping on her face.

Jacob was tempted. For just a moment, knowing there was nothing he could do to bring her back, he thought about trying, anyway. Call her spirit back to its body. Command her to live. But no, that would be wrong. Plus there was the damage to all of these people when they saw their prophet try to raise a body from the dead and fail.

He was only a man. He had no magic that flowed through his hands. He had no power over life and death except for those tools given to him by his medical training. And that training was helpless at a time like this.

Jacob placed his hands on Miriam's forehead. It was still damp with her sweat, still warm from her body heat. Twenty minutes ago she'd been a living, breathing person. A woman filled with passions and prejudices. A mother, a wife, a protector of her people. She had saved lives and taken them. Always, Jacob knew, she had acted according to the dictates of her own conscience, even when they were flawed.

The words of a blessing came to Jacob's mind. He didn't try to shape them or spin them to his own purposes, but spoke the words as he felt inspired. His voice came out strong and confident, filled with power. Maybe, just maybe, he spoke from a divine source.

"Miriam Christianson, in the name of Jesus Christ, and by the power of the Holy Melchizedek Priesthood, I lay my hands upon thy head to give thee a final blessing as thou preparest to meet thy savior."

A collective sob rippled through the gathering crowd.

"And when thou shall look upon the face of the Lord, He will take thee into His arms and say unto thee: Well done, thou good and faithful servant . . ."

CHAPTER TWENTY-NINE

Eliza and Steve hadn't known what to expect when they set off for Salt Lake in the converted armored car they called the Methuselah tank. Panguitch had been deserted, and they knew there was some sort of armed camp at Richfield, because it had stopped the larger group in the Humvee earlier in the day. How fiercely would the survivors in that town resist their passage?

After some discussion, they decided to cut over to I-15 when they reached I-70, which was the rural east-west freeway in Central Utah, passing through Green River on its way to Colorado. Heading north on I-15 would be a dangerous way to approach Provo and Salt Lake, since the freeway was the main artery through Utah. If there were any bandits, rogue army units, or hostile state forces, they would be here. But approaching Richfield a second time also seemed risky.

Foolishly, they didn't have a road map in all their supplies. Eliza hadn't thought to check for one, maybe because she thought she knew the roads of Southern and Central Utah well enough by memory. But it occurred to her that it would be a good idea to have a map in case they reached I-15 to find it unsafe and needed to look for an alternate route.

So when they reached the deserted town of Panguitch, they stopped to search for a map. They found one amidst the looted contents of the old M&D Food Town. The shelves had been emptied of the last can of dog food and the final roll of toilet paper, but the book rack by the checkout was untouched. Nobody wanted to read the latest Harlequin Romance or James Patterson thriller in the apocalypse, it seemed. And neither had anyone taken the Utah road maps.

There was some trouble getting from the I-70 junction to I-15, where the road had washed out at one of the mountain passes, but Jacob had wisely sent them with a chainsaw in case they encountered fallen trees. They used it instead to cut saplings at the mountain pass, which they laid across the gap so they could get over.

By the time they reached the other side of the washout it was almost dark, and they decided this was a good place to spend the night. They drove higher into the mountains, where they found a ranch exit that led to a dirt road. It proved a good place to hide off the freeway.

The night was cold that high in the mountains, but they slept in the sheets and blankets they'd brought from home, cuddled in each other's arms. Soon they fell to kissing and undressing each other. Lying in Steve's arms felt like making love at the end of the world, but when they'd finished, Eliza felt happy and content.

They came down from the mountains the next morning and finally reached I-15. The juncture of the two freeways was a flat, grassy plain, empty between mountain ranges on either side. The interchange itself was littered with the burned husks of semitrucks and motor homes, but continuing north, I-15 itself was deserted.

They'd come onto the freeway between the towns of Beaver and Fillmore. The latter town was abandoned, a picked-over corpse, much like Panguitch had been, so they continued past it without stopping on their way toward Nephi, another hour to the north. Nephi lay on the southern outskirts of Utah's main population center, and had been almost an exurb of the Provo area, which centered on the Mormon temples and Brigham Young University.

Eliza was sure they would encounter people again once they reached Nephi. Maybe even a functioning government. Yet as they approached, nobody emerged to challenge them. The houses on the outskirts of town had either been burned or bombed. Many lay in rubble; others were blackened shells.

The freeway hooked around the bench at the foot of towering Mount Nebo, with Nephi's downtown area lower and to the left. Eliza got her first good look and caught her breath. The town was gone, its trees cut or burned, the houses themselves reduced to their foundations. The hotels, restaurants, and shops, leveled. A handful of old buildings downtown stood with one or two brick walls still upright, but they only accentuated the appalling devastation.

Steve was driving and slowed the vehicle as they passed by the town. "Oh, my God."

Eliza glanced up at the charred foothills. The juniper and scrub oak had burned up the mountainside, and perhaps north over the pass and into Utah County as well. But it hadn't been a recent fire, because the grass was fresh and green from the spring rains.

"Could have been a forest fire," she said. "Lots of grass to burn because of all the rain we had. Probably late last summer when things dried out. Lightning started it, maybe. Or maybe someone's unattended campfire. It got going, and there was nobody left in town to fight it."

"Maybe." He didn't sound convinced. "More likely the fire started in town and spread in the opposite direction."

They rumbled up the freeway. It climbed the lowest shoulder of Mount Nebo, then brought them down into Utah County, with the snow-topped peak of Mount Timpanogos on the far end, thirty-five or forty miles distant.

It had been a few years since Eliza had entered the main population center along the Wasatch Front. At that time, the Salt Lake and Utah Valleys had seemed so lush compared with the desert around Blister Creek. Mile after mile of subdivisions, with their green lawns and wide, leafy trees. And so many cars; between Provo and Salt Lake, there were half a dozen lanes in each direction, and each one had been packed with cars driving at what seemed to her breakneck speeds. People weaving in and out of traffic, always in such a hurry. It was frightening.

The other thing that had tormented her was the pollution. Sometimes, when there wasn't enough wind to push the smog up and over the mountains, a haze would suffocate the valley floors. During her first winter in Salt Lake, a temperature inversion had cut visibility to a few miles and made her lungs burn. People complained, but they didn't stop driving their cars.

No smog now. It was clear from horizon to horizon. And as they approached the southernmost towns of Santaquin and Payson, she saw that the lawns were dead, the trees cut down. Sagebrush and tumbleweeds had begun to reclaim those few farms and orchards that had not yet been bulldozed for strip malls and subdivisions before the collapse.

A giant McDonald's sign still rose next to the freeway at Payson, but the restaurant itself and all the surrounding buildings were gone, as if they'd been wiped from the earth. Instead, nothing but weedy lots.

After Payson, Spanish Fork, then Springville both seemed to have suffered the same fate.

"Where is everyone?" Steve asked.

"Gone."

"Gone, as in they left? Or gone, dead?"

"Thousands of people lived in these towns. They can't have all died."

And yet, by the time the freeway bisected Provo, she'd begun to wonder. The entire west side of the city, between the freeway and Utah Lake, was rubble. Houses had burned to their foundation, warehouses lay gutted. To the right, a row of vacant, windowless houses stared down at the freeway from the ridge.

They came around the bend into Provo's sister city of Orem to see signs for Utah Valley University, but the school itself seemed to have been the site of a battle. Alongside the gutted husks of buildings lay burned-out tanks and other armored vehicles. More wrecked military vehicles clogged the off-ramp and the road up the hill.

They slowed to maneuver around the burned-out wreckage of a helicopter that had fallen or been shot down over the freeway. Eliza stared out the window, and could see only devastation: a swath of burned, destroyed buildings, entire blocks where it was impossible to tell street from house. Not a tree to be seen.

"It's worse than Las Vegas," Steve said. "What the hell were they fighting over?"

They continued into the northern part of the county, where one town after the next lay devastated: Pleasant Grove, American Fork, Lehi. Tens of thousands had made these cities their homes, but now there was nothing. Not a single person, not a sign of life. Most of the buildings had burned, leaving behind only billboards, an entire forest of them lining the freeway like metal trees, advertising long-dead businesses.

It took an hour to cross the next stretch of ten miles. Wrecked vehicles, both civilian and military, clogged the lanes in both directions, and bomb craters had rendered other portions of the road hazardous. Weeds and brush were already growing up through the gaps left by the battle.

They weaved back and forth, pushing aside smaller vehicles, running onto the shoulder, or crossing to the other side to get around the biggest craters. The dead traffic cleared out when they reached the Point of the Mountain, the freeway pass that led up and out of Utah Valley and down into Salt Lake Valley.

When they reached the top of the pass, with its view over Salt Lake and its suburbs, Steve pulled to a stop. They got out and stared, neither speaking for a long moment.

A million people had lived in the valley before the collapse. Now it was a wasteland.

"And the city shall lie in dust," Eliza said.

"What?"

"Something Fernie said to me, once. When she and Jacob lived in the Avenues above Temple Square during his residency, she had a dream, a vision, really, that Salt Lake would be destroyed. In the dream, Fernie was walking the streets of the city and all the buildings were burning. Ash was falling from the sky."

"Is there any point?" he said. "Should we turn around?"

She sighed. "I was hoping . . ."

"Yeah, me too." He squeezed her hand. "It will be okay."

"I hope so."

"It will be," Steve said, more insistently this time. "We're not alone. Our people are still alive and fighting."

Eliza smiled at this. *Our* people. Not your people.

"We'll go home," he added, "tell them what we found, and make the most of it. At the end of the day, we're still the lucky ones, right?"

"Let's be sure," she said.

Eliza grabbed the binoculars and an assault rifle from the truck. She didn't see the slightest risk of attack, but it seemed like a wise precaution, anyway. She handed Steve the gun and lifted the binoculars to study the scene.

She started with the south end of the valley. Ruins and destruction everywhere. More towns completely annihilated. Farther north and west, the towns were in somewhat better condition, with several vast subdivisions seemingly untouched except for their missing trees. But there was nobody on the streets, no movement that she could spot. Tumbleweeds had blown out of the western deserts and piled into house-size mounds in driveways and parking lots. Continuing north, she saw abandoned shopping centers. The LDS temple at Daybreak was a gaunt skeleton on its hill, the spire toppled. Then there was a stretched of burned, emptied land for several miles. East of the freeway was more of the same.

There were still buildings standing in downtown Salt Lake, and she could even spot the main temple at Temple Square, but that was so far to the north that it was impossible to pick out details, even with the binoculars at their highest magnification. No doubt downtown had been gutted by war and fire as well.

"Hey, what's that?" Steve asked. "See that big line?"

"Where? I don't see anything."

"Here, let me have a look."

She handed him the binoculars. He lifted them, lowered them again as if to pick out landmarks, then held them steady. He let out a low whistle.

"Check it out. About 1300 South, follow the freeway exit east toward the university. Yep, it's definitely something."

She was squinting, unable to see what had caught his eye. She could see all the way to downtown, but couldn't pick out anything in particular from this distance except for the larger buildings.

Until Steve handed her the binoculars. Then she found it at once.

It was a wall. A berm of dirt and rubble ran in a straight line from the freeway along the southern edge of downtown, then all the way up to the foothills and the University of Utah, where she lost track of the wall around the football stadium. She'd missed the wall the first time; perhaps sweeping over the berm she'd dismissed it as more bombed-out rubble.

"That's not following 1300 South," she said. "More like Ninth. It climbs the hill and hooks toward the football stadium at the U."

"Yeah, but what is it?"

"A wall." Eliza shifted the binoculars back down toward the freeway and found where the berm cut north. "A two-story wall of dirt and pavement and wrecked buildings. That took an awful lot of manpower to build."

"Must have been vicious fighting to force that. And at the end of the day, that's all they saved? That little square downtown?"

"You save what you can," she said. "Toss it up, protect a few square miles. The rest of the city is lost—hold on to what you can."

"It's like the Dark Ages all over again," Steve said.

The thought was chilling. It had only been a few years since the supervolcano exploded and the crops failed. Already the center had collapsed out of the most powerful nation in the history of the world. There was no government left, no civilization—not in this part of the country, at least. Only a few frightened, huddled communities fighting off the wandering, starving survivors.

They passed the binoculars back and forth. Eliza wondered if there was someone on the wall looking back at them. Perhaps the alarm had already been raised, and the battle-hardened survivors of Salt Lake City were scrambling to prepare a defense against this strange armored car lingering on the outskirts of the valley.

"What now?" Steve asked.

"Somehow, we've got to approach the wall, indicate we're peaceful, and see if they'll let us in." Eliza nodded. "And we find out who is in charge."

★★★

Eliza and Steve rolled up from the southern half of the valley, approaching the city itself at a creeping, unthreatening pace. Before leaving the Point of the Mountain, they'd stuck a pair of rifle butts out the gun ports on either side and tied a white sheet around either one. By the time they reached the 4500 South off-ramp, they were driving slowly enough that any watchers would have time to study the sheets and determine the vehicle didn't pose a threat.

But that didn't mean Eliza wasn't bracing for attack. The world may have lost its governments, its farmland, its networks of trade, but it was awash in weapons and ammunition. Any survivors must by definition have enough firepower to defend themselves. With the National Guard armories in Salt Lake, plus Hill Air Force Base up in Ogden, the survivors would surely have heavy weaponry as well.

And the closer they got to the center of town, the more evidence they saw of a major battle: wrecked tanks, a downed helicopter, gutted Humvees, and armored personnel carriers. There were a few dead, withered bodies, and animal-gnawed bones jutting from khaki pants.

They stopped the vehicle at the 900 South off-ramp. The wind blew from the west, sending plastic bags and tumbleweeds across the roadbed. The off-ramp continued until the curve, where it had been torn up to prevent passage.

"We found them," Steve said, his gravelly voice turning grim. "Look."

What she'd taken for a series of bomb craters between the exit lane and the freeway were really foxholes. Camouflage netting covered a dug-in artillery piece, and the tips of two antitank guns jutted out from behind sandbags, aiming in their direction.

"I don't see people, though," she said. "You're sure they're manned?"

"I saw movement. Stay here."

Steve opened the door and waved his arm before she could ask him what he meant. When that failed to draw a response, he emerged slowly from the truck, leaving the door open. He stepped back and grabbed the white sheet from the rifle butt on his side of the vehicle, then walked in front of the truck with the sheet outstretched.

"Hello? Is anyone there? We come in peace."

This last bit sounded clichéd, but seemed to have the desired effect. Two men with assault rifles climbed out of one of the holes. They wore uniforms, which made Eliza nervous. The men approached warily, while behind them, one of the antitank guns moved back and forth, as if to inform the strangers that they were one ill-advised move from annihilation.

There was no way Eliza would leave Steve alone to face whatever awaited him, so she opened her door slowly and waved her hands before coming out. She put her hands on her head and waited for the men to approach. They crossed the stretch of broken-up pavement and stopped some twenty feet away.

"Who are you?" one of the men asked. "And what do you want?"

He had a Utah accent. Young guy, maybe twenty. Blond, wholesome look, like the families from old-time pioneer stock. The same pioneer stock that had sired Eliza. The other man was Hispanic, but he too, seemed like a young, frightened kid. She could imagine the horrors these two had seen.

When Eliza spotted the uniforms, she'd been afraid this was an army base. Fernie had come back from the Green River refugee camp to tell Eliza that Salt Lake was under partial Federal control. Maybe there was no one left up here but military.

But the appearance of these kids, plus the one boy's Utah accent, gave her renewed hope. She decided to take a chance.

"We're citizens of Utah," Eliza said, "looking to make contact with the state government. Does it still exist?"

The young men looked back and forth between each other. The blond kid shrugged and his companion glanced back toward the foxhole, as if seeking instructions from a superior.

"Is there a government?" Eliza pressed. "Is there a mayor of Salt Lake? A city council? Who is in charge?"

"The governor runs things," the blond kid said. "Jim McKay."

CHAPTER THIRTY

The soldiers didn't abuse the newcomers, but Eliza and Jim were treated like prisoners. After cuffing their hands behind their back, a pair of soldiers led them down the off-ramp and up to 900 South and the outer edge of the wall of rubble and dirt. Behind them, more men inspected the Methuselah tank.

Steve cast a worried glance over his shoulder at her. "Jim McKay," he muttered to Eliza. "Isn't that wonderful?"

The McKays were their old nemeses in the state government. The brothers were cousins of Eliza's father, Abraham Christianson. When he was senator, Jim McKay had instructed his brother Parley, the attorney general, to go after the polygamists to demonstrate to the evangelicals in the Republican Party that he had severed all ties to his fundamentalist relatives. Later, as governor, Jim McKay had been involved in that business stealing Blister Creek's grain to ship it to the Green River refugee camp.

Eliza had hoped to come into the city, tell the government about Blister Creek, report what they'd seen along the road from Southern Utah, and see if they could establish a connection between her hometown and the government. But McKay was their enemy. And he apparently ruled over a walled city like some sort of medieval fortress.

A few blocks later, the wall jogged across the street to enclose a squat brick building that still carried the sign of the credit union it had once housed. Men sat at machine guns on the roof, while others squatted in bunkers on either side of the front doors. There was some discussion between their guards and a uniformed woman who seemed to be in charge here, before the guards led Steve and Eliza into the credit union lobby and through the building.

Eliza blinked in surprise when they emerged on the inside of the city wall. Most of the buildings on the interior were gone: the chain restaurants, motels, condos, and working-class houses that had lined the streets on this side of town.

The ground had been meticulously cleared of rubble, the foundations filled in. In the place of buildings was what appeared to be the world's largest community garden—raised beds and fields and even new vines and tiny fruit trees, crisscrossed by the gridded streets of pioneer-era Utah. Men, women, and children worked by hand weeding and pruning. Irrigation ditches passed through culverts beneath the streets to emerge in fields and gardens.

"Mormons," Steve said, admiringly. "You've got to hand it to them. They know how to organize."

Eliza felt a glow of pride at this, even though these people were mainstream LDS, who had been hostile to the polygamist sects for a hundred years now. But they were cousins of her church, born of the same heritage.

And it wasn't just Mormons who had survived. Modern Salt Lake had been a large, diverse city, and she caught glimpses of people from different ethnicities: Hispanics, Asians, and even a few Polynesians and African Americans. Some of the workers wore tank tops and shorts, which meant they weren't even LDS, since they couldn't be wearing LDS undergarments beneath their clothes.

While most of the land had been cleared for gardens, many of the larger office buildings or apartments remained, and it was here that people lived. Clotheslines hung out laundry to dry, with large, multifamily outhouses out back, together with pens for pigs and chickens. No cattle that she could see, but they would be difficult to care for without fodder or grazing land.

"Where are we going, the Capitol Building?" Eliza asked the guards.

The blond kid gave her a look. "That was destroyed last year in an airstrike. The governor rules from Temple Square."

★★★

"Sorry about the cuffs," McKay said. "People these days can be . . . *zealous.*" He nodded at the two young men who'd brought in Eliza and Steve. "You can leave us."

Eliza rubbed her wrists and watched the departing soldiers as they shut the door to the office behind them. The only light inside the office was sunlight streaming through the windows. McKay had a big map of Utah on one wall, marked with hundreds of pins of various colors. What they meant, she couldn't guess.

McKay himself looked older, thinner, and more careworn than she remembered from seeing him on TV. His hair had gone gray, and worry lines spread from the corners of his mouth. But far from looking beaten down, there was something hard and determined in his expression.

"You know who we are, right?" Eliza asked, surprised that they'd been left alone with the governor.

"Of course," McKay said. "You're my first cousin, once removed. One of Abraham's daughters. This is Steve . . . um, Kravitz? FBI."

"Krantz," Steve said.

"Right. How is your partner? I can't remember her name, but she was LDS, I remember."

"Agent Fayer died last year," Steve said. "Picked up cholera in Las Vegas and we didn't get her to Dr. Christianson in time."

"I'm sorry to hear that. How is Dr. Christianson? And his wife, Fernie. How is she?"

Eliza frowned, her suspicion growing. McKay had seemed momentarily surprised when the guards appeared at his door with the prisoners, but had recovered quickly. Too quickly. He seemed pleased—no doubt he was delighted to have his old enemies fall into his hands.

Eliza had once served as a sister missionary in this very building during her ill-advised attempt to leave Blister Creek and join the mainstream church. All of the old missionary stuff was gone, and it seemed to serve as offices for what remained of the state government, the state itself now reduced to a few square miles and the survivors hiding within the city walls.

"They're good," she said cautiously.

"I'm glad to hear it. I want to thank Fernie someday."

"Hmm."

"I've been inside all morning," the governor said. "Would you two come outside and walk around the square with me?"

Eliza glanced at Steve, who nodded. They followed the governor outside.

She was surprised at how little Temple Square had changed. The temple and its spires still dominated one end, with the rest of the block taken up by the turtle-shaped tabernacle, the visitors' centers, and the outdoor gardens. Miraculously, gardeners were still caring for the flower beds. And there were still trees, their leafy branches spreading welcome shade. The entire scene provided a haven of unexpected and welcome beauty. With the walls of the square itself encircling the block, it was easy to pretend that nothing had changed.

McKay took a deep breath. He led the two newcomers toward the temple. It loomed cathedral-like over them, much larger than Blister Creek's smaller temple. The three of them took a seat on a bench in the sunlight.

"What happened here, Mr. McKay?" Eliza asked. "Who attacked you?"

"Federal troops. The government declared Utah in a state of rebellion."

After the Battle of Las Vegas, the governor explained, the army had withdrawn from Nevada. Technically, the Federal government had won the battle, having thrashed the rebellious Californians and driven them from Vegas. But the army had been unable to mount an offensive to reclaim the Pacific states. Stretched supply lines collapsed, leaving them without food. They'd rolled into northern Utah to scavenge. Civilians who had been living on their food storage found their pantries raided, their gardens picked over by thousands of troops.

People resisted. There were incidents. Martial law was declared. An army general hanged dozens, including mayors, Mormon bishops, and even the president of BYU when he refused to allow the military to turn the campus into a military encampment. Soon, the region was in full rebellion.

"We won," McKay said grimly. "But only because we killed all of them and they only killed ninety percent of us."

"Ninety percent." Eliza couldn't keep the horror out of her voice.

He told how the battle had progressed. The army had destroyed Utah County first, fought a battle with the Utahns at Point of the

Mountain, then swept into the Salt Lake Valley. There, they wiped out one town after another until they were finally stopped at the hastily constructed city wall. And if the army hadn't run low on food and ammo, they'd have overrun downtown, as well.

"Most of our people died from disease and starvation—that's the way of a siege. Hunger weakens you, and disease finishes you off."

"But still, ninety percent. So many."

"Yes."

"Two million people lived on the Wasatch Front," Steve said, his brow furrowed. "That still leaves a couple hundred thousand people. Do you have that many living here?"

"Ninety percent of *what was left,*" McKay said. "We'd already suffered terribly when they came. The current population of Salt Lake is thirty-two thousand. That's all that remains of the two million." He looked at Eliza. "I imagine you've gone through much of the same in Blister Creek."

She looked down at her hands, suddenly guilty that she'd suffered so little while the rest of the world had collapsed.

"No?" he said, a frown spreading.

"I'm sorry, we haven't. We were attacked, and some people have died because of inadequate medical care. But—" She hesitated. If McKay were their enemy, he would show it now. "But there are more people in town than ever. New babies keep getting born."

McKay stared at her. A deep pain flickered across his face, a hint of anger. Steve stiffened next to Eliza, as if prepared to fight if the governor turned violent.

Then McKay turned away with a groan. "I should have known. After what happened with Fernie Christianson, why would I be surprised?"

Eliza had heard of Fernie's encounter with the governor at the Green River refugee camp two years earlier, near the beginning of the crisis. But Fernie had been reluctant to share details. Eliza was now curious.

"What do you mean?"

"Fernie saved my life, you know. The mob was going to tear me apart, and that woman in her wheelchair stood them off. Bravest thing I've ever seen. And the most righteous. She could have let me die, probably should have. She didn't. It was like she had the hand of—well, I don't want to get too mystic about it, but something changed in me that day."

"I can see that, the way you've held this together."

"I haven't managed very well. Our food supplies are gone, and all we have left is what we can grow ourselves. It's not enough. We need more farmland, for one, but there are hundreds, maybe thousands of lawless people out there. Bandits and murderers, rogue army units. Mostly men, mostly young. They're desperate and violent. People venture out, they get killed."

"I still don't understand what you mean when you said you should have known," Eliza said.

"I should have known that if anywhere would be safe and protected, it would be Blister Creek. You were organized. Prepared." He sighed and looked down. "If only we'd pulled together sooner."

"You pulled together better than Las Vegas," Steve said. "That's *completely* gone."

"I know, I heard."

"What else do you know?" Steve asked. "Is there anything left out there?"

It turned out that McKay had been in radio contact with a handful of other towns across the heartland of the continent: Boulder, Rexburg, Helena, Omaha, Duluth, Cardston, Lubbock, Lincoln. Through them, he'd received news from more distant places.

Most of what was left of the country was clinging to the coasts, with the center of the nation a vast, burned-over wasteland. Tens of millions had starved on the East Coast, but there were still a number of smaller towns and some sort of military regime centered in the New York area. But entire states had gone black. Canada and Mexico had fared similarly, with the northern neighbor freezing and the country to the south falling into drought and famine and disease.

Outside of North America, Europe had fared badly, the freezing weather devastating agriculture and leaving them in famine. The Middle East was in even worse shape, torn by conflict and heavily reliant on imported food. After the American war in the Gulf, Israel had expended its nuclear weapons as a last-ditch effort to keep out millions of starving, armed Arabs.

There had been fewer wars in Africa, but most of the continent had simply starved to death, except, people said, the least developed regions. The poor, rural villages had never been connected to the rest of the regional or global economy, and with their tropical climates had better weathered the volcanic winter. Or so it was speculated. Nobody knew for sure.

Nobody had any information about India or Pakistan since their nuclear war, but they were presumed gone. Another nuclear exchange had occurred in East Asia during the Sino-Japanese War. Hundreds of millions of Chinese had died of famine and disease, even though they had ultimately won the war. Nobody knew if Japan had been completely overrun by the Chinese or not.

Southeast Asia had lost its rice crop for two straight years and starved. Apparently Australia had been doing relatively well until a massive flotilla filled with millions of Asian refugees had overwhelmed the country. After that, the country had gone dark, but it was a big continent, with a vast interior. Who knew?

"What about New Zealand?" Steve said.

McKay shrugged. "No idea."

"South America?" Steve asked.

"Doing better than most. Brazil fell into chaos and anarchy, but for some reason the volcano left Argentina's wheat belt relatively unscathed. They still have a central government. So does Chile. I don't know about the northern part of the continent, or Central America either."

"Maybe in a hundred years people will look back and say that this is when Argentina first became the most powerful country on earth," Steve said.

"If there's anyone left to look back," the governor said. "From where I sit, it seems like we're still spiraling down. Maybe it won't stop. Maybe this is the end." He eyed the other two. "Why did you come to Salt Lake?"

"My brother thinks it's time to rebuild," Eliza said.

McKay looked baffled. "Now?"

"Salt Lake is standing. Battered, but alive. Cedar City was too, last time we heard."

The governor gave a grim shake of the head. "Not anymore. The army rolled through on its way up I-15. It was wiped out."

"Maybe so," she conceded, "but there are people in Richfield who were organized enough that they drove us off when we tried to pass through."

"Really?" The governor sounded pleasantly surprised. "I hadn't heard anything about it."

"I'll bet there are more towns," she said. "In fact, I'm sure of it. Come on inside to your maps, I'll show you what I mean."

Back in his office, she explained her thoughts to Steve and the governor. Running on the east side of the mountain range from the freeway, a series of valleys stretched for sixty miles between Richfield on the south and Mount Pleasant and Moroni on the north, with several towns in between, including Manti, with its Mormon temple, and Ephraim, formerly the site of a small community college. There would be lots of shared knowledge there, including people who knew how to live off the land, plus it was heavily Mormon and community-oriented.

Eliza ran her finger along the communities in question. "If the army came straight up I-15 on the opposite side of the mountains, they'd have bypassed all of it. There are enough people to band together whenever bandits or irregulars try to break through. There might be thousands of people, for all we know.

"Now look," she continued. "We have Blister Creek way down here, then the farming communities, then the main valleys of the Wasatch Front. Forget about the I-15 corridor south for the moment. We can't hold it if anyone invades from California or Arizona, anyway. These mountainous regions are easier to defend."

"If only we had a way to resettle Utah County," McKay said. He sounded intrigued as he studied the map. "Then we'd have a near-continuous corridor between Richfield and Salt Lake. You'd still be isolated down there, but you could help protect us from the south."

"What if we brought you fifteen hundred refugees," Steve said with a glance at Eliza, whose eyes widened in understanding. "Could you help them build another fort in Utah County? Then you'd have safe territory for farming between Salt Lake and Provo."

"Sure, if you can get me some refugees, and if they'll cooperate."

"What do you think?" Steve asked Eliza. "Is it worth a try?"

Resettling in Provo had to be better than the miserable conditions at the reservoir. There was plenty of land to clear for fields in Utah County, plus good water and proximity to the hard-earned knowledge in Salt Lake. What's more, she imagined there were thousands more refugees out there, not just in Utah, but surrounding states, who had suffered terribly but somehow stayed alive while their families and friends died. If word got out that there was a stable, protected government on the Wasatch Front, they would come. A chance to escape the chaos, to return to some sort of normal routine, a hope for a real life again.

Eliza hesitated. "People can be stubborn. And there's bad blood between us."

"That's all the more reason to get the squatters up here and away from Blister Creek," Steve said. "Anyway, I bet they'd do it if we promised some of our food storage to help them get established."

"Are you kidding, you still have food storage?" McKay said. "How much?"

"Most of it," Eliza said. "We barely touched it."

"Sweet heavens, you people truly are blessed."

"If the squatters don't take the deal, they're fools," Steve said.

"That's only half our problem," she said. "People like Elder Smoot won't give up our grain without a fight. Not even for a deal that would get rid of the squatters once and for all."

"If *we* don't take the deal," Steve said, "we're even bigger fools."

CHAPTER THIRTY-ONE

Jacob was rehearsing his speech for the funeral when his wives entered the bedroom. Fernie came in first, in her wheelchair, followed by Jessie Lyn. He folded the pieces of paper he'd written his speech on and stuck them into his back pocket.

"Any news from Eliza?" he asked.

"We want to hear the speech," Fernie said.

"You'll hear it in a couple of hours."

"Then let us read it." Fernie held out her hand. "Come on, hand it over."

Jessie Lyn raised her eyebrows. "We're serious, Jacob. We want to see it."

He looked back and forth between the two women. "So this is

what a conspiracy of wives feels like. I finally know what the other men are talking about."

Fernie rolled forward in her chair. "You know why we want to see it."

"This is about us too," Jessie Lyn said. "Not just you. Our kids and families."

"I'm not leaving Blister Creek," Jacob said, "if that's what you're worried about. But it's time to have a hard talk."

Fernie reached him in the chair and leaned forward to try to get the folded-up papers from his back pocket. "Great, then you'll have no problem letting us read it."

He put his hand over the pocket and held out his other hand to keep her at bay. "What are worried about?"

"Are you kidding?" Fernie said. "We're on the verge of the Second Coming and you're going to abrogate your responsibilities. Forgive me, but I find that concerning."

"I have my own worries," Jessie Lyn said, and she did look upset, her earnest face scrunched up, her lips pressed together. "It's no secret what you think about polygamy, and I know this has been hard for you, taking on a second wife. If you give up your calling, does that mean you give up on me too? If you leave and you take Fernie, will you abandon me here?" She put a hand on her belly. "What about our child?"

"I would never do that."

"Do you promise?"

"Can't you both trust me? Just for a few hours?"

"The way you were talking when you came home this morning, no," Fernie said.

"Miriam's blood was still on my hands," he said, frustrated. "My brother was out of his mind. I hadn't slept much in two days. I was saying all sorts of stuff, not all of it well-considered. I'm feeling calmer now, less rash."

"Great, then let's hear it," Fernie said.

Jacob shook his head. "No, not yet."

"You want us to trust you," Jessie Lyn said, "but in a good marriage, trust goes both ways. We're your wives. We love you. You need to trust us, talk this out. If you've got big changes in mind, let us give input before you chisel anything into stone."

Fernie had turned her chair during this, and now she reached back toward Jessie Lyn. The younger woman took Fernie's hand and came to stand by her sister wife. They both looked at him expectantly.

"I can't tell you," Jacob said, "because I'm still trying to work it out myself."

"Let's see what you've written," Fernie said. "Please."

He sighed and reached into his back pocket to remove the papers. "Okay, but like I said, this is an opening. It's not done yet."

"As it should be," Fernie said, taking the papers and unfolding them. "That leaves room for promptings from the spirit."

She read through the pages while Jessie Lyn looked over her shoulder. Jacob turned and stared out the window. The sun was out, the sky blue. Children were playing on the swing set between the two Christianson houses. It looked so peaceful.

But then a cart pulled up in front of David's house, pulled by a draft horse, and led by Elder Griggs. It had come for the casket. In a few minutes Jacob would go next door to help David load the coffin into the back of the cart. Men were already at the cemetery, digging two graves. One was for Grover, killed two nights ago, but not yet buried. The second was for Miriam. Another tragic multiple funeral for Blister Creek.

And what of Eliza? Still no word from his sister or her husband. When he thought about them, the bands of worry tightened around his chest until he could scarcely breathe.

Let it end. Let this be the last time.

But the squatters were still at the reservoir. They had not yet attacked the freshly reinforced bunker, currently manned with twenty men and women from the valley. Maybe they wouldn't—Miriam and Jacob must have gutted the gathering invasion force. But so long as they were up there, Blister Creek would always be at risk.

He'd slept about six hours before getting up to work on his funeral speech. It was enough rest to shake the bone-wearying exhaustion, but not enough to leave his mind clear and sharp. He'd struggled over the words and was unsatisfied with either the content or its presentation.

Fernie rustled the pages behind him. "Jacob, about the speech . . ."

He turned. "So, no word from Eliza?"

"Don't change the subject."

"Is there a part you think is wrong?"

Fernie handed the speech to Jessie Lyn. "Are you sure this is wise?"

"No, I'm not. I'm not sure of anything."

"So many doubts," Fernie said as Jessie Lyn read the pages with a frown spreading across her face. "I knew what I was getting when I agreed to marry you. It takes courage to walk against a huge crowd all marching in the opposite direction. I admire you for that. But still—"

"I'm not sure how much courage I have, but okay."

"But when you speak tonight, promise me you'll do one thing. That's all I ask."

"What is that, Fernie?"

"Open yourself to inspiration. Call it what you want, divine or not, but let yourself be open to whatever comes in the moment."

He looked back and forth between the two women as Jessie Lyn handed him the papers. Footsteps creaked in the attic overhead. From the room next door came the sound of one of Father's widows singing with her daughters. From outside, he could hear his son Daniel shouting excitedly about something. Downstairs, the door banged open. More noisy kids. So many people in the house. Always so many people.

And so much responsibility weighing on Jacob's shoulders, starting in this room and radiating outward. His children, the larger family. The people of Blister Creek. All waiting for him to step forward at the funeral and say something wise. Something that would make sense of it all. Sorry, but his well of wisdom had run dry. He had nothing for them.

"Daddy, Daddy!" a girl cried. Leah burst into the room, followed by Daniel. His son's and daughter's faces lit up with excitement.

"It's Eliza!" Daniel cried. "She's on the radio."

★★★

"Well, big brother," Eliza's voice crackled cheerfully on the other end after he'd shooed everyone out of his clinic. "Took you long enough. Didn't Elder Smoot tell you I'd called? I had expected you to have the radio glued to your ear, waiting for my call."

For a second, he had to put down the receiver, he was so overcome with emotion. Eliza's cheerful voice told him everything he needed to know. She was safe, and so was Steve.

"Are you there? Jacob?"

"I'm here."

"Is everything all right?" Now there was a touch of worry on the other end.

He didn't want to explain, not over the radio. He just wanted her to come home, then he could tell her everything.

"Are you still in Salt Lake City?" he asked. "How can you hear me so well?" The radio didn't have enough power to stretch all the way across the mountains and desert between here and there.

"We're in Richfield, actually. But don't worry, everything is fine. They're friendly."

"When did you get there? Smoot said you'd called from Salt Lake."

Eliza explained, starting with their long journey along the Wasatch Front and its scenes of destruction. To hear that fighting, starvation, and disease had obliterated cities once holding two million people was not a surprise, but left him staggered nonetheless. Provo and Orem were gone. Salt Lake was reduced to a few square miles. And their old nemesis, Governor McKay, was still in charge. Only he apparently wasn't their nemesis anymore.

After leaving Salt Lake, Eliza and Steve had driven down the Sanpete Valley at the head of a small convoy of vehicles, led by the Methuselah tank. They'd established contact with Moroni on the northern edge of the valley, and word had spread through the other towns. The government convoy had then spent the past twenty-four hours speaking with a motley collection of mayors, Mormon bishops and stake presidents, and city councils who served as governments of the surviving towns.

Thirty-two thousand people survived in the Salt Lake Valley, another seventeen thousand in the Sanpete Valley, and now Eliza and Steve were coming back with several representatives from the state government. The government officials would stop at the squatter camp with the promise of land and peaceful settlement in Utah County. The squatters would leave. Together, they would form a string of well-protected settlements from Blister Creek to Salt Lake.

It was everything Jacob had hoped for, a core of survivors who would begin the daunting task of rebuilding. But after last night's ugliness, Eliza would be lucky to make it back to Blister Creek past the reservoir.

"Be careful when you approach," he said. "There was more trouble with the squatters."

"Is everything okay?"

"Another battle. Not like last year, but people were killed. Emotions will be riding high."

"Did we lose any saints?" Her voice was pinched with worry.

Jacob's stomach dropped.

Grover. Miriam. Chambers. Ezekiel.

"Yes, a few. Not like last time, but too many."

She was silent a few moments, and he was about to ask if she was still there. Then she let out a weary sigh. "It feels petty to complain. We've lost so few compared to others. The destruction in Provo and Salt Lake . . . if only you could see it."

That may be true, but Eliza had neglected to ask *whom* they'd lost. She'd have taken Grover's death hard enough—the boy had been a faithful companion during her expedition last year to rescue Steve from Las Vegas. But losing Miriam would devastate her, as it had devastated the rest of the family. What was a million dead elsewhere to the loss of one's own family member?

"I hope this is the end," Eliza said. "No more killing."

"No more," Jacob agreed. He cleared his throat. "About the ones we lost . . . there's something you should know."

CHAPTER THIRTY-TWO

They came by the hundreds from all across Blister Creek, arriving on foot and horse and bicycle. They gathered at the cemetery south of town, where Jacob waited with his family at the top of the grassy hillock, surrounded by weathered, hundred-year-old gravestones.

Fernie, in her wheelchair, took one of Jacob's hands and Jessie Lyn took his other. Children had set out blankets on the grass and sat down amidst their parents, who gathered in knots, talking and whispering.

Jacob extracted himself from the two women to shake hands with Elder Smoot. The older man looked weathered, beaten. He leaned on his black mahogany cane with its beehive handle, and for once it didn't look like an affectation. He seemed to have aged fifteen years in two days. Two sons, taken away so quickly. A third lost last summer.

"I'm sorry for your loss," Jacob said.

Smoot lowered his eyes. "I should be the one apologizing to you, Brother Jacob. If I had been a better father, this evil never would have entered our valley."

There was plenty of fault with Smoot's handling of events. Jacob had wondered a dozen times how things might have turned out differently if the man had said something when Jacob, David, and Miriam confronted him at the bunker that first night. But now was not the time for accusations, not when Jacob was suffering his own guilt for letting Miriam infiltrate the camp.

"A man is only responsible for his own actions, Brother," Jacob said. "Nobody led your son down that dark path. He chose it for himself."

"Then you forgive me?"

"There is nothing to forgive."

Smoot's eyes welled up. "You are too merciful." He stopped, unable to continue for a moment. "My daughter Lillian said . . . is it true? Please tell me it's not."

Jacob glanced up to see that Lillian was approaching with David. Even more awkwardly, David's other living wife was Sister Clarissa, who had been a wife of Bill Smoot, Elder Smoot's son killed by the drone strike last summer. David's two wives each had ties to the Smoot family, while Miriam had been killed as a result of Smoot's son.

Smoot glanced up, saw them coming, and turned away to join his family without waiting to hear Jacob's answer. The Smoots were gathering around Grover's open grave. David watched him go, face unreadable. Then he left his surviving wives and approached Jacob.

The two brothers said nothing, only embraced, looked into each other's eyes, and embraced again. When David pulled away, he returned to Lillian and Clarissa, and the three of them walked to Miriam's open grave. Jacob sighed and looked away.

The sky was clear and blue, as it had been for days. Unlike the cold and rainy spring months of the past couple of years, it was seasonably warm and dry. The grass was a little greener, the wildflowers fresher, but there was no question that the old climate had begun to reassert itself across the desert Southwest.

And looking north toward Witch's Warts to Jacob's right, with the town on his left, everything looked normal: the leafy cottonwoods, the creek carrying its reddish, bubbling current. The white spire of the temple. The salmon-pink cliffs to the north and the mountain ranges shielding the valley on the east and west. Everything was as it had been for generations.

Jacob's father would have recognized the scene. His grandparents. All the way back to Great-Great-Grandmother Cowley, the founder of this town, whose gravestone rested under his hand, the sandstone warm and living beneath his touch.

HENRIETTA R. COWLEY—1872–1969
LAY ME UP ONE THOUSAND BUSHELS OF WHEAT

He was looking back toward the center of town at the last few stragglers when his eyes fell on Eliza and Steve. They walked side by side down the sidewalk, ignoring the stares and whispers. As the two came up through cemetery, Jacob could see people lean in to question them, no doubt wondering what they'd seen in Salt Lake. Eliza and Steve gave curt answers and continued into the cemetery.

After Eliza had finished embracing Fernie and several other family members, she came up to Jacob with her eyes shining. She threw her arms around him and he held him tightly for a long moment, overcome with emotion.

"I'd about given up," he said.

"The business at the reservoir took longer than expected."

"No more trouble, I hope."

"Could have been worse," Eliza said. "They were beaten and discouraged. McQueen was killed in the fight. He'd been single-handedly holding them together, and they'd lost anyone else who might have taken over. Toss in the fact that they haven't had a meal in two days. You could say they were a receptive audience."

"So when do they leave for Provo?"

"As soon as we provide them with food and supplies for the journey. Maybe as soon as the weekend."

That was perfect. Jacob would send up food as a goodwill gesture as soon as the funeral ended, but wait until morning before organizing a full shipment. Then he remembered what he intended to say to the gathered church members.

Eliza studied his face, seeming to notice his scowl. "Important speech?"

"You could say that."

"Don't do anything rash."

"What makes you say that?"

"I know you, big brother. I can read it in your face."

Jacob looked around to see that the crowd was all gathered. The noise of a hundred different conversations had become a low roar. It was time to start the funeral.

★★★

They began with Grover. The young man had only recently received his endowments and his family had dressed him in his temple robes. But his machete wounds had been disfiguring and it would have taken a skilled mortician to make him presentable. There was no such person, so the coffin had been sealed ahead of time.

Elder Smoot dedicated the grave, his voice breaking several times during the prayer. When he was finished, his family surrounded him, so many wives and children that he disappeared in the midst of them all. Then they lowered Grover's simple pine box into the grave, and people shoveled a few scoops of reddish dirt onto the coffin.

Miriam's coffin was open. She appeared almost to be sleeping, except that she was so pale behind her veil that she looked almost translucent. Her two wounds lay hidden beneath the white of her temple robes, with towels wrapped around her chest cavity to absorb any blood that might have leaked through.

David looked almost as pale as his dead wife as he leaned over to kiss her forehead before they closed the coffin. When it was shut, he folded his arms to dedicate the grave. His first words trembled and Jacob worried he would break down, join the soft crying rippling through the extended Christianson family. But David steadied himself, and said the rest of the prayer in a clear, calm voice.

When he was done, they lowered the coffin into the ground, which brought a fresh round of sobs from the crowd. Miriam's adopted son, Diego, tossed in the first shovelful of dirt. He looked so solemn in his tie and white shirt, his black hair neatly parted and slicked down. A lump rose in Jacob's throat. He took a deep breath to calm himself. He couldn't lose it now.

One by one, Miriam's family came to toss in a shovelful of dirt, including Jacob. He had recovered his emotions by this time, and when he passed off the shovel, grabbed his brother in a fierce embrace. David buried his head on Jacob's shoulder. This time he wept openly. Jacob joined him.

When the top of the coffin was covered with dirt and rock, the family members stepped back. The two bodies were in the ground, dressed in their temple robes, their graves dedicated. Miriam and Grover were prepared to rise on the Morning of the First Resurrection.

There were two dead men who would not receive the same treatment. Chambers's body had been recovered from the base of the Ghost Cliffs where Miriam had shot him, and would be quietly buried later. Ezekiel's body should be reclaimed from the squatter camp, but few would be in the mood to mourn him.

The crowd hushed and gathered closer. Expectant faces looked up at Jacob. He paused to think about the past two days and everything they'd suffered. Four years had passed since his father was killed, and it felt like Jacob's leadership had lurched from one crisis to the next.

I'm so weak. Is there no one else?

Jacob made his decision. He lifted his voice, speaking in a clear, commanding tone that could reach the back of the crowd.

"You've all seen Grandma Cowley's gravestone. 'Lay up a thousand bushels of wheat.' Nobody quite knows what that means, except that it speaks to prudence and preparation. Maybe that's all. But maybe not. In the past few years it was impossible not to read those words as a warning to brace ourselves for the coming of the Great and Dreadful Day of the Lord.

"We laid aside our bushels of wheat," Jacob continued. "But that wheat never saved our lives. That's the strange thing. Here we are, three years later, and we've barely touched our stores, because we've been able to grow food, even with the late frosts and the flooding. Others haven't been so fortunate, and I can't help but think if we'd been more generous with outsiders we might have avoided the violent confrontations that have shaken our community."

He stopped to let that sink in. Then he spent a few minutes laying out Eliza and the governor's plan for moving the squatters to northern Utah. To help them survive the journey, Blister Creek would surrender hundreds of tons of wheat, beans, and corn, plus wagonloads of other valuable supplies. All to buy off the squatters and send them away.

Yet nobody protested. There were no whispers, no scowls, only agreement on their faces. Even Elder Smoot nodded solemnly, as if yes, of course, this was the only possible path to take.

Jacob thought about what Eliza had said about the refugees. Beat down and discouraged. They weren't the only ones. A few days ago many of these same saints had been so concerned about the stolen food that they'd been willing to entertain Ezekiel's claim that Jacob was a fallen prophet. Now, after seeing how the alternative had played out—a hard, aggressive posture toward the refugees that led to more deaths—they were willing to give it all away.

"I know you've heard the rumors," Jacob continued. "Two people passed me notes before I left the house, begging me not to leave Blister Creek, and I heard it half a dozen times just walking down here. More worried comments, pleas. Many of you are thinking about it right now."

The crowd had grown tense, people leaning forward to hear what he had to say, women hushing their babies, the elderly in the back cupping their hands to their ears.

"I understand that you're worried, and that most of you don't want me to go. Two different women have told me that if I leave Blister Creek, they'd take their children and follow me into the wilderness. Cursing me all the way, of course, but following." He paused for dramatic effect. "But enough about my wives."

This brought loud laughter, way out of proportion to the mildly humorous nature of the remark. It had broken the tension, which was his intent. Jacob waited for the laughter to die down before continuing.

"I'll set your minds at ease. I'm not leaving. This is my home, and you are my people. Of course I will step down as prophet if you want me to, but this is your choice, not mine."

The smiles and relieved sighs turned to protests at this last part.

"No, Brother Jacob!"

"You're the prophet."

"We love you, Brother Jacob."

Elder Smoot stepped forward. His face was grim; he had lost two sons in two days. But he stood next to Jacob and put his arm around the younger man's shoulder. The crowd fell silent at this, but there were sniffles and watery eyes.

"Thank you," he said, both to Smoot and to the crowd. "If you will still have me as your leader, I will stay on. But I have a few conditions." He glanced at Eliza and Steve. "My sister has returned from Salt Lake with representatives from the state government. They're up at the reservoir now, but they'll be down in the valley tonight. Her journey wasn't only about getting rid of the refugees, it was about discovering if there was still a state government. There wasn't, not really. A few thousand survivors in Salt Lake, a handful of isolated communities in the Sanpete Valley. And us. Everyone else is dead or scattered.

"But there can be. Eliza and Steve met with survivors in Richfield, Manti, Ephraim, and Salina, to ask them to pull together with Salt Lake in the north. Blister Creek can join them as the final community on the south."

More nods and affirmative responses to this, but he didn't think they fully understood what he was asking yet. What he was claiming.

"We were prepared for the Millennium. All our food and weapons and self-sufficiency to survive the apocalypse as we waited for the Great and Dreadful Day of the Lord. But here we are, and the Millennium hasn't come. Maybe it's right around the corner. Or maybe our children and our grandchildren will live their entire lives and never see it.

"I used to shake my head when people talked about the end of the world. People had been predicting the return of Jesus since about five minutes after he left the first time. That was two thousand years ago. But then it seemed that people were finally right. The end was here. I can't tell you the number of times I argued with Sister Miriam about it. You can guess who argued which side.

"It came down to this. Either Miriam was right and the Second Coming is here, or I am right and it isn't. If this isn't the end, then that means we have no choice. We have to rebuild. Not hunker down in our desert citadel, fighting off anyone who approaches, but open up to the outside world. We have so much knowledge here about how to survive, how to thrive, even. We can bring people in to teach them, can sell our surplus food. In return, people up north can help protect trade, can reopen coal mines and power plants. Provide law and order.

"It might take generations, maybe even hundreds of years, but I believe civilization can rebuild. And I want to be a part of it. It will mean lots of changes for our little valley and even for our beliefs as a people."

He stopped and waited for the reaction. There was a long moment of hesitation, where he could see the troubled expressions, knew that it could go either way.

Then, instead of crying out angrily or dropping into a resentful silence, people began to weep and hug each other, and soon huge lines formed as people came up to shake his hand and embrace him.

He took it all in stunned silence.

★★★

Eliza waited for the crowds to disperse before she sought out Jacob. It was a good hour before the only ones left at the cemetery were the adults of the Smoot and Christianson families, who were still standing around their respective grave sites, speaking in hushed tones. David and his remaining wives stood with their children next to Miriam's temporary grave marker.

Steve had taken the rest of the Christianson children back to the house, where the older kids were starting work on a huge family dinner. This would be the scene of another round of prayers and tributes. But Eliza had something to discuss with Jacob before then.

She first came to hug David, who was red-eyed and drawn, which sucked her into further interaction with all sorts of relatives. By the time she pulled away, she found Jacob by himself on the southern edge of the cemetery. She thought he'd be brooding again over the gravestones of children taken in century-old epidemics, but instead he was staring south, into the open desert.

"They're lucky to have you," Eliza said. "You know that, don't you?"

Jacob turned and gave her a thin smile. "Compared to having Ezekiel Smoot or Taylor Kimball Junior as their leader? Yes, they're quite lucky."

"Compared to anyone." She nodded toward the desert. "What are you looking at?"

"Just thinking. Wondering what it would be like to set off into the wilderness. I'll bet there's nothing down there for hundreds of miles. I could find a quiet, watered mountain valley and set up with my family."

"How close were you?"

"To really leaving?" Jacob sighed. "Not very. I tried to work myself up to it, but I couldn't. It wouldn't have been fair to my family—they would have been miserable. And could I leave Blister Creek without a doctor? No."

"That's it? No thought that you're the best they've got?"

He smiled. "Maybe a little. Heaven knows I have my faults, but I'd be gone two days and the fundamentalist stuff would come back. I've got to coax our people through this change." He gave her a curious look. "You were close too, weren't you? To going full-fundie?"

Eliza hesitated at this, unable to answer right away. She needed to be honest with herself, even more than with her brother. "I was caught up in those scripture study nights," she admitted. "The emotion, the rapture of it. A part of me wanted it to be true, to think that the Lord would come and relieve us of our suffering. The alternative, that we were alone, was almost too much to bear."

"And now?"

"I don't know, Jacob. When I reached Salt Lake I was reminded that there are a whole lot of other people out there. People who tell themselves different stories than we do. A thousand different, mutually contradictory stories about how the universe works. But that doesn't mean we're wrong. I'm good with my path in life, but it's not the only path."

"I like that," Jacob said. He was staring south again. "Do you think we could get McKay to send someone to Cedar City to be sure? There might have been some survivors, and we could bring them north. Panguitch is the next place to resettle, and it will be relatively well protected, sitting up above us and below Richfield. Hey, maybe you and Steve could go check it out. As soon as you're ready to leave the valley again, I mean."

Eliza cleared her throat. "Actually, about leaving the valley . . ."

He turned, and his face fell as he studied her expression, and she could see him guessing what she was going to say. Jacob knew her as well as she knew him.

"The governor offered us positions in the state government," she continued. "Steve would be the new attorney general, and I would be head of agriculture."

"It has to be you? There's nobody else?"

"Nobody *better*. Steve has FBI credentials if anyone from the Federal government shows up. I'm a rancher's daughter, with three years' experience with post-collapse agriculture."

There was a moment of uncomfortable silence.

"It's not like you'll never see us," she added, when she could no longer stand it. "We'll be traveling up and down the state. Probably get down here two or three times a year."

"Then why don't you do it from Blister Creek and travel north when you need to, instead of the other way around?"

"Jacob," she said, putting a hand on his arm. "I *want* to leave Blister Creek."

He looked devastated, and more lonely than she could ever remember seeing him. He'd been counting on her, she knew, to be the fellow skeptic in a town of believers. The one who could share his snarky sense of humor, the irony of his position as a doubter leading a community of true believers.

Then the look vanished from his face, and he gave a warm, generous smile. "I get it, I know why you're going. I'm jealous is all. Wish I could go too. Where will you live?"

"Salt Lake to start. Then, when things settle down, we were thinking about the Nephi area, if we can find a few settlers to join us. We'll find an abandoned farm or orchard and see what we can do to bring it back around."

"Nephi," Jacob said. "That's a good Book of Mormon name. Father would approve."

"Also, it's drier than Provo or Salt Lake, more like the desert I'm used to. Beautiful mountains too. And it wouldn't be quite so far to travel to come visit. A good place to start a family, don't you think?"

"A great place. And of course if that doesn't work out, you know where you'll always be welcome."

"Of course."

Eliza took his hand and tugged him back toward where the rest of the family was waiting, including Fernie, who looked at them from her wheelchair, no doubt wondering what they were scheming about.

"I love you, big brother," she said.

"I love you too, kid."

"Things will turn out just fine."

"You know," Jacob said, "I think you might be right."

AFTERWORD

When I first turned my thoughts to writing a series set in a fundamentalist community, I had no idea what I was getting into. An agent who wanted to represent *The Righteous* was the first to convince me that it could be a series, but her idea was to have Jacob be a forensic anthropologist who moved out of the community after the first book. Oh, and could I cut all this talk about angels and never have my main character consider that any of this stuff might be real? She said that the story as I conceived it would descend into the realm of fantasy, and that would never sell. Needless to say, I blew off this advice.

In fact, the only thing I took from that conversation was the word "series." When I wrote the second book, *Mighty and Strong*, I had not yet sold the first novel, so I needed it to serve as its own stand-alone in case someone wanted *Mighty and Strong*, but not *The Righteous*.

However, by the time I wrote *The Wicked*, not only did I have a contract pending from Thomas & Mercer, but I had started to understand what this series was about.

It was not about solving individual murders or having each book be a cult-of-the-day mystery. Instead, it was about the role of belief versus doubt in a faith community, how believers may be motivated to commit either good or evil by following the same teachings, and of course, the role of women in a patriarchal community. One thing I was absolutely sure about was that I did not want my female characters to be either brainwashed fools or dominated by men. More on that below.

I've received a few comments and questions over and over.

What are you trying to pull here? Are you a Mormon, an anti-Mormon, or what? Is this religious fiction?

You don't have to look very far into my reviews to see that The Righteous books make some people angry, and the public reviews are only a hint at what I've seen in my inbox. At first this bothered me, but over time I've taken it as a sign that I'm writing something different and challenging, both for me and for the reader.

It will come as no surprise to readers that I have personal experience with the subject of these books. I was raised in a small religious town in Utah, and I have polygamists in my own family history. About fifteen years ago I went through a difficult period where I had lost the faith of my childhood and felt ostracized, deceived, and angry. Over time, I have come to peace with my own background, with my family and friends from my community, but I have never regained the belief I had as a child.

I think of myself as both insider and outsider. I always wanted to portray the believers of Blister Creek as real people, no more likely on average to be good or bad than anyone else, but sincere about their beliefs. At the same time, I am not naïve about the very real costs of living in such a closed community.

This whole series is really weird. So what are the books about, anyway?

Strangely, I began work on the final volume without knowing how the story would play out. The previous couple of books had focused on the end of the world, but I had not yet decided whether or not it would actually end, or if there would be a rebuilding of civilization.

At its core, this was a question of faith versus doubt, which is where I began the series. Of course, I have wrestled with other issues, the differing and complementary roles of men and women in a fundamentalist religion being chief among them, but also questions of power, of family ties, and the value of community as opposed to individualism. But Jacob's and Eliza's doubt and faith have remained at the heart of the series.

If the world ended, that would be a major nod toward faith, something I dabbled with in earlier books, especially *Destroying Angel*, where it seems for a time that there is a real religious and supernatural element. In this ending, Miriam's vision would be the correct one. Jacob's doubt would be the danger that could destroy Blister Creek when the times called for faith.

However, if the world did not end, if it looked as though civilization could rebuild, then that would be saying something completely different. I thought of Jacob on one side, Miriam and her all-consuming faith on the other, and Eliza as the character who could go either way. Miriam's death, combined with Eliza leaving the community at the end, represents a repudiation of the end-of-times thinking that has penetrated, and some might say poisoned, the community since its founding.

Is the series over?

Yes, for now. But I thought it was over once already. I was starting book #5, *Destroying Angel*, when my publisher offered me the chance to write three more volumes. I decided if I were going to do that, then I couldn't simply repeat what I'd already done. That's when I began to wonder what would happen to this religious community preparing for the end of the world if the world really did end. That was more than enough fuel to write three more books.

I would need some other compelling reason to continue the story, but I will say that I have a few more story ideas like my novella about the childhood of Abraham Christianson, *Trial by Fury*, that would take smaller story ideas and dig into them. That would be the most likely manner for me to continue the story, at least in the short term.

In the meantime, I hope you will take a look at some of my other books. Chances are, if you've followed me through eight books of this series you will find that I have other interesting things to say, albeit in completely different settings.

As I close this chapter of my writing career, I want to thank my friend Grant Morgan, whose thoughts helped shape the series, my agent, Katherine Boyle, and the wonderful team at Thomas & Mercer. To build a writing career takes years of effort, some of it lonely and frustrating. I want to thank my wife, Melinda, for her support during this time. Finally, I want to thank my readers who have stuck with me for eight books, not knowing where I would go, but interested in both the destination and the journey to get there. I hope I have delivered something unexpected and thought-provoking.

ABOUT THE AUTHOR

Michael Wallace was born in California and raised in a small religious community in Utah, eventually heading east to live in Rhode Island and Vermont. An experienced world traveler, he has trekked through the Andes, ventured into the Sahara on camel, and traveled through Thailand by elephant. In addition to working as a literary agent and innkeeper, he previously worked as a software engineer for a Department of Defense contractor, programming simulators for nuclear submarines. He is the author of more than a dozen novels.